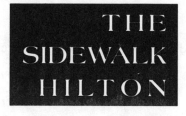

THE SIDEWALK HILTON

Other Chico Cervantes novels by Bruce Cook

Death as a Career Move

Rough Cut

Mexican Standoff

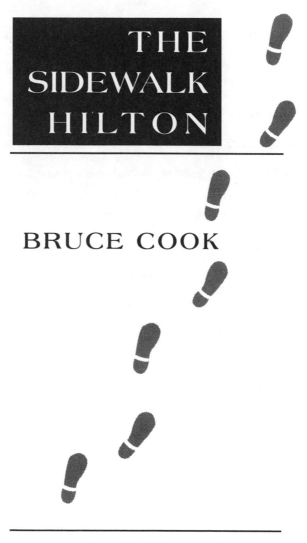

THE SIDEWALK HILTON

BRUCE COOK

ST. MARTIN'S PRESS
NEW YORK

Design by Basha Zapatka

Library of Congress Cataloging-in-Publication Data

Cook, Bruce, 1932–
    The sidewalk Hilton / Bruce Cook.
       p.   cm.
    "A Thomas Dunne book."
    ISBN 0-312-11062-6
    1. Cervantes, Chico (Fictitious character)—Fiction. 2. Private In-
vestigators—California—Los Angeles—Fiction. 3. Mexican Americans—California—Los Angeles—Fiction. 4. Los Angeles (Calif.)—
Fiction. I. Title.
PS3553.O55314S55   1994
813'.54—dc20   94-418
                                                                 CIP

First edition: May 1994

10 9 8 7 6 5 4 3 2 1

FOR DAVID DURAN

Fitzgerald: "The very rich are different from us."

Hemingway: "Yes, they have more money."

1

The sun glistened so bright on the blue Pacific about a block away that I got tired of squinting and put on my sunglasses. What the hell, I thought, make me look like a man of mystery.

We were playing a game at the bar. The way I remember, it was some version of what they used to call Truth, or around here, Honest-Honest. The woman down at the other end who had started it all had taken the part of the Grand Inquisitor. She came up with the questions and each of us—the four sitting at the bar and the female bartender—had to answer them. Truthfully. (I know this sounds dumb, but it's how you pass the time in Santa Monica on a Sunday afternoon.)

Anyway, she asked questions. Questions like what? Oh, questions like (trying to get it down now the way she said it), "If you were, like, an animal? What kind would you rilly, rilly like to be?"

"A coyote," I said. I guess I was thinking about the trickster in the old Indian stories. Then I flashed on those cucarachas down in Tijuana, and I was sorry I said it.

"Uh-huh, uh-huh, okay. That's rilly neat. But how about if you were a plant?"

"A Venus flytrap." That seemed about right for the work I did. Nobody questioned it. They all just sort of nodded like I'd said something profound.

I forget what answers the rest of them gave to those two questions. I wasn't really paying close attention. Would you? Besides, I had a lot on my mind just then.

Look at me sitting here, stuck on a barstool—no, not a barstool, it's one of those chairs with four-foot legs, blond wood, leather seat, very tasteful. The whole place, meaning the little bar and the dining area beyond, is just dripping with taste. But what would you expect? This is the classiest hotel in Santa Monica. Because it's the middle of the afternoon, nobody's eating, but the waitresses come and go, and the woman behind the bar keeps fairly busy filling orders for the people lounging poolside out in the sun. And what am I doing here? I'm supposed to be working.

It was sort of a missing person's job. There seemed some doubt, however, whether Benjamin Sterling really was missing, or whether he wanted to be found. First of all, he'd been out of communication with his family for less than a week. (It takes longer to get an official posting by the police.) Then, too, he was out here on a vacation from Chicago, "a little business, mostly vacation," his daughter had told me on the telephone. He was still registered at his hotel, this hotel, and there were indications that he came and went from his room irregularly. One of the maids claimed to have seen him leaving it two days ago. But it was certain he wasn't sleeping there. How old was he, after all—seventy-two and a recent widower. Maybe he'd found someplace else to sleep, somebody to sleep *with*. It's been known to happen that way, with men older than Sterling. Why not? I had a great-uncle in Guanajuato who remarried at seventy-five, got the male heir he'd always hoped for, and died at ninety-two.

But just try to suggest this even subtly to Sterling's daughter, Clarissa! She conceded that he was in good physical condition for a man his age and was *very* independent. But, according to her, he'd been acting kind of odd lately. She said she was afraid he might be wandering around "in a fugue state." I had to look that up. It's like amnesia, except it comes and goes. Which might explain his erratic visits to the hotel room, but when he made a stop it was evidently just to shower and shave and change his clothes, and then he'd head right out again.

Anyway, she sent me a photograph—one of those studio portraits—and I'd had copies made. I walked around Santa Monica, showing them, leaving them where I thought it would do some good. I checked the hospitals, of course—St. John's, Santa Monica, and County—and checked in with the cops. "I know you can't list him yet," I said to the sergeant at the bureau. "Just keep it in case he turns up in the hospital or something, okay?" He shrugged and tossed the photo indifferently onto a pile in his in box.

Yeah, I'd stuck pretty close to Santa Monica. Benjamin Sterling had rented a car at the airport, but after the first day it hadn't left the hotel garage. He had to be around here somewhere.

Somebody punched my arm. Lightly. The bartender. "Hey," she said, "are you still playing or aren't you?"

"What? Oh yeah. Sure."

"Well, answer the question."

"What's the question?"

"Oh, hey," said the Grand Inquisitor, "maybe we just better quit."

"No, no, go ahead. Ask me again."

"I said, you know, *outrageous*."

"Outrageous?"

"What's the most outrageous thing you've, like, ever done?"

Now what was I supposed to say to that? I'd done things in the last year and a half or two years that would have shocked them. Jesus, they shocked me. I never *really* thought I was capable of killing a man, and yet I'd killed three. So what now? I wasn't about to tell this little crowd at the bar what I hadn't yet been able to tell a priest in the confessional.

"Come on now," whined the questioner, "honest-honest."

"I guess I'll pass on that one."

"You can't!" from the bartender. And from the couple at the middle of the bar: "No, no, you've got to tell!"

So I don't know what I said. Well, yes I do, but it was just something dumb from when I was a kid in Boyle Heights. Okay, what I did, I told them about the time a carful of us got chased all over the East Side by the local gang. It wasn't a gang like they have today, guns and drive-bys, and all that. But they were tough kids, and they were out to get us, and they would have whipped our asses if they'd caught us. It was a real chase, up and down Whittier Boulevard, through red lights. We were hoping the cops would stop us—and the guys following us. But wouldn't you know it? This was the one night they weren't out. So I got this idea; I said, turn down this alley, which we did, and then we pulled into a lot beside some other cars, switched off the lights, and we all got down in our seats. The gang car just sailed on down the alley. Before they could come back, we pulled out of there and parked on a side street. They went by a couple of times, but they never spotted us. So we waited around, and I got an idea: hit 'em where they live, create a diversion. By this time we figured they'd be back in this rundown bungalow where they crashed, so I phoned in a false alarm. Then we went back to watch. The hook-and-ladder was there, a squad unit, everything. The firemen were pretty pissed off, of course. And even though they didn't think for a minute the gang guys had phoned in the phony fire alarm, they cited them for a lot of fire code violations just to teach them a lesson.

Then the punch line: "And you know what that got us from the gang?"

"Oooh! I'll bet!" said the guy sitting just down from me. "How long did it take you to recover?"

"No!" I slapped the marble top of the bar. "It got us *respect*! They knew we could get at them in ways they hadn't thought of. They had to respect that. They left us alone."

Silence. The bunch at the bar thought that over. I'd entertained them, and that was what it was all about, wasn't it?

Finally, the Grand Inquisitor herself spoke up. "So, like, turning in a false alarm was the most outrageous thing you *ever* did?"

"I've led a pretty quiet life."

"Yeah, sure," the bartender laughed. "What were you, in another gang or something?"

"What we were was the *non*gang. We were the independents."

That would hold them for a while. They moved on. I tuned out. I took a gulp of the Dos Equis I'd been nursing and wondered if maybe I shouldn't pay up and go check again with the concierge. It seemed at this point that the hotel was my best bet. So after covering all the necessary spots, and just generally looking around town the first couple of days, I'd been sticking pretty close to this place, waiting for Benjamin Sterling to come back and change clothes.

I'd posted a five-hundred-dollar reward and passed the word around the staff to let me know if he showed up. I figured, these people are pretty well paid, but nobody's going to turn up their nose at that kind of money. Besides, the retainer Clarissa—what was her name? Clarissa Edwards—had wired to my account gave me the chance to be generous. Grace Jarrett told me not to worry about expenses. She was the contact on this. I called her out in San Marino after I talked to Sterling's daughter, and she assured me that if Clarissa said that money was no object, then it wasn't.

The game at the bar had gotten interesting again. The question was: What is the most outrageous thing you've ever *seen*?

It was the bartender's turn. She looked around kind of sheepishly and said, "Well, it was just the other night at a club I was at in Silverlake." She hesitated. "It was the first time I ever saw people beating each other, you know, with cat-o'-nine-tails. It was really weird."

"Truly outrageous," said the guy down the bar from me.

"That's sick," said the girl with him, "pathological." They were from out of town.

"Wait a minute," I said. "Silverlake?"

"Yeah."

"Was it the Club Fuck?"

"My God," said the bartender, capping her hand over her mouth like she'd said too much. Then, "Were you there? Wasn't it awful?"

"No, I wasn't there, but I heard about it."

The Grand Inquisitor: "Okay, yuh, hey, right, Mister Man of

the World, what's the most outrageous thing *you've* ever seen? And no false alarms this time."

Again I slapped the marble bar top. "That's *easy*." I bellowed it. "I saw something on TV this week that was just outrageous. There was this new sitcom, *Lupe,* about an illegal, you know, a wetback, and it was just total, total bullshit! What does she do? She goes to the state employment office, and they give her a job! I mean, what is this? Where's the reality?"

I'd fairly erupted. This, in case you hadn't guessed, had also been on my mind. It was personal. I shouldn't have opened my mouth about it.

"Oh, hey, I saw that," said the bartender who had been present at the S-M revelries. "I thought it was cute."

"So what are you, a critic?" said the Grand Inquisitor. "It got good reviews. Everybody liked the star. What's her name? Alicia somebody."

"Excuse me, sir, excuse me." This was the guy from out of town. He was frowning—not in an unfriendly way, just showing himself to be speaking very seriously. "Am I correct in assuming that you are of the Hispanic persuasion?"

"No," I said, "I'd say I am of the Mexican persuasion, Mexican-American." I felt a tug at my sleeve. "And I really object to that kind of bullshit on TV."

"Well, obviously you bring a certain perspective to bear on this. If you could just, you know, be more specific about your objections."

That tug on my sleeve again. Right at the elbow.

"Señor, por favor."

"Well, just for starters, there's this whole thing of the green card." I was really worked up.

"Señor, por favor, venga conmigo."

"And look, if you really—"

"¡VENGA!"

With that, a great pull on my arm landed me off the bar chair, nearly tipping it over. What was this? *Who* was this?

I was being pulled bodily away by a chunky woman not much more than five feet tall. In my confusion, it took a moment more to register that she was wearing a hotel maid's uniform and that she was, in fact, the one who had spotted Benjamin Sterling leaving his room a couple of days ago. Finally it dawned on me what this was all about.

"Okay, okay," I said to her, *"momentito, eh?"*

I grabbed into my pocket, came up with some bills, and tossed them down on the bar. "That cover it? Gotta go. Business." They were staring. The maid was pulling. I was out of there.

All the way up to the third level on the service stairs, she was making these exclamations of misery. *"¡Ay, que lastima, que verguenza!"* And I'm running behind her, trying to get her to tell me what happened. Is he in the room? What is it? And all she'll say is, "You'll see, you'll see! *¡Que verguenza!"*

Once up there, I could see her cleaning cart parked out on the landing at what I knew was Sterling's room. The door was shut and locked. She fumbled a moment with her passkeys. Then, unlocking the door, she rolled her eyes so expressively that I expected some scene of horror just inside.

But there was nothing. Some clothes thrown on the bed, an open closet door, an open suitcase thrown on the floor, bureau drawers open. Disorder, sure, but . . .

She was into the room, dancing around the suitcase, waving me ahead. In this way she brought me on to the bathroom, stood at the doorway, and gestured inside.

There he was on the floor. The space was tight so that he had fallen in a crumpled heap between the lavatory and the toilet stool. The white terry-cloth robe he had on had bunched forward, covering the back of his neck and leaving just the hair on his head visible. There was blood right there on the robe and on the back of his head, but a lot more on the light green tile beneath him.

I leaned forward carefully and touched his neck on the right side to see if there was any sign of a pulse. Not a chance. He was cold to the touch. If rigor hadn't set in already, it wouldn't be long.

"Es muerto," said the maid.

"Sí," I said, *"sin duda."*

I told her to report it to the concierge, and she leaped to the telephone. *"¡No!"* I yelled at her. Her hand froze in the air just above the receiver. *"No toca nada."* She nodded, intimidated. "Go tell him to call the police and bring him here." Then, as she was leaving the room, I called after her, "You did well to tell me first." And then she disappeared through the doorway.

I'm not sure I really meant that. This would give me a couple of minutes to look around, but it was going to be awkward explaining my presence to the cops once they got here.

I stepped carefully all the way into the bathroom and saw what had happened. The mirror above the washbasin had been shattered. There were bits of blood and maybe bloody bits of tissue plastered on the glass and broken bits of the mirror scattered over the basin and in it. There was water in it. I touched it. Cold. He'd been shaving. The guy came up behind him and popped him in the back of the head. How many times? I counted three holes in what was left of the mirror. Benjamin Sterling must have had at least a glimpse of the guy before he got it.

I leaned over the body again, pulled the collar of the robe back carefully, and counted three entry wounds right up where the spinal column joins the skull. There was another one higher, behind the left ear. That was about as professional as you could get, except the caliber of the weapon used was larger than usual. It had to be a .38 or a 9mm from the look of the entry wounds. All the blood on the floor was from the exit wounds in his face. He would look like hell from the front.

Then, looking close one last time, I saw something interesting, maybe even strange. There were still traces of lather on the face, but it had dried enough to see the beard beneath. There must have been four days' growth on his right cheek, maybe five—really heavy. It looked like he had started to grow a beard, then changed his mind. That didn't quite tally with the maid's report that she had seen him two days before, that he had been in to shower and shave and change his clothes. Two days will give most men a thick stubble. But this—well, maybe Sterling's beard just grew faster than mine.

With that, I left the bathroom and began looking around the

hotel room, trying to establish the sequence of events. The assailant had evidently entered through the door while Sterling was in the shower, but how? Did he have a key? Did he hide in the closet? How long was he there? Or maybe it was the other way around. Could the guy have been here first, looking for something? He hears Sterling's key in the door, ducks into the closet, waits until Sterling was occupied in the bathroom. Taking a shower? Who says he didn't start shaving first? I mean, just because he had that robe on, what does that prove? So the assailant goes in, pops him, and continues to look for what he came for.

So what's wrong with the burglary scenario? The room sure looks like he was searching for something. It looks tossed. It was meant to look tossed. And there's probably money missing. But whoever was in here was after more than pocket cash and credit cards, if he was after anything at all. What was it Sterling did? His daughter said he had a seat on the Board of Trade. That was like a seat on the stock market, wasn't it? That's money, of course, big money, but what do you carry around with you that would give somebody access to it? I was out of my depth there completely.

"My God, is it true?" It was the concierge, a young guy, handsome and stylish in a dark double-breasted suit, the way those guys dress. I'd talked to him earlier. He seemed okay. The maid peeped into the room behind him, staying out in the hall.

"It's true," I said, walking over to him. "If you want to, you can take a look. He's a mess, though, lot of blood."

"N-no." He hesitated. "No, that's all right."

A big guy pushed past the maid and into the room. Hotel security. I talked to him before, too. Him I didn't like so well. He looked around the room. "Another fucking burglary!"

"You've had a lot of them?"

"Enough," he said. "Too many. Where's the body?"

"In the bathroom."

He headed past me and straight into the bathroom. All the way in. "Jesus!" he wailed. "This could mean my fucking job!"

"Don't touch anything," I yelled in to him.

"You think I'm some kinda amateur?"

Frankly, I thought, yes. He emerged from the bathroom, wiping his hands on his pants. I wondered where they'd been.

"I'm not so sure this one's really a burglary," I said to the concierge.

"Really? It certainly looks like—"

"Whoever was here was after something." Hotel security picked up the empty suitcase and waved it at me.

"Look, what do you say we all go outside and wait for the cops?" To the concierge: "You called them, didn't you?"

"Oh yes. They should be here any moment."

"It'd look better if we weren't all in the room."

"I suppose so."

I herded them out into the hall. On his way, the hotel detective tossed the suitcase down on the floor about three feet from its original position, and stopped to take one last look around. Then, outside the door, he suddenly turned on me like he'd just decided to be angry. "Who the fuck are you to tell us what to do?"

"Really, Alex," said the concierge, "I think he's right."

"And whatta you mean you're not so sure it's a burglary?"

"Burglars don't usually shoot," I said. "If they're caught in the act, they usually say, 'Oops, wrong room,' or something."

"Funny, really funny."

"I'm not trying to be funny. I'm trying to tell you it looks like a hit, an assassination."

"Who was this guy? You were asking about him. You must know something."

"He was a businessman from Chicago."

"Why would anyone want to kill him?"

"That I don't know. But whoever did it had to use a silencer." Then I asked the concierge, "None of your guests reported hearing gunshots late last night or early this morning, did they?"

"Certainly not!" said the concierge. He seemed shocked at the idea, as if the noise would have been more offensive than the corpse in the bathroom.

"I didn't think so. That was no BB gun he used. You would've heard it all over the hotel—without a silencer." I turned to the hotel detective. "And you know who uses silencers."

But I wasn't getting eye contact from him. He was looking over my shoulder and beyond the maid, who seemed to have attached herself to me. The five-hundred-dollar reward, of course. I guessed that in a way she'd earned it.

"Well, that's your theory," said the big guy. "You can tell it to the cops. Here they come now."

I turned and looked. He was right. Here they came.

2

This was crazy. The way the homicide guy said he had it figured was that I had just been waiting around the bar for the maid to finger Sterling. She came and got me. Then I went up and took him out and sent her downstairs to call 911.

Detective Lorenzen grinned at me. "How does that sound to you?"

It was bullshit. It was harassment. That's how it sounded.

"I think your theory has a couple of flaws in it," I said.

"Yeah? Tell me." He was a little too young, too blond, and too soft around the eyes to play the hard-guy role he'd chosen for himself. He was trying to act his way through it. I wondered if he practiced in front of the mirror.

"Well, for one thing," I said, "where's the weapon? They patted me. I'm clean. You check, you'll find I'm registered for a thirty-eight Smith & Wesson Police Special. It's at home."

"Sure it is. You got one off the street for this. Maybe you threw it out the window. Maybe the maid hid it. Whatever. We'll find it."

"Okay, then there's the matter of the time of death. Medical examiner cuts him open, he'll tell you he's been dead six, maybe eight hours."

"Yeah? How do you know so much about that?"

"He was cold to the touch. The blood on the floor had dried."

"Hey, you touched him—disturbing a crime scene. That's a no-no. A p.i. like you's supposed to know better than that."

"Just checking for a pulse, detective, the way any informed citizen would do."

"Oh, that's cute. That's what you are, huh? An informed citizen?"

I hesitated, not consciously counting to ten but giving myself time to choose words besides the obscene ones I was choking back down my throat. Then, quietly, I said, "Yes. I am also a private investigator, duly licensed in the State of California, who was hired by the dead man's daughter to find him. They had been out of touch for four days. She was worried about him. Now, before we discuss this any more, I think you better call her and check that out."

It was his turn to be quiet. Maybe he was just thinking it over. "No," he said at last, "you call her." He pointed to the telephone.

We were in the room next door to Sterling's. The layout of the place was just like his, only in reverse, so that the two bathrooms were back to back, sharing a wall, sharing pipes, the usual arrangement. I'd noted it when Detective Lorenzen brought me in for our little talk. Something had occurred to me.

"Look," I said to him, "I wouldn't try to tell you your job, but if I'm right, and the guy who popped Sterling went into his room specifically to do that, then he had to have someplace to wait, didn't he? He couldn't hang around in the hall. So you might check with the desk if this room has been rented in the last couple of days, particularly last night, and by who. Bed's not been slept in, but somebody's been here. Somebody left some butts in the ashtray. Marlboros. Somebody was waiting."

I was getting to him. I could tell. Lorenzen's eyes had shifted around the room as I talked. They were now fixed on the ashtray.

"The maid hadn't gotten to this room yet," I continued. "But we've been here a little while and about all we haven't dirtied so far is the bathroom, that ashtray, and the telephone." I paused. "So why don't we use another telephone?"

When he looked back at me, his face had flushed. He jumped to his feet. There was an instant when I thought he was going to land on top of me and knock me off my chair. The thought probably passed through his mind. But no. He simply jerked a thumb back toward the door and said, "Come on."

I followed him out into the hall. He walked me back to the door to Sterling's room. "Wait here," he said, and went inside.

After he had been gone a few moments, I leaned into the doorway and looked. Just as I suspected, he was talking to the chief of the crime-scene crew and pointing in the direction of the room we had just left. I ducked back and waited.

But before Detective Lorenzen reappeared, the boys from the L.A. County Morgue banged out of the room, wheeling their prize on a stretcher. Some prize. The corpse was zipped up in a body bag, as usual, but there was a big, hulking bulge in the middle, and it was flat where the legs should have been. Inside, Sterling was still crumpled, the way I'd first seen him on the bathroom floor.

The guy in the white coat at the back of the stretcher was having a hard time working his end through the door. Once it was free, he looked up and saw me staring at the lump in the bag. "Rigor," he said. "They're a lot more trouble this way." I guess he thought I was one of the Santa Monica cops.

Lorenzen followed them out. He knew the condition of the body, but he wasn't giving an inch, still playing the hard guy. "Downstairs," he said. And as the morgue team headed for the elevator, he led me to the service stairs.

This guy couldn't have been more than thirty, more likely a year or two younger. He'd probably been a good uniform cop, distinguished himself with a tough collar or two, and been rewarded with a civilian-clothes job. All cops want to work homicide, or think they do until they've had a taste of it, so he must have tried hard to get where he doesn't belong. No eye for detail. No imagination. He was more interested in intimidating me than he was in listening. He was still running his act like a street cop.

Well, at least he took my advice and checked on the room next door to Sterling's. We stopped at the desk while he had a hurried conference with the clerk. The room bill was pulled from the files. I heard the clerk promise a photocopy and direct Lorenzen to an empty office around the corner and down the hall where he could use a telephone. Then I heard Lorenzen ask if there was an extension in there.

"An extension? No," said the desk clerk. "If you need an extension, better go to the second office on the right instead of the first. Somebody's in there now. Maybe you could—"

"Got it," said the detective. And to me: "Come on."

So again I followed, to a door marked ACCOUNTING and into a big office full of empty desks, except for one. A black woman about fifty years old sat at that one. There were six or eight piles of paper ranged across her desk on either side. She sat in the middle of it all, her fingers flying over the keyboard of an electronic calculator. They continued to fly for a moment or two until she had shifted a sheet from one pile to another. She looked up then, frowning at the interruption.

"Police business," said Lorenzen. "Out." He jerked his thumb toward the door to show her the way. He seemed to use that a lot.

She took off her glasses and looked at him coolly. "I beg your pardon."

Flustered, he produced his police ID, flopped it open, and waved it at her. "Santa Monica Police," he said. "We need the telephones in this office, and we need them secure."

"Secure?"

"No listening in."

Something like a grunt, or maybe a "hrrumph," escaped from her. Then, "The work I'm doing requires extreme concentration, I can assure you. Now, you just go over there, and make your phone call. I won't be eavesdropping."

"Lady, this is a homicide case—murder, serious business." He'd taken a couple of steps toward her, not exactly threatening but pleading his case.

She waved her hand over the desk. *"This* is serious business, too. If I don't finish today, there'll be no garbage-in for the computers tomorrow."

"The desk clerk said we could use this office."

"Did he say you could kick me out? No. You'd have to do better than the desk clerk, anyway. You get the day manager to tell me to leave, and I'll leave. Not until."

Lorenzen panted in exasperation. He wasn't used to this. At last he waved me on, and I followed him to the rear corner of the room, where she had told him to place the call. As I passed her desk, I gave her a wink and raised a fist in approval. She winked back.

That woman had lightened my load a little. Given me distraction from the job ahead, which I dreaded. Wouldn't you? I mean, telling somebody their son/daughter/mother/father is dead, *murdered,* that's got to be maybe the worst message you can deliver. Oh, I've done it before—a few times as a cop and once as a p.i. But you know how they talk about killing the messenger? Well, nobody ever tried that, really, but once there was a woman just started beating on me with her fists wherever she could when I told her her daughter was dead, until finally her husband wrestled her away. And then another time, I told this guy his father had been hit (the old man had been into some pretty heavy stuff, money laundering for a bunch of Peruvians), and the son just hauled off and clipped me on the jaw. What was I supposed to do? Arrest the guy for assaulting an officer? At least on the phone I was safe from physical violence.

Anyway, that was the kind of call I had to make, and I wasn't looking forward to it at all, especially not with Lorenzen listening in. He was already sitting down at the desk across the aisle from me, his hand on the receiver. "You really have to hear this?" I asked him.

"Sure," he said, "how else am I gonna know if she put you up to it?"

"Jesus," I said and, shaking my head, I dialed the number in the 708 area code I had pulled from my wallet.

A female voice answered, prim and proper—not Sterling's daughter, probably a maid. I asked for Mrs. Edwards.

By this time Lorenzen had the phone up to his face and was breathing heavily into the mouthpiece. Did he have a sinus problem or something? I could hear him clearly at my end. I gestured for him to take the mouthpiece away from in front of his face.

"Oh. Oh, yeah," he said loudly in my ear, then took it away. This was going to go great, I could tell.

"Hello? Yes? This is Clarissa Edwards."

"Mrs. Edwards, this is Antonio Cervantes out in Los Angeles."

"Oh, do you know something? Have you found him?"

"I'm afraid I've got bad news."

"Tell me," she said. Her voice was steady but tense.

"A man's been found in your father's room. Shot. He's dead."

"Oh, *God!*" A whisper. She said nothing at all for a long time, until, "Well, but, is it *him*? You said a man was shot. Was it *him*?"

Then a voice booming in my ear: "That's what you'll have to tell us, Mrs. . . . Mrs. . . ." It was Lorenzen, of course. This was embarrassing.

"Edwards. Who is this speaking?"

"Detective Lorenzen, Santa Monica Police Department."

"Were you listening in before? I don't think I like this. Please get off the line."

He glanced in my direction, looking confused, almost like he was asking for help. Not from me, buddy. I looked away and just stared at the busy fingers of the lady up front, waiting him out. Finally, he tried to bully his way through. "Now, look, what I'm trying to tell you is that you or some member of the immediate family—"

"Please get off the line."

"Mrs. Edwards—"

"Off! I'll talk *only* to Mr. Cervantes. Unless you hang up, I will, Detective Whoever-you-are. I mean it."

I couldn't resist taking a look. Lorenzen sat, holding the receiver away from him, staring at it red-faced. His jaw was clenched so tight he couldn't have said a word if he'd wanted to. Then suddenly he jammed the receiver down in its cradle, jumped up, and without a look in my direction, stormed down the aisle and through the door, slamming it behind him.

"Mr. Cervantes?"

"Yes, Mrs. Edwards, I'm still here."

"And that man is gone?"

"Yes, he is."

"Good." She sighed. "Where were we? I . . . I was asking you if you were sure the . . . the dead man is my father." She was tough, all right—going to see it through, no matter what.

"I honestly can't say for sure," I told her. "They wouldn't let me have a good look at him. But I would say that indications are that it's him." I paused, waiting. She didn't say anything, so I went on: "I'm afraid somebody will have to come out to identify the body."

She didn't hesitate. "I'll come."

"It's going to be pretty unpleasant," I said. "His face will be . . . well, pretty disfigured. Maybe you could bring his dental records along."

"I'll come. I'll be on the first flight out tomorrow."

"Okay, look," I said, "I don't know how long they're going to keep me here at the hotel—I'll explain it all later—so if I'm not at my home number, just leave the time of arrival and the flight number with my answering service, and I'll meet your plane."

If Lorenzen didn't decide to book me out of spite.

"I would appreciate that. Yes. Thank you." And then, without another word, she hung up.

I waited a moment longer to make sure she was off the line, then I replaced the receiver. It was my turn to sigh. If I had dreaded this phone call, I dreaded the next day a whole lot more. I knew I'd have to walk her through the whole nasty procedure, answer her questions as well as I could, and give her a shoulder to cry on. Or maybe there wouldn't be any crying. Just from what I'd heard on the phone, it sounded to me like she might be out for blood.

Still mulling it over, I hauled myself up out of my chair and started for the door. The lady at the calculator broke off suddenly, turned, and gave me a serious look.

"Your friend left in kind of a hurry."

"He's no friend of mine," I said.

"Glad to hear it. People like that, they can give you a lot of trouble, if you let them. What's the phrase? Ah, yes, a 'loose cannon.'"

"Thanks, I'll keep that in mind."

"Have a nice day," she said, and went back to her calculator.

The moment I stepped through the door, Lorenzen had me up against the wall and was breathing heavily, blowing his breath in my face. "Listen," he said, "listen to me. I don't like you personally, and I don't like you professionally. You get a p.i. around the edge of a case, and it's dirty. He always messes things up. Now you stay out of this one." He was panting. I wasn't giving him any resistance. It was all emotional. "Understand?" Fairly shouted.

"I understand."

"She's coming out here?"

I nodded.

"Okay. Now, I only want to see you one more time, and that's at Los Angeles Street to eyeball the old man—and then after, you bring her back to the station. I want to talk to both of you." He fumbled out his card and pushed it into my hand. Then he turned away and left me staring after him as he disappeared around the corner and into the hotel lobby. This guy was off the wall. Completely. It's true, cops don't like p.i.s involved in their cases, none of them do, but this was pathological. Bad attitude, none too swift, and some real problems with female authority. Not a cop I'd want on my side.

I tucked and straightened, then followed him out to the lobby. Lorenzen was nowhere in sight, probably on his way back up to Sterling's room. That left me free to leave. And I was on my way, more than ready to get clear of the place, when just short of the exit to the boulevard, a hiss and the wave of a disembodied hand brought me over a dense jungle of potted palms and ficus. Hiding behind them was the maid. I was glad to see she didn't look the worse for wear. Her eyes were wide. There was a little half-smile on her face.

"Is exciting, huh? Jus' like TV."

"Yeah," I said, "just like TV. I hope they didn't give you a hard time up there."

"Oh, no' really. When I find the *muerto—ay de mi, horroroso!* But when he as' questions . . . was in'eresting."

Interesting? Detective Lorenzen? "Who did you talk to? Was he big and blond, have a moustache?"

"Oh no." She was digging through the pockets of her apron, evidently looking for the card cops always leave. "Was a little guy. *Japones*."

"Japanese-American or Japanese-Japanese?"

She shrugged. "I don' know. I only get my green card las' month. Ah, here." She found the card at last and handed it over. The name on it was Robert Shinahara, Lieutenant, Homicide Division, Santa Monica Police Department.

Who was he? And then it hit me—I'd seen him. He had to be the little guy Lorenzen had been talking to in Sterling's room, the one I thought was the chief of the crime-scene squad.

"I shou' tell you," she said, "I inform him about the *premio*—*cómo se dice?*"

"Reward."

"Yes, re-ward." She sounded it out carefully. "Is okay I do that?"

"Sure, of course it's okay. It was the truth, and you should always tell the truth to the police." Listen to me, would you!

"Bueno. Good." She nodded, then waited. "Señor? The reward?"

Of course. It wasn't her fault she had delivered Benjamin Sterling dead instead of alive. She had come to me first. She deserved it. I took out my checkbook, asked her to spell her name for me, and wrote out the check.

The name, her name, Pilar Ramirez? A question formed in my mind. "What part of Mexico do you come from?" I tore off the check and handed it to her.

"From Sonora, near Hermosillo. Why you ask?"

"I knew a Ramirez who came from Sinaloa."

"Es un nombre muy ordinario."

"Sí," I said, *"muy ordinario."*

She waved the check at me. *"Gracias, Señor. Dios bendiga."* She made a little curtsy and in another moment was gone, leaving me there among the potted palms.

3

"That's not him."

She said it with such certainty and so quickly that the rest of us around the gurney turned from the body and looked at her in surprise. I know I was surprised. That's how Lieutenant Shinahara looked, too—but also suddenly very interested; his eyes became lively, exchanging looks with me, with her, all the way around. Her husband (what was his name? Oh yeah, Roger), he seemed to glance at her sharply, suspiciously, then back at the body. And the morgue attendant? Well, he just appeared slightly annoyed— an unnecessary complication to his day. After all, he'd prepared the body, gotten it out from the drawer and onto the gurney, washed it, draped a towel over what was left of the face, done all he could for this next-of-kin ID, and now what?

"No, really," said Clarissa Edwards. "I'm sure of it. Roger, aren't you? Just look."

And he did, frowning over it from bottom to top, turning back to her. "What is it," he asked, "that makes you so sure?"

"Him," she said, "that, the body. Look at him."

"What is it?" asked Lieutenant Shinahara. "I'd really like to know, Mrs. Edwards."

She inhaled, looked around, exhaled, and began, "Well, all right, there were his scars from the war, just above the stomach and all over his shoulder. I saw them as a child, every time we went swimming. They're not there. And the shape of . . . this person is all wrong."

"How is that?"

"Well, it's just wrong, that's all. First of all, I think my father was an inch or two taller, and then, too . . ."

"Yes? What?"

"Look, my father played tennis every day he could for as long as I can remember. He was in good shape. But this man, just look at his legs, how skinny they are, and even though he's sort of skinny all over he's got a belly, which my father never had."

"Interesting," said Lieutenant Shinahara.

She turned to her husband. "Wouldn't you say so, Roger?"

"I . . . oh, I don't know. Could we see the face?"

"Is that really necessary?" I asked. I'd pretty well pictured his face the day before. It had to be a mess. Four exit wounds, after all. "There couldn't be a lot there."

"Well," said Roger, "let's see."

The morgue attendant shrugged and pulled the towel away. Clarissa Edwards stared, evidently fascinated by what she saw. What she saw was not quite as bad as I'd expected. From the nose up, the face was intact. The mouth, the jaw, were a mess. I wondered how much use the dental records would be to anybody.

She was tough. "That settles it. That's not my father." Again, that authority. She turned to me. "Mr. Cervantes, you know the photo I sent. Does that look like him?"

I felt like I had to take a good, long look. Finally I said, "No, I don't think so. No."

"Roger?"

"I guess not. No."

"The nose is wide. My father's was narrow. The eyes of this . . . person's are set closer together. This is *not* my father."

Before we left, Clarissa Edwards surrendered the dental records she had brought with her. The morgue attendant took them with a shrug. After such a positive nonidentification, there was really no point in sawing off the jaw of the corpse and checking out his molars and eyeteeth. Of course, the medical examiner would have to decide about that.

As the four of us walked out to the parking lot we didn't say much. In fact, we didn't say anything at all. Once outside, we stood for a moment there on the pavement, just looking at each other.

"Well," said Clarissa, "I guess we're back where we started."

She said it to me, but Lieutenant Shinahara answered her. "Not exactly, Mrs. Edwards. We've got a body on our hands we have to identify."

She blinked at that, looked a little embarrassed. "Yes, of course, Lieutenant. I didn't mean that quite the way it sounded."

He nodded. "I'm glad it wasn't your father. But I'd really appreciate it if you'd come by and make a statement."

"That shouldn't be necessary now," said her husband. "Why should that be necessary?" He was very emphatic, sounded almost angry.

"I'm afraid it is," the lieutenant said. "The victim was in your father's room, after all. If it wasn't a simple burglary, then it was Mr. Sterling who was the intended victim." The lieutenant said it with one of those little polite smiles that come so easily to the Japanese. But he said it firmly.

"Why shouldn't it have been a burglary?" Edwards insisted. "Things were taken, weren't they?"

"Roger, please!" Mrs. Edwards gestured sharply to her husband, cutting him off. "Lieutenant, we'll be happy to make a statement. Any way we can help."

"I won't," said Edwards.

"You won't?" The lieutenant seemed more confused than surprised, as if he thought he might have misunderstood.

"No, I've got to get back to Chicago. Got a business to run. I only came out here to give my dear wife support. It's obvious, though, she didn't need any."

This was directed at her, and she responded to it. "Then go, Roger, by all means, go. I intend to stay at least until tomorrow.

Mr. Cervantes and I have work to do. Isn't that right, Mr. Cervantes?"

"Uh . . . yeah . . . well . . . sure." She caught me off guard. I'd been watching and listening so closely—really as a spectator, a member of the audience—that it was almost like I'd been grabbed out of a seat on the 50-yard line and sent in with a play.

She seemed to wince at my weak response, but she went right on. "Lieutenant, will that be satisfactory? I'll come, give you your statement, and my husband can go right back to his . . . business."

"That'll be fine, Mrs. Edwards. Say, two o'clock?"

She nodded. "Well, then. Roger?" With that, they walked off together to the big Lincoln he had rented and held a hurried conference there in the parking lot.

"Are they always like this?" asked Lieutenant Shinahara. I looked at him. He wasn't smirking or smiling. It really seemed like he wanted to know.

"Well," I said, "I've only been around them for about an hour and a half, but on the basis of what I've seen, I'd say . . . yeah."

He shook his head, and with a wave and a see-you-later, he headed for his car.

What surprised me then, as I was waiting for Mrs. Edwards, was how she kissed her husband good-bye. This wasn't your average peck on the lips, see you later, honey. This was the real thing. She stood on tiptoe, pulled him to her, and gave him a long, deep one. They stood there for a moment looking in each other's eyes, then she pulled away from him and started over in my direction.

Married people! I'd never understand them! I didn't even understand myself when I was married.

It was a pretty interesting hour and a half I had spent with Mr. and Mrs. Edwards. I'd met their plane at LAX. Arriving early, I sat for a while with a paperback I carry around in the glove compartment for such occasions. Then, glancing down at my watch, I saw that it was only a few minutes until scheduled arrival time. I got up and took my place with the rest of the welcomers. A lot of them were brown-faced like me. They pressed forward eagerly, ready to greet their more prosperous relations from the East. Why was it that so many of us Californians seemed to look across the map for reassurance and—what did they call it?—validation. Sure, we had the movies and TV here, but even those guys waited for the big money men to come in from New York. Well, this flight was just in from Chicago. Maybe I didn't need to be quite so humble.

The gate attendant went over and opened the door right on time. And as the first passengers emerged from the jetway, I held up the sign I had earlier lettered in Magic Marker, EDWARDS, just like a limo chauffeur meeting his passenger. Passenger—singular. That's why I was surprised when a well-dressed man and a woman, who had been talking heatedly from the moment they came in sight, suddenly stopped in front of me. But they kept right on carping away at each other.

"But really, we're not here on holiday," said the man. "We simply don't have time."

"Oh, I know, Roger, but she'd be hurt if I were in town and didn't at least look in on her."

"Surely a telephone call would do. I've got to get back."

The two weren't even looking at me. Who were they? At this point I wasn't so sure. I edged away from them a step or two and held the sign up again.

But the woman reached out and touched my arm. "Don't go away, Mr. Cervantes. We'll be right with you." Then to the man, "Well, let's leave it at that for now, shall we, Roger?"

"That's *fine* with me."

Then at last Clarissa Edwards gave me her full attention. "As you may have guessed," she said, "this is my husband, Roger."

I started to offer my hand but saw he was staring off intently in another direction. Was he really looking for something or just trying to avoid my hand?

She shook it instead. "Clarissa Edwards," she said. "Call me Clare. I know you were only expecting me, but Roger wanted to come along. He thinks I can't handle anything by myself."

He turned and looked at her but said nothing.

"Well," I said, "maybe not this."

She nodded. "Yes, well, we'll see." Peculiar response.

I made a grab at the leather overnight bag she'd brought off the plane. "Here, I'll take that."

"No," she said, swinging it away, "no, I'll manage it."

Roger Edwards thrust his slightly larger, matching bag at me. "In that case," he said, "you can have mine."

I weighed my options and decided I really didn't have any. I reached out and took it. With a nod toward the corridor, I said, "Shall we?"

Of course, the discussion didn't end there at the gate. They kept going back and forth all the way to the short-term parking lot where I had stowed my car. Somehow I had managed to get stuck in the middle. The question was whether or not she would work in a quick visit to Grace Jarrett after the visit to the morgue. It did seem to me a rather strange plan. After all, that was presumably her father on the slab.

Anyway, we get to the lot. I walk them to my car. Roger takes a look at it, stops dead in his tracks, and says, "You've got to be kidding."

I looked at him. "What's wrong? What's the matter?"

"We're all supposed to fit in *that*?"

"Oh, Roger, come on. Don't be difficult."

I like my car. I'm proud of my car. I like it so much that one of these days I'm going to get the gray primer on the fender painted red like the rest of it. "It's got a backseat," I said, "not a big one, but it'll be okay."

"No, it won't," he said. His lips were tight, hardly moved at all, but somehow the words came out. "Take us to Hertz."

So that's what I did. He made a big deal about pulling his legs in and shifting in his seat, trying to get comfortable. He wasn't *that* big. He insisted on going directly to the Hertz lot. At one point on the drive over I caught Clarissa Edwards in the rearview mirror. She sort of rolled her eyes, or raised her eyebrows or something, very expressively, as if to say, What can you do?

Just like I figured, they gave him a hard time at Hertz—no reservation, why didn't he go to the counter in the baggage claim area? etc. But in the end, he got what he wanted. People like him usually do, just by being the way they are.

In the meantime, I was busy writing out directions to the L.A. County Morgue. We'd settled it that they would follow me, but I knew from experience that we'd probably get separated on the freeway.

And that was just about what happened. He stayed close behind me in that big Lincoln as far as the 405. But once on it, he began a pattern of alternately lagging behind and speeding up that put a row of cars between us. He switched lanes then and passed me by, so it was up to me to get in ahead of him. I managed to do that just in time to lead him onto the 10. After that, in heavier traffic, he began that lag-and-speed process again, and by the La Brea exit I'd lost him completely. Well, he had directions. The rest was up to him.

As it happened, the Edwardses arrived at the morgue parking lot about twenty minutes after I got there—had taken a wrong turn, of course, and headed out toward Anaheim. I spent part of that time standing around in front of the entrance talking to Lieutenant Shinahara. He seemed like an okay guy. I was glad he showed up instead of Lorenzen. The less I saw of my interrogator the better I liked it.

I remember that after he'd introduced himself and I'd given him the situation with the Edwardses ("any minute now"), I made some neutral comment about Lorenzen. Something like how I expected to see his "partner" there.

"Partner?" he asked. "My partner?" He seemed genuinely puzzled.

"Detective Lorenzen."

Shinahara smiled slightly and looked away. "My trainee, you mean."

"New on the job, huh?"

"He's learning." Then his eyes shifted back to me. They were smiling—just his eyes. "He give you a hard time?"

"Well . . ." I shrugged.

"He's learning." Then the lieutenant asked me bluntly, "You pay off the maid?"

"Yeah," I said. "She did her part."

He nodded, satisfied. "That's good."

Then, in a conversational way, so casually I didn't realize what he was up to until we were well into it, he took me through the story I'd told Lorenzen. Probably checking to see if I'd changed any of the details, or maybe just wanting to hear it from me. About the only point he checked me on was the time of my arrival at the hotel yesterday. He seemed to accept it when I fixed it at a little before noon. "I went to the concierge first and told him I was just going to hang out there for a few hours," I said, "and then I walked around the place a little."

"Did you go up to Sterling's room? Try the door?"

I sighed. "No. I probably should have. But I'd been in there the day before—Saturday, I guess. Mrs. Edwards fixed it up with the hotel people. The concierge let me in and waited while I took a look around, just a short look. So I didn't go back on Sunday. Didn't seem any point. Just walked around the lobby and outside on the patio a little and headed into the bar. I remember it was still before noon when I sat down because I ordered a Virgin Mary first drink. You can check all this with the concierge and the bartender."

"I already have." This guy was a pro. "Could you fill me in a little on these people, the Edwardses?"

"Yeah, well, I could, but here they come now."

I'd been so involved with the lieutenant that I hadn't noticed the Lincoln slipping into the lot. But here they were again, the Clare and Roger Show, direct from Chicago. Let's give them a big L.A. welcome, folks.

"I like your little car. I really do."

I was waiting for her to say she thought it was cute. While she didn't go quite that far, that seemed to be what she had in mind. Because Lieutenant Shinahara had asked us to come by in about an hour's time, and since neither of us was much interested in eating after what we'd seen at the morgue, I had taken Clarissa Edwards on the scenic route to Santa Monica, pointing out the sights along the way—Chinatown, lower Sunset, an old movie studio or two—none of which interested her very much. Well, I couldn't blame her. She was worried about her father, of course—afraid, as I was, that wherever he might be, he was probably in danger. That John Doe in the morgue had served as his stand-in. But she didn't want to talk about that, either, not just yet. No, what she wanted to talk about was my car.

"Is this one of those from Japan?"

"No," I said, "it's Italian. It's an Alfa Romeo."

"Oh, I've heard of them. That's better. More romantic, somehow. Maybe that's why Roger was so against it. The man hasn't a romantic bone in his body."

I got her to talk a little about Roger Edwards. He was, as I'd figured out, in business with her father—not an employee, it seemed, more of a partner. What sort of business? "They're on the Board of Trade," she said. I know that should tell me more than it did. I had the idea that it was something like the stock market, but beyond that, I would have been guessing. Anyway, it was money, big money, and it looked like Roger had married the boss's daughter. What was it they used to say in Hollywood? The son-in-law also rises, and right up next to the top in this case. Well, there was no crime in that.

"Do you have any brothers and sisters?" I asked her.

"No," she said, "I'm an only child, and a late arrival at that."

With that, she lapsed into silence. She seemed to want it that way. So, although I had some questions for her, I put them off until later. Driving down Wilshire now, passing under that bent arc that marks the entry into Santa Monica, we had almost reached the turnoff to the cop house anyway.

Once in the parking lot I found a visitor's space near the entrance. Our names had been left at the gate by Shinahara. Jumping out of the car, I hurried around to Mrs. Edwards's side to give her a hand and show her the way. I found her fishing her overnight bag out of the backseat. That seemed a little strange to me, but maybe she had something inside to show the lieutenant.

As we entered the station and stepped up to the reception desk, a heavyset man a little older than thirty, well barbered and manicured, dressed in a pinstripe suit, white shirt, and paisley tie, walked up to Mrs. Edwards and introduced himself. Whatever his name was, and I didn't really catch it, he was a lawyer. He explained that he'd been asked by the Edwardses' law firm in Chicago "to assist her in making her statement to the police."

She nodded, accepted that, and allowed herself to be guided over to one corner. I stood and watched, heard nothing, as they held a quick, whispered conference.

Shinahara appeared. He looked over at them curiously, then back at me with his eyebrows raised in a question mark.

"Lawyer," I said.

He nodded and waited there a moment or two longer. Then, "Mrs. Edwards?"

The two of them came over together, but she stopped and said to me, "I won't be needing you further. I'll be getting a lift over to San Marino. I'll give you a call tonight, or perhaps in the morning, and we'll plan our day."

I turned to Shinahara. "Lieutenant?"

He shrugged. "You can go."

And so I went. Dismissed. Just like that. She knew the lawyer would be there. That's why she had grabbed her overnight bag from the backseat. They had probably arranged it before they took off from Chicago.

Don't get me wrong. The lawyer was a good idea, a precautionary measure, you might say, just in case the cops get too aggressive asking questions. In the ideal world, everybody should have one along in a situation like this, but not everybody can afford one. Money makes the difference. It insulates you in ways most of us never considered.

Somehow I resented that.

4

With time on my hands, I pulled out of the police lot wondering which way to turn, where I ought to go. Clarissa Edwards had given me the afternoon off. I didn't *want* the afternoon off. If the guy in the morgue wasn't Benjamin Sterling, then Sterling was still out there somewhere waiting for me to find him. But where should I look?

With nowhere better to go, noplace better to start, I decided to resume my search where I had left off—back at the hotel. I headed west, just about as far west as you can go in the Los Angeles area, to Ocean Avenue, Santa Monica.

Parking there has gone up, as just about everything else has. If you're lucky enough to find a space, you'd better have a pocketful of quarters, because that's all the meters take. As it happened, digging deep, I discovered four. That gave me two hours to dig around, ask questions, and show that photo of Sterling I had been carrying around with me for the past couple of days. It occurred to me that maybe I'd better pick up some more change along the way.

I was a good block and a half away from the hotel when I started out, walking along the little park that overlooks Pacific

Coast Highway and the beach beyond. It's a nice little strip of green where they hold arts-and-crafts shows a couple of times a year. The rest of the time it seems to belong strictly to joggers and the homeless.

That's the thing about Santa Monica; it's probably the most schizophrenic town in America. Yes, it is a town—or a small city—less than a hundred thousand, separated from Los Angeles by history, politics, and a border that runs along a jagged line just west of the San Diego Freeway. Santa Monica has its own mayor, city council, police force, even has its own bus line. Visitors probably think of it as just one of the nicer parts of L.A., like Westwood or Brentwood. But if you live there, or go there to hang out the way a lot of people do, then you better believe you know the difference between the big town and the People's Republic of Santa Monica.

Schizophrenic? You bet.

On the one hand, it's the glitziest community this side of Beverly Hills. It may not have those Rodeo Drive boutiques, but it's got the restaurants, the movies, the bars, the energy, everything that geriatric Beverly Hills probably never had. It's got style. It's got the Third Street Promenade. It's got chic Montana Avenue. It's got real celebrities, not has-beens. And they live in houses that cost in the millions, just the way they do in Bel Air, Holmby Hills, and, yeah, in Beverly Hills, too.

On the other hand, Santa Monica also has a conscience. It goes back to a renters' revolt that led to the election of a new city council and eventually to a new mayor. What followed was not just a rent control law tougher than L.A.'s, but also a slow-growth, keep-Santa-Monica-funky policy that put a brake on development at least along the beach. That's when the landlords and the developers began calling it the People's Republic. But in a way, what pleased those guys even less was the treatment given the homeless: the city administration told the cops to go easy on them, began serving free lunches, opened up shelters. Word got around, and a migration westward from downtown L.A. began— the unshaven and unwashed, pushing shopping carts that dangled plastic bags crammed with God knew what, panhandling their way to the promised land.

And here they are, more of them every day, or so it seems. On a warm, sunny, early-spring day like this one they chill out along the Ocean Avenue strip park, men and women, old and young, sitting on the benches, stretched out on the grass. They seem satisfied just being there. Were they hurting anyone? No. Were they bringing down property values? Well, maybe just a little. They weren't even much bother to the few, like me, hiking along the sidewalk like they had someplace to go—once in a while an outstretched palm or a hand jingling coins in a Styrofoam cup. These had to be the least aggressive down-and-outers in the Western world.

One guy stopped me, though, not so much by what he said— "Hey, man, welcome to my enterprise zone"—as by his appearance. He was black, or I guess African-American, because he wasn't much darker than me. Clean-shaven and in a clean shirt, he didn't look like he belonged.

"You're out of uniform, soldier."

He gave me a long, slow smile at that, looking around at the begrimed bunch around him. "I like to keep up . . . well, appearances, anyway," he said. "At least that."

"How long you been at this?"

"Too long," he said. "GM plant in Van Nuys shut down. Took about a year for me to get here. Tried too hard to hold onto my, uh, lifestyle. Where I went wrong, see."

I just said, "Yeah," imagining myself in the same situation, filing it away.

He waggled his coffee cup at me. Coins jingled at the bottom. "How about it, man? Am I victim enough for you?"

There was an edge to that, of course. I ignored it. Instead, I hauled out the picture of Benjamin Sterling and handed it over to him. "Have you seen this guy?"

"You a cop?"

"Private."

He nodded, then he held the picture up and gave it serious

consideration. At last he nodded and said, "Yeah, I think I've seen him. Here. Recently."

"What do you mean, 'here'? In Santa Monica?"

"Sure, in Santa Monica. But I mean, right here, in the park."

His eyes narrowed a moment, frowning, thinking. "Or *maybe* down on the beach."

"Are you sure?"

"I'd be lyin' if I said I was. No, I'm *not* sure. I *think* I saw him. That's all."

"What kind of shape was he in? Did he seem dazed, out of it?"

"Oh, man, I don't know. Just a face I *think* I saw in the last couple of days. That's all."

"Okay," I said, "I accept that." I shoved a ten-dollar bill into his cup, reminding myself to expense it.

"And I accept *that*! Thank you."

"Look," I said, "here's my card. You see him, you call me. Okay?"

"Will do, man. No doubt about it." He waved at me as I started away. "I'll keep my eyes open for him. I will!"

Well, that was interesting, in a way encouraging—the first good news I'd had since I'd seen that body in the bathroom. Buoyed by it, I made it the rest of the way to the hotel at a fast clip.

There were no panhandlers anywhere near it. It had been a problem when the place opened a couple of years earlier. They ganged up around the entrance. You don't pay a couple of hundred a night for a place to sleep and then expect to get hit for a handout on the way out. So now I heard the management paid them to keep away, maybe paid the cops to see it stayed that way, too.

I caught a flicker of the wrong kind of recognition from the doorman as he held it open wide for me. Persona non grata? Probably. As far as the hotel staff was concerned, I'd brought them only trouble. All, that is, except for Pilar Ramirez: as far as she was concerned, I'd brought her five hundred bucks. It was her I wanted to see, anyway.

Because I was halfway sure that the doorman would be on the

phone to the front desk at just that moment, telling them of my arrival, I dodged behind the shrubbery, heading for the bank of elevators. I jumped into one as the doors were closing and headed up to the third level in the company of a couple in their fifties.

Once up there, I paused for a moment to look for the maid's cart. I looked and I looked, but no cart, no direct sign of her anywhere. There was, however, a door open, exactly the room I wanted to see. I headed over there, past the door with the yellow police bands across it, to the next one, the room where I'd spent the worst part of yesterday afternoon.

I came in, calling out, *"Señora Ramirez. ¡Tengo una pregunta para Usted!"*

Uh-oh, my mistake—for who should come out of the bathroom but Detective Lorenzen, looking for trouble, as usual. He stood there, hands on hips, and shouted across the room at me, "What're *you* doing here?"

I stood my ground. "Looking for the maid," I said to him.

"She ain't here."

"So I see." I turned and started back out of the room.

"Wait a minute, you."

I stuck my head back reluctantly. "Yeah?"

"Come back in here."

I weighed the possibility of just walking away, running away if I had to. He had no reason to detain me. He couldn't justify it. But maybe he didn't know that. He was, after all, just a detective-trainee. In the end, after a moment's hesitation, I stepped back inside and waited.

He came over to me, walking very slowly and purposefully. His face was hard to read. There was a sort of solemn scowl on it. When he stood before me within punching distance I began mentally measuring the space behind for a backward jump. I shifted my weight slightly.

He was breathing heavily, practically hyperventilating. Finally, he managed to come out with it. "The lieutenant said I should apologize to you next time I saw you. So . . . I'm sorry. I guess I was out of line yesterday."

He thrust an open hand at my belly. It was all I could do to keep from ducking away, but in the end I had no choice but to shake it. Expecting a bone-crushing squeeze, I got no more than an indifferent wiggle. What to say to him? "Yeah, well, no harm done," I muttered. "Don't mention it."

He let go of my hand. We stood awkwardly. Not much eye contact. Then he said, "Okay," meaning, I guessed, that I could go.

But as I backed out of the room, I decided to press my luck. "You turn up anything in here?" I asked. "Find out who was in this room and smoked all those cigarettes?"

Suddenly rigid, he snarled, "None of your fucking business. It's a police matter. Stay out of it."

With that, he restored my faith in human nature. Something like, you can make a leopard apologize, but you can't change his spots. I gave him a nod and left, chuckling to myself.

I never did find Señora Ramirez. When at last I located a cart outside one of the rooms in the back corridor, I looked inside and saw that the maid busily making the bed was Asian. She looked up at me, startled. I gave her a wave and a smile I hoped would seem reassuring and went on my way. Maybe it was the good Señora's day off, or maybe she'd phoned in sick and gone out to spend the five hundred.

With no better prospects inside the hotel, I decided to wander around outside and study the faces back there in the park. Who knows? I might get lucky. But on my way out, the moment I stepped out on the lobby floor, I had a temporary change of plan.

I spotted the lady from the accounting office.

She was just walking by, a sheaf of papers in her hand. Maybe she'd picked them up at the reception desk, or maybe she'd been back to check on something. Anyway, there she was, and seeing her, I got an idea.

I called out quietly, "Ma'am? Hey, please?"

She continued on a couple of steps but turned as she did and saw me. Not knowing quite what I wanted, she gave me a tentative smile of recognition and a nod, then continued on her way. But by that time I had caught up with her.

"You remember me? Yesterday? I was with the cop, the . . . the loose cannon?"

She nodded. "Oh, I remember, all right. The odd couple."

She started walking again. I matched her step for step, looking all around as we went to see if we'd been noticed. So far so good. "I, uh, was wondering if you could do me a favor."

A wry smile. "Probably not," she said.

"See, I'm a private investigator. That's why that cop was giving me such a hard time."

"Oh?" Definitely noncommittal.

"And I was just wondering, there's a piece of paper that's got to do with the investigation that I'd really like to see. *Need* to see."

"And what might that piece of paper be?"

By now we were headed down the hallway toward the accounting office. I had to pull this off pretty quickly or I'd lose her. Something told me that the last thing I should do was offer her money. "Ma'am, I'll tell you, the police get what they want just by asking. What I have to do is beg."

She stopped and faced me. "Is that what you're doing? Begging?"

"Well, more or less."

"Just who're you representing?"

"The daughter of the man in room three-oh-eight."

"The man who was killed?"

I sighed. "Well, it's sort of complicated. She hired me to find him, and then this corpse turns up in his room. But I was just with her at the morgue, and she says it's not her father."

"Really? The plot thickens."

Ah-hah! I had her hooked. Now, if I could just land her.

"Understand, that's confidential information," I said. "I'd appreciate it if you didn't mention it, even to the people here at the hotel."

"Oh, I won't, Mr. . . . ."

"Cervantes. Here's my card." I whipped one out and pressed it into her palm.

Holding it up, she read it carefully and looked back at me. By this time I had my wallet out and my State of California p.i. license up where she could look it over. That's just what she did. At last, satisfied, she said, "What is it you want?"

"I'd like to see the bill for the party who checked out of room three-oh-six yesterday morning."

"Three-oh-six, not three-oh-eight?"

"That's right."

"The room next door?"

"Yes."

She looked around, not like she expected to see anyone but just taking a moment to decide. Then she said, "Wait here." In another second or two she had disappeared through the door. The glimpse I got into the office told me it was fully staffed today. I just hoped nobody came out of there before she did and asked me why I was hanging around. Well, if they did, I'd think of something.

In a few minutes—less than five—she came back out, waving the document. I reached for it, but she held it out of reach.

"Any chance I could get a copy of that?" I asked.

"I don't think so. It might look just a little suspicious."

"Well, okay. Let's see it then."

She held it up, and I crowded in close for a look over her shoulder. The name of the party in room 306 was William Hill—a bit more imaginative than John Smith, anyway—with an address in Denver. There was no credit card impression, so I could only assume that he had paid in cash. There was a check mark in front of the room number he had been assigned. I pointed at it. "What's this mean?" I asked my friend from the accounting office.

"It means that he requested that room in particular," she said.

"Well, isn't that pretty unusual?"

"No, not really. People come back, they like the room they had, they want it back. Couples for sentimental reasons, sometimes."

"This guy wasn't a couple."

"No."

"So then?"

"The view? I don't know. This room had a nice view of the ocean. Maybe that was it." She seemed oddly defensive. Why?

"But look," I said, pointing to the time stamp, "he checked out at eight-sixteen in the morning. He didn't hang around long enough to enjoy the view."

She sighed. "No, he didn't."

More than likely he got out of there just as soon as he'd put away the guy in the next room. I stared down at the document. Then I pointed down at some numbers down in one corner—3/16. "What's this?" I asked. "Some kind of code?" They'd evidently been put there by the desk clerk.

"Yes, it's a code," she said, "for internal use." A barrier had suddenly gone up. These three numbers just bothered the hell out of her.

"Well, what does it stand for?"

She turned away and took a step toward the door. It looked like I'd lost her. Then she turned back and, in a loud whisper, said, "It means Mr. Hill was black."

Then she explained that the hotel kept a running record of minority registrations—1 for Asians, 2 for Hispanics, and 3 for blacks.

"Is that legal?" I asked.

"Probably not. They justify it by claiming that if they ever get sued they can prove they don't turn away anybody. But they do. That's what the 16 means. Mr. Hill hit sixteen on a scale of twenty—well-dressed, quality luggage. He passed the eyeball test. Anything below ten, there would have been a problem with his reservation, all rooms booked." She hesitated, then added, "Naturally, being the color I am, I don't approve of this practice, but I want to keep my job, so . . ."

She put her hand on the doorknob then and gave me a curt nod of good-bye.

"Hey, wait a minute," I said. "Do the cops know about this?"

"I don't know," she said, "you'll have to ask them yourself." With that, she opened the door and stepped into the accounting office.

★   ★   ★

As I wandered out of the hotel and onto Ocean Avenue, my mind shifted back to the homeless guy I'd talked to about twenty minutes earlier. He was black and notably better dressed than the rest of those in the park. Maybe he was the party in room 306.

That made me annoyed with myself. Typical copthink. You got a complaint on a black/Hispanic/Asian? Then just grab the nearest black/Hispanic/Asian, and you've got a suspect. Isn't that the way it works? Yes, far too often that was just how it worked.

I picked away at it some more. After all, just say for the sake of argument that the black guy in the park was the one who had put four bullets into the shaver. If he had, he wouldn't be hanging around the next day. He'd get as far away as he could—go back to Denver, if that was where he was from. Which, of course, was highly unlikely. He had no way of knowing the man he killed was not Benjamin Sterling.

Even so, when I came to the little strip park that ran along Ocean, I slowed down and kept an eye open for the black guy. For Benjamin Sterling, too. A couple of times I left the sidewalk to get a closer look at groups stretched out under the April sun. No luck. But since I had nothing better to do that afternoon, I kept right on looking, going past my car, pausing just long enough to check the meter, and continuing all the way past Wilshire and the statue of Saint Monica to the turnoff leading down to Pacific Coast Highway. Still no luck.

On the way back, I showed Sterling's picture a few times to homeless guys who hit me for change.

"Have you seen him?"

"No."

"Let me know if you do." Passing my card, stuffing a bill into a dirty palm.

And so on down the line. Not a single yes, not even a maybe.

It was pretty discouraging work. I'd half intended to do a tour of the beach, showing the picture to the permanent residents there, but by the time I got back to my car, I decided I was hungry. The effects of my visit to the morgue seemed to have worn off. So I drove a few blocks up Ocean to Chez Jay's, hung a left, and pulled into one of the parking spaces in the lot.

Jay's is one of the few real places in Santa Monica, as far from the chichi of Montana Avenue as Hollywood is from Beverly Hills. It's a dark bar that serves good food. The decor is kind of nautical but nice. There's just one problem I have at Chez Jay's.

"What'll you have?"

"Gimme a Dos Equis."

"No got."

"What *do* you got? Mexican beers, I mean."

"Zero, friend. Sorry."

"Not even Corona?"

"Not even Corona."

I settled for a Beck's and ordered a cheeseburger to go with it. It was well into the afternoon by that time, and the place was pretty empty. The waitress seemed to believe I'd be lucky to get fed at all. "Cook's on his break," she informed me. "This may take a while."

That didn't matter. I needed time to think.

I still believed my original theory on Sterling had some validity. He might have found a comfortable bed partner and simply dropped out for a week or so. That didn't explain why somebody wanted him dead, of course. (Jealous lover? Not likely. Burglar? Even less likely. Business? Probable, but at this point I knew nothing about that.) It did, however, suggest why the guy had been so darned hard to find.

Maybe I was going at this from the wrong angle. It looked like whoever shot the guy in room 308 thought he was taking out Sterling. Maybe that wasn't the way it was at all. It could be that he knew exactly who he was hitting. It didn't seem likely, but I had to admit it was a possibility. In that case, the identity of the victim would be the key to it all.

Yeah, but that wasn't my problem. I was quite willing to leave the homicide to Lieutenant Shinahara and the Santa Monica Police. Clarissa Edwards had hired me to find her father; that was my job. Now, with the murder, it was more important than ever.

I kept batting all this around in my brain as I sipped away at the Beck's. At one point I found myself trying to remember if the black guy I talked to in the park had been smoking a cigarette—

remembering that mighty pile of Marlboros in the ashtray there in room 306. So I guess I hadn't given up on that entirely. Copthink.

Then at last the cheeseburger came, with the usual heap of fries. I ordered another Beck's and got to work on the cheeseburger. About that time the door to the place opened, and a figure stood for a moment just inside, blinking, trying to adjust his eyes to the dark interior. He looked familiar, a guy I used to drink with at Barney's Beanery—Bill . . . Bill? I couldn't remember his last name, so I went with what I had. "Hey, Bill, come on over." I motioned to the barstool next to mine.

"Chico! How you doin', my man? It's been a while." He heaved himself up on the barstool and offered his hand. I wiped mine on the paper napkin and shook it.

It hadn't really been so long since I'd seen him—just last fall at Majestic Pictures. I wondered if he remembered the day as clearly as I did. It was when that whole mess began that got me kicked off the lot. I also remembered his name now. It was Bill Schmidt, and he was a gaffer.

"What're you doing down here?"

"Oh, I live here now." He said it like I should have read about it in the newspaper or something. "Nice little two-room and kitchen within walking distance of the beach. And it's"—he paused dramatically and rolled his eyes at the sweetness of it—*"rent-controlled!"*

"How'd you luck into that?"

"The usual. I knew somebody who knows somebody. You know how Santa Monica is."

"Yeah, I guess."

The bartender came over, and Bill Schmidt ordered a Bud.

We talked. Oh, we talked about whatever it is that grown men talk about when they really don't have much in common. Probably about the Lakers and how they weren't the same without Magic, how amazing it was to see a team tumble like the Dodgers did last season. Basically kid talk is what it was, flavored with the sour disappointment of maturity: Things would never be as good as they'd been before.

He slugged his Bud down right out of the bottle the way he used to do at Barney's. I finished my cheeseburger. Then I got around to asking him what he was working on. Crew guys always like to talk about that. The new movie is always Academy quality.

"Oh, well." He shrugged. "I'm between jobs. Things are tough right now. Production's down all over. Last job I had, they didn't even release it—that Tommy Osborne biopic, *Cold Wind*. It was Academy all the way, then there was this big mess when they found Osborne where he was hiding out up in northern California. You probably read about that."

"Yeah," I said, "I saw something."

He sighed. "But this D.P. I work with has a start next month. I guess I'll be crewing on that one."

"That's good."

"Yeah, but TV, they just keep churning that stuff out. Some of it isn't so bad, though. Majestic's got a new three-camera show. You seen it? "Lupe"? Real cute."

"Uh, yeah, I . . . uh, saw it."

"Little seenyorita who plays the title role—she's a knockout, isn't she?"

"Oh, yeah, really . . . nice."

"And funny! Really funny, got some talent. Like that first episode when she shows up at the State Employment Office looking for a job. Oh, man, *that* was funny."

"Look," I said, "I'd better be going."

"Come on, Chico, stick around. I'll buy the next one."

"No, really, I'm working."

"Working? You mean, like, a case?" He was impressed. "Anything you can talk about?"

"Just the usual—a missing person's beef."

"Well, I respect that. Man, what you do must be so *interesting*."

As I settled with the bartender and the waitress, Schmidt insisted on writing out his new address and phone number. "If this one next month doesn't work out—God forbid—we could get together and write scripts—or treatments, anyway. You gotta have a hundred stories in your files."

I hear that a lot.

There was still some afternoon left when I left Chez Jay's, so I decided to proceed with my earlier plan to walk the beach. I drove onto Santa Monica Pier, left my car there, descended to sand level, and marched south.

I knew who I was looking for but not *what*. Would Benjamin Sterling be with a woman? Had he decked himself out in jeans by now? Would he be sitting alone on the sand, studying the incoming tide? What was his attitude? *Why* had he disappeared?

Because it was a Monday, the crowd along the walkway was thin, mostly couples, male and female, male and male, female and female. A few skaters flashed by on brand new Rollerblades. I felt kind of out of place in my jacket and tie, so I peeled off the tie, rolled it up, and tucked it into my pocket. That felt better.

This was the California that people in the East dream about. They don't think desert. They don't think mountains. They think of the whole state as one long strip of beach with just a few palm trees to break the monotony. Out there, too, the blue Pacific with some surfers dotting the seascape. Life under the sun. I wondered why it was I seemed to do most of my work on dark streets at night.

Along the way, I was stopped from time to time by panhandlers. The same routine with the picture over and over again, with just about the same results, until I was hit on by a creepy-looking character with wild eyes and a full beard. He also didn't smell so good.

I showed him the picture of Benjamin Sterling.

His head began bobbing up and down like a puppet's. "Oh yeah, man, I saw him, I did, just yesterday. Uh-huh. No doubt about it."

He was not what you'd call a reliable witness. "Are you sure?" I asked him.

"I said I was sure, didn't I? I mean, it was him. What can I tell you? I remember him because of his aura."

"His aura?"

"Oh, yeah, man, everybody's got one. You got a pretty good

one, kind of hums a little. Good. Not great, but good." He gave a great nod of certainty. "His was great. Like, a saint."

"Yeah?" I must have sounded dubious. That wasn't really how I thought of Benjamin Sterling.

"Oh, yeah, right. His was terrific. The guy he was with, though, not so good. Huh-uh, no, not so good."

"Who was he with?"

"I don't know, some guy. But the guy, the guy in the picture, him I remember. He was outstanding. He gave me, like, some change, said he'd give me more but he had his wallet stolen. I told him, 'No problem, man, it's a pleasure to meet you. You're, like, a saint.' You know what he did then? He laughed. Weird, huh? Didn't know his own power."

"So what happened?"

"Nothing. *That* happened, what I told you. He and the other guy just went on their way."

"Tell me about the other guy."

"Nothing to tell. Just a guy. Light red aura. Kinda pink. Not good."

"Black? White? Asian? What?"

"Oh, I don't know. White, I guess. I don't pay much attention to skin color."

Somehow I believed that. I believed *him*.

"This was yesterday? What time?"

"Oh, I don't know. I'm not real good on time."

I believed that, too.

I started to push my card at him and give him my pitch about calling me if and when he might see Sterling again, but he refused it.

"Can't take it, man. I don't deal with telephones. They're evil, man, like, part of the devil's design. You know what I mean?"

"Uh, maybe. I think I do."

"You come back tomorrow. I'll let you know if I saw him again."

I promised to do that, stuffed a ten in his cup, and moved away. Looking back at him, I decided that it was because of all that aura bullshit that I believed him. He wasn't looking at me, though. He kept right on shaking his cup, examining the passing auras. Maybe he was crazy, a burnt-out case from the sixties, but I was sure he had seen Benjamin Sterling just yesterday.

I walked all the way down to Ocean Park Avenue, then started back again, with the sun off to my left lowering toward the horizon. This time I stayed close to the surf line and managed to get my feet wet a couple of times along the way. It seemed the way to go, though. The few people still out on the sand were sitting close to the water. I could keep an eye out for Sterling this way, see some faces I'd overlooked before. But why not admit it? I'd punched out. The day was over, as far as I was concerned. I figured I'd given Mrs. Edwards her money's worth. Now I was just loafing along the waterline, enjoying the beach at sundown the way I used to when I was a *mozo*.

What the hell, I'd found out a couple of things that day, hadn't I? By the time I got back to my car up on the pier, I was telling myself what a tough, tenacious fellow I was. Well, a bulldog detective like me deserved a drink before plunging into rush-hour traffic. Why not? I knew a quiet little bar there on the pier. That's where I headed.

This, as you will see, was a mistake.

Not a big one, but a definite error. One Cuervo Gold on the rocks, no more. I sipped at it and made it last half an hour as I watched the news on the TV behind the bar. When I left it was dark. My driving was fine. I had KLON tuned in, listening to jazz all the way up Santa Monica Boulevard, just keeping up with traffic. I was relaxed.

If I hadn't felt quite so relaxed, I might have noticed those two guys when I pulled into the parking garage beneath my building. I mean, I was so relaxed I even held the elevator door for them. New neighbors? Visitors? Come on in, fellas.

They looked kind of big and athletic, but what did a tough, tenacious fellow like me have to fear? Plenty, as it turned out.

They beat the shit out of me. It was all very fast and done with amazing precision. One of them grabbed me and held my arms tight behind me while the other one hit me ten or twelve times hard in the midsection. Then the elevator hit the lobby floor and, as the doors opened, I was thrown to the floor and given a kick in the gut by each of them.

They jumped out, but one of them hung back, holding the doors to the elevator open as he watched me rolling around on the floor like a beetle on its back.

"The message is: Lay off. Give it up. Forget about it." That's what he said, and then he ducked back out and let the doors close.

The next minutes I don't remember so well. The elevator stopped at my floor, and I managed to crawl out. I must have half-walked, half-crawled to my door, unlocked it, and gotten inside, because the next thing I knew I was in the bathroom, on the floor, vomiting into the toilet bowl. It all came out—cheeseburger, beer, tequila, followed by a lot of nasty fluid that just sort of squirted indiscriminately through my nose and throat. Finally, the dry heaves came, then subsided, as I hung on to the toilet bowl, panting.

The telephone rang. Jesus, I thought, let it ring. And that's just what it did. But I didn't answer, not that night.

5

"Well, you certainly don't *look* like you've been beaten up."

I guess it was up to me to prove it. I began unbuttoning my shirt, just the buttons around my chest.

"Mr. Cervantes, *please!*" Grace Jarrett wanted no vulgar displays in her living room. "You don't have to show us."

But Clarissa Edwards clearly had her doubts. She waited, her mouth pressed into a firm line as I exposed the adhesive wrapping just above my middle.

"Satisfied?" I asked. "For some reason they left my face alone. I suppose I should be glad they did."

"Who bandaged you up?" she asked.

Did she think I did it myself? One of the two good-bye kicks had cracked a couple of ribs. After I'd emptied my stomach into the toilet bowl, I became acutely aware that there was something wrong there on my right side, a pain that kept getting worse. It hurt to breathe. So as soon as I was able, I managed to take myself off to the emergency room at Cedars-Sinai, tell them I'd been mugged, and get X-rayed and wrapped with a broad band of adhesive, about the only thing you can do for cracked ribs. The painkiller they gave me helped, though.

Did I tell Mrs. Edwards all this? No, I just said that I'd been to the emergency room. But then I added, "Maybe you'd like the whole show," and undid the two buttons above my belt. I tugged open the gap and gave them a view of my colorful belly. Red, yellow, blue—the bruises were only beginning to bloom, but they were impressive just as they were.

Grace Jarrett fluttered her hand at me. Sympathetically. "Oh, you poor man. But please now, button up."

What was this? Indecent exposure? I did as she told me.

"I assume," said Mrs. Edwards, "that you're covered for that trip to the hospital. Health insurance, that sort of thing."

"I'm covered."

"Good." Her face relaxed into a tentative smile. I could see I was going to have some trouble getting that five hundred bucks out of her.

Tucking my shirt in carefully—it still hurt plenty down there—I gave Mrs. Edwards one of my killer stares. "This is all to explain why I didn't return your call last night." She had plainly been annoyed, and I had been annoyed at that. I don't know if it was right at that moment or earlier, but I remember thinking, You don't own me, lady, you just rent me.

"Well, of course," she said, "that's perfectly understandable." Her mouth had gone tight again.

"Now, the big question in my mind is why somebody who we can assume thought your father was already dead would tell me to lay off, to stop looking for him. It doesn't make good sense."

"No," she said, "it doesn't."

"The newspapers didn't carry the story until this morning, so how did they know?"

"I have no idea."

"Maybe the killer knew he'd shot the wrong guy just as soon as he'd done it. Maybe there was enough of the victim's face left so the killer could tell."

"Perhaps."

"I have to say, though, it's really got me puzzled."

"Hmmm. Well . . ."

"Now what was it you wanted me to call you about?"

"Oh, yes, of course, *that.*" Clare Edwards proceeded to tell me that she'd gotten a call from her father's housekeeper, the one who paid the household bills. As it happened, she'd just gotten one from the telephone company, and checking the long-distance calls, the housekeeper noticed that there had been a couple there to the West Coast just before he left on the trip out here.

Aha! I thought, the girlfriend!

But no. "She gave me the number, and I called it myself," said Mrs. Edwards. "It belongs to a Mr. Cosentino." She said it like I ought to know who he was. The name meant nothing to me.

"Who's he?"

"Well, I don't know, really, but I called him, and he's someone who had dinner with my father just last Wednesday."

"The day before your father disappeared."

She nodded emphatically. "That's right," she said. "I thought we ought to see Mr. Cosentino."

"I think so, too."

"Good. I told him we'd be out to see him at . . ." She looked at her watch, a big-faced, man-sized Rolex. "Well, in less than an hour. Is San Pedro some distance away?"

"Pretty far. We'd better get started."

The drive out to San Pedro was uneventful and pretty quiet. Through most of the trip, Clarissa Edwards just stared out the window. Since there wasn't much to look at along the way, she could only be considering the case—her options, the possibilities. Who knows? Maybe she was thinking of firing me and hiring somebody else. That had never happened to me in the middle of a case before, but there was a first time for everything.

Grace Jarrett had gotten me the job. She and Clarissa Edwards had been roommates at some college in the East and had kept in touch, so when this problem with Benjamin Sterling came up, I was recommended. I'd never worked for Mrs. Jarrett before, but I put her ex-husband out of the drug business, and that sent me to the top of her preferred list of Mexican-American private eyes. I liked her. She was a decent woman who'd had some tragedy in her life. I'd hoped to have a few moments to talk privately with her, but that hadn't worked out—not that morning, anyway. I was curious whether she had heard anything about her ex-husband, Thomas Jarrett. He was an enemy. It's always good to know what your enemies are up to.

I was on automatic pilot through most of the trip, trying to sort through the little I had picked up the day before. I wondered about the identity of the man traveling with Sterling, the one with the bad aura. Not that I took any of that stuff seriously, but good aura or bad, who was he? What were the two of them doing together? What did they have in common? What sort of influence did he have over Sterling?

Then there was the question of the black man in room 306. Although I didn't know who he was, it seemed like we'd met. The night before, as I knelt on the bathroom floor, retching my last into the toilet bowl, the whole episode of about forty-five seconds' duration began rerunning in my mind like a bad dream. I'd been through it a couple of times when I finally realized that the guy who held me for the hitter had been black. Could I be sure? I hadn't paid much attention when he stepped onto the elevator, couldn't see him while I was being worked over, and I was too far gone when they'd finished with me. The other guy was white. Him I wouldn't forget. Dark-haired, maybe Italian, he seemed to enjoy what he was doing. He wore a kind of fixed smile as he went about his work. Let's look at that beginning part again. And so, staggering to my feet, holding my hand to the pain in my right side, I concentrated on the two of them, jogging to the elevator wearing—what?—workout clothes (a nice touch), then on the elevator, one of them leaning over to push the button for the lobby. Yes, that guy was definitely black. His face? No clear impression: young, clean-shaven, bright-eyed.

I guess I was lucky he didn't put a gun to my head.

I glanced over at my passenger. She now sat staring straight ahead, her arms folded in front of her.

"Mrs. Edwards?"

"Yes?"

My eyes went back to the road. "Did anything come up in that interview you had with Lieutenant Shinahara?"

"How do you mean?"

"Well, for instance, did that lawyer object to any of his questions?"

"No. He was ready to, eager I might say, but nothing came up. He seemed sort of apologetic afterward that he hadn't been of more use to me." She paused. "It went well. Why shouldn't it have?"

"No reason."

"You came up."

"Oh?"

"Yes. The lieutenant wanted to know how I'd happened to choose you. I told him through Grace."

"I see."

"He seemed to want to put me at ease then, so he told me that he'd run a check on you and that you had a good reputation. He said you were cooperating with the investigation."

"Good. I'm glad he said that. I am cooperating." But maybe not a hundred percent. "Did he say anything about the investigation?"

"How do you mean?"

"Oh, like, for instance, do they have anything on the killer? Any idea who he might be?" (What color?)

I glanced over at her again. She was looking at me, frowning. "No," she said, "but would they tell me that?"

"Probably not. Just one other thing. Are they still calling it a burglary?"

"I don't know what they're calling it, Mr. Cervantes. I do know, however, that the lieutenant said that the Santa Monica police were looking for my father now, and that when they found him we should get him out of town right away."

Out of their jurisdiction, anyway.

"Sounds right to me," I said.

Out of mine, too.

Al Cosentino lived on his boat. That makes him sound like sort of a playboy. He was anything but that. He had started out as a commercial fisherman, he told us, just after the war when there was still a pretty healthy industry in the towns along the Santa Monica Bay and farther south. But gradually, as the bay became polluted and the fish ran out, he, like most of the rest, cashed in, got what he could from his boat, and went into another line of work.

"It was either that," he said, "or upgrade, become a corporation, get an ocean trawler and stay out a couple a weeks at a time. Didn't appeal to me. Didn't like the debt. I didn't like being away from my wife that long, either. Mostly, I guess I was just getting too old to make that kind of change in my life."

He was showing us around the boat, walking us from bow to stern, giving us what amounted to the grand tour.

"She's a beauty, isn't she? It was finding her that decided things for me."

I haven't been on many boats, only been out on the water a couple of times, but this one impressed me. It was sort of like going back to the real thing, the age of sail or something.

"She's kind of an antique, really," he said. "Wooden-hulled, built up in Washington in nineteen forty-one. Fifty feet, two masts, with a good, solid in-board auxiliary engine. People see that wooden hull, and they can hardly wait to get on board. I had to learn sailing to make it work."

He had a sport-fishing business. As he explained it, he would take them south, off Baja, and out into the deep water, keep them overnight, maybe two, three at the most, whatever they wanted. In the beginning, his first few years in the new business, his wife would sometimes come along and cook for the fishing parties. They both liked that. It was fun for her.

"But then," he explained, "she got the cancer, and we had to quit that. There were about three years there when I stayed pretty close to home."

She died, and after that, there seemed no point in having a house as well as a boat, and so Cosentino sold off everything and moved onto the boat.

"I got a regular little home here," he said proudly. "My own captain's cabin, a galley, and the saloon. Come on down to my living room." Then he added, "I made some coffee for us."

How had Clarissa Edwards reacted to all this? It was hard to tell. She had followed along behind Cosentino, giving little nods, asking nothing at all. To tell the truth, she seemed sort of vaguely annoyed. Maybe, still, at me. Cosentino had said all the right things when we came aboard—how glad he was that the man in the morgue wasn't her father and so on—but then he had taken us around the boat and nothing more had passed between them.

"You take cream? Sugar?" he asked once we were settled in the saloon.

"Both, thank you," she said.

He went back to the galley, and Mrs. Edwards flashed me a look I couldn't quite interpret. Maybe it meant she wanted me to take the lead with Cosentino—I had expected to—or maybe she wanted to ask the questions herself. I wasn't used to having a client along. I didn't like it much.

But he didn't need much prompting. He took a place across from us at the swing table, and as she proceeded to denature her coffee, he launched right in. "You know this wasn't the first time Ben and I got together," he said. "Oh, no. It seemed like any time he had business in Los Angeles, or once in San Diego, we'd get together. It wasn't all that often. Every few years. But we kept in touch. I got him out on the boat last time, just the two of us and my little crew. He loved it. Said he'd wasted his whole life." He paused, sipped his coffee.

"I don't remember him mentioning you," she said. She made it sound like he was an impostor or something.

"Well . . ." He shrugged.

"How did you two meet?" I asked him.

"Oh, that was during the war. He was a twenty-one-year-old ensign commanding an LSM—that's a landing craft for personnel, smallest ship in the Navy—and I was his second, same age. We'd been assigned together, trained together, and I came to respect him. I figured a guy from his background could've had a pretty soft job if he'd wanted it, but he wanted to be where the action was. We got plenty at Tarawa.

"See, it was our job to put the Marines on the beach, then go back for another load. Supposedly just shuttle back and forth. But at Tarawa you couldn't get to the beach. There was a reef there, and the LSMs were grounding on the reef. The Marines had to go over the side and wade ashore. Not many of them in that first wave made it, the way it looked. The Japanese had pillboxes all over and big stuff our sixteen-inchers hadn't knocked out, and they were putting out, oh, just a withering fire. Those poor fucking Marines—excuse me, Mrs. Edwards—they were floating dead in the water, some of them piled on top of each other on the sand. Water was running red."

The corners of his eyes glistened. I noticed his hand shaking slightly as he took a gulp of coffee.

"Anyway, we came in the second wave—me, your father, McCarthy, and a load of Marines. Ben saw what had happened to a lot of the LSMs ahead of us. They were just hopelessly stuck on the reef, never got off, sitting ducks. So he took us in real slow, and as soon as we grounded on the reef, he cut the engine so our propeller was free. That way, see, the Marines could still get off over the side in front, and we had at least a chance to get off the reef and get back to the ship. But we were stuck pretty good, so McCarthy and I went over the side, and we just heaved and pushed at it like you would a car that was in the mud. Mind you, there's bullets zipping all around. We're up to our shoulders in water. But we got it moving, and the propeller's churning away in reverse. McCarthy started clambering aboard—he made it, and a good thing, too—and I was hanging on because it was starting to move off now pretty fast.

"Just then, a Japanese mortar round landed right next to the LSM, didn't hit us, but it came so close that it chewed up a big piece of the reef—coral is just like glass—and it showered Ben at the wheel, shrapnel, too, cut him all up, and it blew him right over the stern into the deep water. Well, I hung on and dropped off after him. The thing was, the explosion had stunned him, knocked him more or less unconscious, and he just went down, couldn't help himself at all. But I found him and brought him up. McCarthy brought the LSM back, close to the reef, and tossed us a line, and got us aboard. By this time Ben had come to, and he just insisted on taking the wheel when we came alongside the transport. That part's kind of tricky. I ought to know. I rammed the ship the next run. That one trip was all for him that day, though. As a matter of fact, that was the last time we saw each other until after the war ended. He got reassigned—to a minesweeper, I think it was—after he got out of the hospital in Australia.

"Ben always insisted I saved his life, got me a medal for it. You ask me, McCarthy saved both our lives coming back for us, but he didn't make it through the day. Ben got one, too—a medal, I mean. Well, he got two; the Purple Heart was automatic. He ever show them to you, Mrs. Edwards? Ever tell you any of this?"

"No," she said, then hesitated, "No, he never did. He never talked about the war at all. I knew he'd been wounded, but . . ."

"I'm not surprised. You can't really talk about it to anyone who hasn't been there. But that's why I told the story. He behaved about as well under fire as a man could. I wanted you to be proud of him."

"Well, I am," she said. "Of course."

"I also wanted you to know why your father and I kept in contact all these years," he continued. "He kept me up to date on his family. He was proud of you and those grandchildren you gave him. But I'll tell you, when his wife died, your mother—what was her name? Julia, wasn't it?—that hit him pretty hard. I know what that's like. He talked about that last Wednesday. Talked about a lot of things."

"Such as?" I put in.

"Well, you know, when a man gets to be our age—Ben and I are only a couple of months apart—you begin adding things up, kind of taking stock. He felt like he really didn't have much to show for it all. 'Just made a lot of money,' was what he said, 'and some of that was trading on other people's misery.' He talk to you about that much, Mrs. Edwards?"

She shook her head, no. Once more her mouth had formed into a tight, straight line.

"That was the theme that night," Cosentino said. "Soul-searching, I guess you'd call it. He seemed to have some sort of vague plan to do better, some kind of project, I don't know."

"He wasn't specific about it?" I asked him. "Didn't give you any idea what it might be?"

"No, like I said, he was pretty vague." Then he hesitated. "Well, there was one thing."

"What was that?"

"Well, he had a lot of questions about the homeless: why there were so many where he was staying in Santa Monica, how many were in Los Angeles, what was being done for them, and so on."

"Really," I said. "That's interesting." And it was. It connected with what I'd heard from the aura guy, and with some other things, too.

"Yeah, he said they'd moved them all out of the skid row section of Chicago, just flattened it into one big parking lot. Where they were now he didn't know, but they were still around. There were panhandlers in the Loop, certain parts of it." Then Cosentino suddenly chuckled, remembering. "He did say something that struck me as funny, though."

"What was that?"

"Well, he wanted to know how he could meet some of them. And I laughed and said, 'Jesus, Ben, you might try talking to them.' It was like he needed an introduction or something. Then I said, 'As a matter of fact, you have met one.' And I told him that Pete Patterson, who cooks for us out on the fishing runs and just sort of all-around crews for me, was sleeping on the beach when I got to know him. He wanted to work, and he could cook, so I hired him. Been at it for over a year. He's got his own little place over by the docks. I pay him enough for that and then some. Most of these people want to work if you give them the chance. Pete had cooked our meal that night, nothing real special, steaks and home fries, but they were good. Ben was impressed by that."

Mrs. Edwards stood up and stuck out her hand, ending the interview right there. "I want to thank you, Mr. Cosentino. You've really been most helpful," she said.

He rose, with a glance at me, and I got up, too. I was a little puzzled by this sudden departure. It seemed to me that we were just getting at the good stuff. I decided I definitely *didn't* like clients trailing along.

Al Cosentino shook her hand. "Well, I sure hope you find him," he said. "Let me know if you do."

"We will," I said. I would, anyway.

He gave my hand a little extra squeeze, not a bone crusher, just a little added pressure. "Good to meet you, Mr. Cervantes."

"Likewise," I said. "Absolutely. And thanks."

And then he gave me a wink. Sympathy? Understanding?

Up on deck Mrs. Edwards was halfway down the gangplank before she remembered to turn and wave good-bye.

"One other thing," said Cosentino as we walked across the deck in pursuit. "When you find Ben—and I'm pretty sure you will—keep an eye on him. He's fundamentally a pretty naive guy." He left me then with a pat on the back and a whispered "Good luck."

Mrs. Edwards was clipping along the marina wharf so rapidly that I had to jog to catch up with her. She said nothing, simply nodded.

"Well," I said, "that was interesting, wasn't it?" Was I baiting her? I'm not sure.

"Not terribly helpful, though."

"Oh, I don't know. It gave me some ideas about where to look." More of what I'd done yesterday was what I meant.

"I want to go to the hotel and take a look at my father's room."

"Sure. We can do that."

No more was said until we got to the car. As I unlocked the door and opened it for her, I tried her one more time. "That was quite a story about your father at Tarawa, wasn't it?"

She made a face. "Man talk," she said. Then she ducked in and adjusted herself into the seat.

I slammed the car door after her.

I walked Mrs. Edwards over to the concierge's desk, identified her, and told him she would like to see her father's room.

"I'll see if that can be arranged," he said and reached for the telephone.

I put my hand on his. "Don't bother," I said. "We're going up."

"Well . . ."

"Just send somebody with the key."

Then, with my hand at Mrs. Edwards's elbow, I turned her around, and we started for the elevators.

"Well *done*, Mr. Cervantes." She had a smile on her face. Or was it a smirk?

When we got up there, it turned out we didn't need a key after all. The police bands were gone, and the door stood open. I looked at her, shrugged, and nodded her inside.

There was a workman in the bathroom replacing the mirror and medicine cabinet. Life goes on. He looked in our direction, called out a "Hi," and returned to his work. Mrs. Edwards was no more interested in him than he was in her. She began ambling slowly around the room, taking it all in.

"This surely couldn't have been the way they found it," she said to me. "My father was a meticulously neat man."

"Well, the cops are supposed to put everything back where it was, but sometimes they forget." I surveyed the room. It was your average, run-of-the-mill, luxury hotel room, a little bigger and better furnished than what I was used to at the Holiday Inns I stayed at but otherwise not much different. "Actually," I said, "it looks a little better than it did. That suitcase on the bed, for instance, was on the floor. Things out of it were scattered. Remember, the guy who killed whoever in the bathroom wanted to make it look like a robbery."

"Yes," she said dryly, "of course." She continued to roam around the room.

I walked over to the bathroom, leaned against the doorjamb, and watched the man do his job. I enjoy watching people work. What I mean is, people who work well with their hands fascinate me. There's an economy to their movements, a grace, that's kind of like manual poetry, fingers thinking for themselves.

"Bullets go right through into the wall?" I asked.

"Oh, sure," he said, "this stuff isn't strong enough to stop much." He somehow managed to tap the flimsy metal with his screwdriver without missing a twist. "Cops dug 'em out, and I plastered them over last night." He worked swiftly, anchoring the cabinet into place. Two bolt-sized screws in, six to go.

"You a cop?"

"No, not really. Private cop."

"Oh." It made no difference to him.

This was the first real look I'd had at the scene of the crime since my hurried inspection Sunday morning. It was fairly evident that there was more work to be done. Although the floor had been carelessly mopped, there was still a good deal of dried blood trapped in the spaces between the ceramic tiles. One of the tiles between the sink and the toilet bowl was missing, too—just a nasty bullet-sized hole where it had been. That confirmed my hasty reconstruction: The victim had been shot behind the ear after he had fallen. Coup de grâce, quite unnecessary. They would probably have the whole room retiled.

"Guy who got shot here, he wasn't a guest, was he?" He talked as he worked, looking me full in the face.

"Doesn't seem like it. No."

"I didn't think so."

"Oh? How come?"

"Well," he said, "just look at the bathtub. There, I mean, behind the shower curtain. Go on. Take a look."

I stepped gingerly over the threshold and behind him. I grabbed the curtain—a very soft, clothlike plastic—and threw it back. The bathtub was filthy; a deep layer of dirt and sand covered the bottom like so much dried silt.

"At first I thought the cops did that. You know, tracked it in or something. But you can tell, somebody just turned off the shower and left it that way."

"Yeah," I said, "you can see the drain pattern."

"Guy must have had a month's worth of dirt on him."

I nodded, staring down at the mess. "Right."

"A year's worth."

"Maybe."

"Could only be one of those guys off the street. How do you s'pose he got in?"

"Guess he had the key."

Whoever he was, the poor guy probably thought he'd just grab a shower and a shave, dress up in new clothes, and get a new start on life with Benjamin Sterling's credit cards. But the man in 306 put an end to that before it had begun.

Mrs. Edwards appeared at the door. "Something interesting?"

I beckoned her inside and started to explain, but a voice boomed out behind her: "Who's in here? How'd you get in?"

It was Alex, the hotel security man. We went out to meet him.

"The door was open," I told him.

"It's okay, Alex," came the call from the bathroom. "I'm in here."

"You were sent up with the key, I take it," said Mrs. Edwards.

"Well . . . yeah, but I was also supposed to find out what you wanted in here."

She exploded. "What we *wanted*! A man was shot here because he was taken for my father. My father's clothes are strewn all over this room. There's no telling what's been taken *or by whom*. After the way the hotel has handled this, there's simply no telling *where* my father is, or if we'll ever find him!"

I wasn't sure about the logic of that, but it was great to see this overgrown hotel dick start to crumble bit by bit in the face of her attack.

"Oh, well, now, listen, ma'am——"

"You listen!" She was panting with rage. "You tell me. Doesn't this hotel have any security system at all? Who's in charge of security here?"

Just as Alex was trying to figure out how to talk his way out of that one, the telephone rang. He leaped for it, a lifeline, and grabbed it up so fast he fumbled and nearly dropped it. But he did manage to get it up to his ear.

"Hello? Yeah? This is Wickowski."

He listened then, and as he listened, his eyes widened. He kept nodding and saying, "Uh-huh." Finally he finished and said, "I'll tell her," and then hung up.

"Uh, ma'am, there's a man downstairs making a big fuss. He wants a key to this room. Maybe you should talk to him. He says he's your father."

6

It was Benjamin Sterling, all right. I'd carried his picture around too long, showed it too often for there to be any mistake about that. He was standing with one hand on the registration desk, turned away from the clerk and looking exasperated, as we stepped off the elevator. Mrs. Edwards began walking toward him at the same fast clip she'd traveled the wharf in San Pedro; it was hard to keep up with her. Then she broke into a trot and finally a run, and I didn't even try. She threw her arms out, encircled him, and almost pulled the man down. "Daddy," she called out so loudly that her voice rang out across the lobby, "are you all *right?*"

"Well, of course I'm all right," he said. "If I could just get them to give me another key to . . . but—but what are you doing here, Clare?"

"Oh, God, you don't know what's happened, do you?"

"N–no, I guess I don't."

She'd taken a step back from him and was addressing him directly. I noticed they were just about the same height—around five feet ten. (Of course, she was wearing heels.) "Well, Daddy, a man was killed, murdered, in your room." Quite a little crowd had gathered around them. The expressions of interest and smiles of approval on their faces suddenly faded. Looks of concern and shock were exchanged. They were nothing to the looks on the faces of the hotel staff, who began pushing through to Sterling and his daughter. Alex Wickowski was there, and he produced the extra key, pressed it into Mrs. Edwards's hand, and began clearing the way for them back to the elevator.

One face in the crowd didn't belong. It was about as brown as mine, unshaven, sharp-eyed, and . . . familiar. He moved along behind Sterling, keeping close. He seemed to have attached himself to the little party headed for the elevator. Or maybe he had been with Sterling all along. Maybe he had come in with him. He looked like he might have a bad aura.

I joined them about halfway to the elevator and fell in beside the stranger. He looked at me curiously. I simply nodded. He smelled, well, kind of gamey. Fairly clean—I'd seen a lot worse wandering around Santa Monica—he carried a sports bag that probably contained a couple of shirts but no change of pants; the jeans he had on were pretty dirty. I could tell, too, that under the Dodgers baseball cap he wore his black hair was matted and in need of a wash. A street guy, for sure.

Father and daughter were already on the elevator, talking intently. Wickowski followed, leaned over, and pushed the button for three. But just as the guy beside me was stepping forward to climb aboard before the doors shut, I grabbed his wrist and held him back.

The elevator doors closed.

"Hey," said the guy, "what you do that for, mahn?"

I recognized the accent. East L.A., Boyle Heights, maybe. "I wanted to talk to you," I said to him.

"Who d'fuck are you?"

"Funny. I was about to ask you the same thing."

"Well, who *are* you?" he demanded.

"I'm a private investigator who was hired by Mrs. Edwards to find Benjamin Sterling. Now, who are you?"

"Me?" He broke into a wide grin. "Mahn, I'm his fuckin' consultant."

★ ★ ★

His name was Julio Alviero. If I thought he looked familiar, it was because we were in high school together—Roosevelt High, just outside the Heights. I'm not a hundred percent sure, but Julio might have been one of the gang in that car chasing us the night I phoned in the false alarm. Yeah, he was a gang guy, but being in a gang back then, as I explained to the people at the bar, didn't mean what it does today. There were turf wars, but they weren't fought with Uzis and Berettas, and the drive-bys didn't start until ten years or more after I'd left Roosevelt. The way I remember it, Julio was never that tough anyway, more of a *chulo*, a wiseguy, always ready with a remark. He probably cooled more situations than he created that way. That is, he cooled them if it was in his interest. Because the big thing about Julio—and I remember this very clearly—was that he always had an angle, was always looking out for what was best for him. Like that time he negotiated a peace between the Pumas and the Piratas, his gang, kidding them through it all the way. It turned out he had a new *novia* in Puma territory; he wanted to date her without getting hassled.

"So you're a homeboy, huh?" Julio looked at me, sizing me up.

"Boyle Heights. Right there on St. Louis Avenue across from Hollenbeck Park."

"Yeah," he said, "yeah, I remember you."

I was sure he didn't. Julio would have told Bill Clinton the two of them were big buddies in high school if he thought he could con him into believing it.

"You're a long way from the old barrio," I said.

"Yeah, well, I don't miss it. Figured I'd take a little oceanfront vacation, grab some rays here in SM."

"Not hot enough for you back home?"

He looked at me oddly, like I'd said something I shouldn't have. "Things are *very* hot back in the Heights. Maybe you haven't been back there in a while."

"Not for a while," I agreed.

He nodded and said nothing, his suspicions confirmed. Finally, "So, homeboy, you're a private eye, huh?"

"Duly registered with the State of California's Bureau of Investigative Services."

"Hey, wow, that's some shit, huh? What do you do, go to school for that? Take some special course?"

"No, mostly you put in ten years on the LAPD."

"You were a cop?" He seemed surprised at that. I wondered why. "I don' know, mahn, you look too good in a shirt and tie."

"Cops wear ties."

"You know what I mean, more like a businessman."

I knew what he meant.

"Hey," he continued, "when this deal goes through with the old man, I'll be a businessman, too. How you think I'll look in a tie?"

I thought about that a moment. "Different," I said, "very different."

We were talking in the corridor outside room 308. By the time Julio and I had caught the next elevator up there, Sterling and his daughter were inside. The door was still open, so I stuck my head inside. The two of them were sitting on the bed, still talking; that is, Sterling was talking, and Mrs. Edwards was listening. She looked back and caught sight of me in the doorway. She waved me away briskly. I ducked back and eased the door shut but left it ajar. We waited outside.

So that was where Julio and I continued the conversation we had started on the elevator, each leaning against an opposite wall and talking across the width of the corridor. He told me that he had been panhandling on Ocean a few days ago—it would have been Thursday—when this old guy walked up to him and started asking him questions about what it was like to be homeless.

"Questions like what?" I asked Julio.

"Oh, mahn, I don' know, the usual shit, I guess. Like, how does it feel? Where do you sleep? Do you get enough to eat?"

"So what did you tell him?"

"I don' know. I gave him some kinda rap, laid some shit on him, you know. I don' do too bad out on the street, but I figure I can't tell him that because that isn' what he wants to hear. You know?"

That sounded like Julio, all right.

"Anyway," he continued, "this *viejo* keeps on asking questions. He put, I don' know, a coupla quarters in my cup, and all these people are going by. I'm missing them, see, and he's still askin'. I can't shake him. So finally, I get kind of pissed, you know, and I say to him, 'Look, you wanna know about the problem, it's gonna cost you.' I put it up to him, he should pay me, and I'll take him aroun'. People will talk to him, I tell him, because he's with me. I'll show him around, tell him who to watch out for, all that shit. So he thinks that over, and he says, 'Fair enough. You'll be my consultant.' I think, 'Go for it, Julio,' and I tell him it's gonna cost him fifty bucks a day. He pulls it out of his pocket and counts it out jus' like that, and I think right away, I shoulda ask' for more, and so I say, 'Plus expenses,' and that's cool with him."

And so, with Julio as his guide, Benjamin Sterling began the kind of fact-finding tour through Santa Monica that no Congressman has been on yet as far as I know. They walked the park and the Third Street Promenade, then went up Wilshire to the park where the winos sleep it off. Sterling's questioning became more detailed, more sophisticated. He wanted to know what percentage were out on the street because they'd been released from some state mental institution; how many were winos or junkies hustling for pills or crack. Julio had no idea, of course, so he simply made up figures—he admitted that to me. But what Sterling was getting at, it *eventually* became clear, was just how many of these homeless people might actually be able to hold a job if it were given to them. On that point Julio refused to lie. He told Sterling that the longer people were out on the street the harder it was to make it back to the straight life. It depended on what they were doing before they fell through the cracks. If they were living on the edge before, then this wasn't so different, just kind of an outdoor version on their former life indoors. But on the other hand, if they were plugged into the system before, then there was a good chance they could plug into it again. Julio told him it was different in every case: "You gotta go out and talk to these people. Then you decide."

And so, during the next couple of days, they did that, and then a couple more days, until by the end of the tour Sterling had heard a lot of hard-luck stories, some of which he believed and some he did not. He had heard about UFOs sending messages down to Earth, about miniature radio receivers implanted in the brain by the CIA, and gotten the real dope on who killed Kennedy. He had also met Haile Selassie, Hitler, and Jesus Christ (three times).

At the end of their first day out, Sterling had thanked Julio, shook his hand, and asked if they might get together the next day. By this time, though, Julio was really getting into it. So he tossed him a challenge. He said, "Hey, you wanna know what it's like out on the street? Then stay out, spend the night at the Sidewalk Hilton and see how that feels." To his surprise, Sterling accepted the challenge. They spent the night under the stars on the roof level of a Santa Monica city parking garage. They got rousted once by the cops, waited, then went back and finished the night where they'd begun it. "The only thing was," Julio explained to me, "Ben's got this thing about dirt, see. It's un'erstan'able. He's not used to it, you know? Anyhow, in the morning, he leaves me for about an hour, showers, shaves, all that shit, and he comes back really ready for action—he didn't wear a tie this time! ¡Hombre! What a trip, huh?"

So that's how it went the next night, too. But on Saturday night, when they slept out on the beach, it turned colder. Sterling had been using his jacket for a pillow. That kept his wallet and his hotel key tucked away safely under his head. He tried it that way Saturday night, too, but he woke up shivering during the night and threw his jacket over himself, using it for a blanket. Sometime between that time and morning, his wallet and hotel key had been lifted. The unlucky thief managed to get into the hotel, probably by a service door, found his way up to Sterling's room, and that was where he bought it, a stand-in for Sterling.

So then Julio issued a second challenge: "Okay, Ben, you're one of us now. You lost your credit cards, your hotel key, your ID. You're down to zero. Why don' you find out how that feels? Stay out another day or two. I'll get you a cup. Let's see what you can hustle with it."

Again to his surprise, Benjamin Sterling accepted that challenge, too—though not before going to a pay phone and making a call to report the theft of his credit cards. He may have been pretty adventurous for a seventy-year-old man, but he wasn't foolhardy.

On Sunday Sterling did pretty well with his Styrofoam cup. The beach was crowded. They were lining up for movies on the promenade. Julio worked away from him—you never hustle in pairs—but kept him in sight and checked in with him from time to time.

But Monday was another matter. Sterling jingled the coins in that cup for all he was worth on the beach, the pier, the promenade, up and down Ocean Avenue, and all he had to show for it was $6.75—hardly enough to eat on, as he complained to Julio. When Tuesday started out no better, he declared his fact-finding mission completed, said he'd learned enough and needed a bath. And that was when he went to the hotel desk and demanded a key to his room.

What had he learned? Well, here I'm guessing, but I imagine that those last two days in particular, which he spent shaking a cup, gave him a whole new perspective on a lot of things. What he said later suggested as much. For one thing he told me that it was the first time he'd ever been looked at like he was so much dogshit—people just making a face at him and walking on. For another, he must have gotten just a hint of what it felt like to be brought down to zero. And maybe he'd learned, too, just how flimsy this contrivance called identity really is. Are you who you say you are? Not if you don't have the credit cards, the driver's license, and the Social Security number to prove it. Not if you don't dress the part. Not if you're alone, without family, business associates, or friends to vouch for you. If he had learned that, he'd learned a lot. Anyway, people around him seemed to agree that he'd come back from the experience a changed man, a man with a mission.

Maybe that's all Mrs. Edwards was saying when she raised her voice on the other side of that closed door. What was it she said? Something like "Daddy, you can't be serious!"

Julio and I both heard it, though I can't swear we both heard it the same way. We exchanged shrugs. I wasn't eavesdropping, and just to prove it, I moved off a little farther from the door. Julio had apparently said all he had to say about those days when Benjamin Sterling was missing. I wanted to keep him talking. And so that was when I told him we'd been in high school together. Then, in the middle of that little conversation, the guy from the hotel maintenance staff came down the hall, looked at Julio a little skeptically, then turned to me and said, "They're still in there, huh? Both of them?"

"Still in there," I said. "Talking."

"Boy, that lady, she's somethin' else, ain't she? She got me out of there *so* fast!"

"So fast that what?"

He studied his shoes, not the big work jobs you'd expect but Nike Playmakers. "So fast I left my tools in the bathroom—you know, where I was working? I got other stuff I could do, but I need my tools to do them." He seemed embarrassed about it. What's a maintenance man without his toolbox? He's a maintenance man with an identity crisis.

Just as I was about to urge him to stick around a little while longer, Sterling and his daughter emerged from the room carrying suitcases. Julio leaped across the corridor in a single bound and took the heavier one from him. I relieved her of the lighter one; she didn't argue this time.

The hotel manager showed some class and tore up Sterling's bill. Probably corporate policy when homicides occur on the premises. Paragraph five, subsection eight.

Sterling gathered us around him then in the middle of the lobby and began setting out the order of the day. "Now, look," he said, "here's how we'll proceed. Clare and I will go to this woman's home—Jarrett, I believe, is her name—we'll overnight there, and—"

"But Daddy, don't you think it would be better if you came right back home with me? We can be on a plane in an hour."

"Clare, please, we've been through this once. I have at least another day's work to do here. Now, please."

Mrs. Edwards had slipped into her family role, as many of us do with our parents. I could tell she wanted to say more. She was literally biting her lip.

"Where was I? Now, you," he said, pointing at me. "What was your name again?"

"Cervantes," I said. "Antonio Cervantes."

"Fine. Okay. You, Mr. Cervantes, have the rest of the day off. I'll need you tomorrow. Not today."

That kind of surprised me. "Well, thanks, Mr. Sterling," I said to him, "but don't you think it would be a good idea if I stuck pretty close to you? I mean, somebody tried to get you. The fact that another man died in your place was just your good luck. I believe you need twenty-four-hour protection."

"I think he's right, Daddy." She said it with a bit more authority than before.

"No, I'm sure I'll be perfectly safe out there at Mrs. whatever-her-name-is. Besides, that unfortunate business in my room was probably a burglary, anyway."

"Burglars don't shoot," I said. "It's not in their job description."

He frowned a moment, then allowed a brief smile. "Oh, I see," he said, "a joke. I like a man with a sense of humor, Cervantes." Then he turned away; I felt like saluting. "Julio," he said with a sigh, "we've *got* to do something to make you look more presentable. A bath would do you a world of good, my friend, make you smell better, too. We'll fix you up with a motel room. Then, of course, you'll need some clothes. Better throw away those you've got. And, oh yes, a decent-looking, inexpensive suitcase—you'll need one of those, too."

"Suitcase?" echoed Mrs. Edwards.

"Oh yes, of course. He's coming with me to Chicago. Aren't you, Julio?"

"I'm wit' you all the way, Ben," declared Julio. "Jus' like I say."

"Good man."

What was at first open consternation on Mrs. Edwards's face became nothing at all—that mask with its straight-line mouth and expressionless eyes.

"Clare," he said, turning to her, "give him some money for that."

"Money?" she said. Her voice had gone kind of dead. "You mean cash? I have none. Just credit cards."

"Well, I don't even have those." He turned to me. "What about you, Cervantes? Got any cash?"

"Well, yeah," I said. "Not much. About fifty bucks."

"Credit cards? A bank card?"

I hesitated. Almost anybody would, under the circumstances. Finally, "Yes, I guess so."

"Fine, then, I'll put you in charge of Julio's new image. You'll be reimbursed, of course. Keep the receipts. Find a motel for him, then the two of you go out shopping. How does that sound?"

"Well, okay, sure."

"So I guess you don't have the rest of the day off, after all."

Just as long as I get paid, I thought. Just as long as I get paid.

Outfitting Julio was just as much fun as I expected it would be—a constant battle to keep from going wild with my money—for which I'd be reimbursed, of course. (Yeah, I'd heard that before.) Anyway, I talked him into a motel up Wilshire, promising he'd look a lot different when they saw him again. Then I took him to the Gap.

He took the place in and looked at me in open dismay. "I don't know, mahn, I kinda thought, like, something wit' more style, you know?"

In spite of that, I got him out of there with a corduroy suit, a pair of slacks, a couple of pairs of jeans, and some shirts. That would hold him, wouldn't it? I guess not.

Out on the street, he pointed down at the worn-out, flapping pair of running shoes he had on and said, reasonably enough, that these wouldn't go so well with the new clothes. So we bought him new shoes and some socks. No, not the pair of Western boots he had his eye on but your basic pair of penny loafers.

Then, finally, the suitcase. I told him to stay in the car on that one, and minutes later I came back with what I thought filled the bill. Decent-looking, inexpensive? Sure, it was plastic, but it seemed pretty strong, and it was big enough to hold all we'd bought and then some.

Julio took one look at it and said, "Din' they have nothin' in red?"

That annoyed me. I could've told him a lot of things, but I didn't. What I said was, "Only stuff for women," which was true—I think. He made a face, nodded, didn't say a word.

Then, up Wilshire, on the way back to his motel, Julio suddenly sat erect in his seat. "Hey, mahn," he said, "do me a *favorito*, huh? See that little store coming up on your left on the corner? Stop there, okay? They got parking in back."

Why not? I pulled into a space behind the store, killed the engine, and Julio jumped out. "This one's on me," he called as he left, disappearing into the place.

It was one of those old-time fancy tobacco shops—you know, pipes, blended tobaccos, imported cigarettes, and a humidor room full of cigars. That much I'd noticed as we turned left past the place. I wondered what he wanted in there. He hadn't lit up a cigarette while we'd talked, and he sure as hell wasn't a pipe smoker. Maybe a cigar.

No, the cigar was for me. He tossed it in my lap as he jumped back into the seat beside me—a nice, long Macanudo. "There's your *premio*, homeboy. Everybody like a good cigar now and then, huh?" What had he bought for himself? Nothing that I could see.

I didn't get the answer to that until we were back in the motel room. As the water ran for his first bath in who knows how long, Julio went rummaging through the red sports bag he had been carrying. I went back for the last load of packages from the car. When I returned he had hauled out a glassene bag with a good ounce or more of grass inside. He opened it up and smelled it, then offered it to me. "Take a whiff," he said. "This is the *best* shit ever. Hawaiian."

I whiffed. To tell you the truth, I wouldn't know the good stuff from oregano. But just to make him feel right about it, I practically breathed my appreciation: "Mmmmm. Terrific."

"I been carryin' this shit aroun' for a long time, homeboy.

Makin' me *loco,* you know? Number one, I can' smoke it outside with the street boys because it draws a crowd—cops, too. Number two, I can' smoke it because I got no papers. But now"—he whipped out a packet of ZigZags—"ta-*dah!* That's why I had you stop at that shop. Good shit deserves good papers, you know? Can't roll this stuff in newspaper."

Julio crafted a big banana-sized joint, lit up, and offered it to me. I took a very tentative puff. What can I say? I didn't inhale. I handed it back to Julio.

The last I saw of him that day he was up to his neck in soap bubbles, smoking his banana joint, reading—well, examining—a copy of *Playboy* he'd rummaged out of his sports bag. It occurred to me then that Benjamin Sterling was going to have his hands full with Julio.

And maybe vice versa, too.

Around the first of the year I had dropped my answering service and got an answering machine. No, that's not right; they dropped me. Let's try it one more time. Around the first of the year, the answering service I'd used for ten years or so informed me by mail that they were cutting me off the next day. Just like that. I'd be billed up to that date, but it was up to me to find a replacement service. That made me crazy. What had I done to offend them? A few years ago or so I hit a dry spell, and I was slow paying my bills, but that was a few years ago. Since then I'd been up to date, first of every month. So I called Darlene, my regular operator at the service—I remember this was at night and there was no one else to talk to there—and I asked what the shit this was all about. (Yeah, just like that; I was kind of abrasive.) And Darlene started to cry and told me they were going out of business.

"Well, why didn't they say so in the notice?" I was really puzzled.

"Oh, Chico, old Mr. Levine feels so *ashamed*—bankruptcy, all that. Everybody's got answering machines now. You know."

"Yeah," I said, "I guess I do. But what about you?"

"Well, he's paying us girls as much as his creditors will let him. I'll go on unemployment and look for a job. I'll find something.

But poor Mr. Levine, all those years, and he feels like such a failure."

I told her I understood and asked her to remember me if she needed a job reference. That was the last conversation I had with Darlene.

In the months since then I've thought a couple of times about Mr. Levine, his shame, and this big thing Americans have about failure. *Financial* failure—that's the only kind there is, isn't it? I didn't suppose for a minute that Mr. Levine had joined those nameless men on the beach in Santa Monica, but that was his fear: the abyss, the black hole that's waiting to suck us in if we ever stop running at full speed or are unlucky enough to stumble and fall. Is this the way it is everywhere in America? All over the world? I don't know, but it sure is the way it is in Los Angeles. I feel it myself. Those guys in Santa Monica scare me, too.

So anyway, now I've got an answering machine just like everybody else. You know the drill; you come in, first thing you do is check the light on the machine, rewind, play, listen to the hangups. I hate hangups. Then there was a message from Sterling—my marching orders for the morning. Report in San Marino with Julio at 10 A.M. sharp. Was I working for Sterling now? I wasn't sure.

I thought at first that the last message on the tape was somebody's idea of a joke. There was nearly a minute of heavy breathing—a kid? a woman?—and then a voice that stopped me cold, speaking through tears: "Chico, how could you do this thing to me?" More heavy breathing, and then a hangup.

I listened to it again and again. How many times? I couldn't even guess. I was still backing it up and playing it the next morning. It was unmistakably the voice of Alicia Ramirez. I knew it too well, had heard it too often in this very room, every room in the apartment, for there to be any doubt about that. Yeah, we'd lived together here before and after the baby was born, her baby, Marilyn. I guess I felt kind of bitter about the whole experience. She stayed just as long as it was in her interest to stay. But it's not like she had hidden her intentions. She was headed for stardom. She told me; she warned me. So how could

I have been surprised that when her chance came, she took it? Yeah, she was Lupe, the star of the new hit on television. Everybody was talking about her—the people at the hotel bar, Bill Schmidt at Jay's, everybody. It drove me crazy. And she'd gotten a lot of attention in the press, too—*TV Guide,* the *L.A. Times,* and probably a lot of out-of-town papers, too. The idea of a Mexican playing a Mexican was just so new and fresh and totally original that it seemed to take all the television journalists by surprise. What could you expect? After years of watching TV, it wouldn't take a lot to surprise them.

So here she is, calling me up out of the blue, asking me how I could do this to her. Do *what* to her? Just what could I have done to get her to talk to me after all these months? I didn't know where she lived and didn't know her phone number, either, so there was no question of returning her call. I didn't know that I would do that, anyway. If I responded, I'd be half admitting to the accusation, wouldn't I? Sort of like, when did you stop beating your wife? No, it'd be better if I approached the problem from a different angle.

There was just a chance that I might still catch Casimir Urbanski at Majestic Studios. If so, his secretary would have gone home—it was after six—and he'd pick up the call himself. I dialed. I waited through three rings, and there was Casimir, formerly a cop, now a producer.

"Yeah? Hullo?"

"Hi, Casimir, this is Chico."

"Oh . . . uh, how you doin'?"

"I'm doing all right, except I got a problem."

He held back. I wondered if there was someone in the office with him. "Yeah?" he said at last. "What's the problem?"

"I got a call from Alicia on my machine, and I can't figure out what it's all about."

"You got no idea?"

"None at all."

"That's what I thought."

"That's what you *thought?* Hey, come *on,* what's this all about?" I hesitated. "Listen, are you alone there? Can you talk?"

"No," he said. No emphasis. Very mildly.

Well, I asked myself, should I send him a coded message or what? No, I handed him an ultimatum instead: "Okay, Casimir, I am gonna eat breakfast tomorrow at eight A.M. down at Zucky's, the deli at Fifth and Wilshire in Santa Monica. It's on your way to the studio, so that shouldn't cause you a problem. You want to explain this to me, you can do it there."

"Sounds good to me," he said cheerfully. "See you then." And he hung up.

Jesus, I thought, what's going on at that place? Obviously he had to pretend he was talking to somebody else. Strictly routine. Had Casimir just suddenly gone paranoid, or was there really some reason behind all this? I kept thinking about him and Alicia's message on the answering machine, and that crazy studio where I used to work. I was trying to put some of this together, trying to get a handle on it. But nothing I came up with seemed to work. Nothing.

I broke out the bottle of Cuervo Gold, telling myself, against all reason, that it might help me think a little better. It didn't. It did sort of ease the pain in my ribs, though. For that much, at least, I was grateful.

If I hadn't already downed a couple of tequilas, I might not have switched on the television at nine o'clock and tuned in "Lupe." Yes, it was that time of the week again. Here she comes, America, out of the wilds of Sonora, right into your heart. She may be undocumented and underprivileged, but she's undaunted and ultimately unbeatable. That's our girl Lupe, all right.

And here she is in the film intro, squeezing through the barbed wire at the border in a company of pathetic-looking illegals. Her face is suddenly illuminated by a border patrol spotlight: she's beautiful; she's scared. She runs. They all scatter. But the border patrol Jeeps come barreling down on them from every side. Fast cuts as the illegals are rounded up. Lupe, hidden behind some rocks, sees it all happen. Only she, it seems, has made it successfully across the border. Final cut: she tramps alone in the early morning along a dusty road northward, but in a closeup we see the determined smile on her face.

That gets me, that smile—it did last week, too—because I know it all too well. That's the real Alicia Ramirez y Sandoval behind that look. And if that realistic bit at the beginning of the show wasn't the way *she* crossed the border, well, the route she took was even more devious and dangerous. She's tough, that woman, tougher than I am, tougher than I want to be.

To go from that to the silly sitcom stuff that followed proved a little too much for me that night. There were the obvious jokes turning upon her faulty English and her ignorance of ordinary kitchen appliances. Why, the show practically wrote itself.

I switched it off at the commercial break.

7

Zucky's is a Jewish deli like any other—a little bigger maybe, the Formica a little shinier, the clientele a bit more affluent—but just as noisy as any of them. People talk so loud there you couldn't possibly hear anyone at the next table, so it's a great place to have a confidential conversation. And that was the kind I wanted to have with Casimir Urbanski.

Although the place was fairly full, I managed to locate him sitting alone in one corner of the place. He didn't see me. He wasn't looking. The big guy sat, his thick shoulders hunched, staring into a coffee cup that he held nearly hidden in his hands. He didn't look happy.

But when I loomed over him he looked up and forced a smile. He pushed up to his feet and stuck out his hand. "Chico," he said, "I'm really glad to see you." As he pumped my hand, he gave my shoulder a squeeze. "Hey, you're lookin' good. You goin' by the gym?"

"As often as I can."

"Well, it shows. Me, look at me, hey, I'm gettin' fat."

It was true. In the six months since I'd seen him last, he must have put on fifteen or twenty pounds. The stylish, loose-cut jacket and pleated pants he wore did a lot to cover it up, but there was a push to his middle that was never there before. His face had plumped out, too.

"Sit down," he urged, "sit down."

Casimir had come a long way from Hamtramck, Michigan. As a cop—first in Detroit, then here in L.A.—he'd been happy, happier than he was now as a movie producer, I'd bet. What looks like great good fortune—love, opportunity, a new life—sometimes isn't. There's an old Spanish proverb: "God says, 'Take what you want, but pay for it.' " I learned that not at my mother's knee but in a movie, probably one by Sam Peckinpah, so I can't vouch for its authenticity, just its validity.

"How's the movie coming?" I asked as I took the chair beside him. "I hear it's in production."

"*Post* production," he said, "we're rushing it, like. Got a rough cut already. Music goes on next week."

"You pleased with it?"

He shrugged. "It got changed some."

"I hear they always do—get changed, I mean."

He shrugged again. "They say."

The waitress came, liberating us from such small talk; well, it was small talk for me, anyway. The moment she was gone, I put my elbows on the table, leaned into his face and said, "Now, what's this all about?"

"You don't know," he said. "You *really* don't know, do ya?"

"If I did, I wouldn't be here."

"What I told them that. Right before you called."

"Told *who?* Who was in the office with you? Somebody was."

"Aw, it was that fucking Hans-Dieter. I hate that Nazi son of a bitch. I told him then. I told Uschi before." Then he added, "That you weren't involved."

"In *what,* dammit? Tell me!"

Casimir sighed. "Well," he said, "you know Alicia, she's doin' pretty good now. She's got that series. Network just put in an order for fall. That's good, I guess, but who knows about TV, not me. Anyways, she's doin' good, she's a hit, right?"

"Right," I said, "I hate the show, but I wish her well. I guess it's what she always wanted."

"What I told them that."

"Will you go *on?* What's that got to do with me? With that call I got from her."

"Yeah," he said, "if they knew she talked to you—"

"She left a message."

"Worse. It's on tape. If they knew that, they'd really be pissed at her. They told her not to have any contact with you at all. If they knew I was here, telling you this, they'd fucking die, that's all."

"So?"

"So somebody's trying to blackmail her."

I didn't say anything. My mind went into computer overdrive. Things began to suggest themselves. Connections previously ignored became possible, even probable.

Then Casimir went on to clarify. "Well, no, not exactly. Actually, they're not blackmailing *her,* they're blackmailing the studio *because* of her."

"What're they saying?"

"Well, it's embarrassing. I don't like to talk about it."

"Try."

"Okay." He took a deep breath, came in close, and said, "They're saying that she was, like . . ." He had begun to whisper. *"you* know . . ."

I looked around at the tables around us and noticed that conversation had stopped, just like in the Paine Webber commercial. People were looking in our direction, or very carefully the other way.

"Casimir," I said, "whatever you have to say, say it out loud. Otherwise, everybody will hear you."

He frowned at that, but he seemed to get the idea. "Okay, Chico." He said it louder than he really needed to. "I guess you're right."

Conversation around us resumed.

"They're saying she was a prostitute, before, down in Mexico."

"Who's saying that?"

"Well, that's it, see, like, we don't know. Hans-Dieter, and I gotta admit, Uschi, too, they think it's, uh . . . you."

A lot had come clear by now. "What does Alicia think?"

He seemed insulted. "I already *said!*"

"Okay, okay, take it easy." I weighed the situation, trying to decide what to tell him—how much. Finally, I decided to take the plunge: "I guess she hasn't told you, so you'd better know this. The . . . information you got, this secret, well, it's true."

Casimir said nothing, but I could tell from the expression of hurt on his face that he took it personally. There was doubt and anger there, too. I'd told him something he really didn't want to hear.

"So my advice is, pay up. I know about blackmail. You may only be buying time, but for now, time's what you need. What's the threat? What've they got?"

His lips worked silently for a moment before he was able to speak. "A sworn statement, pictures."

"Pictures? Oh, shit." You could impugn a statement, but pictures? It'd depend on what they were. "You seen them?"

"No. The guy just said. I thought it was all bullshit, a whatta ya call it, a bluff. You know, a shakedown."

"You never considered the possibility it might be true?"

"You mean it? About Alicia?" He fell quiet a moment, looking for the right words. "She seems so innocent. And that kid of hers . . . *your* kid."

I sighed. "Not my kid, Casimir. She was pregnant when I met her. I owe her a lot. She saved my life. But no, not my kid."

"Oh." He looked down into that coffee cup again. "Uschi said you didn't even care about your own. Just let her go."

"Maybe she got that from Alicia."

"Maybe."

The waitress came with breakfast. Neither one of us was very hungry. Casimir dipped his toast in egg yolk and nibbled. I spread some cream cheese on my bagel and chewed away at it thoughtfully. The coffee tasted good, though.

"What does the old man say about this?" I asked.

"Toller? He's out of the country. Hasn't heard nothing about it."

"Well, he's the Majestic CEO. Don't you think he should at least be notified?"

"Not my call. Uschi's head of the studio, says she'll handle it herself. Kind of a father-daughter thing going there."

"Must be tough living with that," I suggested.

"You got no idea. I thought I knew about stress when I was a cop. But this is way beyond that. I wasn't made to be almost-married to the woman I work for. All I wanna do is just get this movie made to prove I can do it, to prove I ain't just the boss's cutie."

"Tough times for guys."

"Tell me about it."

"Maybe turnabout's fair play."

"Maybe."

We sat there silently for a while, each lost in his own predicament. Casimir pushed his plate away. He took a deep gulp of coffee, turned to me, and asked, "Got any ideas?"

"Yeah, I got one. You said, the *guy* claimed to have a statement and pictures. It was a man? A phone call?"

"Yeah, a guy. There were two calls, both of them to Uschi—right to the top. They got the second one on tape. I heard it."

"Anything distinctive about his voice?"

He thought about that and suddenly brightened. "Yeah. Definitely was something. The guy had, like, an accent."

That figured. "Not Latino."

"Oh, no, not, definitely. Like, back in Detroit they got all these Arabs—more Arabs in Detroit than any place in the country. I'd know an Arab accent anyplace. That's what this guy had. He was an Arab."

That figured. Saheed made the call.

"Okay, look, Casimir, there is absolutely *no way* I am going to get involved in this, but I'm going to give you a name, and I want you to be very careful about using this. You understand?"

"Yeah," he said, "really."

"This guy is tough, and he doesn't play fair. He's also connected, very well connected politically. His name is Thomas Jarrett. The last I knew he was living down in Newport Beach. I'm not going to give you the whole story, but you can get some of it from a DEA agent named Rossi. The guy on the phone works for him. His name is Saheed. Both these two are my enemies and Alicia's. My bet is they're not just out for the money, they're out to destroy her. How much are they asking, by the way?"

"A million," he said.

"Nice round figure. But look, I'm going to say it again. These are very serious bad guys. Don't think for a minute you can send a couple of guys down there to rough them up and tell them to lay off and it's actually going to happen. I wouldn't force their hand at all. Just find out all you can about the guy, and then maybe we can talk again."

Casimir nodded very seriously. "Just like you say, Chico." Then he brightened a little. "Hey, it's funny you should say what you did about don't send a couple of guys to, like, discourage them. That's what Hans-Dieter wanted to do to you, Chico. He said he knew a couple of guys, stuntmen, who did that stuff. I talked him out of it, though."

"I'm glad you did, Casimir. But don't even think about it with Jarrett and Saheed."

"Just like you say."

Somehow, I didn't have it in me to tell Casimir Urbanski that he hadn't, in the end, talked Hans-Dieter out of it. He was in a bad spot as it was. Why add to his conflict? Besides, no move like that could have been made without Ursula Toller's okay. If I knew Casimir, that would have put an end to things between him and her. Maybe not a bad thing? Maybe not. But for him it would have been too early. He needed to walk out of it with something, something solid, a movie—or maybe just his self-respect. But who knows? The two might put a patch on it and go ahead and get married. What people do when they're in love is beyond me. I'd been telling myself that regularly ever since Alicia left.

Anyway, I decided on the short drive up Wilshire to Julio's

motel that my decision at Zucky's to say nothing about those two guys in the elevator had been the right one.

It was nearly nine o'clock by the time I got to the place. I'd told Sterling I'd be in San Marino to pick him up at ten. If Julio was ready and waiting, the way he'd promised, we'd probably make it on time. If not, well, I might find myself offering explanations to his daughter again. I didn't want that. Besides, now more than ever I wanted a chance to talk to Grace Jarrett about her ex-husband.

I rapped hard on the door of his room, waited, then knocked again. There were vague stirrings inside. I looked left and right. There was nobody around, so I yelled out pretty loud, "Julio, it's Chico. Open up!"

With my ear to the door, I listened—to what? Voices? I banged on the door even harder, rattling the thing in its frame. Then suddenly there before me, Julio stood naked in the wide-open doorway, scratching his pubic hair. "Hey, homeboy, how you doin'?"

I hesitated just an instant, then pushed past him and into the room. The high, sweet smell of last night's pot still hung heavy in the air. Julio stared stupidly at me as I took a quick look around, trying to decide what to do first.

The blonde in the bed, she had to go. She was sitting up, eyes wide, the sheet pulled up demurely to cover her breasts. But she didn't fool me; she left demure behind about a quarter of a century ago. With one hand I scooped her clothes up off the floor, and with the other I hauled her out of bed. I pushed the clothes at her. "Here," I said, "get dressed and get out."

"Julio, you gonna let him get away with this?"

Still standing in the doorway, he shrugged. "Can't help it, querida. He's the boss. We got someplace to go." At least he remembered that much.

With her clothes under her arm, she started for the bathroom. I caught her by the shoulder. "Not in there. I need that for Julio."

She stood there, frowning, her jaws clenched tight. Angry. "Well, if I have to get dressed out here," she yelled at him, "then shut the goddamn door!"

"What? Oh . . . yeah, sure." I pushed it shut. Julio seemed vaguely amused by all this.

"Come on!" I yelled at him. He came. I pushed him into the bathroom, then into the shower, turned on the cold water, listened to him scream and curse—"*¡Chinga! ¡Chinga! ¡Chinga!*" Then I pulled him out, tossed him a towel, and put him in front of the mirror. "Shave," I said. "Once over lightly should do it." I left him there in the bathroom and went out to check on the blonde. She had her hand in one of Julio's pants pockets and was pulling out a bill.

She waved it at me. It was a five. "Don't worry," she said, "I'm only taking cab fare."

I looked at her, really saw her for the first time. She was over forty, but then, so was I: so was Julio. Her jaw was tight again, but her cheeks sagged so that in spite of the deep red lipstick she'd put on, her face had kind of the pouched look of a dog, a boxer. Suddenly I felt like shit, pushing her around the way I had. I dipped into my pocket and pulled out the little bunch of twenties I'd picked up at the cash machine on the way to Zucky's. "Look," I said to her, "I'm sorry the way I came in here. Maybe you should have some more."

Her eyes went cold, something beyond anger. "I'm not a whore," she said. I started to say something, a more heartfelt apology or whatever, I don't know. But I saw she was struggling to add something. Finally, she came out with it: "I have to pee."

I nodded and got Julio out of the bathroom. He was smirking, half-shaven, fully awake. She slammed the door behind her, stayed no longer than it took, and walked past without a look at either of us. Pushing Julio back inside, I told him to hurry up, and then turned back to the blonde, just in time to see her, purse in hand, on her way out.

She hesitated at the open door, looked at me, and said, as if explaining, "He was nice to me. More than I can say for you." Then she left, pulling the door shut after her.

Somehow, pressing as hard as I could, I got Julio out of there, showered, shaved, and dressed, in not much more than ten minutes. It was 9:07 by the dashboard clock when we pulled out of there and headed for the freeway. Because I was stoked, angry, and ready to do battle out there with the traffic, we made it to the Jarrett house in San Marino with a few minutes to spare. I don't think I spoke a word to Julio during the trip. But about halfway there I must have pulled back a little, eased off enough to ask myself just what I was so angry about. So Julio had gone out and celebrated his first night off the street, so he had sweet-talked a woman into his bed—so what? Why was I so pissed off? I knocked that around in my head awhile and came reluctantly to the conclusion that it all had something to do with Alicia and me. I didn't like that. I didn't like it at all.

It was moving day. Benjamin Sterling was packed and ready to leave with us. His daughter would return the car he had rented a week ago and fly back to Chicago. There were things he had to do today, and I was expected to chauffeur him and baby-sit all the way. Was I armed? Mrs. Edwards wanted to know. I flapped open my jacket, exposing the butt of the old Police Special I carried. She nodded, satisfied, and went into the hall to say an earnest good-bye to her father.

I looked around for Grace Jarrett and found her out on the sun porch. This was where we had eaten lunch that day over a year ago after I'd come back from Mexico with Alicia. Things were different then. But Thomas Jarrett was now back in the picture.

She looked up from her newspaper, set down her coffee cup, and offered her hand. "Mr. Cervantes," she said, "how're you feeling after that awful business night before last? Do have some coffee."

I sat down as she poured, told her I was feeling better, then got right to the point: "I was wondering, Mrs. Jarrett, if you've heard anything from your ex-husband."

"From Tom? Oh no, we never communicate. I will never see him or speak to him again, not after . . . well, you're the one person in the world to whom I need not explain—or conceal."

I nodded. "Sure," I said, "of course. Nothing at all about him then?"

"Oh, *about* him? That's another matter entirely. I *hear* he's having problems, financial problems, and I can only say that I'm delighted. As a matter of fact, what I said wasn't quite correct. We have been in communication, indirectly, his lawyer talking to my lawyer. There was a bit of property up in Santa Barbara County, something that for some reason hadn't been covered in the settlement. He wanted to sell it, needed me to sign off on it so he could. I told my lawyer to tell his lawyer to tell him to go to hell. Just my words. He will anyway. Doesn't need me to point the way. But Tom's in trouble, no doubt about it. People I know down in Balboa tell me he sold the boat. He swore once he'd never give that up." She'd stopped talking to me a few sentences back. Her eyes had gone distant, unfocused. But suddenly she was back with me. "Why?" she said. "Why do you ask? What's he up to now?"

I hesitated, then, "Blackmail, I think."

She nodded. "He's capable of that. You and I both know, Mr. Cervantes, that he's capable of anything."

I might have asked her more, but just then Clarissa Edwards appeared, frowning impatiently. "He's ready to go, just as soon as you finish your coffee."

8

Julio and I sat cooling our heels in an anteroom of the Office of
Human Services, City of Los Angeles. Sterling was down the hall,
talking to the director. Had it been difficult for him to get an
appointment on short notice? A guy with his money connections?
Are you kidding? People like Benjamin Sterling have a kind of
golden key that opens doors like this one, and bigger doors than
this one, too.

I have to admit, though, he didn't flaunt it. Actually, I kind of
liked the guy. All the way downtown on 110 from Pasadena he
sort of interviewed me, asked me questions about myself, but in
a friendly way, like he was really interested. I got the idea from
Julio that once the barrier was down, this was how he talked to
the street people, too. He wanted to know stuff like how I'd
become a private detective—everybody wants to know that; how
long I'd been on the LAPD; why I'd left; educational background. All that stuff. By the time we got to Chavez Ravine, I
thought the guy was actually going to offer me a job.

Sterling had been with the director of the Office of Human
Services for nearly an hour, and I was pretty bored. I wished that
I'd brought something to read, but that wouldn't have looked too

cool, would it? I mean, you never saw Kevin Costner curl up with a book in that movie with Whitney Houston. A bodyguard's supposed to be on his toes every minute, constantly alert, never off-duty. Yeah, sure. The truth is, every aspect of private detecting involves a lot of waiting. You wait for somebody to come out of a house and jump in a car so you can follow him. You sit around waiting for a telephone to ring to get a lead or a piece of information. Or maybe, as in the baby-sitting drill, you just sit around waiting for your guy to show up.

Julio had his own way of passing the time. He was trying to make time with the receptionist. She was Latina, in her thirties, built for comfort and not for speed. Except that she was a *morena,* she could have been the younger sister of that blonde back at the motel. For the most part, she managed to ignore him, but he worked so hard tossing out his sly little witticisms and bits of flattery—*"¡Ay que bonita!"*—that he began getting little smiles from her. When a pair of no-nonsense, briefcase-bearing, downtown lawyers showed up for an appointment with an assistant director, she phoned on to check it out, then sent them down the hall to the right door.

Julio jumped up and watched them go, pulling a long face, impressed. I was staring at him, fascinated in spite of myself. "Hey, *querida,"* he called in a loud whisper to the receptionist, "those are pretty important guys, huh?"

"They're lawyers," she said.

"Lawyers, huh? Where are they when you need them?" Strange thing to say. He grinned at her, winked, and in his baggy, off-the-rack suit pulled himself erect and duplicated the pompous custom-tailored bearing of one of the two men in exact caricature. He was a good mime, a natural, and he was rewarded with the first real laugh he had yet received from the receptionist. She was delighted. I was impressed. He was inspired to further feats of mimicry.

The second lawyer offered more of a challenge because he was older, shorter, and fatter; he also had a slight waddling limp. But throwing out his belly, sagging down into his suit, and puffing out his cheeks, Julio got him just right, even down to the limp. By now the receptionist was breaking up, and he was mugging funny faces at her just to keep her laughing. Unfortunately, though, he wasn't watching where he was going, and before I could yell out a warning he collided with Benjamin Sterling.

To be fair, Sterling wasn't watching where he was going, either; he had his nose in a sheaf of papers he had carried away from the director's office. The papers went flying. He lost his balance and nearly followed them down to the floor. But Julio grabbed him, held him upright until he was again firm on his feet, and all the while he babbled apologies.

"Hey, boss, I'm sorry! *Lo siento mucho,* you know? You okay? My fault, all my fault. Here, let me help you pick those things up."

What followed was like a routine from one of those old silent movies, Chaplin or Keaton or somebody. First of all, they bumped heads going down. Sterling survived that. Julio went down on his ass. More apologies.

"Hey, did it again! Sorry. *¡Chinga!* Pretty clumsy, huh?"

Sterling hadn't said a word yet. That seemed sort of ominous.

The receptionist kept right on laughing, now quite out of control.

I found myself on my feet, but I resisted the impulse to rush over and join in. I'd only add to the confusion. Also, I had the good sense to keep my mouth shut. Julio, meanwhile, was moving around the floor on his hands and knees, grabbing up sheet after sheet, wrinkling some in the process, smoothing them out, presenting them to Sterling, all of it in kind of goofy, exaggerated movements. He was clowning his way through this, too.

It worked. Sterling suddenly burst out laughing. Right where he knelt, shuffling the papers back into some kind of order, he began barking out a series of great guffaws. And just as suddenly, I understood something more about the odd relationship between these two. Julio may have been, as he claimed, Sterling's consultant on the homeless. He might be part of Benjamin Sterling's grand plan for Chicago, whatever that might be. But he was also the court jester. If Sterling had slept out on the beach, played at being poor for the better part of a week, it wasn't all in the interest of research; it had to be because he was also having fun. Julio must have clowned his way through that, too, conned Sterling so obviously that he knew he was being conned. He probably gave the old guy the best time he'd had in years. And later, thinking back, I decided this was exactly consistent with the way he'd been in high school. Probably in grade school and junior high, too, though I wouldn't have known about that.

At last, Sterling got hold of himself and, calming down to a series of abrupt chortles, he managed to say, "Julio, stop scooting around on the floor like that. You'll get your suit dirty." Then he added, "You look very good in it, too. I don't think I told you that."

Where were we? Downtown, certainly, but where? On Fifth, I guess, pointed west, headed for the freeway. We were on our way back to Santa Monica. It seemed that Lieutenant Shinahara wanted a statement from Sterling, too. Julio was sitting beside me up front, and Sterling had taken over the little backseat of my Alfa Sprint, browsing through the papers he had been given—no, engrossed in them, tossing them aside as he read, littering them across the narrow, upholstered bench.

I had pulled up at a stoplight—yes, it had to be Hill Street because I remember pointing out Pershing Square to Sterling— what used to be Pershing Square, a park where a mob of the homeless had hung out. To get rid of them, they had started construction on a new shopping mall. Nobody knew whether the mall would draw any shoppers. Nobody seemed to care. Promoters of downtown development touted the project as a way of coping with the homeless problem: get them out of sight.

I glanced in the rearview to see if he had taken in any of this. He was looking over at the construction site. "Interesting," he muttered, then went back to his papers. Then I looked back into the mirror. Something had caught my eye when Sterling lowered his head. The two guys in the car behind us were talking with great animation, gesticulating. The one on the passenger side kept pointing ahead.

At us? Why would he be pointing at us?

Not for any *good* reason, as I found out when the light changed and I pulled away briskly. I thought I might just leave them behind, remember them as one of life's little mysteries. But no. They stayed right behind me, about three feet behind me, until suddenly they disappeared completely. Then, at the next stoplight, they reappeared on my left, the next car to mine. I looked it over quickly—a pickup truck, Toyota or Nissan or something, a low-rider, maybe from the East Side. The guys inside were Latino—they looked Mexican to me—and one of them, that guy on the passenger side again, was opening the car door, and—My God, he had a piece in his hand, an automatic! Just that glimpse was all I needed. I glanced in the rearview and saw I wasn't hemmed in. I swung into the curb lane then, red light or not, and blasted across the intersection; a squeal of brakes to my right, I didn't care. I kept going, gathering more speed, moving into the Harbor Freeway South lane.

But they were right behind me. They must have leaped the light, too. What was this? A carjacking right in downtown L.A.? Were they so hot for a five-year-old Alfa Sprint with gray primer on the fender that they just had to have it, no matter what or where? Nah, impossible. They wouldn't be chasing us if it was the car they were after.

I glanced over at Julio. He was looking at me, his eyes wide. He said nothing, just shrugged. Well, he must have seen the gun, too.

Then back into the rearview. I was on the Harbor Freeway now, but they were still there behind us, not gaining but keeping up. It was hard to keep a steady fix on them because Sterling blocked my view. Sterling, of course! They had to be after him! I hadn't taken my baby-sitting seriously enough. If they were after him, they might just begin shooting out on the freeway.

I swung off the Harbor onto the Santa Monica Freeway, and yes, there they were. I had them in the side mirror now. Had they moved up on me? Yeah, maybe a little bit. Well, I ought to be able to give them a run for it. Traffic was midday light. I double-clutched down to third, and wound it out to 6,000 rpm before shifting to fourth. There was still plenty of torque left in that gear, and I kept right on accelerating but held it down to 85, about as fast as I could safely maneuver through traffic there on I-10. But then I hit a knot of traffic around Crenshaw and had to brake and downshift to 70 to get around it, then right back up to speed.

The mirror told me I'd opened up quite a gap, but they were still in sight. The trouble with the Santa Monica Freeway was that it was too damned straight. If there were curves, a good-sized bend or two, I might have been able to sneak off at an exit and lose the low-rider that way.

"My gosh, listen to this." Sterling spoke up suddenly from the backseat. It shook me up. My hands jerked on the wheel. I heard a sudden intake of breath from Julio beside me. "There's forty thousand homeless people in Los Angeles, just an estimate, probably on the low side, too. Now, would that be just the city, the Los Angeles area, or the county, Julio?"

"G-gee, boss, I don't know." Julio's voice quavered. He was scared.

"Remind me to ask this Lieutenant Shinahara about that."

"Sh-sure."

Sterling returned to his research. He hadn't noticed a thing.

Somehow they'd moved up on me. They were a good 50 yards, maybe 75, behind us, but there was nothing in between. Another slowdown ahead might put them right up beside us. Where were the cops? The highway patrol? I needed a moving violation like a hole in the head, but . . . No, that wasn't right. I needed a moving violation *instead* of a hole in the head. That's why I was looking so desperately for a black-and-white who might cut in behind us, its domelights flashing.

When I saw the junction with the San Diego Freeway announced on one of those green menu boards posted at regular intervals along the way, I got a flash of inspiration, or maybe two flashes all at once. If the first plan didn't work, there was the more drastic second one to fall back on.

This was going to be tricky. I had to let the low-rider get close without braking. If they saw my brakelights go on with nothing up ahead, they'd know something was up. I eased back on the accelerator, eased back some more. Finally, I took my foot off altogether as he moved up on me.

Also, the traffic in the lanes to the right had to be spread in a good pattern for me to pull this off. Approaching the southbound turnoff for the San Diego, it looked like the traffic spread was favorable, and the low-rider was now only about 25 yards behind me and coming up fast.

I jammed the gearshift lever into third, slammed down on the accelerator, and swung the wheel wide to the right—all just about simultaneously.

We swung in a wide arc across three lanes. I inserted the Alfa into the slow-moving line of traffic heading toward the southbound ramp. My brakes held. We moved up the ramp.

As we did, I looked back on the freeway we had just left and saw that the low-rider had come to a dead stop in the number-one lane and had traffic at a halt as they tried to right-angle their way across the lanes that separated them from the ramp. Lots of honking and screeching of brakes. It was a mess down there. Would they make it across? I sure as hell hoped not.

"Pretty reckless driving there, Cervantes," Sterling spoke up sternly from the backseat.

"Yeah," I said, faking a chuckle, "I almost missed the turnoff. Sorry about that, Mr. Sterling."

"You'd never get away with it in Chicago."

We had now looped over the freeway, and we were just about to join the southbound traffic on the San Diego when I looked into the side mirror and saw the low-rider about ten cars back still on the ramp. Damn! They'd made it across.

Plan B.

I shot out onto 405, winding the Alfa out through second and third, and ducked off at the first exit. Maybe, just maybe, I'd lose them there. I couldn't see the pickup in the rearview or the side mirror, but that didn't mean they couldn't see me. Down the exit ramp, Venice Boulevard to the right, Washington to the left. They'd have to guess which I took. I hung a left, then turned right on Washington. I moved along at a nice rapid clip but not fast enough to call attention. One block, two blocks, three blocks, no sign of the low-rider in the rearview. I stopped for a traffic light, waited it out, pulled ahead on green. Still no sign of them. I felt a hand on my shoulder. It was Julio, a pat on the back. He hadn't said a word the whole trip, but the grin of relief on his face right now said an awful lot.

"Good driving, homeboy."

From the backseat: "What was that, Julio?"

"I said it's a good drive he's takin' us on, boss, down by the ocean. Real pretty."

"Well, we don't have time for sightseeing, Cervantes. The sooner we get through with the police, the sooner we'll be able to get out of here."

"Sounds good to me, boss." Julio said it like he meant it.

I'd begun to relax. My mistake.

They must have taken Venice Boulevard, realized their error after a few blocks, then shot over to Washington, because suddenly they were there beside us in the lane to my right. The window on the passenger side was down, and the shooter was leaning out, gun up, yelling something. I didn't stick around to find out what it was.

"Duck, Sterling!" I yelled. Then, digging down into second gear, I stood on the accelerator and was out of there before the guy could get a shot off.

"What is this, Cervantes?" Sterling sounded puzzled, not scared.

The race was on. They were right behind us. Whatever was under the hood of that pickup wasn't standard Japanese—too much torque—but it was still a low-rider, no more than three or four inches off the ground, and that gave me an advantage.

I stretched a yellow light into an early red, and made it through the intersection at Lincoln Avenue. A squeal of brakes behind me told me they'd run into some trouble. But a glance into the rearview told me they'd gotten out of it. They'd fallen a bit behind, but not too far. They were positioned just about right for what I had in mind.

I'd used this route about a year ago. It worked then. It ought to work even better with a low-rider. I just hoped *my* car would hold up.

I found my marker—Alan's Market—turned right on Dell and yelled out, "Everybody got their seat belt buckled up?"

Up ahead the bridges over the separate branches of the old Venice Grand Canal were the speed bumps to end all speed bumps. One after another they rose a good three or four feet above street level, intended to slow traffic on the bridges down to a crawl. We were going to hit them at about 55 mph. The low-rider pickup behind us seemed to be going even faster. They were gaining on us.

"Jesus Christ!" yelled Sterling. "What're you doing?"

Julio's eyes were wide.

We sailed over the first one, came down hard halfway up the second. The shocks on the Alfa held—God bless those Italians! I felt sure enough about all this that I applied the brakes at the top of the second and continued over the rest at something like a reasonable rate of speed.

Julio was turned around in his seat, peering out the back window. He waited. "They didn't make it," he announced. "Hit it like a fockin' kamikaze, and the bottom just collapsed. Fockin' low-riders ain't worth shit. Good move, homeboy."

There was something in Julio's voice—was it gloating?—that made me glance over at him. He was looking straight ahead, chin up, lower lip out, like those old pictures of Mussolini. Was this some sort of personal triumph? I began to wonder about him.

"Just what in the world do you think you're up to, Cervantes?" Sterling demanded.

"I'll tell you, boss," said Julio. "While you was busy readin', he was busy savin' your ass."

I wasn't sure that Julio completely convinced Sterling that he had been in mortal danger all the way from downtown to Venice, but it wasn't because he didn't try. He sang my praises, gave a detailed account of my performance behind the wheel, going on and on until it actually got kind of embarrassing. But somehow Sterling remained skeptical.

"Is this all true, Cervantes?"

"Well . . . yeah," I said.

"You actually saw a weapon brandished?"

"Brandished? Well, he didn't exactly wave it around. He brought it up that second time, though."

"He was gonna shoot, boss."

Sterling was one of those guys who'd led a kind of sheltered life. His money had insulated him so effectively from all those urban miseries the rest of us know all too well that he seemed to believe that nothing really bad could happen to him. He might read about things in the newspaper, shake his head, and make some solemn remark about anarchy abroad in our society, the need for more police, longer jail terms, bigger prisons, whatever. But he didn't seem to think of violence as something he might experience firsthand. What he said next made that clear.

"Well, I, personally, can't think of any reason why somebody would want to harm me," he declared. "That's why I haven't been able to take seriously that shooting in my room at the hotel. That was all a mistake."

"You bet it was a mistake!" I exploded. "It was *you* the shooter was after!"

"Well . . ." A verbal shrug. I didn't actually see his shoulders go up and down. We were almost to the Santa Monica cop house, and I was giving all my attention to getting us there without any more problems. To tell you the truth, my hands were shaking on the steering wheel. The way it is with me, I'm okay in the crunch. It's only afterward that I start to fall apart. I get the shakes. My stomach jumps around. I sweat. It was all I could do to keep myself under control just then. I didn't need this conversation with Sterling, but he wouldn't let go.

"I think I should have been informed," he said. "After all, who's in charge here?"

"*I am!*" I yelled. "As long as I'm paid to protect you, then I call the shots. I make the decisions. You don't like it, you fire me. But I don't think you want to do that, Mr. Sterling, because like it or not, somebody wants you dead."

Quite an outburst. I was practically panting afterward.

Julio reached over and gave my arm a squeeze. Solidarity. Barrio boys forever. Benjamin Sterling didn't say another word all the way to police headquarters.

When we got there, it wasn't Lieutenant Shinahara who came out to meet us but my old pal, Detective Lorenzen. Again, he was apologetic. Maybe Shinahara really was teaching him humility. He explained that the senior detective had been called out on a case. Just when he might return would be uncertain.

"He wanted me to ask where you'd be tonight," said Lorenzen.

"Well," said Sterling, "we were planning on being in Chicago."

"Really? Geez, that's a long way off, isn't it? Could you stick around maybe one more night? Because I know the lieutenant really does want to talk to you. See, he got called away real suddenly. So if you could stay, he'd sure appreciate it."

My God, I thought, is this the same Detective Lorenzen who had slammed me up against the wall in the hotel and made threats and promises? No, this was a different guy entirely. It seemed to me that these Santa Monica cops, maybe all cops everywhere, were kind of two-faced. They had one style for the rich and famous and another for the rest of us.

"Oh, I don't know," said Sterling at last, "what do you think, Cervantes?"

He was deferring to me. Maybe I *had* made some impression on him. "Your call," I said, "strictly your call. I warn you, though, if you do decide to stay over another night, I'll be sleeping in the next bed."

Sterling gave one of those ha-ha-ha phony laughs at that, and then he asked, "What was the name of that motel where Julio's staying?" Julio had, oddly, chosen to wait for us in the car.

What was it? Would I have to run out and ask him? But then it came to me. "It's the Travelers Inn."

"I know the place," said Lorenzen. "It's up Wilshire."

"That's it," I said. "It's just a nuts-and-bolts motel, no luxury spot."

"Where I've been sleeping most of last week," said Sterling, "almost anyplace would seem luxurious." I had to acknowledge that that was probably true. "Unless you hear otherwise from us," he said to Lorenzen, "that's where we'll be. All right?"

"Fine," said Lorenzen, "we'll call before we come over."

"We'd appreciate that," Sterling said to me, "wouldn't we?"

Now it seemed he was checking with me on everything. "Yeah, sure, of course," I said.

That settled, Sterling and I turned to leave and got as far as the door when Lorenzen called me back. "Cervantes," he said, "just one more thing."

While Sterling waited, I went back. "Yeah?" Very business-like. "What is it?"

Lorenzen lowered his voice to a whisper. "I hope you two will be very happy together." He left, giggling. You can't change human nature.

9

As soon as we had registered at the motel, Sterling led the way into the room, tossed his carryon bag onto one bed, and went straight to the telephone. By the time I got inside with his suitcase, he was on the wire to his son-in-law, telling him that he'd be remaining another night.

"We ought to be able to get away fairly early tomorrow, though. I'll let you and Clare know the time and the flight number as soon as it's set." They talked a little longer. Sterling listened impatiently to some business talk, then cut him off sharply: "Roger, you know you're perfectly capable of making that decision yourself . . . Oh, come *on* . . . All right, the number here is—they don't have it on the phone. Well, it's been defaced, written over, can't read it." Not without his glasses, anyway. He turned to me, "Cervantes, what's the name of this place again?" I told him, and he repeated it into the phone. Then, "What? Oh yes, he's working out just fine. Very able young man, very professional . . ." He wound up the conversation then and hung up, frowning.

Sterling busied himself unpacking then, hanging a couple of things in the open closet space, bringing his toilet kit into the bathroom and spreading out its contents on a shelf before the mirror. There wasn't much I could do to help, and besides, I didn't want to. I wasn't his valet. Did he have one? Probably not. He was too capably neat himself to need somebody to pick up after him, match tie to suit, and so on. Besides, nobody had valets anymore, did they? or butlers? Chauffeurs, maybe, but—well, the truth was, I didn't have much firsthand experience of how the very rich lived. There were the Tollers, of course, but they weren't exactly rich. They were movie people.

It had been a while since anyone called me a young man, but I suppose that's how I must have looked to Benjamin Sterling at—what? Seventy-two, I guess. He looked pretty good for his age, certainly—dapper, lean, and he moved well, too, must play a lot of tennis, or whatever those guys do to stay in shape. He looked like he could last another twenty years if he just stayed out of harm's way.

There was a knock on the door. I motioned for Sterling to stay in the bathroom, and, with my hand on the butt of my .38, I went to the door and called out, "Who is it?"

"It's Julio, homeboy."

Hand still on the gun, I swung the door open and let him in. He was alone. I relaxed.

"Hey, boss," he called to Sterling, "I'm going over to Fatburgers to get a couple. You wan' anything?"

"Nothing for me. Thank you, Julio."

"You wanna go out to a restauran'? Izzat it?"

"No, just not hungry."

"How bou' you, homeboy?"

"Yeah, I could go for a cheeseburger."

"Everything on it?"

"Everything."

Julio stood for a moment in the doorway, looking away, waiting. Then he looked directly at me. "Well?"

"Well what?"

He lowered his voice: "I could use some bread, mahn."

I dug into my pocket. "For mine?"

"For mine, too. I spen' all I had las' night. She took my las' five."

I glanced over my shoulder at Sterling. "Okay, sure," I said, and handed Julio a twenty.

"He ain' got nothin' till he gets back home," said Julio. "Credit cards gone. No more cash. Didn' they tell you? You're bankrollin' the whole fockin' expedition."

I sighed. "Okay," I said, "get a receipt and bring me the change."

"You got it, bro." He gave me a grin, a little two-fingered salute, and was out the door.

I went back, sat down in a chair, and watched Sterling putter around, put a couple of pairs of socks into a drawer, underwear, clean shirts, just like he was moving in to stay. What was it his daughter said about him? He was "meticulously neat." Well, there was no arguing about that, was there?

He pushed the drawer shut and looked up at me suddenly. "You got any kids, Cervantes?"

"No," I said, "not exactly, no." That was a hell of an answer, wasn't it? Alicia? Her kid? Did that make me a father? I had thought for a while it did.

"Well, we only had the one, Julia and I, Mother Nature saw to that. But Clare was a terrific kid, terrific young woman, wanted in the worst way to be a trader like me. She came right out and asked me when she finished college. But I—oh, I don't know . . . You ever been to Chicago? Ever gone to the Board of Trade, had a look at the trading floor?"

"No," I said, "I've never been to Chicago at all. Just to change planes a couple of times."

"Too bad. Great city." He sat down opposite me at the foot of the bed I'd picked out as mine. "But the trading floor, that's my life. It was my father's life and his before him. My grandfather started our trading house, Sterling Partners, way back in the last century. It's one of the few real old family houses on the Board. Anyway, what goes on there on the trading floor is just absolutely crazy, very slightly ordered chaos, all the yelling and jumping, the money that changes hands. There's nothing like it. And some of it, I admit, is kind of dirty. The deals that are made and the way they're made just wouldn't stand up to close inspection. It's not for nothing they call it 'the pit.'

"But it's been my life, you see, and I've played dirty and rough and tumble just like the rest of them down there. And to tell you the truth, Cervantes, I didn't want her to know that. I wanted my only daughter to keep the high opinion of me she had. I admit she had the mind for it, the instincts, and she would have made a terrific trader. But I told her no, it was out of the question. So she got married. And what did she do with this mind, those instincts? Tennis. She became a regular Lake Wood lady, but a killer on the court. I really regret not taking her into Sterling Partners, and I know she resents it. I don't think she's ever forgiven me."

"Oh, I don't know about that," I objected mildly. "She was sure concerned when you disappeared."

He shrugged and waved his hand dismissively. "That's family stuff. Any daughter would feel that way if her father turned up missing."

"Maybe," I said. "I don't think so, though."

"Be that as it may," he continued, "one of the reasons I regret not taking her in is because I did take her husband into the firm, more or less in her place." He hesitated. "Now, you've met Roger, haven't you?"

I nodded, said nothing. I'd just as soon he left me out of it.

"What did you think of him?"

"Mr. Sterling," I said, "I don't want to comment on members of your family. It's not professional. Basically, it doesn't matter what I think of him, just so I do my job."

He took a moment to think that over, then he nodded, "Good response," he said, "reasonable. But I can tell you what you thought of him. You thought he was a pain in the ass. Everybody thinks that. He's overbearing. He uses bluster to cover up fundamental weakness. Why do you think I've stayed in the business so long? It's because I don't want to hand it over to him. Now I've got this new project I'm going to be giving all my attention to, and frankly I'm scared to death what's going to happen to the firm."

Sighing, he rose from where he'd been sitting on the bed and paced a few steps away. "I don't know why I'm burdening you with all this, Cervantes. But as you get older, you sort of survey your life, try to set things in order. It seems like that's what this trip out here has been about, setting things in order. I guess I just needed somebody to hear me through."

That sounded familiar. Al Cosentino had said something similar on his boat down in San Pedro. "I was wondering, Mr. Sterling, if you've talked to Al Cosentino."

"That's right, you've met Al, haven't you? Clare told me you two went down there. Good man, really solid."

"He's got a high opinion of you, too. Told us about the war."

"Jesus, Tarawa. What a day that was. . . . The worst and the best."

"Why don't you give him a call? Tell him you're back among the living."

He smiled, nodded, and went to the telephone. As he punched out the numbers, there was another knock at the door. Same routine. Hand on the butt of the .38, Julio identifying himself, and so on. By the time I got my cheeseburger and the receipt, Sterling had hung up. Julio asked him if he wanted him for anything more. Then, dismissed, he left. It was only after he'd gone I realized I hadn't gotten the change from the transaction. I promised myself I'd get it later.

"Not there," said Sterling. "Harbormaster said he was out on a day trip."

"Well, maybe tonight," I said.

"Yeah, maybe tonight."

With that, he kicked off his loafers, hauled his feet up on the bed, and went back to the great pile of papers he'd carried away from the Office of Human Services.

I was fairly desperate for something to read, so I asked him if I might have a look at some of the stuff he'd already been through.

"Sure," he said, indicating the smaller pile of papers on his left, "help yourself."

I went over and picked up about a half inch of photocopied reports, unwrapped my cheeseburger, and munched as I read. I liked the cheeseburger better. The reports and memos—there must have been five or six of them stapled separately—were set out in that sort of bureaucratic jargon that seems intended to cover up problems rather than reveal them. There was a whole lot of "interfacing" going on here between the "clients," which meant the homeless, I guess, and the agencies. But I struggled on, and gradually I got the drift of it.

Los Angeles has a hell of a homeless problem, probably the worst of any city in the country except New York. Considering the fact that New York has a population of 13 million or so—I read it in *Time* magazine so it must be so—and L.A.'s is about half that, we're more than holding up our end; we're going for the gold. Here in Los Angeles, they have the homeless problem spotlighted pretty well, and judging by all this paperwork they've got it pretty well analyzed, it's just that they don't seem to have enough money to do anything about it, except maybe build a shopping mall over Pershing Square to get them out of sight.

But Jesus, I thought, what can they do? There're so many of them!

"It's not very elevating reading, is it?" said Sterling from the bed.

"Yeah, I guess you could say that."

"It makes sense that so many come out here just to keep from freezing in the winter. We don't even think of that in our warm beds back home. You know, it gets really cold back in Chicago."

"That's what I hear."

"And when it does," he said, "we just put an extra blanket on the bed. We don't stop to think that a twenty-degree drop in temperature could mean so-and-so many could freeze that night."

"It's a good argument for hitchhiking out to L.A.," I said, "if that's how they come."

"Yes, that's how they come. At least I heard that from a lot of them in Santa Monica."

"Hey, I'm getting cheeseburger on some of these," I said, waving the memo I'd been reading. "Fingerprints, anyway. Sorry."

"That's okay. You can deep-six them when you're done."

"Not much help, huh?"

"Well, yes, in a way they are. They give you a good idea of what's *not* the right approach."

"Yeah, I can see that."

"You take this one I'm reading," he said. "A few years ago they put up a tent city for them on some industrial plot downtown. Good idea, good project. They fed them, provided secondhand clothes in reasonable condition. The idea was to get them into shape so they could get jobs—you know, service, maintenance, low-level work. The city and county agencies provided job leads, set up meetings, coached them through interviews, did all they could for them."

"Yeah," I said. "What happened with that?"

"Well, some good things happened. Some people got jobs. A few of them even kept them."

"A few?"

"Yes. You've got to realize that at best only about fifty percent of these people are employable. That's my estimate, anyway. I'm trying not to be starry-eyed about this. Now, with the fifty percent who are employable—not alcoholics or addicts or mentally incapacitated—a couple of things worked against them. In the first place, the longer they've been out on the street the harder it is to adjust to the workaday world. The street has its own rhythm, you know. There's a lot of freedom in being down and out. You get moving when you want to, go where you want to. It's a little bit like being on permanent vacation."

"And taking a job is like coming off vacation?"

"That's right. Who wants to put up with a time clock or a boss when you've been your own boss for so long? Now, the other thing that worked against them is peculiar to Los Angeles, and it's the size of this city, the physical size."

"It's huge. And public transportation's not that great."

"Exactly! So some of these people would land jobs, all right, but they'd face a two-hour bus commute every morning. Naturally they're going to be late to work some of the time. That made them look undependable, so . . ."

Sterling threw up his hands in a what's-the-use gesture. "Well, this was the major effort, the big project. The city and the county showed they cared. It wasn't planned as permanent. They didn't have the money to keep it going indefinitely—no city does these days—so after a while they took down the tents, and the people just went back to the streets. The man I talked to up there at the city office tried to put a good face on it, but it was a failure by any measure."

I waited for him to go on, but he didn't. He just sat there staring at me. Finally, I said, "So what's the answer?"

He chuckled then. "Why, I thought you'd never ask." With that, he began talking and kept it up the rest of the afternoon. It was almost like a performance, a preliminary run-through for a presentation he'd be making sometime soon. But who to? He spoke without notes. If that seems like a dumb thing to say, considering the fact that we were in a motel room, and it was just me he was talking to, it should give you an idea of just how well ordered his presentation was. Through part of it he was up on his feet, pacing the floor. For about an hour he was sitting on the foot of the bed, opposite me, where he'd been before. He talked quietly, earnestly, like he was really trying to convince me. Why me? Once in a while he'd stop and wait for the obvious question, the one that had to be answered at that particular point. I'd ask it, then he'd go on and talk some more.

This was his big idea, the project that Julio had hinted at, the one for the homeless in Chicago. Would it solve the problem? No, he made it clear he wasn't as naive as all that. But if other projects like it were started, he declared, they might go a long way toward cutting it in half. It was that employable fifty percent that he was after. Others like it? That explained the presentation aspect of all this. He was going to go out and pitch his idea to the business community in Chicago. "That's one of the things that went wrong with the tent city project here in Los Angeles," he said at one point. "They didn't get the business community sufficiently involved. That's where it has to come from." He gave me all kinds of reasons for this, among them: Because government at every level is broke; because ultimately, at least in Chicago, support for social action has always come from the business side; and "because, damn it, we ought to do it."

Obviously, the last of them was most important to him personally. He elaborated on it, explaining that a trader wasn't exactly like a stockbroker, that he took more chances, was more of a buccaneer. But like a stockbroker, he dealt in paper, not products, in deals and not tangibles. "Which is a roundabout way of saying that for my working life, Cervantes, I've been a parasite on the economy. I haven't produced a thing, haven't built a thing, haven't grown a thing. I just . . . traded. Now, I know my colleagues on the Board would yell plenty if they heard me say that. But I've been at it longer than just about any of them. By God, it's my life, and that's the way I look back at it."

Okay, by now you shouldn't be surprised to learn that his big plan for the homeless in Chicago was for him, Benjamin Sterling, to become a producer at last, a manufacturer. There was obviously a certain amount of ego involved here, but if it worked, why not? He would open up a factory and hire the homeless. Not just for minimum wage, he insisted, but for a real living wage. The important thing was to get them off the street. When they were hired, they would be loaned enough to rent apartments, the amount to be taken out of their pay a little at a time. There'd be advances for clothing, for food, "whatever it takes to put them on their feet again."

He went on and on like this, until I put a question to him, the only one he seemed not totally prepared for. "Okay," I said, "just what are you going to manufacture? Nothing high tech, I hope. I mean, these people aren't exactly rocket scientists or they wouldn't be out on the street."

But as it turned out, he was not totally unprepared, either. "No, no you're right, not high tech. What would I know about it? What could I contribute? Nothing, absolutely zero. Now, I could brush that question aside and say the product is yet to be determined. But it's not unimportant. If this enterprise is going to be anything more than make-work, we've got to respect the market. It's absolutely germane. So what does the market say that Americans are most interested in?"

I shrugged. "I don't know. Television?"

"No, no, no, not television. The Japanese have that completely covered. We'll never get back into TV manufacturing again. Besides, these days it amounts to high tech. No, television is out. But you're on the right track. You're thinking recreation, leisure time, and so am I. What I'm considering now—considering, mind you; it's not carved in stone—is a fishing reel Al Cosentino has designed; built a prototype, too. It's new, it's original, it's different from anything on the market today. He's even applied for a patent on it."

Sterling then spent about half an hour explaining its revolutionary action to me. He drew a diagram and everything. I kept saying, "Uh-huh, uh-huh," just like I understood it all. But to tell you the truth, I've never been fishing in my life. How would I know what was a conventional design, much less what was new and different?

So in the end, all I could do was point to the diagram he'd drawn and ask, "You think you can get a bank loan on this? Attract investors?"

"I've no idea."

"But starting up from scratch with a new product like this, marketing it, that could cost a lot of money."

"It could, yes."

"Millions."

"I've got millions."

In Hollywood, they've got a rule: Never invest more than your own time and talent in a movie; let somebody else take the financial risk. So, at that moment, in spite of his enthusiasm, I became doubtful of Sterling's big project. I mean, after all, he had no experience in manufacturing, and God knows Julio didn't. He'd better invest one of those millions in a production manager, get the very best, because nobody else involved would have any idea what they were doing. What was it his daughter said? "Daddy, you can't be serious!" Well, I had news for her. Benjamin Sterling was definitely serious.

10

He continued to talk off and on through dinner. Lieutenant Shinahara had called toward the end of the afternoon and said he'd be around about 6:30. Sterling had then hung up the telephone and asked if there was anyplace we could go and get a meal this early; it was around five. "I'm starving," he said. "I guess I get kind of pumped up just talking about this. Raises the metabolism. Good sign, don't you think?"

So I called Jean-Claude down the street at the Café Reni and asked if the kitchen was open. He told us to come ahead, he'd fix us up with something. When Sterling found out how close it was, he wanted to walk it. But remembering our experience with those two guys in the low-rider, I didn't want us going anywhere on foot—too exposed. (There was something that bothered me about that; I had to think about it.) So I packed Sterling and Julio into the Alfa and headed back down Wilshire.

Jean-Claude came through. Although we were alone there until just before we left, we ate well and had a good bottle of wine. I could tell Sterling was impressed. His private eye proved he had some class. His private eye paid the bill, too—and kept the receipt.

In the middle of all that, I heard all about Julio's part in Sterling's planned enterprise. He was to be—are you sitting down?—director of personnel. I guess the theory was that it took one to know one. He was to separate the employable from the unemployable, the sane from the crazies.

"An' community relations, too, boss," Julio added. "Don' forget that."

"Yes," said Sterling, "Julio feels it's important for us to locate right down among them."

"See, then they got no excuse for clockin' in late. That way, too, I go out and let them know what we're doin'. Make a place for ourselves, get a good image in the 'hood, you know?"

Yeah, I knew. I was just glad I wouldn't be bankrolling *that* expedition.

Lieutenant Shinahara arrived right on time. He brought with him Detective-trainee Lorenzen, who followed, smirking his way into the room, giving me a wink as he passed me by. This guy was really too much.

Shinahara apologized again, probably three times in all, for failing to keep the earlier date. And then he asked if it would be all right with Sterling if he tape-recorded this. Sterling said it was okay. So then Shinahara coached him through a little preamble in the beginning in which Sterling identified himself, gave the date, said he knew his statement was being tape-recorded and had no objection.

I expected Shinahara to ask him about the reason for his long absence from his hotel room and to hear once more about his firsthand research, how he had his wallet stolen, the whole business. But no. Shinahara might have gotten around to that, but the answer to his first line of questioning surprised us—astonished me, at least—and pushed the entire case off into a new direction. Here's how it went.

Shinahara: "Mr. Sterling, your daughter, Clarissa Edwards, said in her statement that your trip here was part vacation, part business. Could you tell us about the business you transacted here?"

Sterling: "Oh, well, that didn't come to anything. That was just a meeting I had the first day I was here. My son-in-law arranged it. As I say, nothing came of it."

Shinahara: "The details, please."

Sterling: "All right. I was to meet with a lawyer and his client on a U.S. government bond purchase. We deal those at the Board of Trade, you know. Anyway, there was a complication to it that I didn't like, and so I'd requested the meeting. The lawyer was there, so was the client."

Shinahara: "Where did the meeting take place?"

Sterling: "Oh, right at my hotel. They were very obliging about that. The lawyer's office was way down in Little Tokyo, and I—"

Shinahara: "Little Tokyo?"

Sterling: "Yes, you know—downtown?"

Shinahara: "Certainly, of course. But he was Japanese?"

Sterling: "Japanese-American, a very slick young man named—oh, what is it? At my age my memory for names isn't what it ought to be. [Pause] Richard, uh, Nakamura. That was it."

Shinahara: "And the client?"

Sterling: "Well, there you've got me. He was Japanese-Japanese. Didn't even speak English. Nakamura's Japanese was good, though—at least I assume it was. He served as interpreter. But the name of the client? Well, I couldn't possibly come up with his first name. It was very . . . Japanese. But the last name was easy—Ito—a little too easy, probably. I understand Ito's like Smith or Jones in Japan. In other words, it was probably phony."

Shinahara: "Why do you think that?"

Sterling: "Well, because of the nature of the deal, because of *him*. As I said, it was a purchase of U.S. government bonds, a few million dollars' worth. They never gave me the specific amount. Now, the Japanese buy government bonds all the time, nothing unusual in that. But what this fellow Ito proposed, or maybe it was the lawyer's idea; who's to say? In any case, the deal was that it not be a bank transaction, a transfer of funds, but a cash purchase, millions in cash, in dollars. Now, we could handle that, they must have known it. We're currency traders, too. But frankly, the whole deal smelled to me like money laundering. They said, or Nakamura said, that they realized this was unusual, and they were willing to pay us above our usual commision. They wanted to negotiate right then and there. That smelled bad, too.

"This meeting was kind of a late breakfast or early lunch. Anyway, we were there together in the hotel dining room around eleven, just about alone there, as I recall. Let me tell you about this fellow Ito. He wasn't tall, about your height, Lieutenant, but he was burly, stocky, make about two of you. And he sort of growled when he talked, made the language sound sort of ugly, if you know what I mean. Well, he was formal and polite—shook hands, bowed, all of that. We had coffee, but all I saw on the table was his right hand. When the waitress brought us croissants, I guess he was hungry because he really attacked his—grabbed it up, broke it apart, and started smearing jam all over it. That was the first real look I had at his left hand. The little finger on it was missing down to the second joint. You could tell it had been cut off there. I knew what that meant. Up to the moment I saw that stump of a little finger, I'd intended just to stall them and back out of the deal once I got home. But suddenly I just got furious. The idea of even a part of the national debt being mortgaged with what was probably drug money to gangsters just made me livid. And so I told him that. Nakamura started arguing with me, or actually trying to placate me. I cut him off. I said, 'Tell him,' and he did. Ito didn't like that. He growled something back, which Nakamura translated as, 'He's very unhappy to hear that.' I'll bet what he actually said was a lot more colorful.

"Then I made kind of a speech. I told him, 'Look, I fought a war to keep scum like you away from here, and I'd fight another one, if I had to. What I'm certainly *not* going to do is help you buy this country out with dirty money. And I'm going to spread word among the traders not to do business with you.' I didn't wait for Nakamura to translate. I just jumped up and started out of there. The way it seemed to me, Ito had understood some of it, because as I passed him on my way out, he grabbed hold of me, my arm. The fellow had a grip like steel; I couldn't move, and he gave me what I would call a threatening stare and started growling at me again. So I simply drove the index finger of my free hand into his eye. He let go then, howled plenty, and I walked away."

Shinahara [after a pause]: "You insulted him."

Sterling: "I suppose so. It was certainly my intention to."

At that point, Shinahar switched off the tape recorder. He'd gotten more than he'd expected, maybe more than he wanted. He was visibly shaken by what he'd heard.

Not only did he have a laundering scheme for what was almost certainly drug money, which he would have to turn over to the feds, but since the meeting Sterling had just described took place in Santa Monica, he also had evidence of activity within his jurisdiction by the Yakuza, the Japanese Mafia. That's what that missing finger meant. It's a little way of saying you're sorry to your capo when you fuck up; you present him with one of your fingers. I could tell Lieutenant Shinahara was excited, but he also seemed a little overwhelmed. Sometime during the two or three generations his family had been here, the Shinaharas had lost their inscrutability.

Although I hadn't said a word and was sitting well back from the others on the bed nearest the door, the lieutenant suddenly became aware of my presence there. He seemed to be thinking things over, his eyes wandering around the room, when they rested on me.

"Uh, you," he said, "Cervantes, I'm going to have to ask you to go."

"Go where?"

"Well, leave the room, anyway. Also, you're not to repeat anything you've heard here. You understand that?"

"I understand."

"Come on," Lorenzen yelled at me, "the lieutenant said go, you go."

We both got up. I started for the door. He started after me, probably hoping to push me out. But I beat him there and was practically through the door by the time he arrived. Then I had the opportunity to push it open in his face. "I'll be next door with Julio," I called. The door behind me shut with a loud slam.

I was as good as my word. I didn't tell Julio anything about Benjamin Sterling's encounter with the Yakuza. I suspected that Julio had worries enough without adding the possibility of a murder for honor by some insulted Japanese gangster. Shinahara certainly took this all very seriously. And certainly the growling Mr. Ito could have arranged for the hit in the hotel bathroom that left the wrong man dead. But I was less sure about that crazy chase on the freeway. I needed to talk to Julio about that.

"Hey, homeboy! ¿Cómo le va? The cops chase you out?" He threw the door open.

"That's just what they did." The television was on, some game show. I walked over and shut it off.

"Hey, I was watchin' that!"

"Sit down," I said, nodding at the bed. "There's something we've got to talk about."

"Don' you hardass me, mahn. I'm in with the boss. Remember that!" But he sat down, anyway.

Not me. I began pacing up and down in a narrow space there in the motel room, my hands clasped behind my back. I'd seen an L.A. county prosecutor do it that way in a trial I testified in once. He didn't say a word then, neither did I now—not for about three or four trips across the carpet. Finally, I stopped suddenly and confronted Julio.

"Look," I said, "I checked my car over from the outside, and it's pretty hard to see anybody in the backseat—I mean, see them well enough to identify them."

"So? I don' get it. What's that prove?"

"Sterling was sitting in back. I kind of remember those guys in that low-rider pickup moving along beside us on Fifth before they wound up behind us at Fifth and Hill. I don't think they saw Sterling in the backseat at all."

"Get real, homeboy. They knew the car. They had your plate."

"Maybe," I said, "or maybe they spotted somebody sitting in front who got them excited enough to chase us. Now, those guys didn't know me. I'm pretty sure about that because I got a good look at them, and I didn't know them. You tell me, Julio—did they know you?"

"No *way,* man! What is this shit, anyway? What you tryin' to prove on me?"

"I'm not trying to prove anything. I'm just trying to get it straight in my head who they were after. I don't think it was Sterling. I know it wasn't me. That leaves you."

Julio said nothing. His eyes shifted around the room.

"I give you my word, Julio, anything you tell me stays with me. My interest in Benjamin Sterling stops when I get him on a plane to Chicago in the morning. But you'll be along on that trip to the airport, and I want to know if you should sit in the back or the front."

Nothing from him for almost a minute. Then at last we established eye contact, and he said, "In the back would prob'ly be better."

"Tell me about it."

And he did, surprising me not much at all. I'd wondered about Julio—not from the start but pretty early on. The truth is, you don't see too many Latinos among the homeless, certainly not in Santa Monica. First of all, the ones who come up here from the South are more ambitious than the ones who stay at home.

Sometimes that gets passed on to their kids, and sometimes it doesn't. When it doesn't there seems to be a kind of net in the Latino community that catches them before they hit bottom. Maybe it's a holdover from the Indian side, an old tribal virtue or something, but we try to look after our own. During those days of mixing among the homeless, searching the beaches and the parks for Sterling, the only face I saw like mine was Julio's. Here's how he got there:

He told me that he'd been dealing up and down Whittier Boulevard—just a street dealer, the end of the chain, but he was doing pretty well, had a 1982 Cadillac Seville that was in pretty good shape and looked great, had money and the clothes. He was doing all right. The thing was, he explained, he got into the trade late. He'd had various hustles. In the old days, when they used to bring the illegals in by the truckload, Julio worked the end of the line for a very respectable coyote in San Ysidro, a very profitable business, he assured me. Eventually he came away with enough money so that he was able to invest in one of those meat-market employment agencies they run on the East Side. He worked it, too—got paid on both sides. The Migra, the emigration people, put them out of business. That cost him lawyer money, but he came out of it with enough to go into partnership on a bar. That went all right for a while, years in fact, but then things got tough, and his partner cleaned out all the money and beat it someplace East, and Julio wound up working for an importer, selling Mexican beer, some brand nobody ever heard of, bottled in Chihuahua.

"It was okay," he said, "I was gettin' by, but I got divorced, she divorced me, and I got hit by alimony. Mahn, that hurt! I'm tellin' you."

But he was a familiar figure on the Boulevard, calling on bars, clubs, package goods stores. He blended into the picture.

"All this time," he said, "I wasn' too much into shit myself. I mean, I always smoked, right? Once in a while some blow when I could afford it, which then wasn' so often. But I got nothin' agains' it, you know what I mean.

"So anyway, these two guys approach me, I'd seen 'em aroun', you know? They say they got a deal they wan' to talk over. But they're pretty young, see, flashy but young, half my age. I had a pretty good idea what they wanted to talk about. So yeah, they wanted me to deal. They make it soun' good, how much I can make, all that. I say, 'Why you wan' me? There's people all over the Boulevar' dealin'.' They say, 'Because you're not a fockin' junkie. You're a businessman. You make your roun's, nobody notices you. All the business you do would be in bars, nothin' on the street.'

"So I got to admit that sounds attractive. I keep my job dealin' beer, an' along the way I deal their shit. You know what? My beer sales go up, suddenly I got respec'. I'm dealin' grass an' blow, some crack—what the fock, it's still coke, right? An' maybe a little of the hard shit, too. I ain' too crazy abou' that. I ain' a pusher, see, I'm a seller. If they wan' it, I got it. It goes on like that. I'm doin' great. A year an' a half of that, an' I'm pullin' in more money than I thought there was. But I keep my beer job, see, because that's my, like, cover. The suppliers are happy. They tell me I'm movin' more product than three or four of their people on the street. I had the *niñas,* I had the clothes, but I figure I'll keep the ol' car because that's part of the cover. They like me so much, they take me to meet the next man up. He's pretty young, too. His name is Nacho Gonzales. He's the distributor. You hear of him?"

It seems that I had. The name rang a bell, anyway. What was it? A trial?

"Anyway, he wanted to know, were there any businessmen I knew who might be in'erested in moving product. He was especially in'erested in those guys, they go aroun' the barrio collecting rents. Did I know these guys? Would they be in'erested? Well, I said I knew a couple, which was bullshit, an' that I'd look into it.

"So wouldn' you know? The DEA's been on me a couple of mont's. Jus' watchin'. They do a pinch on me, but real quiet, you know? Nobody aroun'. You were a cop. You know the drill. I'm dead if I don' wear a wire. They tell me I'm lookin' at twenty, federal conviction, no parole. So what can I do, you know? I'm too ol' to go to jail. You got any idea how ol' I'd be when I got out? In my sixties! I can't defend myself, either, mahn. There's some bad dudes in there.

"Yeah, you got it. I turn over. They wanted Gonzales. I gave him to them. I took an undercover cop to him, said he was a rent collector. Gonzales laid out what he wanted. The cop knew his stuff, got him to be specific, an' then the bust was called in—an' that was it.

"They put me away in protective custody, not so bad, out of the general population. The trial comes, and I testify agains' Gonzales. He's convicted. That's it. They say, 'Okay, Julio, good-bye. You cooperated, charges dismiss'. I say, 'Hey, mahn, how 'bout the federal witness program? They talk about it a lot, but I admit it wasn' a promise. So they remin' me of that—no promise. They say, 'Charges dismiss', Julio. Take a walk. Go back to sellin' beer.' I wen' all the way for these guys, an' all they can say is 'Take a walk?' "

Julio was sweating. Just going over this had made it happen all over again. Is there such a thing as emotional memory? Why not? Fear is the strongest of them all. Why shouldn't it stay with you longest? He was still sitting on the bed. He'd drawn his knees up to his chest, rested his head against them, circled them with his arms. If he was on his side, you'd say he was in a fetal position. His shoulders began to shake slightly. I waited one minute, two, maybe three, giving him time to get control again.

Finally, I asked him, "Okay, what happened then?"

He made a great sniff, wiped his eyes, and cleared his throat. "Well, I knew I couldn' go back home again. Nacho sent me a message, real simple. 'You're a dead man.' What did I have back there, anyway? The DEA seize everything. The car was auctioned off by the time I testified. No more money. So what could I do? I took a bus down to Santa Monica, an' I start livin' on the beach. I figure they won't find me there. That was maybe two months ago—yeah, about two months.

"Then Ben comes along. I figure, this is a guy I can make some bread off him, maybe get out of town. But he starts talkin' about this big plan he's got, see? I start makin' suggestions. All of a sudden, jus' like I planned it that way, I'm part of the project. I'm

119

goin' to Chicago with him. Mahn, far away. They'll never fin' me there. I been prayin' for somethin' like this—I mean, really prayin'—and here it is."

He stopped. I knew it wasn't a full stop. He had more to tell. I had more to hear. Julio faced me then.

"So what happened today, that was outta left field, a freak. I'll tell you who those two guys were in the low-rider, that was Pepe and Paco, who got me into it in the firs' place. When the DEA guys wen' lookin' for them, they were gone. Who knows where? To Tijuana, maybe, I don' know. So anyway, they're back, an' they know I'm aroun', so I *gotta* get out of town, you know?"

"Yeah, I know, Julio," I said. "Tomorrow morning for sure."

"For sure!"

"Get up early. You got an alarm in that bag of tricks you carry?"

"I got nothin', man."

"Well, get up early. Not like this morning."

"I'll be ready. Don' worry."

I got as far as the door when Julio called after me, "Homeboy?"

"Yeah, Julio?"

"A funny thing. Out on the freeway, you know? When they were chasin' us?"

"Yeah?"

"I knew it was my ass if they caught us. I knew they'd shoot you jus' to get to me. But I wasn' scared. I was excited, but I wasn' scared. Weird, huh? I figure you'd get me out of it, all of us, and you came through. You're a hell of a driver, homeboy. Thanks."

Back in Boyle Heights, guys like Julio grew up to some sort of macho standard. They tried to stay on top of everything—be cool, man, be cool. Well, he'd blown his cool tonight, all right. First tears and now gratitude. He didn't seem as though he'd be real big on gratitude. So I guess he surprised me.

What could I say? I opened the door, trying to think of some sort of response. Finally, all I could come up with was, "Don' mention it, Julio." Playing it cool, I guess.

Outside, I stood for a moment, just breathing in the night air.

That felt good. One after the other, the two rooms I'd been in had seemed to shrink on me. The air in them had gotten thick with revelation. Julio had worn me out emotionally. I felt for the guy. I didn't like him, but I felt for him.

Digging into my jacket pocket, I pulled out my weekly pack of cigarettes and lit one up. Why didn't I give them up altogether? Why did I keep on smoking ten or fifteen a week? For moments like this one, I guess, so I could be alone, get away from it all. As I stood there drawing on the dry cigarette, I wondered why I didn't like these people better. Back in the old days, a guy like Sterling would have been satisfied just leaving a shitload of money to the church. But this was today. He had to have a project, a big plan. Who knows? Maybe it would work. Maybe it was exactly the right approach to the problem. But I suspected his motives. He had an awful lot of ego tied up in all this. And Al Cosentino was right: Sterling *was* naive. He might be a terror on the trading floor, but he was sure an easy con for Julio. Well, they probably deserved each other.

Al Cosentino—him I liked. He'd given me the best half hour I'd spent on this job. Would Sterling get around to calling him back? Probably not. I dug through my wallet and found the card Cosentino had given me with the San Pedro phone number at the bottom. I decided to pass the word on Sterling to him myself. Sterling could call him later. I'd seen a pay phone just outside the motel office. I tossed down the cigarette and headed for it. Julio's room was the last along the row. The way he looked when I checked him in, I would have tucked him out of sight myself. So it was a bit of a walk. There must have been six or eight rooms along the line before I came to the office and the telephone outside.

I put in a quarter and dialed. I looked into the motel office. There was a guy in there talking to the manager. He was in some kind of uniform, from a messenger service or something. There was a package on the counter between them.

A recorded message came on. The number I had dialed would require an additional fifty cents. Luckily, I had it. I put in two quarters and waited.

The messenger finished up with the manager. He grabbed up the package and the clipboard he had also laid down on the counter and headed for the door of the office.

I listened to the telephone ring at the other end of the line—once, twice. Cosentino picked up.

"Hello. Al Cosentino here."

"Yeah, hi, Al. This is Antonio Cervantes. You remember me from yesterday?"

The messenger rounded the corner and walked past me there at the pay phone. A black guy, early thirties. His eyes barely grazed over me as he walked by. I really didn't get much of a look at him. But there was something about him that seemed familiar.

"Sure, I do. How you doing? Was it you who called earlier?"

"No, that was Sterling. So that should tell you he's okay. Came into the hotel demanding his old room. There he was. I just wanted you to know he's okay."

"Well, thanks, Cervantes. That sounds like Ben, all right."

"He'll probably call you back later on himself."

The messenger had reached a door on down the line. Yeah, it had to be Sterling's . . . mine. He knocked on it.

Then it hit me just why the guy looked familiar.

Without another word to Cosentino, I hung up the telephone. I started walking back to the room. I was moving fast, just as rapidly as I could, while I was trying to haul that .38 of mine out of its shoulder holster. It's a full-sized Smith & Wesson, really too big for a shoulder holster. It jammed inside the holster.

The guy in the messenger suit was there at the door, talking, handing over the package.

I pulled again. The .38 came free. I pushed off the safety, and with my finger off the trigger I started to run toward the room and the guy at the door.

He must have heard me coming because he turned toward me.

I skidded to a halt a good twenty paces away, went down into the shooter's crouch, and aimed the pistol at him.

He backpedaled from the doorway as he grabbed inside his jacket.

"Hold it right there," I yelled.

But no. His hand came clear of his jacket. In it was an automatic.

He glanced at the doorway, looked back at me, and brought the automatic down in my direction.

It was the wrong call. From just inside the room, so close to the door I could see the muzzle flashes, three rounds exploded. The guy was literally lifted off his feet. He went down in a heap without ever getting a shot off. Lucky for me.

I ran to him, my .38 still extended. But by the time I got there, he was wheezing, gurgling, breathing his last. There is such a thing as the death rattle, and I heard it just then, standing over him, staring down. The look in his eyes, terrible surprise, was something I'd always remember.

Then I was pushed away, bodily, by Lorenzen. He came down on top of the guy, pushed his own automatic into the dead man's face, and said, "Shit."

"He's gone," I said.

He looked up at me. He was like a kid, the playground bully. "Yeah, well, you didn't even get a shot off."

"Didn't need to. You took care of him. I mean, you *really* took care of him. No answers from him." I tucked the .38 away.

He stood up, looking down at the corpse. "Shit," he repeated.

Then Shinahara was beside me. "Who was he?" he asked. "You recognized him?"

A number of people had come out of their rooms. They stood back, watching, talking in low tones among themselves.

"Yeah," I said to Shinahara, "the last time I saw him he was out near the hotel panhandling. He said he thought he'd seen Sterling. I gave him my card and told him to call me if he saw him again."

"This was when Sterling was missing."

"Right."

Shinahara turned to Lorenzen. "Go inside and call it in," he said. "Ask for a morgue team and a shooting team as well as the regular people."

Lorenzen made a face at that. The shooting team meant he'd have his piece taken away, would have to answer questions and face an inquiry board. But he did as he was told, squeezing past Sterling, who stood in the doorway to his room looking slightly dazed. Julio was nowhere to be seen, but the door to his room stood open.

Shinahara turned back to me. "Let me get this straight," he said. "You saw him panhandling, and then he turned up in a messenger's uniform, and you thought that was suspicious?"

"Yeah," I said, "but it was more than that. The guy who did the shooting at the hotel, at least the one registered in the next room, was black."

"How did you know this?"

"Didn't you?"

He didn't take that kindly. "You withheld this information?"

"I didn't withhold it, but evidently the hotel staff did. It's in their records. You can check it out."

"I will." He turned and walked away toward the crowd that had gathered, and he made a little speech, assuring them the excitement was all over and urging them to return to their rooms. There was some shuffling of feet at that, but nobody left.

I looked back at Sterling and saw that he had ventured out at last, and so had Julio. The two of them were talking in low tones far from the body.

But there was Detective Lorenzen kneeling in the doorway, just starting to unwrap the package the phony messenger had delivered.

"Hey," I yelled at him. "Don't do that. It might be a bomb."

Wide-eyed, Lorenzen dropped it to the floor and jumped away.

About an hour later we found out that, sure enough, it was a bomb.

11

A little after nine the next morning I saw Benjamin Sterling and Julio Alviero off on American's flight 84 direct to Chicago. As I watched them disappear through the gate, it seemed to me that I had never before been quite so glad to get rid of two guys. And I was sure that if Lieutenant Shinahara were there beside me, he would have said the same. He wasn't, of course. Sterling had given him enough to worry about for the next six months or so. He may already have invited Richard Nakamura in for a friendly talk. Or, playing it by the numbers, he may have contacted the feds. However he played it, this was going to be a big investigation, and he had a piece of it.

There had been no smile back at me, no final wave from Sterling or Julio as they started through the ramp to board the plane. In fact, there hadn't even been a thank you from either of them, unless you count the limp handshake I got from Sterling. He did, however, give me a pat on the back and assure me that a check would go out just as soon as my bill came in. That was to ease the pain that was written all over my face as I was asked to hand over my Visa card to the lady behind the counter to cover Julio's first-class ticket to Chicago.

"Can't he go coach?" I whispered to Sterling.

"Of course not," he said indignantly. "That is *not* the sort of image I wish to foster among my employees—the master and his serfs. Besides, he and I have matters to discuss. I want him sitting next to me."

So I tossed the card on the counter and received my assurance of prompt payment from Sterling.

Have you ever flown first class? I haven't. And I didn't like the idea of financing a first-time experience for Julio, either. Well, I didn't have to like it, just as long as Sterling covered time and expenses.

I waited until they shut the gate, then took a place at the window and watched the big plane roll slowly away. Satisfied, I turned and took a fast walk back to the short-term parking lot.

There was an accumulation of messages on my answering machine from yesterday, last night, and even a couple from that morning. Most of them were from Casimir Urbanski. He made it pretty plain he wanted to talk to me. He didn't say it was urgent; he didn't say much of anything except "Chico, this is Casimir. Call me." Over and over again. The urgency was in his voice. But in fact, on the last message on the tape, he added, "I really need to talk to you."

So, a little reluctantly—I really had determined to stay as far away as possible from this blackmail scenario—I picked up the telephone, sat down, and punched out Casimir's office number at Majestic. I felt, and feel right now, that I had every right to stay out of it. My ribs hurt plenty. The bruises on my midsection had turned a deeper shade of purple. I was still a mess. I wanted to keep my distance, because, frankly, I had mixed loyalties. I had no sympathy for Jarrett either, as a drug dealer or a blackmailer. But I thought Majestic Studios, particularly Ursula Toller and Hans-Dieter, deserved some trouble. I felt lots of different ways about Alicia. Casimir, on the other hand, was a friend who had problems that, in their own way, were bigger than mine.

As soon as I gave my name his secretary put me right through to him.

"Yeah, this is Urbanski."

"This is Chico. You've been trying to get hold of me."

"Uh, that's right." Again, conversational. There must be somebody in there with him again. "I was wondering if we could get together and, like, talk," he said.

"Not on the phone?"

"I don't think so."

"How about Zucky's again at breakfast?"

"Maybe a little before that."

"You mean tonight?"

"That'd be better."

"Okay," I said, "how about this? Meet me at the Pacific Dining Car on Wilshire in Santa Monica. It's on your way home. You get off Ten at Cloverfield, and you wind up at Twenty-sixth and Wilshire. It's about a block east of there on the south side of the street. In the bar at seven."

"That'll be fine. See you around that time sharp."

And then he hung up.

Poor Casimir. Did he have reason to be so careful, or was he just acting paranoid? It didn't seem his style at all.

I spent a lot of time assembling a detailed expense account, complete with receipts, for Benjamin Sterling, a job I hate. But doing that part first got it out of the way so that I could get on to what really interested me. I had decided to write out a detailed, day-by-day report so that Sterling would know just what I had done for him. He had volunteered to pay for those days when I was officially in the employ of his daughter. "After all," he had said, "it was me you were looking for. It seems only right." And that was true: it seemed only right.

There were six days to cover, and I guess I worked hardest explaining what I had been up to during those four days that he was missing. One point I really labored over was the five hundred dollars I had paid to Pilar Ramirez as a reward for finding "Sterling's" body. In hindsight, it seemed like an excessive amount, of course. But when I posted it, I didn't stipulate I wanted Benjamin Sterling alive only. And when, the next day, the dead man in the bathroom turned out not to be Sterling, we were all surprised. By then the reward had been paid. I couldn't very well stop payment on the check, since Pilar Ramirez and I had both acted in good faith. What was particularly embarrassing was the fact that I hadn't asked her for a receipt. Except for Julio's first-class ticket to Chicago, it was the largest single item on the expense account. I had no paper to back it up and wouldn't have until the canceled check came through. Since I didn't want to wait that long to get paid, I used all my powers of justification and persuasion to defend the reward.

I also made a pretty good case for myself as a fearless bodyguard, detailing our escape from "unknown assailants" out on the freeway and the city streets, as well as my part in stopping the phony messenger with the bomb. (I was pretty sure he wouldn't have gotten the word from Lorenzen.) An interesting thing: when they lifted the guy's wallet to do an ID—James Clark, with an address in the Valley—it turned out he had an old General Motors plant ID card from before the shutdown. What was it he had said to me that day in the park? Something about trying too hard to keep up his old lifestyle. Well, he had told the truth about that, anyway. There's no telling what kind of work a man will take on to keep up his lifestyle. Even murder.

Writing through all this gave me the chance to sort through it all in my mind. Nobody had asked me to find out who it was who wanted Benjamin Sterling dead. I had been asked, first, to try to find him, which I hadn't done, exactly, though I'd given it a good shot. Then I'd been asked to guard him, which I'd done spectacularly well, in my opinion. But things occurred to me as I wrote— speculations and guesses—and while I didn't include any of them in the report, I did urge Benjamin Sterling very strongly in my cover letter to hire another bodyguard to go with him there in Chicago. "You may feel like you're safe now that you're home," I wrote, "but I think you're still in a lot of danger." That was putting it pretty dramatically, but I felt I had to do it that way to make any impression on him at all.

Well, putting together the expense account and writing the report and the letter took most of the day. When I finished I had just enough time to put the package together and get it to the Federal Express office over on Sunset. I figured if Sterling received this the day after he arrived, he'd understand I wanted to be paid right away. With all that I'd spent on Julio and him during the last couple of days I had a couple of thousand invested in this case. I wanted it back. The old cash-flow problem.

That done, I settled in for a long drive through rush-hour traffic to the Pacific Dining Car at the other end of town. Still, I arrived early and killed a little time at one of those big chain bookstores nearby. When I went into the bar and settled into a table far from the main action, it was seven o'clock on the button. As it happened, Casimir was about half an hour late, but that was okay, because now I had something to read. It was pure pleasure to sit, sipping a Cuervo Gold, finding out what Dave Robicheaux was up to down on the Bayou Teche. After all I'd been through in the past few days, I thought I deserved a little R and R.

Enter Casimir Urbanski, full of apologies.

I calmed him down, eased him into a chair, and got a beer in front of him. Then, for a long time—over a minute, anyway—he just sat, saying nothing at all, staring fixedly at the label on the beer bottle. I wondered if he could even see it. His mind was obviously elsewhere. This was strange behavior for Casimir, probably the most open and least secretive person I knew. He would always tell you what was on his mind. But now, he seemed to be weighing what he could tell me and what he couldn't. The television behind the bar was going loud enough to cover any tale he had to tell.

"Chico," he said at last, "this business with Alicia has me so fucked up I can't hardly work on my movie." Casimir didn't usually use words like that. He was basically a good Catholic boy.

"Okay," I said with a sigh, "tell me about it."

"Where do I start?" Was he asking me or himself? Only he knew. "Good tip on Rossi, that DEA guy. I tracked him down, and it turns out he's on comp time, so he can see me any time he wants. So I invite him to have lunch with me at the studio—you know, the stars of movies and TV right before your eyes! Dazzle him, like, you know? Anyway, he gets there at the commissary, and believe me he's not, like, impressed, you know? He's been here before, and maybe every other studio in town. It turns out he's been pitching a DEA series for TV all over town, and I guess he thought what this was about was, like, a callback. So he starts pitching me right there in the dining room."

He broke off suddenly, frowning, then asked, "Can they do that? I mean, he's definitely still by the agency. I mean, there's rules, right?"

"Rules were made to be broken, Casimir," I said mildly.

Taking a moment to think about that, he shrugged and said, "Yeah, maybe." Then back to his story: "Anyways, I had to tell him I got nothin' to do with TV, I'm strictly on the movie side. Then he starts pitching it like a movie. And then I had to tell him, 'Look, maybe this would make a terrific movie, but I'm just finishing up my first, and I'm in no position to take on something else. What I really need from you is some information about somebody.' Then he got really pissed off like I was taking up his time or something, and I thought he was going to jump up and get out of there. But then I mentioned your name, and then everything was okay. He's got a very high opinion on you, Chico."

"Always nice to know." I didn't say it as smugly as that might seem. "Did you tell him you'd been a cop?"

"Yeah, I told him that, too. I guess that helped. Anyways, I asked him what he could tell me about Thomas Jarrett. And holy shit, I was impressed. I guess I don't have to tell you, huh? You know all about him. I mean, you ought to. You went down there to Mexico, am I right? After that night at Tiny Naylor's? He says you put Jarrett out of business all by yourself."

"No, I didn't. Alicia helped."

"Yeah? Then I gotta do an apology to her. Anyways, he says that Jarrett was so connected they hadda let him go. All the way to the top. They saved his neck; Rossi thinks he had some shit on them, but they wouldn't save his business. Rossi says, 'How would it be if it comes out one of the boys in the kitchen was a big-time dealer?' What'd he mean with that, Chico?"

"Later, Casimir. Go on."

"Yeah, sure, okay. Rossi says from what he hears, Jarrett's feeling the pinch. Had to sell his boat and his house in Newport Beach. He's got a ranch, too. That's where he's living, but it's on the block, too. Hard to sell those five-million-dollar places now."

"Except to the Japanese."

"Maybe not even by them." Casimir said it like he had some inside dope. "So it, like, makes sense he might do a blackmail on Alicia. Am I right? He needs money."

"You didn't tell Rossi about that, did you?"

"Oh, no, Chico! I might not be smart, but I ain't dumb. You know what I mean?" I knew what he meant.

"What's this about owing Alicia an apology?"

"Yeah, well, that was after."

"After what?"

"After I talked to the guy Rossi."

"Come on, Casimir. Tell me the whole story."

"I will! I'm gettin' to it." He took a big swig of the beer, right out of the bottle. Storytelling was hard work, but somebody had to do it. "So after I wind it up with him—I had to promise I'd look at a script when his partner finished it, some woman—that's when I called you the third time." He hesitated a moment, then looked at me almost accusingly. "Where were you? I mean, I know you ain't working for me or anything, but jeez, Chico, you're really hard to get hold of."

"Well, you're right," I said, "I'm *not* working for you. I was working for a guy named Benjamin Sterling from Chicago, a baby-sitting job. I did him a lot of good, too."

"Yeah, well, okay, I'm sorry. Anyways, what I wanted to do was, like, get it absolutely straight about Alicia. Like, was what this guy Jarrett saying about her *really* true?"

"I said so, didn't I?"

"Yeah, well, that's the way I figured it. I figure I'm going nuts with this. Like when you called me back, I'm afraid to talk because there's somebody with me, the editor, one of my own people! I'm afraid he's a spy on me. This has gotta stop. So I took a hike over to Uschi's office. There's somebody in with her. Even *I* gotta wait to see her these days except at bedtime or in the morning. I have the secretary call in and tell her it's important, can't wait till then. So finally she gets rid of this guy. I don't know, it's some director, new movie on the lot. And I go in, and I, like, put it in front of her. I told her what you said. I told her what Rossi said. And you know what?"

"She didn't believe you."

"Well, that's not exactly what she said, but I know her, see, and I can tell I got her thinking, see. I mean, it makes sense. You put this guy out of business, so now he needs money. He comes up with blackmail. Also, he wants to get back at you by Alicia. I don't know if that part's right, but I just, like, tossed it in, you know? Anyways, she calls up and gets Alicia on the phone and tells her to come over after she's finished. This isn't the day they shoot, just the run-through.

"So okay, she comes over about six o'clock—tonight, see. And Uschi sits back and has me tell her what she just heard. So first I tell her about Rossi. It turns out she remembers him, says he came to your place once or twice. She listens and says, yes, it could be like that. It could be Jarrett who's making trouble for her. Then I tell her what you told me, that it was all true what Jarrett said, and—"

"And," I interrupted, "she was shocked, hurt, *insulted* that anyone should think such things about her—such lies!"

"Yeah," said Casimir, "that was sort of what she said, stuff like that. And then she wanted to know who said she was once a . . . a *puta,* is that the word?"

"That's the word. And you told her I said it."

"I had to, Chico. And she says, 'That proves it. He's in on it, too.' Then she starts in on you. Man, you were the worst! You were—well, she said some things in Mexican I couldn't understand, but they sounded pretty bad, even if I couldn't understand them. She's screaming and stomping her foot. And then I, like, take a look at Uschi to see how she's taking this. And you know what? She's smiling. I wonder, is she smiling because Alicia's saying such terrible things about you? Or what? But I didn't say anything, and Uschi didn't either, just sort of let her wind down, you know?

132

"So finally, Alicia finished, you know. And Uschi opens up her desk drawer and pulls out a file—it's Alicia's file, contracts, all that shit. And right off the top she takes a sheet of paper. Maybe it's a couple of sheets, I don't know. Anyway, she says to her, 'You remember this, Alicia? This is your professional résumé, your list of credits down in Mexico. You gave this to me the first day here at the studio.'

"Alicia gets real quiet, doesn't say anything, just stares at the paper.

"Uschi says, 'When this blackmail business started, I fax a copy to our office in Mexico City and ask them to check it out. The answer came today. There isn't one name on it, one production that is real. It is all one big lie. You know what I think of this?' And then she starts ripping it up, Chico, until it's all in little pieces all over her desk.

"Then, you know how it is, starting then on, it's all just breaking Alicia down. First she said you did it, then you made her do it, then some of what you said was true, then all of it. By the end, she's bawling, see. I mean, Uschi really kept after her, like in the Gestapo, those fucking Germans. I woulda backed off, prob'ly."

Once he got started, Casimir told a good story. I could certainly picture the scene. And I was sure that Ursula Toller would have been a ruthless interrogator—"like in the Gestapo." So what were we left with?

He took another gulp of beer and moved his chair a little closer to mine. "Anyways, Alicia's crying, so Uschi pushes a box of Kleenex at her across the desk and then gives her a lecture. She tells her that with blackmail you always have to know whether you're dealing with lies or the truth. The truth makes it harder, but it's not impossible. 'The big thing,' she tells her, 'is you've got a hit show. The critics like it, and the overnights on the second show were a big jump over the first one. That's the big thing,' she said.

"So she sends her out, tells her to go home if they're through with her on the soundstage, which she knows they are. Alicia's sniffing, starts to, like, apologize, and Uschi just waves her out—you know, get lost. She goes. Uschi looks at me.

"All this time I been sitting there, not saying nothing, just taking it all in. So Uschi says to me, 'Well, I hope you're happy.'

" 'Happy?' I say. 'Why should I be happy?' I really thought it was a weird thing to say.

" 'You know what I mean,' she says. 'You and your big friend Chico were right, and I was wrong.' Like this was all between me and her, not about Alicia at all. She's like that about a lot of stuff.

"So finally she says, 'Okay, you can hire him, your friend Chico.'

" 'For what?' I say.

" 'To take care of this business, to get rid of this man—Jarrett.'

"She's talking like the godfather, Chico, letting out fucking contracts. So I try to explain to her. I say, 'Chico does *not* want to get involved. He says no way will he get involved.'

"She just laughs and says, 'Offer him money.'

"So I'm offering you money, Chico, like I told her I would. I think you could name your own price as long as it isn't a million."

I didn't even have to think twice. "I wouldn't work for her on this, even for a million," I said. "No. Absofuckinglutely not."

12

A couple of days went by. I performed all the usual rituals that in the past have kept me from going nuts during periods of unemployment—cleaning out my files, trekking off to the gym, answering letters, and then, finally, paying bills. By the time I put my checkbook away, I had less than five hundred dollars in my account. Sure, I had some in savings, but that was my fuck-you money. Everybody needs that, especially people in my business, so they can say fuck you and walk away from any job, any situation, any client.

That was more or less what I had said to Casimir that night at the Pacific Dining Car. No, not to him, to Ursula Toller, the head of production at Majestic Studios. He knew that. He was just the messenger.

The more I thought about that scene he'd described in Uschi's office the worse I felt. You take the matter of the phony résumé. Alicia said I made her do it. Not true, of course, but it was my idea. I knew that actors had to have them, and I also supposed that the chances of them checking on one that was mostly in Spanish and was spread around between places like Culiacán, Guanajuato, and Ciudad Mejico were practically zero. *Practically* zero, as it turned out. I remembered the night that she and I put it together, giggling over the names we invented for the theater companies, the titles of the plays. (One I remember—Guanajuato, a university town, had to have an experimental theater so we came up with her role as Eva in El Teatro de la Futura's production of *El Cabrón,* by José Barba.) We had a good time that night. We had a lot of good times, and remembering them made me feel sad. Thinking of Alicia, in tears, confessing to Uschi a past she wanted to forget, made me even sadder.

So it was not a great couple of days. Around nine or ten o'clock the second night, I decided to hell with it and went around the corner to Barney's Beanery. It was a weeknight, so there wasn't a big mob there. Just the regulars, of which I was considered to be more or less one. Or maybe I was more of an irregular, because it seemed like the bartenders there were always giving me greetings like the one I got that night.

"Hey, Chico, how you been?" He reached across the bar and shook my hand. "Haven't seen you around in a while."

"I've been working," I told him.

"Big case, huh?" Everybody at Barney's seems to know what I do. I wish they didn't.

"I'll be able to pay some big bills when the check comes through."

"Great. What'll you have? The usual?"

"What's the usual?"

"Well, the last time you were in, and the time before that, you had Cuervo Gold, didn't you?"

"Yeah, probably. Maybe I'll work up to that. Give me a Dos Equis."

"Comin' up."

And it came up, just the way he promised. He asked me if I wanted a glass, and I waved him away. I sucked at the beer. It tasted just as good as it ever did—the way German beer would have tasted if it were brewed for you to drink in hundred-degree temperatures. Cold, wet, and tasty. How could anybody drink American beer?

I'm just sitting there, pulling away at my beer, when along

comes Elaine and sits down beside me. We say hello and all of that, and I do the gentlemanly thing and offer to buy her a drink. And she does the expected thing and turns me down.

Elaine dances the day shift up at the Body Shop, the local strip joint, on Sunset. She makes no secret of that. I've never gone up to see her there, so I take her word for it. It would seem kind of rude to go see somebody you know with clothes on walking around naked, so our acquaintance is limited to our meetings here at Barney's. I like her. Never apologize, never explain—that's Elaine.

She ordered a White Russian. Her only weakness, she drinks dumb drinks.

"So, Chico," she said, "how you doing?"

I shrugged. "I don't know," I said. "You want the stock answer or the real one?"

"Well, obviously the stock answer is you're doing fine, so give me the real one."

Again I shrugged. "I'm not really sure. I just finished a job. The money's coming through pretty soon, so that's good. But I just turned down some work, too, and I've got the feeling that's bad."

Her drink comes. We sort of toast each other, her with that milky concoction and me with my bottle. Once the courtesies had been observed, she asks, "Why'd you turn it down?"

"Because I didn't like the client."

"Sounds reasonable. Why do you feel bad then? Just the money?"

"No, it felt good turning down the money. But there's another party involved. I feel like I'm deserting . . . that party."

"Oh, a party, huh? Not a him or a her, just a party?"

She was getting too nosy. "Forget it, Elaine. Let's talk about something else."

"Ho-ho!" she said, "my favorite Latino suddenly shows a chink in his macho armor. What are we to make of this? Since he has given every sign of being heterosexual in his preference, I would speculate that the 'party' he speaks of is—ta-*dah!*—female! So you feel like you're deserting *her,* Chico. Am I right?"

"No doubt about it, you should've been a detective."

"I have a long life ahead of me. It's not out of the question."

"Let me know when you want to join the firm."

"Oh, I will," she said, "but let's pursue this further. Would this mysterious 'her' by any chance be that beauteous Latina lady you kept company with a while back? Very close company, I believe."

"How'd you hear about her?"

"Oh, Chico, come *on*. For about three or four months you didn't come in here at all. Everybody's saying, 'What happened to Chico? Did he move out of the neighborhood, or what?' Then there were sightings. Stu said he saw you helping this young lady out of your car, very pretty and very pregnant. Other reports. Then I—I myself!—driving down Olive, saw you with her, and she's not pregnant anymore, but she's pushing a baby carriage. That really gave me a turn."

"What do you mean?"

She sighed. "What do I mean?" She stared off at some point behind the bar and took a sip of her drink. "Okay, seeing you two together like that made me kind of squishy inside. I suddenly got all those female-maternal feelings I work so hard to suppress. I had to take myself by the scruff of the neck and give myself a good talking-to."

She remained out there somewhere just a moment longer. Then she turned to me and said, "And you! All at once you turn up here, and it's like you're trying to make up for all those nights you missed. Stu told me you were in every night for a month, easy; drank too much. He said he would've cut you off a couple of times, except he knew you weren't driving. I think it must have been one of those nights I was in here, and you tried to pick me up."

"I didn't do that!"

"You sure did."

"Well, maybe we had a conversation or something, but . . ."

"Noooo. You were sort of gallant in a way—but very explicit."

"I don't remember it. I honestly don't."

"I'm not surprised, the shape you were in."

This was really pretty embarrassing. It was not the kind of guy I wanted to be at all. But I believed her, all right. One thing I'd found out about Elaine in the course of about a dozen conversations with her: she was one of those rare people who doesn't have it in them to lie.

"Well," I said, "I'm sorry. I really am."

She gave my hand on the bar a pat. "Don't be. I was sort of flattered." Winking, she flashed me a smile. "Then you tapered off, didn't come in so often, didn't drink so much when you did. It was the old Chico. You remember that night you told me about Yeats and that woman—what was her name?"

"Maud Gonne. Yeah, that was crazy. You were arguing in *her* favor."

"What I *said* was, she may have made him an unhappier man, but she made him a better poet." She threw up her hand, closing off further discussion. "Whatever. Anyway, that night I decided that at last you'd gotten over her. Then the other night I thought I saw her on TV, and now you come up with this. You're afraid you're deserting her. Chico, just who deserted who?"

I didn't say anything. I couldn't think of anything to say.

"That was her on TV, wasn't it?" she asked.

"That was her."

"She looked great," said Elaine. "The show, however, was to vomit."

"I'm glad somebody thinks that besides me."

"I understand it's a big hit."

"Yeah."

We were staring straight ahead, looking in the mirror behind the bar. Suddenly, she turned and punched me in the shoulder—not hard, just enough to rouse me. "Pay up, Chico." She dug into her purse and threw a five down next to her drink. "I'm going to take you someplace." I slid off the barstool, frowning, trying to figure this one out, and managed to get a few bills down on the bar before she grabbed me by the wrist and half pulled, half dragged me out of the place.

She seemed to be in an awful hurry. Starting down Santa Monica Boulevard, she moved so swiftly I could barely keep up, and not a word from her. Then she turned up Olive, her heels going click–click–click on the sidewalk, still saying nothing. She threw a glance at me. If I didn't know better, I would have said she looked a little scared.

She stopped. Unprepared, I overshot her a couple of steps, maybe three, and came back to her.

"Here," she said.

I looked around. I saw where I was. "Here?" I asked.

"Well, this is where you live, isn't it?"

"Well . . . yeah."

"Aren't you going to invite me up?"

I invited her, and she accepted. I noticed that as we rode up in the elevator we stood apart. No eye contact. And though she stepped out first, following my nod, she trailed me all the way to the door at a slow pace. By the time I got the door open she had just arrived. I switched on the lights, and she walked inside.

"My God," she said, "what a lot of books." I guess it's the first thing you notice about my place—one whole wall.

"Well, you know, I read. I don't watch much TV."

"I guess not," she said. And then she tossed her purse on a chair and walked over to the books, pulling one down, replacing it, and then another, making little exclamations to herself as she moved along the shelves.

"Would you like something to drink?" I asked. It seemed a shame to interrupt her.

"Oh, sure, anything. White wine, if you've got it."

As it happened, I did—refrigerated Chardonnay, unopened. I don't drink the stuff myself. Who knows why I had it? Maybe for an occasion like this. Would this be an occasion? Jesus, I hoped so.

She took the wineglass with a murmured thanks, kneeling, hardly lifting her eyes from the book she held in her hand. It was an old copy of *The Second Sex* by Simone de Beauvoir that I'd rescued from a used-book shop on Hollywood Boulevard. She looked up at me. "Chico, I can't believe you have this book. Have you read it?"

"Well, yeah, some parts harder than others. It was when my marriage broke up. I was trying to figure things out."

"The lady on TV?"

"Oh, no. We were never married. This was years ago."

"I see." Her eyes rested briefly on the page again, then she stood and returned it to the shelf. She turned and faced me then and took a sip of her wine, staring at me. "What's your first name? Everybody just calls you Chico. That's, like, a nickname, right?"

"Right. Antonio," I said. "Antonio's my first name."

"Well, Antonio Cervantes, you are a rare fellow." She said it with great seriousness, but then she smiled a big smile at me.

We were standing about three feet apart. All of a sudden, I didn't know what to do with my hands. I tried clasping them behind my back, but that didn't seem right; then I tried them on my hips. That didn't seem right, either, but I kept them there, and I said, "I don't know your last name, Elaine."

She kind of laughed at that. "You really want to know? It's Norgaard, two *a*s. I'm from Minnesota."

And somehow—I don't know quite how it happened—as she told me that, we must have moved closer together, because quite unexpectedly the three feet that separated us was no distance at all, and we were kissing; not chewing each other up, the way they do in the movies today, just kissing. I seemed to be holding her face between my two hands. She seemed to have her eyes closed.

But then they opened. We studied each other for a long moment. And then she took a step back. "I must . . ."

"It's in there," I said. "The first door on your left." She nodded, unsmiling, and went into the bathroom.

I didn't know what to do with myself. I took a gulp of her wine. It seemed sort of tasteless but vaguely sour to me; I hoped it didn't seem that way to her. I lit a cigarette, then after two puffs I put it out. My God, beer, wine, a cigarette—how would that taste? I wanted to brush my teeth with Gleem, gargle with Listerine, squirt with Binaca, whatever it took. And all this while, I could hear water running in the bathroom, and then not running, then running again.

And finally the door opened and Elaine stepped out, nude,

smiling solemnly. "Such as I am," she said. Her lean, muscular dancer's body rested lightly against the doorjamb. She extended a hand toward me.

I don't know who led who, but somehow we found our way together into the bedroom. We sat together on the bed, and we kissed again. I couldn't, I don't know why, bring myself to touch her body just then. But I could kiss her, and I did that; her mouth, of course, but also her closed eyes, her nose, her throat. She liked that. Her chin tilted back, and she exposed her throat to me, like I was Count Dracula, and she was offering herself up. I kissed it softly.

I felt her opening the buttons of my shirt. She didn't get far before she exposed the adhesive wrapping around my ribs. Running her hand lightly around it, she whispered, "What's this?"

"Cracked ribs," I said.

The only light in the bedroom came in from the living room. But as she finished unbuttoning my shirt and it fell free, she reached over and turned on the light next to the bed. I saw her leaning over me, blond-brown hair streaming over her face as she looked down. She saw my bruised belly. Throwing her hair back in a motion so beautiful I couldn't possibly describe it, she looked at me then and said, "Jesus, Chico, what happened?" There was more than concern in her eyes.

"I got beat up," I said.

"It hurt," she said. It wasn't a question.

"Yeah. It hurt."

Then she reached over and switched off the light, and in a moment or two more I was as naked as she was. We were naked together, and so I was able then to touch her body. I touched it often with different parts of my own.

If you're looking for a detailed description of what happened next, you won't find it here. To tell you the truth, I don't know what happened next. It was more like a sustained sensation—the sensation of floating, moving through a dimension where there was no time. Space travel? Yeah, maybe a little like that: toppling, joined, floating free. We did what our bodies told us to do. It was as simple as that. All I know is that afterward, when we lay on pillows facing each other, I looked beyond Elaine and saw by the face of the illuminated alarm clock that it was well after midnight.

What happened then was easier to remember—or maybe hard to forget. We lay there on our pillows, peering at each other in the dark. I'm not sure how I knew, but I could tell she was smiling.

"Chico?"

"Yes?"

"Would you do me a favor?"

"Anything. I really think I mean that."

"You know that poem that Yeats wrote after he'd seen Maud . . ."

"Gonne."

"Yeah, her, for the first time in years? Would you read that to me?"

I rolled out of bed and, naked except for the wide swath of adhesive around my diaphragm, I padded into the living room and pulled Yeats down from the shelf. I shuffled the pages and found it without much trouble, just a little eight-line thing titled "After Long Silence."

Back in the bedroom, I found the light on and Elaine sitting up in bed, her pillow propped up behind her; she'd arranged mine the same way. I sat down beside her, leaned back against the pillow, and handed the open book to her. I said it from memory.

"Very impressive," she said, "very beautiful." She leaned over and kissed me on the lips. " 'Young we loved each other and were ignorant.' A rare fellow."

I couldn't help but laugh. "You mean me or William Butler Yeats?"

She gave me a nice, lazy smile. "Both, of course." Then the smile faded. She leaned forward, so that her face was very close to mine, and then she said, "But we're not worth it, you know."

"Who's not worth it?"

"We aren't. Us—women, not worth all the grief we cause. We're as fucked up as you guys are, only in different ways—new and different ways. The Latina lady isn't worth it, Chico." She sighed. "And Maud Gonne probably wasn't even worth it, either."

"I hate to sound logical at a time like this," I said, "but you said before she made him unhappy but a better poet. Remember? Maybe Alicia makes me unhappy but a better detective."

"That's dumb," she said. " 'A foolish consistency is the hobgoblin of little minds.' I forgot who said that."

"I do, too."

Then, laughing, we kissed. "I'm going to go," she said.

"You can stay all night, if you want to," I said. I wished she would. One of the things I missed most about Alicia was just having a warm, female body beside me in the bed.

"No, I look like hell in the morning, and I'm a bitch, too."

"I'll walk you home."

"No. Don't. I live close by. I'd like you to stay right here, right where you are."

With that, she threw her feet down and started to rise. I remember her naked back at just that moment, the muscles tensing as she pushed upward, then suddenly relaxing. She dropped back down on the bed.

"One thing I want to ask, though," she said. "Why Yeats?"

"Well . . . because I think he was great, the greatest—in English, I mean."

"That's just it. Why not García Lorca? Why not—oh, that Mexican poet who won the Nobel a few years ago?"

"Octavio Paz."

"That's who I mean. Why not him? I mean, you're Latino, Hispanic, whatever it is we're supposed to call you guys now. Why Yeats?"

"I like Lorca," I said. "He's terrific. *Jaca negra, luna roja, y aceitunas en mi alfombra.*' See? I know some García Lorca."

"I'm impressed. And what about the other guy? Paz?"

"I was trying to impress you," I admitted. "Why not Paz? Well, I don't like his poetry as well, but I liked his book on Mexican identity."

She hesitated a moment, then she said quietly, "That's what we're talking about, isn't it? Mexican identity?"

Why did she have to get into this? It was turning out like one of our talks at Barney's. "No," I said, throwing my hands in the air, "what we're talking about is a living, breathing, walking, talking identity crisis. That's me. I know it. I've been living with it most of my life, Elaine. I grew up in Boyle Heights—"

"I know that. You told me a while ago."

"Yeah, well, I wanted to get out of there just as quick as I could. I went to UCLA, which was about ninety percent Anglo back then, and I was an English major—Yeats, see? I moved out of the neighborhood, and I stayed out. I married a blond nurse from Seattle. That didn't work out, and maybe all this had something to do with it. Look, I don't need a shrink to tell me about this. I've been through it one way or another every day of my life for the past twenty years. I've got some problems about who I am and what I am. I know that."

I was breathing heavily, plunging on: "Look, you're—what? Swedish-American. You're not especially into Ingmar Bergman, are you? Why can't I just be Mexican-American the same way and leave it at that?"

Her hand had been resting on my shoulder, probably for about a minute. She moved it then, fingertips tracing a slow path up my neck and onto my face. They came to rest on my lips. "It's okay by me, Chico," she said. Her fingers stayed there. It was unnecessary. I'd said all I had to say. I nodded. She understood and took her fingers away.

"Look," she began, "I just want to put something in front of you, give you something to think about, so don't interrupt, okay?"

I nodded. "While you were saying all that, it sort of came to me that this woman—Alicia?—is all tied up in your head with who you are and what you are. I mean, I'm no shrink, and I don't want to be, but it seems to me that as long as you were with her, you'd sort of resolved your problem, you had a better grip on this whole Mexican thing. You were paying your dues. You see what I mean?"

I nodded. I saw what she meant. But it was all more complicated than that. She didn't really understand, did she?

"And when the baby was born, that sort of made it all the more real. Here you were, a real *hombre,* good macho. Let me tell you, Chico, when I saw you two out that day with the baby carriage, you really looked *proud,* like your father must've looked when you were a baby. Probably for the first time in your life you felt like your father, and that felt good."

"He . . ." There was something in my throat. I had to clear it a couple of times. "He was a terrific man."

"But the kid wasn't yours, was it?"

I shook my head, no.

"And you didn't kick Alicia and the baby out, did you?"

"No!"

"Alicia walked, right? Left you behind."

I nodded.

"Showbiz," she said, like she knew all about it. "So now there's a problem. You don't want to get involved in it, probably for good reason. But you feel guilty about that. You feel like you're deserting Alicia. You know why?"

"Okay, why?" I was looking around the room, unwilling to agree with any of this but willing to hear her out. I'd promised Elaine that and nothing more.

"Because by now, in your head, she *is* the whole Mexican thing, and you feel like you deserted that a long time ago."

We made brief eye contact. I began to feel sort of silly having this conversation without any clothes on. I wanted to jump out of bed and at least put on my pants.

She got up and faced me, hands on hips. "Well," she said, "thank you for your attention. Something to think about." She turned and started out of the room.

"Elaine," I called after her, "I owe her a lot. She saved my life down in Mexico."

She turned and faced me in the doorway. "Oh? A one-way street? You owe it all to her? She doesn't owe you anything?"

A long moment passed as Elaine stood in the doorway, waiting for an answer. Somehow she forced the truth out of me, or at least *a* truth. "All right," I said, "I guess I kind of saved her, too."

"I rest my case."

146

She disappeared into the bathroom but was gone only about a minute. I didn't know women could get dressed that fast. But here she was, back again to say good-bye. I started to get up, but she pushed me back down again and gave me a quick kiss on the mouth. Perfunctory—that's the word for a kiss like that.

"Stay there," she said. "I'll let myself out." But she stood, hesitating awkwardly, like she had something more to say. She had that almost-scared look I'd seen on her face before. "I was wondering, Chico, I was wondering if I could borrow the Yeats book."

"Sure," I said, "of course." I picked it up and handed it to her. I'd probably never see it again, but what the hell.

"Well . . . okay. I hope I didn't, like, offend you or anything."

"No, it's okay, really."

She was backing away. "See you then."

"See you."

She disappeared, and I waited to hear the sound of the door open and close. It took a while, though, and I wondered what she was up to there in the living room. Then at last it came—open and, *slam,* shut, like she was angry or something. Why should *she* be angry?

Then I put on my robe and went out there to lock up and pour myself a drink. I needed to come down. Finally, drink in hand— Gold on the rocks—I took a tour of the room, switching off lights. And I noticed that on the pad next to the telephone Elaine had written her address and telephone number. That was what had held her in the living room. She lived just up Olive near the corner of Fountain. I had no idea she was so close.

13

I had a dream that night about my father. I was in it, too, and I guess my mother as well, but it seemed to be about him; he was the focus. We were back in Boyle Heights, he and I, in front of our old house there. He was all dressed up—suit, tie, white shirt—the way he looked when he went to church, because he was going to have his picture taken with me. I was standing beside him, looking up at him. From the way he towered over me I must have been about five or six. I had this sense of a strong presence beside me, the way I always did with him when I was a kid.

My mother must have been the photographer. She took all the family pictures. But when I faced the camera with him, I don't really remember seeing her at all. The picture was taken, or it must have been, because it was handed to me. We never had one of those instant cameras, just an old Kodak box model, but somehow the photo was ready and right there in my hands. I looked down at it, and it wasn't a picture of my father and me at all. I was the only one in it—me, as I am now. That was frightening. I turned and looked for him beside me, but he'd vanished. I was all alone, and that scared me as much as it would have if I'd been five years old.

And so I woke in something like a panic, gasping, blinking, up on my elbows, unaware for a moment that it had actually been the ringing of the phone that had wakened me. I jumped out of bed and ran to the living room, pulling on my robe as I went, promising myself I'd put an extension in the bedroom when the next check came through.

The next check was what the call was about.

I plopped down in the chair and grabbed up the receiver. "Hello? Hello?" I was panting.

"Hello, who is this? Is it you, Cervantes?"

"Yeah, yes, it's me. Who's this?"

"This is Ben Sterling. Don't tell me I woke you up! What time is it out there anyway?"

I looked down at my bare wrist. I'd taken off my watch along with everything else last night. From where I sat, I couldn't see the clock in the kitchen. "Uh . . . I don't know."

"Well, it's eleven-thirty here. What kind of a shop do you run, anyway? Never mind, I called you to talk about this bill of yours. I know I promised to pay it right away, but frankly, I've got a problem with it."

More or less in control of myself at last, I said, "Okay, what's the problem?"

"Well, it isn't with the bill itself, it's your list of expenses." Why was I not surprised? "It's this item of five hundred dollars to Pilar Ramirez. Now, you explained in your report why you thought it was necessary. I suppose I accept that. But was it authorized? I haven't had a chance to talk to Clare about this, but that seems like one hell of a lot to pay a hotel maid."

"I had to make it enough to get the attention of the staff, all of them," I said. "And no, I mean, it wasn't *specifically* authorized by your daughter, but she did say 'spare no expense,' or something like that."

"It seems high, though, Cervantes. I have to say that. And besides, there's no paper with it, no receipt, nothing. You're just asking me to take your word for it, aren't you?"

"Okay, look, why don't you pay everything *except* that, and I'll send you a copy of the canceled check when it comes through?"

That seemed perfectly reasonable, didn't it? Well, needless to say it didn't suit Benjamin Sterling. We went around and around about it, and finally we agreed that he would pay my bill for services but would shelve the expenses pending receipt of a copy of the check. In the meantime, he'd talk to Clare about it.

Terrific. Who was it who said that the rich got to be rich by holding on to their money? Whoever he was, he was right.

Eventually we got around to talking about his business there. He assured me that everything was going just fine. "Julio and I are looking for the right location," he said. "I'm really serious about this, Cervantes. I hope you realize that."

"Yeah, I guess I do." After that afternoon-long lecture in the motel room, how could I not? "But tell me," I said, "have you gotten any protection there in Chicago?"

"Protection?" He didn't seem to know what I meant.

"A bodyguard."

"Oh, I hardly think that's necessary. Julio's with me wherever I go."

I wasn't sure whether I should laugh or cry at that. "Well, look, Mr. Sterling, I was entirely serious about that in the letter. I think you need somebody 'round the clock. I mean it."

He chuckled at that. "The long arm of the Yakuza, eh? I hardly think it stretches all the way to Chicago."

"Lieutenant Shinahara certainly took it all very seriously," I said. "He's a good cop. He warned you before he left that night at the motel. I heard him."

"Well, I'll give it some consideration. I appreciate your concern. Really, I do. And I'll see that that check gets off to you today."

We said good-bye then and hung up.

Sitting there by the telephone, I told myself I'd done all I could. After all, I couldn't force him to hire a bodyguard, could I? No, and neither could Lieutenant Shinahara. But Sterling had not only insulted the Japanese guy, he'd threatened to spread word of the scam. In my opinion, he was definitely at risk. But I'd done what I could, hadn't I? Even got him to say he'd consider it. Somehow, though, I felt bad about it—guilty, like if anything happened to him it would be my fault.

Or maybe I just felt generally bad, full of—what was the word? angst—because of the way I woke up, that dream that stayed with me, vivid and frightening. And then my eyes fell upon the pad beside the phone, with Elaine's name, address, and phone number scribbled on it. *That* was why I felt the way I did. *That* was why I'd dreamed that damned dream. It was all about last night, wasn't it? How could anything that had started so well suddenly have turned out so badly?

In a surge of anger that took me by surprise, I ripped the top sheet off the pad, wadded it up, and threw it down on the carpet. Then I went into the kitchen and made myself a pot of coffee.

All that day I argued with Elaine. I was so pumped thinking about the night before that I had to get physical—clean the house, wash the windows, do *something!* And so I did it all. Starting in the kitchen, gulping coffee as I went, I washed all the dishes that had accumulated since I'd seen Sterling and Julio off at the airport. I cleaned the stove, inside and out—hadn't done that in a while, I'm afraid. I mopped the floor. Man, I even cleaned the cupboards! Then I got the old Sunbeam out, hooked it up, and started in on the living room. And all the while I was having these conversations inside my head with Elaine.

Jesus, I really told her off! You know when she said, "I'm no shrink, and I don't want to be?" You know what I told her? I said, "Bullshit you don't. That's what's wrong with people today. Everybody's a shrink. Everybody thinks he's got the answer to somebody else's problem. Just back off, okay?"

And when she started talking about my father, I didn't just say he was a terrific man, listen, I told her how terrific he really was—all the details! I told her how he was a man of learning and sensitivity, and that maybe he was never completely comfortable in English—he made mistakes we kidded him about—but his Spanish was wonderful. He wrote editorials that Unamuno would have been proud of, essays that were beautifully developed, wonderfully articulated, more than that newspaper he worked for deserved. And I told her how he'd raised us kids, keeping us in line in a bad neighborhood that was going worse, seeing that somehow we all got off to college—UCLA, Cal State L.A., wherever—and that we finished.

The difficulty was that once in a while Elaine answered me back. This time, she said, "Chico, that's what I mean about *good macho.*"

I said to her, "What do you know about *macho,* good or bad?"

And she said, "Chico, I've got a history, too, you know. You realize you didn't ask me one thing about myself last night?"

"That's because you were too busy psyching me out, telling *me* what was wrong with me."

"And what about all those talks we had at Barney's? We always talked about neutral subjects. We had discussions. Believe me, I loved our discussions. Once in a while you'd tell me something about you. But you never asked me about me. Why not?"

"Well," I said, "I had a problem, I guess. Look, when you reduce what I do for my living to its basics, what I do is ask questions. I'm professionally nosy. The people I know away from business, like you, I try to leave them alone. If people want to tell me about themselves, then great! I listen. I have to say, though, if I didn't ask you questions, you didn't volunteer much, either."

"No, I suppose I didn't," she said. "I guess you'll have to ask me questions."

"There's some things you want to hide?"

"You'll have to ask me, Chico."

By this time, I'd been all around the big living room with the Sunbeam except for that little corner over by the telephone. I knew I'd been avoiding it. I looked at that little wad of paper under the table where the telephone sat. I knew how it got there. I wondered if the Sunbeam would pick it up. I wondered if I wanted it to.

Finally, as I got closer and closer to it, I made a kind of nondecision, switched off the vacuum cleaner, picked up the wad of paper, walked into the kitchen, and tossed it on the table. Then I went back into the living room and finished up there. I dusted. I actually *dusted* with the tail of a shirt that had long ago fallen apart. Then I got out the Windex and did the windows with newspapers the way I'd been taught at home. The bathroom wasn't disgusting, so I left it alone. And what did I do in the bedroom? Well, I made the bed, at least—and had some thoughts about what went on there last night.

What had it meant to Elaine, anyway? Was she just playing Florence Nightingale? Bringing me back to life? Did any of it have any meaning for her? Try as I could, speculate as I would, I couldn't get her to enter into conversation about that. She just smiled, as she had smiled at me in the dim light a number of times the night before. She wouldn't talk about that.

Most of the morning had been taken up by this wild orgy of cleaning. I was still in my robe, still sipping coffee, still nearly as angry at Elaine as I had been when I began it all, still pounding with unexpended emotional energy. So I went to the gym.

Half an hour on the Lifecycle. Lots of time to think.

What did Elaine know about what happened down in Sinaloa? Nothing! She couldn't even imagine a situation like the one Alicia and I survived there. The battle on the mesa—it ran and reran in my mind like a video on a short loop as my legs pumped away on the bike. I remembered rolling around on the floor with the captain, trying to keep that pistol of his pointed away, feeling myself weaken, then seeing his face collapse as Alicia put a gun to his head and pulled the trigger. Could Elaine do that? Maybe her great-great-grandmother could, out there on the prairie in Minnesota, but Elaine? I doubted it. That was the thing, see. Mexican women—Alicia, anyway—would do what had to be done. I mean, you had to admire that, didn't you?

Crunches and roman-chair dips, crunches and roman-chair dips, back and forth in alternating sets, still sweating heavily from the bike, panting a little. I stopped to rest for a moment. And what do you know? Elaine spoke up right there in the gym.

"She'll do what it takes, huh?" she said to me. "Including walking out on you. That was part of that TV deal, wasn't it?"

"Whatta you know about that?"

"Showbiz," said Elaine. "I know about showbiz."

Then a guy nearby, with big, bunchy pecs and deltoids and no waist at all, gave me a kind of funny look. He'd just finished up on the curl machine, and his biceps were pumped.

Stepping over in my direction, he called out in a loud whisper, "You're talking to yourself, Chico."

Oh, Jesus, this was embarrassing. Shut up, Elaine. "Thanks, I'll watch that." His name was Roy. "You know what they say, Roy."

He stretched his arms almost lazily. He'd been working the machine at around 150 and hadn't even worked up a sweat. "Yeah? What's that?"

"It's okay to talk to yourself, but when you start answering yourself, that's when to get worried."

He gave that a smile it hardly deserved. "Yeah, well, maybe," he said. "I've got a good therapist, if you want his name."

I couldn't believe he'd said that! "Uh, no thanks. Maybe later on."

I dropped down onto the slant board and started another set of crunches. With a shrug, Roy went on to the deltoid machine. Well, at least he didn't try to play shrink and treat me himself.

By the time I got back to my place, it was getting toward the end of the afternoon. I was exhausted and hungry and had cooled down considerably. At the gym, I'd worked myself so hard that I knew I'd be sore the next day. Somehow that seemed right; all day I'd been punishing myself for something, some offense, some sin. Hungry? I was so hungry I could have a cow, but I settled for a good-sized piece of one I'd bought at Mayfair Market the day before. I got the skillet very hot, then I tossed in the steak. As it smoked and sizzled, I barely had time to throw together a salad. But it all came together at the same moment, and I took a seat there at the kitchen table to wolf it down. I was halfway through the meal when I discovered I still had on my Dodgers cap. I decided to leave it on.

And yeah, I'd cooled down, too; I wasn't having any more of those crazy conversations with myself, or imaginary Elaine, or whoever it was who kept answering me back. That's not to say I wasn't thinking about it—what she'd said the night before, how

I'd responded, or refused to respond. But I was thinking about it more rationally. I mean, I had to admit she'd made a few points.

For instance, as I sat there chewing my steak, I remembered something she'd said earlier at Barney's about maternal feelings. Nobody denies them, right? I mean, they're there. So what about paternal feelings? Elaine was probably right. I probably did look proud behind that baby carriage. And maybe I felt like my father; and yeah, that felt good. So I give her a point there—keen observation. (But how did that lead to my weird dream, and why was I in such a panic when I woke up from it?)

I guess what really calmed me down about Elaine was not what she'd said but that she'd said it. She really got to me, didn't she? Favorite movie of mine—*Happy New Year,* the French one with Lino Ventura and Françoise Fabian, not the Billy Wilder remake. I've got it on video. There's this long scene in the middle, a restaurant lunch where two grown-up people fall in love. The talk is terrific, maybe even better in French than it is underneath in English. But in the course of it, what does she do? She sort of challenges him, asks something like, "For you, what is a woman?" He's stymied for a moment, hesitates, then he says, "A woman is . . . a man who cries." I liked his answer. But her question was even better. You know, sort of—*bam!*—in your face. If I liked that in the movies, why couldn't I handle it in real life? Anyway, Lino comes away from this, and he's really pumped, he sort of exclaims right out loud, "My God, a woman you can talk to!" Well, that was Elaine, wasn't it? A woman you could talk to, who'd talk to you, ask you questions you didn't want to answer, tell you what she thought whether you wanted to hear it or not.

So that's what I was thinking as I finished up that steak. I pushed the plate away, reached over, and grabbed the wad of paper I'd thrown on the floor that morning. Very carefully I loosened it and smoothed it out on the table top. There was a tear across the top where I'd ripped it from the pad, but the address and phone number were intact.

I got up, went into the living room, and sat down in the chair beside the telephone. I put my hand on the receiver. Then I asked myself what I wanted to say to her. I didn't know. I just wanted to talk to her. Maybe it'd work out. I picked up the receiver and started to punch out her number. Then I slammed the receiver down.

She wouldn't be there, and I didn't want to talk to her answering machine. No, she'd be up there at the Body Shop, wouldn't she? The day shift; made it sound like a factory, which it was, sort of. Funny, but all those nights we talked at Barney's, I never minded that she worked where she did, did what she did. I liked her for being so up front about it—never apologize, never explain.

But all of a sudden I minded. Life is complicated, isn't it?

Then the telephone rang.

No, it wasn't Elaine, as I certainly hoped and half expected. It was Casimir.

"Chico, I *gotta* see you."

We'd been through this once. "Come on, I said no, and I meant it."

"This isn't about that. . . . Well, it is and it isn't, you know?" He sounded scared, almost desperate. "I can't handle this with myself. I need you to come by."

"You don't want to meet someplace?"

"No, no, come by here."

"The studio?"

"Yeah, sure. I'll leave your name by the gate."

"I thought there was a standing order I was to stay off the lot."

"Fuck it. I'll come out and bring you in myself if I have to. I really need your help on this."

"You want me to come over right now?"

He hesitated. "No, you better wait. Say, like, seven. It woulda emptied out by then. You remember where my office is?"

"Sure, yeah, it hasn't been that long."

"Okay, seven then. They give you any trouble at the gate, just have them call me."

"See you then."

"Chico?"

"Yeah?"

"Thanks." And he hung up.

I pulled in at Majestic Studios' main gate about five minutes to seven. The car ahead of mine pulled away, and I rolled up to the guard station.

"Well, well, well, look who's here." The black woman in the gray uniform leaned down and gave me a big smile.

"Alta Jean! They got you working nights now?"

"One week out of four," she said. "I like it. It's quiet. But I sure never expected to see you back here again, Chico. Not after the way you messed them up."

"*You're* not mad at me, though."

"Shoot, no. Just as long as I get paid, I ain't mad at anybody."

"You gonna let me in?"

"Course I am. It wasn't personal before. Just orders is orders, you know."

"I never took it personally."

"You know where to go? Mr. Urbanski's expecting you."

"I know where to go."

"Well, come back soon, sugar. Great to have you here."

She gave me her official wave-through, and I pulled away with a waggle of my hand. I knew my way, all right, but I knew it in the daytime. I realized only then that I had never been on the Majestic lot at night. There is something almost sinister about these empty streets and huge, dark soundstages after dark—a perfect setting for a horror movie. Creepy.

I pulled in at one of the assigned parking spaces in front of Casimir's building. The rightful owner would have left for the day. If he came back, he could complain to Alta Jean.

My footsteps echoed hollowly from the tiled floor. From a door far down at the end of the hall, Casimir's head popped out.

"All the way, Chico," he called out. "Right down here."

I couldn't have missed it. His was the only office where lights still burned. As I came nearer, he stepped out into the hall, threw open his arms, and greeted me with a big hug.

"I knew I could count on you," he said. "Come on inside."

He ushered me through the secretary's empty outer office and into his own. He paused there then, saw me inside, and shut the door behind us.

"I got something to show you," he said, beckoning me over to his desk. "Look, I'm sorry how I was on the phone. I was pretty freaked up then. I just seen this, and it all seemed so weird. I didn't know what to do, Chico, so I called you."

"What to do about what?" I asked.

There was a sturdy cardboard box on his desk, about a foot and a half square and a foot high. I assumed that whatever had set him off was inside it. In the silence that followed my question I found myself listening, as if I might hear noise from the box, like there might be something alive in there. As it turned out, I couldn't have been more wrong about that.

"Okay," said Casimir, "here's what happened." He stood at his desk, a little tense but under control. "One thing I definitely told Uschi and Hans-Dieter was what you said about don't make a move against this guy Jarrett. I told them that early, right when I gave Uschi his name. But after that big scene with Alicia I told you about, we don't hear anything from Jarrett. We expect to, but he's keeping us dangling.

"So Uschi calls a meeting, the three of us—her, Hans-Dieter, and me. Wants to talk about what we do next. I tell them, 'What do we do? We wait.' They don't want to hear about that. You know, she shakes her fist and says, 'We've got to do *something!*' And then Hans-Dieter says something to her in German, and she says something back the same way. And then they're off, the two of them talking German with each other. I might as well not be there at all. I get kind of pissed off at this, and I get up, ready to go. She turns to me and says, 'We've decided to send this man Jarrett a warning.'

" 'From what I hear, it won't work. It's dangerous,' I told her.

"Then Hans-Dieter gets this smile on his face, and he says, 'Why not? It worked with your friend, Cervantes.' Then he tells me, and I swear, Chico, it's the first I heard about him sending those two guys after you. You remember I told you I talked him out of it. He let me think that. I swear, Chico, I didn't know a thing about it."

"I believe you, Casimir. I never thought for a minute you knew."

"But why didn't you say nothin'?"

"It wouldn't have done you any good to know."

"Maybe. Anyways, Hans-Dieter's version of it is that you were in on it from the beginning with this guy Jarrett. He sent those two guys to rough you up. You got scared off and gave me Jarrett."

"Oh," I said, "is that right?"

"I almost popped him right there." Casimir sighed. Then he lowered his eyes guiltily. "Only I couldn't. I gotta finish this damn movie. I gotta prove I can do it!"

"It's okay, Casimir. I understand the problem."

"So I walked out, Chico. There wasn't nothing I could do or say, so I just walked. I guess they went right ahead with it; I know they did, because this morning this package was delivered to the main gate for the personal and private attention of Ursula Toller. See, it's right there on the box." He pointed to the label. "And see here what it says for a return address? Just one word—Jarrett. Take a look inside."

I stepped up to the desk and looked down at the box. The label was just as he'd described it. I wasn't at all sure what I'd find in there, and frankly I wished that Casimir had just told me instead of making me look. But I had to prove I was tough enough to meet the challenge, I guess. So I opened it.

Inside were two human hands on a bed of excelsior. You could tell they were the real thing because of the mess of ligaments and veins at the stump ends—each cut off at the wrist. But they weren't a matching pair. They were two right hands—one black, actually light milk-chocolate color with a pale palm, and the other white, Caucasian, hairy. I had no wish to touch them. Looking at them didn't make me sick at my stomach or anything; they made me sick in my head.

"There was a note inside," Casimir said, "typed. It said, like,

'For purposes of fingerprint identification,' something like that. Like this is all that's left."

"It probably is. The two guys who did the job on me, one was black and one white."

"Figures. Hans-Dieter says they were stuntmen, just did that shit on the side."

"So what was Ursula's reaction?"

"She freaked up completely. Had to go home and lie down. Left it all in my lap. I guess I don't have to tell you, Chico, she acts a lot tougher than she is."

"Like a lot of us."

"Yeah. So what are we supposed to do?"

"Are you including me in this 'we'?"

He looked at me sort of regretfully. "No, I guess not," he said. "But Chico, this is murder."

"Looks like it."

"Well, jeez, blackmail's one thing. This is something else. We can't just forget about it, chalk it up to fucking experience. We gotta report this."

"If you do, the whole blackmail angle's going to come out," I said. "You know that."

"Yeah, that's what Hans-Dieter says."

"He would. Look, Casimir," I said, "I'm not telling you *not* to call the cops in. But just be prepared. Jarrett's daring you. He even put his name on the package. It's also a warning. 'Don't mess around with me,' that's what he's saying. Look, didn't Rossi tell you he was in with Mexican drug Mafia? Didn't I? This is the kind of stuff they do. He learned some tricks from them, or maybe some of them are still working for him, I don't know."

Casimir closed up the box. I was glad he did. "Yeah, okay. I guess I was just a cop too long. I still think like one."

"That isn't bad," I said. "Just be prepared for the consequences. To tell you the truth, I'd blow the whistle, if it was me. But I don't have what you have to lose. It's your call."

Then Casimir and I both heard it at the same time—the sound of footsteps outside in the hall. He swept the box off his desk, contents rattling inside, and tucked it out of sight down below. We heard the door to the outer office open, then a moment later Casimir's door flew open, and in walked Hans-Dieter Geisel. His hand was upraised, his fingers pointed at Casimir like a pistol.

"Urbanski!" he shouted, "you have no *right* to do this!"

"I took the box out of his office," Casimir remarked almost casually to me.

"How dare you do such a thing? Where have you hidden it, you stupid Polack?"

"I wouldn't call him that, if I were you," I said to him.

Up to that moment, I don't think Hans-Dieter was aware of me. Oh, he must have known there was someone there in the office with Casimir but must not have cared who it was. But then he turned and recognized me.

"You! Cervantes!" he screamed. "This is *all* your fault." He stamped his foot. Hitler used to stamp his foot a lot. "I warned you to stay out of this. Get *out* of here! Get *off* the lot!" He stamped his foot again. He was having a real tantrum.

Hans-Dieter had four or five inches and a good forty pounds on me, but I figured, what the hell.

He had to see my first punch coming. I stepped in close and threw a straight right to his face. He staggered back, his eyes wild, not so much with anger as disbelief. He really didn't think I'd dare. Guys like him think they can't be touched. And I guess that's what really made me go kind of crazy, because suddenly I was all over him, just punching him, left and right, no real style to it, mostly in the midsection. He went limp, sagged to the floor. I wasn't even tempted to kick him.

I felt hands on my shoulders. Casimir.

"You better go, Chico," he said.

"I hope I didn't mess things up for you too much."

"Don't worry about it. He deserved it."

I stepped away from Hans-Dieter and walked around him to the door. "See you, Casimir."

"See you, Chico."

★   ★   ★

The phone at the other end of the line rang once, twice, three times. I had taken the receiver away from my ear and was about to hang up when I heard the pickup and a rushed hello.

"Oh, yeah, hi, this is Chico. . . . I hope I didn't wake you up or anything."

"No, oh no, I was in bed, but I was reading. As a matter of fact, I was reading that Yeats book I borrowed. God, some of that stuff . . ."

"I know, yeah. . . . Look, Elaine, I was wondering if maybe you'd like to go to dinner tomorrow night, maybe to Butterfield's, up at the top of the hill."

"A date?"

"Yeah . . . a date."

"Well, sure, of course, Chico. I'd like that. I'd like that a lot."

"I'm sorry I didn't call earlier. I was out—on business, I guess."

"A new job?"

"No, it's that job I turned down. I'm . . . I'm still out of it, though."

"Let's not talk about it, okay? I really think I stepped over the line last night, the things I said. I guess I got carried away. Sorry."

"That isn't like you, Elaine."

"What do you mean?"

"Never apologize, never explain."

"Well, every ten years or so I apologize, and sometimes I explain."

Pause.

"Come by about eight then?"

"Eight's fine. We can walk. It's so close."

"See you then."

"See you, Chico."

14

The next morning I felt good every way but physically. Just getting out of bed I was sore from that long workout in the gym. (It was really dumb to do crunches with that bruised belly of mine.) On the other hand, once out of bed, I had a sort of surge of energy, an adrenaline rush, that sent me into the bathroom for a shower instead of into the kitchen for my usual morning caffeine fix. I felt good, clearheaded, alert. And all that steamy hot water pounding down on my body helped relax my stiff, tight muscles so that by the time I stepped out of the shower I could stand almost erect again.

The usual stuff in front of the bathroom mirror. While I was shaving, I caught myself humming—who knows what tune?— but *humming* as I performed a chore I usually detest. Where had this sudden sense of well-being come from? I put the question to myself as I raised my chin and went after the thick, wiry growth on my throat.

Was it punching out Hans-Dieter that made me feel so good? Man, I walked out of Casimir's office with my head held high, my shoulders back, and a spring in my step that took me all the way back to my car. Anything that felt that right just couldn't be wrong.

Maybe it was working through that whole business with Elaine during the course of the day. Yeah, that felt good. Was she right with all that shrink stuff? I had absolutely no idea, still haven't. But one thing I was sure about: it was great to have somebody around who cared enough to come out with it, to let me know what *she* thought.

Or maybe it was just that I was going to see her that night. If that was it, then I hadn't felt this way since I was a kid, a teenager, and I started dating Maria-Luz Barca. Whatever happened to her? Six kids and a divorce? No, she was headed for better things— more likely a law degree and a job with the state.

Showered, shaved, dressed, and I was still so stoked that I decided to run around the corner to Barney's for breakfast. I grabbed up the *L.A. Times* from in front of my door on the way out, and within five minutes I had a cup of cofee in front of me and was waiting for my order of huevos rancheros to come up. The newspaper—what an ordeal! You know, I can really understand those guys who grab out the sports section and throw the rest of the paper away. That's not me, but sometimes I wish it were. If the problems of Washington and the world beyond weren't bad enough, there's always the Metro section to bring you down. All the drive-bys and the drug-burn shootings, the five-year-olds who are gunned down when a corner gets sprayed, not to mention the arsons, the more spectacular robberies, and the freeway slaughter; they make you wonder if Los Angeles will ever make it into the next century. I used to wonder that as a cop ten years ago, and things have gotten a lot worse since then.

I seldom do more than glance at the pages of Calendar and View. Calendar is the entertainment section, which tells me every Friday what new movies are in town. Useful. If I've got View figured out, it's just the women's pages dressed up in Calvin Klein. Lifestyle stories up in front, and inside, fashion, Dear Abby, and society notes. Yeah, that's right, society notes. You wouldn't think that in the age of the drive-by, in the city where it had been developed to an art, it would matter much which millionaire was at what party for the benefit of which particular charity. But I guess it does, because you still get those items that tell you who was there, what witty remarks they made, and, maybe most important of all, you get their pictures. You've seen those pictures, of course, usually in groupings of four—husband, wife, wife, husband—all with the same resigned smiles fixed on their faces.

Well, paging quickly through the middle of View, something caught my eye. I went back for a closer look. One of those society faces looked awfully familiar. It was him, wasn't it? The caption below confirmed it. Thomas Jarrett was there, smiling with the rest, handsome as ever in a tuxedo. It seemed he was giving his support at a hundred dollars a plate to a charity dedicated to aiding victims of Alzheimer's disease; a hospice of some sort was planned. How nice. He'd made his reentry into society—or maybe he'd never been away. I may have missed his face and name in View a half dozen times since we'd last met. It just went to show you that a good old California name was worth a lot more than a bad reputation.

I was glad I'd finished my breakfast by then, because I don't think I could have eaten afterward. It wasn't that it made me sick to my stomach exactly—more that just seeing his picture reminded me of those severed hands, and thinking of them would surely have taken away my appetite. I guess the fact that I woke up with such energy and in such a positive state of mind meant that I'd managed to blank them out. All of which goes to prove that my memory is just as selective as the next guy's.

Paying the bill, leaving the tip, tossing the paper aside, I left Barney's feeling a lot different from the way I had when I came in. What would I do? Slink back to my place around the corner and hide out? From who? From Jarrett? Why did I feel he was daring me, that he wanted me to get involved? Probably because he did. I knew I was on his list, too. Feeling intimidated, refusing to feel intimidated, I set off briskly in the opposite direction—west—across La Cienega and up the hill.

Man, this was radical therapy; I was taking a walk! You got any idea how much people in this town hate to walk? No wonder cops stop pedestrians as suspicious characters. Take me. I might go to the gym and spend a half hour or forty-five minutes on the bike, even give some time to the dreaded Stairmaster, but I wouldn't think of walking to the gym. And it's something like six or seven blocks away. No more than that, and the walk that morning wasn't much longer, to and from. I decided about half-way there that I was headed for the bookstore at the top of the hill. When in doubt, when in periods of stress and/or frustration, buy a book. Good rule. Even if you don't read it right away, you'll feel better for it. It's sure to improve your outlook.

I know what I got because I did read it right away; in fact, I read it through two or three times that very day on the plane. It was Stephen Mitchell's translation of the *Tao Te Ching,* a little paperback edition. I still read it. I find it useful.

I'd wandered around the shop for about a half hour, picked up the book along the way, and had it tucked under my arm as I made my last stop there at the store's magazine rack. It's pretty vast, takes up the front of one whole side of the store. I can browse with the best. I'd put in an extra five minutes at least thumbing through a lot of magazines I wouldn't buy on a bet; I even looked at *Elle,* though I can't say why. But I can't guarantee which one was in my hands when I became aware that somebody was standing opposite me and staring.

Now, to stand opposite me, on the other side of the knee-high magazine rack, he had to be outside, for the rack stands right up against the plate-glass window. I almost jumped right through it—for who should my audience of one turn out to be but Jarrett's right-hand man, Saheed. He stood there on the sidewalk, giving me his version of a mysterious, all-knowing, Middle Eastern smile. It had been nearly a year, but I recognized him immediately.

Just as he turned and started to walk away, I dropped the magazine, whatever it was, and ran for the door. Near the cash register I bumped into an exiting customer but kept right on going without so much as a pardon me, sir.

Out on the street—where was he? He had turned west, but the sidewalk was empty in that direction for a block or more. So I looked east; he was nowhere to be seen. But then a car pulled away from in front of the shop, a Cadillac, and I realized he'd gotten away. No, I didn't see him, but I was sure he must be inside. Dammit!

"Just where do you think you're going with that book?"

I looked around, distracted, slightly confused, and found the guy behind the register no longer behind the register but confronting me, fist on his hips. What book? Oh . . . the one in my hand.

"I saw somebody I knew," I said. "I'm—I'm sorry."

He surveyed the empty sidewalk. "You see him now?"

"No, he got away."

"Too bad. Suppose you come back inside now and pay for the book."

So that's what I did, shamefaced, reduced to a bumbling, apologetic clod before this guy's icy professionalism. *He* knew a petty thief when he'd caught one. What was the matter with me, anyway? I guess I used to be a lot more intimidating when I was a cop than I am now.

So what the picture of Thomas Jarrett in the pages of View had failed to do, the live, in-person appearance of Saheed direct from the streets of West Hollywood had certainly accomplished. It brought me down. Where was all that energy I woke up with? I trudged back home at an old man's pace, a black cloud over my head on that sunny Southern California morning. What would I have done to Saheed, what would I have said to him, if I had managed to catch up with him there in front of the bookshop? I have no idea. I only know that I wanted to get at him. Maybe I thought I would punch him out the way I had Hans-Dieter. And what good would that have done? None. It could only have had a negative result. And it certainly wouldn't have demonstrated what I wanted to make clear, what I wanted understood—that I was going to sit this one out, that for my own reasons I didn't want to get involved in his little scam with Alicia and Majestic Studios.

But Saheed's appearance at the window made it clear that Jarrett thought I was involved, or maybe he wanted to get me involved. What was the message? We've got our eye on you, Chico. Don't turn around because we'll be there. Had Saheed wanted to give me a start (and I guess he had), or had he wanted to frighten me away? It's what's known in the trade as an open shadow. Or could it be he was just driving along on Sunset, spotted me in the window, and said to himself, I think I'll jump out here and scare the shit out of my old buddy Chico.

Whatever.

Anyway, I approached my building carefully, looking up and down the block on both sides of the street for the car I had pegged as Saheed's. Not a Cadillac in sight. Even so, I was wary going into the front door, scoping out the territory ahead. I unlocked the inner door and decided to go on up the stairs and stay away from the elevator. Fool me once . . . etc., etc. But the hall was clear, and in a minute or less I was inside my apartment. He had me looking over my shoulder, all right. Was I going to start wearing that .38 of mine wherever I went?

There was a message on my machine. Were they harassing me by telephone? Expecting the worst, I reversed the tape and played it back. A female voice:

"Hi, uh, Mr. Cervantes? This is Kathleen McGucken of the Cook County Public Defender's Office. I've been assigned as Julio Alviero's attorney, and I was just wondering if you could give me a call. Practically any time. I'm through in court for the day, and I eat lunch at my desk, so, you know, any time. The area code is 312, and the number is 435-4907. Hope to hear from you today." Click.

Cook County. That had to be Chicago. What kind of trouble had Julio gotten himself into there? Was smoking dope a big deal in Chicago, or in—what was Sterling's town? Lake Wood? Whatever it was, Sterling wouldn't like it. Poor Julio, he'd screwed up again.

I replayed the tape to make sure I had the number right, then punched it out on the phone. The switchboard answered. I hoped I got her name right.

"Kathleen McGucken." That's how she answered. No nonsense, businesslike, but she sounded pretty young.

"Yeah, hi," I said, "this is Antonio Cervantes. You called me about Julio Alviero."

"Oh, yes, Mr. Cervantes. Thanks for getting back to me so promptly. I had my first client conference with Mr. Julio Alviero just before arraignment, and—"

"Arraignment? For what?"

"Oh, of course. It's all over the papers here, but there wouldn't be anything about it in Los Angeles." She sighed audibly into the phone. "Well, it's homicide. The assistant prosecutor at the arraignment said they're going for murder one. I, personally, think he's bluffing. I don't think he can put together that kind of case."

"Hold it a minute," I said. "Back up. Julio's up for murder? Who's he supposed to have killed?"

She giggled in embarrassment. "Not too swift, McGucken," she chided herself, "leaving out important details. Okay, yes, Mr. Cervantes, the victim's name is Benjamin Sterling. It's a pretty big case around here because he was on the Board of Trade and all. You know, old Lake Wood money, the—"

"I know about him," I interrupted. "I know him, or I *knew* him, I guess. I baby-sat him a couple of days out here. I was, you know, like, his bodyguard."

"Yes, that's what Mr. Alviero said. It's at his request I'm calling you. He says he didn't do it; well, naturally, they all say that, and I'm pleading him not guilty, of course. But you know, I have to say, he's sort of convincing. For what it's worth, I tend to believe him . . . sort of."

"Well, good. He couldn't have done it."

"There *is* physical evidence that puts him at the scene of the crime."

"I don't care. He couldn't have done it."

"He must have known you'd feel that way."

"Why?"

"Well, you're a private investigator, aren't you? That's how I got you—through your business listing."

"Yes, but . . ."

"My client wants to hire you. He says you're the only one who can save him."

15

It was a long walk to get there, that much I remember. I went up a wide flight of stairs, along which were ranged visitors to the Cook County Jail of the usual ethnic diversity. Was I getting in ahead of them? Maybe my way had been paved by Kathleen McGucken. Or maybe, because I was visiting one of their star inmates, I was receiving special treatment.

Anyway, down a hall and into a big room, and there was Julio, sitting behind the glass, leaning forward tensely. He didn't catch sight of me at first. There were a couple of people ahead of me as I came in. Then I separated from them, and he saw me. The grin that spread over his face was pure Julio—triumph and relief. The relief was there in his eyes. He jumped up from his chair. If the glass hadn't separated us, he would have thrown me an *abrazo*.

"Homeboy! I knew you'd come! Can't forget the ol' barrio, huh?"

"Yeah, well . . ." I sat down opposite him. Was that why I was there? I still wasn't sure.

The grin faded slightly as he sank back down into the chair. "Anyway, you came. Thanks."

"Look, Julio, we're not going to have all that much time here, and there's some things I have to know."

"Firs' of all, I didn' do it."

"I know that. It's understood."

"Good." He nodded soberly. "Ask me anything."

"Where were you when Sterling was killed?"

"That was early afternoon, I guess, according to the cops. I'll tell you what I tol' them. I don' know, exactly. I was on Blue Island Avenue clear at the other en' of town. The boss wanted me to check on some ol' warehouses an' factory buildings there, but I never made it."

"How come?"

"It turns out the places I'm s'posed to look at are right in the middle of a real ol'-time barrio, right down there."

"So what happened? I don't understand."

"I went to some places. I had some drinks. I talk to some people."

"Good," I said, "maybe I can work up an alibi for you."

"Maybe." He shrugged. "I don' remember the places so well. Jus' the firs' one—Tito's or something like that—big Tecate sign in the window."

"Will they remember you there?"

"Prob'ly. I drank a lot, try to make out with the waitress, shit like that. See, the boss kep' me on a pretty short rope here. No drinkin', no smokin' dope. I'm goin' nuts, you know? So anyway, when he sends me out to look over these buildings for his big project, I guess I wen' kin' of crazy, you know?"

Yeah, I knew. I could imagine Julio unleashed at last, suddenly discovering he'd found a home in Chicago. After days on his best behavior, with a little money in his pocket, he'd backslid with a vengeance.

"Okay," I said to him, "this woman at the Public Defender's Office, she said there was physical evidence that put you at the scene of the crime."

"Yeah," he said, "that's why I'm here."

"What was it?"

"A wallet."

"Yours?"

"Not really, no."

"What's that supposed to mean? Either it was or it wasn't."

"Then no. It wasn' mine. It look' like mine. My driver's license was inside—you know, California DMV—behind a little glass window, there's my face, my ol' address on the East Side. But the wallet's not mine. I never saw it before. I wouldn' own a wallet like that."

"Like what? Whatta you mean?"

"Well, it was the long kind, the kind you carry around in your suit jacket. I like the kin' that fits in your hip pocket, you know?"

"Is that the kind you've got?"

He shrugged. "I don' have one. I never got it back when I left L.A. County Jail. They gave me the shit that was inside, my license, but not the wallet. It was new, snakeskin. Somebody like it, somebody took it. Happens all the time."

"What about the other one, the one they found?"

"Cheap. Cowhide, maybe plastic. I wouldn' own a wallet like that."

"But your license was inside. How did it get there?"

He shrugged a big shrug, palms up. "I don' know. The firs' I miss it was the morning of the day all this happen. *Madre!* was it only day before yesterday? Anyway, the boss says, 'Take one of the cars.' He's got three—some shit, huh? So I go digging through my bag for my driver's license—you remember my red bag? An' I can' find it. Anyplace. So I don' say anything about it—I mean, driving without a license, I done worse things, right? An' I go down to take a look at those buildings aroun' Halsted, which I never really looked at, like I said. But there at the cop house they had it when they questioned me. It was inside this wallet, which was new, like somebody bought it just for this. My driver's license and a few bucks was all that was inside—no cards, no receipts, nothing, just the license and a few bucks. That makes it mine. The cops showed it to me in an evidence bag. They say, 'This look familiar?' They open up the bag and offer it to me, so I reach in an' grab it, an' take a look inside. There's my license, there's my picture—"

"There's your fingerprints," I put in. "If you hadn't touched it, it would've been clean."

172

"Homeboy, I figured that out already."

I sighed. "Okay," I said, "where was this wallet found?"

"Under the boss's body, like I lost it in the struggle or something."

"While you were beating him to death?"

"That's what they say."

"Okay, Julio, maybe you better go back and tell me just what happened that day—say, from the time you went looking for your license."

It wasn't a long story, because he couldn't supply many details, but I took careful notes. I went over it a couple of times as I drove from the huge complex at Twenty-sixth and California—felony courts in front, county jail located in back. Convenient, huh? You could be arraigned, housed, tried, convicted, and executed—Cook County has its own electric chair—and never leave the premises.

Julio said he got lost driving from Lake Wood to the inner city. It was the local freeways that messed him up, just like they will any visitor to Los Angeles. He arrived over an hour late for the appointment with the real estate agent that Sterling had made for him. The agent had left by then. Julio, feeling frustrated and angry, went off to get a drink. That was when he found Tito's or whatever it was. He figured he must've been there a couple of hours before he went on to another place—he was kind of vague about this—and then he kind of woke up in a diner, guzzling coffee, sobering up. By the time he'd had something to eat, vomited it up in the men's room, and had more coffee, it was late afternoon, nearly five o'clock. He decided he could drive then. Fighting rush-hour traffic, taking another wrong turn, he didn't make it back to Sterling's place in Lake Wood until six-thirty. They were all waiting for him then—the Lake Wood cops, the Chicago cops, even Clare and Roger. They read him his rights, then took him back to Chicago, and after they showed him the wallet, they booked him.

Time was up. A guard came and clapped Julio on the shoulder. But just as he was getting up to leave, Julio said to me, "Try

Josefina at the house." He pronounced it the Spanish way, with a *jota*. "She's one of the maids there. Maybe she knows who lifted my license."

"You think she took it?" I asked.

"I hope not," he said. "She's a good kid. But she's a Salvadoreana—scared, you know?"

The way he said it, I thought I got the picture.

I was on my way to have lunch with Kathleen McGucken. If she usually ate at her desk, she was making an exception in my case. I was glad of that. There were some things I had to settle with her. I wasn't at all sure what my status in Chicago was with my California p.i. license. Was I going to have to sneak around? Would they chase me out of town? I had no idea, really.

The part of Chicago I was driving through looked grungy—gray, industrial, pretty rough. A dark day, it looked like it might rain. I'd glimpsed something of what I guess was the Loop as I drove around it, heading for the Cook County Jail. Anyway, I saw a great cluster of buildings fifty stories and higher, a bunch that made L.A.'s downtown look like Fresno's.

I had no sense of the city at all. Sure, I had a map. I had a car. (What good is an Angeleno without a car?) I'd seen a little of it. But Chicago itself—the way the city operated, the power brokers in town, what to watch out for and what to look into—all this was an absolute mystery to me. It's really pretty hard for a guy like me to operate off his turf. Maybe Julio would be better off with somebody from Chicago. I knew I'd be happy to go back to Los Angeles.

I had fought with myself for about an hour after I first talked to Ms. McGucken. I mean, just because he said I was the only one who could save him didn't mean I caved right in and said I'd catch the next plane there. No, what I said was, I'd think about it, and that's what I did. After all, there were a couple of pretty basic questions to be answered. The big one: Was Julio worth saving? We're talking about a drug dealer here. So what if he stood up in court and sent the big guy to jail? He was forced into it. He turned over to stay out of San Quentin or Chino, or wherever they would have put him. Oh yeah, he was a dealer, all right, in it for the money and the *niñas*. He liked the life. He'd be making his rounds today if some undercover guy hadn't made a good pinch on him.

And then there was the matter of money, no small consideration, as far as I was concerned. Ms. McGucken said Julio wanted to hire me. That was a major laugh. I hate doing pro bono work. It isn't professional. And not only that, but it so happened that this wonderful opportunity that Julio had extended to me came at a time when I was cash poor. I wasn't exactly hurting, but I was hoping hard that Benjamin Sterling had managed to get that payment for services off to me before he went to that big trading floor in the sky. Reimbursement for expenses? I'd be lucky if I ever saw that, even after I'd submitted proof of payment to Pilar Ramirez. I'd probably have to sue Sterling's estate to get it, and it wouldn't be worth hiring a Chicago lawyer to handle it.

But overriding both these considerations was my absolute certainty that Julio could not have, would not have, committed the crime he'd been accused of. It made no sense. Benjamin Sterling had offered him not just a ticket out of Los Angeles, which he badly needed, but a ticket back into the world. Killing him would have canceled the ticket. Besides, I knew the kind of guy Julio was. He may have been everything I'd grown up with in Boyle Heights, everything I wanted to leave behind when I left, but I knew he wasn't a killer.

And yeah, okay, when I'd thrashed that all out, but not until I'd done it, that's when I called Kathleen McGucken and told her I'd be flying out that afternoon for a late arrival. And that's when she said she'd fix it up so I could interview Julio at Cook County Jail, and why didn't we have lunch afterward and talk about the case.

The name of the restaurant was Marconi's. She'd given me very explicit directions—on Oakley between Blue Island and Cermak, turn left, turn right, and so on. And there it was, coming up ahead of me. It was early enough so that I was able to find street parking. It seemed that a mist had settled just as I stepped out of the car. But by the time I reached the entrance to the restaurant, it had established itself as a light rain.

Inside, just your basic Italian restaurant. I asked at the door for her and was ushered through the usual maze of tables, already half-filled at noon, to one in the corner occupied by a woman with red hair dressed in a black power suit. It was the hair that you noticed: there was a lot of it. As she rose, with a serious face, to greet me and shake hands, the light caught her hair, and it shone vermilion. She didn't look to be more than twenty-five.

"Mr. Alviero holding up?" she asked as she settled back down in her chair.

I was confused for just a moment. "Oh, you mean Julio. Yeah, he seems to be all right."

"I understand that this isn't an entirely new experience for him—being in jail, I mean."

She'd done her homework. "No, he was in L.A. County awhile."

"For dealing," she said crisply. "Charges were dropped, eventually."

"He was a witness for the state. That was the deal."

"So I hear—or read, actually, on a fax I got this morning from the Los Angeles Prosecutor's Office."

She was certainly cooler than she had been on the phone. "Ms. McGucken," I said, "when I talked to you yesterday you said you sort of believed Julio when he said he didn't do it. Do you still sort of believe that?"

"I'll tell you, Mr. Cervantes, I haven't been in the Public Defender's Office very long, just about three years. I got the job right out of law school. I guess you can tell I'm pretty young. Well, I didn't realize how young—and naive—I was until I started working here as a PD. Mr. Cervantes, they're *all* guilty. It is my *profound* conviction that I have *never* defended an innocent man—or woman, for that matter. And with my caseload, around ten at any given time, usually more—well, that's a *lot* of guilty defendants."

I got the feeling she had more to say on the subject, but just then a waitress came up to take our order. I hadn't bothered to look at the menu; Ms. McGucken already had. So I just doubled her order and pointed at the bottle of designer water in front of her—San something-or-other.

I was glad for the interruption. She was venting her disappointment not so much with the job as with what she had to work with. Once, as a cop, I talked to a PD in Los Angeles who said just about the same thing but a little less passionately.

The moment the waitress turned away with our order, I leaned across the table and said, "Okay, look, I understand what you're saying. When Julio came along you thought you might—just *might*—have somebody who was for real, a guy who really didn't do it. You said he was pretty convincing."

"He cried."

"He wasn't putting on an act," I said. "But then you found out he'd been through the system out in L.A., and now you're quite naturally a little less convinced than before."

"The system!" She sort of snorted. "Listen, these people know the routine better than I do. Next time I see him, he'll probably ask me what're his chances of copping it down to aggravated assault—too bad the victim died." A little irony. She stopped for a sip of San something-or-other and eyed me a bit suspiciously. "I suppose you two are old friends," she said at last.

I thought a moment. "We were in the same high school at the same time." That wasn't saying we were there together. That would have implied something different.

"You're saying you were there at the same time, but you weren't friends."

"Exactly."

"Did you know him? Were you acquainted?" Very lawyerly.

"Everybody knew Julio. We may have spoken on a few occasions."

"And afterward? Did you keep contact with him?"

"I didn't see him again until a few days ago, a little less than a week. Listen," I said, "I didn't even *like* Julio. I still don't."

She frowned at me, looked honestly perplexed. "Then why did he say you were the only one who could save him? And why were you so sure he *couldn't* have done it? I mean, I even brought up the matter of physical evidence—a wallet, by the way, with his driver's license in it."

I nodded. "Yeah, I heard about the wallet from Julio. I'll tell you about that later. Listen, I can't speak for Julio. He's probably got an exaggerated idea of my powers as an investigator, but he knows that I know his situation—or what his situation was. And it's because I know it that I said he couldn't have killed Benjamin Sterling."

"You've lost me," she said. "This is pretty vague."

"Okay, Ms. McGucken, a lot of my work I get from lawyers. I don't exactly hang around with them, but we talk. And there's a phrase they like to toss around that you probably know, too—cui bono."

"To whom the good," she said. "Who gains?"

"Yeah, and when I found out what it meant, I realized it was a principle in investigation, too. Who gains? It won't always tell you who did it, but it's sure good to use when you want to eliminate suspects. You look at the case in its whole context and you ask yourself, Who benefits from this criminal act, whatever it is? And anybody who doesn't benefit, who has nothing to gain, you can eliminate as a suspect, no matter what their opportunity, no matter what the physical evidence."

I could tell I was getting to her. She was nodding with me as I made my points. When the waitress brought our orders she hardly seemed to notice. The pasta sat steaming on the table.

"But," she said, "motives aren't always clear. Sometimes it's not always clear how people benefit."

"Okay," I said, "that I'll grant you. But in Julio's case, he not only had nothing to gain by Sterling's death, he had everything to lose by it."

"You'd better eat your food."

And so we did, and I told her about Julio and Sterling—Julio on the beach and Sterling with his ambitious plan to help the homeless, how they came together in Santa Monica, and how Julio showed him around, taught him what it meant to be homeless. Then I told her there had been two attempts on Sterling's life while he was there in Santa Monica. I explained them, told her that the first, a case of mistaken identity, had resulted in a homicide, and the second, a bomb attempt, had resulted in the death of the perpetrator. And I pointed out that all this time Julio was with Sterling, he had a hundred opportunities to put him away. But it was obviously not in his interest to do that because Sterling had more or less adopted him, made him part of his plan. Admittedly, Julio was sort of a con artist, but Sterling had bought the con, had taken him with him to Chicago, given him a job in the enterprise.

"But," she objected, "maybe they quarreled or something. Maybe Sterling fired him, and he got so angry that—"

"Do we know that? Has anybody come forward with that?"

"No. But they might."

"You're right," I said, "they might. But if it didn't come out in the initial questioning I'd be pretty suspicious, wouldn't you?"

"Well . . . yes." There was a long moment when she sat frowning at me. It was a frown of concentration. "You're pretty persuasive, you know that?"

"Good," I said. "I meant to be. But listen, you'll want confirmation on what I've been telling you; I mean, about the attempts on Sterling's life and all, so here"—I whipped out Lieutenant Shinahara's card and pushed it across the table at her. "Call this guy, Santa Monica Police. He won't know much about Julio. As far as he was concerned, Julio was more or less in the background. But I think he could tell you, if you made a point of it, that Julio was with Sterling when both attempts took place."

"Hey, this is cool," she said, "a real mystery. I had no idea!" Her professional demeanor had slipped a little.

"Yeah, well, it gets even better. Shinahara's going to tell you all about the Yakuza connection. I didn't even go into that."

"You mean Yakuza, like the Japanese Mafia?"

"That's right. He probably doesn't even know Sterling's dead, been murdered. I didn't think to tell him before I left—I should have—and police departments don't really talk to each other. So yeah, he'll be interested, all right. He'll probably give you a whole theory on the case, very sexy. Let him tell you, though. Then we'll talk about it."

She nodded. "All right, sure. There really are a lot of . . . implications to this, aren't there?"

"Yeah," I said, "too many." And then, because it had just occurred to me, I added, "That stuff I ate was really good. What was it?"

"Linguini and pesto."

"Is that what that green stuff was? I'll have to remember that."

"I hope you don't mind paying for your own. Private detectives are definitely not in the budget."

"Yeah, I was wondering about that—I mean, me with a California license and all. You know."

"I know. I'm finding out about it." She sighed. "I'll tell you later, okay?"

When the bill came, I made a grab for it, but she wouldn't allow it. We split it down the middle; even split the tip, because she insisted. Then, as I was getting up from the table, she asked if I was free for the next hour and a half or so.

"I'm free all day. At this point I don't have a lot to work on. Why?"

"I think you ought to see the crime scene," she said.

"That'd certainly be helpful. Can you arrange it?"

"Come on. I'll take you there."

It was a drive through the rain, coming down harder now, but she knew the way. She took the Dan Ryan Expressway (who was Dan Ryan, anyway?) to some other one, and after a stretch of some fairly swift wet-weather driving—they don't creep in Chicago the way they do in Los Angeles—she took a turnoff to Wilson Avenue. She headed in a direction I took to be east. We talked intermittently along the way, though not as much as in the restaurant. I guess that was my fault, because I kept looking out the car window at the city, still trying to get some sense of it. As the windshield wipers marked time, I asked her questions.

"How big is it? Chicago, I mean. What's the population?"

"Oh, I don't know. It's big—four or five million, I guess. Maybe more."

Then later, still on the freeway, after we'd passed some Polish cultural center or something:

"I understand Chicago's pretty, well, ethnic—ethnically diverse, I mean."

"Oh, yeah, more Poles than Warsaw, biggest archdiocese in the world, we've got everything."

"Even Mexicans, I hear."

"Even Mexicans. And lots of Puerto Ricans and assorted Central Americans."

"But who owns it? Who runs it?"

"That's a good question. Probably more blacks than any single group, but I've got to say I think the Irish still run it."

Kathleen McGucken glanced over at me as she said that. It was clear she wasn't bragging. If anything, she seemed sort of embarrassed.

Then she said, "You ask unusual questions for a visitor."

"I'm interested in cities," I said, "how they run, how they tick. This one is sure different from Los Angeles."

"I'll bet it is. No movie stars. Funny you've never been here before."

"Yeah, isn't it."

Wilson Avenue wasn't much, mostly middle-class apartment buildings and bungalows. But then, as we drove further, the street seemed to deteriorate into a slum—rusting cars, rain-drenched refuse in the street and out on the sidewalk. The buildings, though no older than the ones we'd passed earlier, looked ramshackle and untended. Just ahead, I saw stores, a fast-food location, an office building or two. It became commercial without rising economically or socially: it was still a slum.

"This is sort of a skid row area," she said. "As a matter of fact, I've taken you here through the backyard of the city. If we've got time, I'll go back by the scenic route."

"This shouldn't take long," I said. "I'm sure the cops have been over it. I just want to get a sense of the area."

She signaled a left turn just before the big commercial corner. Looking over to my right, I was mildly surprised to see a college campus opening off in that direction—HARRY TRUMAN COLLEGE, the sign said—right in the middle of this urban blight.

At a break in traffic, she made her left turn into a narrow street, then an immediate right up a short alley, where she came to a halt at the familiar yellow tape that police everywhere use to mark off a crime scene. A single uniformed cop stood by, off to one side. Although he was dressed in rain gear, he looked pretty unhappy out there.

Ms. McGucken jumped out of the car, grabbed an umbrella from the backseat, and opened it up as she went over to the cop. I got out and followed her. About all I could do was raise my collar against the rain. I hadn't even thought to bring a raincoat along from home.

She showed him her ID, and he made a vague gesture that passed us both under the yellow tape. I went first. Before she ducked under, she handed the umbrella to me.

"You hold it," she said. "You're taller." Not by much I wasn't.

So we started through the alley close together, huddling against the rain. It was cruddy and junk-strewn. Along its borders it was thick with a kind of muddy peat made up of dirt and newspaper pulp from which weeds were growing. Mother Nature having her way even here.

There was a great rumble and rattle above us. I looked up, tilting the umbrella in the process so that we got spattered with rain. There was a train up there beyond the wall where the alley ended. It had come to a halt just beyond us.

"What's that?" I asked.

"It's the el," she said, "the elevated train. It goes into the Loop from here."

"I thought you had a subway."

"We do. Some trains go down, and some stay up on the el tracks."

"Is it possible anybody up there on the train could have looked down and witnessed the homicide?"

"I suppose so," she said. "If it happened that the train pulled into the station at just the right moment."

"Long shot, I guess." I nodded toward the left. "Come on, let's go find the chalk marks."

We started off around the corner on that side. While the alley ended just ahead at the el tracks, there was a kind of open yard behind the building over there, probably meant to accommodate trucks. We looked around there and saw nothing. Anyway, there was a loading dock at the back of the building that offered shelter from the rain. We climbed the six stairs that brought us up to tailgate level and, glad to be out of the rain for a little while, I folded up the umbrella and shook it out. Then I turned around, and there it was. I nudged Ms. McGucken and pointed down at the floor of the loading dock.

It's always kind of creepy to see the outline of a body chalked out, right where it fell. A little shiver ran through me—maybe a chill from the rain.

So this was where Benjamin Sterling bought the farm. He didn't seem like a bad man at all, in spite of what he'd said. He'd called himself an old buccaneer, a pirate. But he was probably no worse than most in his line of work; probably better. The man had standards, after all, as he proved to that gangster from Tokyo. And he had a noble ambition. He might really have done some good with that fishing-reel factory of his. It was certainly his intention. We'd probably never know now.

Looking over at Ms. McGucken, I caught her making the sign of the cross, maybe even saying a prayer for the repose of the soul of Benjamin Sterling. She looked at me a little sheepishly.

"Wow," she said, "it's really something, huh? Right here."

I nodded, and we walked around the continuous chalk line, careful not to step on it. Sterling had fallen with his head toward the back wall of the building, both arms outstretched, his feet a yard or more from the edge of the dock. I looked back at the truck yard and then up, and I saw that although the roof of the truck dock was fairly high it effectively shut off any view from the el tracks above. So this was a much more secluded spot than I'd thought at first—maybe not a perfect place for a murder but not a bad choice, either.

"What time did this take place?" I asked.

"Probably around one in the afternoon. Between twelve and two, they're saying. The body was found just after two by a couple of street guys. I'll save you a copy of the coroner's report."

"And what was the weather like?"

"When? Let's see, that was . . . day before yesterday." She thought a moment. "Just about like this," she said then, "only worse. Yeah, it really came down that day."

I looked back at the truck yard. Although it was paved, the blacktop was cracked and bumpy. There were pools of water all around it. If it was raining harder then than today, any tire tracks would have been washed away.

"What about Sterling's car?" I asked. "Where was it parked? Out on the street, or back here?"

"That was a funny thing," she said. "He'd left it on the lot downtown. He must have taken a cab out here."

"Have the cops checked with the cab companies? Maybe he met somebody here. He'd been looking at buildings for that factory of his. Maybe a real estate agent or something."

"They haven't come up with anything yet, but I don't think they're trying very hard."

"Probably not. Once they found that wallet with Julio's license in it, they must have figured they had it wrapped up. The license had an L.A. address on it, back when he had one. How did they know he was staying at Sterling's in Lake Wood? Julio said they were waiting for him when he got back there at six-thirty."

"I don't know," she said. "It'll be in the file, though."

I walked around the loading dock a little. It was literally clean. At least the forensic guys had evidently done their job well. I went over to the big double doors that led from the loading dock into the building. A big hasp and staple held them shut. An oversized padlock made sure they would stay shut. I gave it a tug. It held. Then I turned back to Ms. McGucken and shrugged.

"I'm ready. I've seen enough."

And so we put up the umbrella again and went back down the steps, crowding together against the rain. As we crossed the truck yard, heading for the alley, something caught my eye just above my line of vision, a movement. I tilted the umbrella up for a look. More rain in the face.

"Hey! Watch it! Come on!"

"What's that building over there?" I pointed. There were four rows of windows, one on top of the other, leading up to the flat roof. Each of the windows had shades, at least. A few had curtains, too. Maybe I'd seen some movement behind the curtains. The brown brick of the building's back wall was smoked and dirty. It seemed to be in far worse shape than the factory building behind us.

"That one? Oh, I don't know, some skid row hotel or something. We'll be passing by. Take a look then."

"I'll do that," I said.

Then we started for the car at a quick jog.

Standing by the door, watching the crowd go by, I waited for Kathleen McGucken in the big downstairs lobby of the Felony Courts Building. Her office, it turned out, was right upstairs in this same building next to the County Jail. She'd probably arranged that we meet at Marconi's, away from the office, because she was unsure about my status there in Illinois—and probably because she was unsure about Julio, too.

The people who passed in and out there in the lobby were of two types, generally, and easily separated. There were the official court people—briefcase-carrying lawyers, public defenders, and prosecutors, court reporters, maybe even a judge or two—and they were in the minority. The majority were the relatives and friends of the defendants, if the defendants had any friends. They looked just like their brothers and sisters in Los Angeles—same colors, same blank, defeated expressions on their faces, same bewildered kids tagging along behind them. They'd probably look the same in New York, too.

I spotted Ms. McGucken as she crossed the lobby from the elevators. She waved at me. Actually, what she waved was a big manila envelope, the kind that was big enough to hold almost anything. But she wasn't quite so open about handing it over. She moved me over to one side, away from the doors, and, standing close, put it in my hands.

"Here's most of the file," she said. "Maybe I shouldn't be showing you what I've got here, but I'm letting you have it on the basis that you've been hired by Mr. Alviero. I guess that makes it okay. What do I know? I've never worked with a private detective before. I don't think any of us have."

I nodded, gave her a kind of solemn smile. "Thanks, Ms. McGucken."

"I'm also giving this to you because I guess I trust you. You're either okay, or you're the best bullshitter I've ever met, Mr. Cervantes."

"Call me Chico."

"Okay, you call me Katy. Anything else? I'd better get upstairs."

"Yeah, just one thing. I want to canvass the places Julio was drinking yesterday. I need a picture for that. Could you get me a copy of his mug shot?"

"I'll see what I can do. I'll have to let you know about that."

She started to back off, raised her hand to wave good-bye. Then I remembered and pursued her a few steps.

"Last thing, I promise. How do I get down to the Board of Trade from here?"

16

The ride up on the elevator was swift, decisive, nonstop. It wasn't that I was the only one on board. It was just that the three other people—two chattering traders in bright jackets and a tall, nifty black woman—were all riding beyond the eighteenth floor.

That was where I got off. I walked down the long corridor, checking numbers and names on the doors as I went, turned a corner, and found the door I was looking for at the far end—Sterling Partners. Would they change the name now? That seemed unlikely. What outfits like this one wanted to emphasize was age, solidity, continuity. That was certainly what the name on the door said, along with the line underneath, "established 1889."

I felt slightly intimidated, as if I ought to knock first or something, but I knew that would be all wrong. So, taking a deep breath, I turned the knob and pushed the door open.

It wasn't quite what I'd expected. I must have visualized some ultramodern, open space right out of the movies, with a gorgeous receptionist doing her nails at a desk ten feet wide. What I got instead was a cramped little reception area with a middle-aged woman, who looked harried, giving her attention to a compact telephone switchboard. She worked it efficiently, answering brightly, "Sterling Partners," switching whoever to where. Somehow she worked a finger free and with it directed me to one of the four chairs in the little anteroom. I sat. I waited. Finally, at a welcome lull, she asked me just who it was I wanted to see.

I rose, stepped forward, and said, "Roger Edwards, please."

"Is he expecting you? Got an appointment?"

"I'm afraid not," I said. "I'm from out of town, just stopping by. He, uh, ought to know my name, though."

"What is it?"

"Antonio Cervantes."

"I'll try."

And so she did, working in her attempt between incoming calls. At one point I heard her pronounce my name into the telephone headset and wait, listening. Then she turned to me and asked, "What is your visit regarding?"

"Regarding the death of Benjamin Sterling."

"Oh." She did a quick take on me and repeated what I'd said into her headset. Then, "If you'll just take a seat, Mr. Edwards will be with you soon."

The telephone had started up again. She attended to it. I sat back down and studied my shoes. They were wet.

I knew I was taking a chance seeing Roger Edwards. I didn't want to scare him, just let him know I was around, give him something to think about. It was a funny thing, but people usually made more mistakes when they were on the defensive than when they were indifferent. So the idea was to put him on the defensive.

It took about five minutes of patient sitting for me to be invited down the hall in search of his office. It wasn't hard to find. All along the way were partitioned work spaces where young men worked the telephones, but there were two private offices beyond them, each with a secretary stationed in front. The door to one of the two stood open. The secretary there, not exactly young but good-looking and busty, scrambled to her feet and gave me a quick smile.

"Find your way? I should've gone down and brought you,"

she said apologetically, "but I was on the phone, and her highness over there said she was too busy."

I glanced across the aisle at the other woman—much older, into her sixties. She was obviously Sterling's secretary and, with the death of her boss, on her way out. I gave her a quick smile and a sympathetic wink. She kind of puckered her chin and nodded.

"You can go right on in," said Edwards's secretary.

"Thanks."

I speeded up as I crossed the threshold into his office, crossed it in three big strides, and stretched my open hand across his desk. He had to shake it.

"Mr. Edwards, Antonio Cervantes from Los Angeles. I hope you remember me. I was in town, and I just had to come by and tell you how sorry I was to hear about the death of your father-in-law. I know I should've phoned first, but I was here in the Loop, and I just looked up, and there it was—the Board of Trade Building. So I just barged in on you. I hope you'll forgive me."

I was pumping his hand for about half the time it took me to say all that. He was sitting down. I'd given him no chance to rise. He seemed sort of taken aback by my high-energy entrance. I believe I'd shocked the bluster right out of him.

"Oh, of course, uh, Mr. Cervantes. Sit down, sit down, please."

I took the chair he nodded to and pulled it closer to the desk.

"You know, Mr. Edwards, when I heard Ben had died, and the *way* he died, well, it just hit me here." I gave a mea culpa chuck to my chest. "You know, I'd never lost a client before. He was the first one—ever."

"Well, you can hardly blame yourself. After all, you were two thousand miles away . . . weren't you?"

"Yeah, but when you spend twenty-four hours in a day with a guy, with him every minute, the way I was with Ben, you really get pretty close, or at least that's how I felt about him. Close. I guess that's why it hit me so hard."

"If you don't mind my asking, how *did* you hear about all this? Surely it wasn't in the papers or on television out there."

"Oh no," with a strong shake of my head, "I heard from one of my Chicago contacts. See, I talked with Ben the morning he was murdered—isn't that something, that *very* morning? Anyway, he called me, and we discussed a few things; I remember he complained about the wet weather you were having here, like today, I guess, and said he wished he was back in sunny California. But at one point we got pretty serious. I told him, 'Ben, I think you really need protection—'round the clock, the way it was in L.A. Somebody wants you dead.' Then I recommended a private investigator here in town, an ex-cop, just like me. But you know how Ben was, kind of stubborn; all I got him to say was he'd give it serious consideration. Well, after that I called the guy I'd recommended, and I told him, 'If a guy named Benjamin Sterling calls, give him A-number-one treatment.' Then a day later this same guy calls me back and says, 'Chico, I hate to tell you, but you know that guy Benjamin Sterling? . . .' Well, it was a shock, I want to tell you, a real shock."

"It was for all of us, Mr. Cervantes, I can assure you. I remember how I got the news myself; well, I'll never forget, really. I'd come off the trading floor and had a bite to eat when the police came and told me—two detectives. I'd been on the floor all day, well, since nine, didn't even break for lunch until afterward. You get kind of pumped up down there, don't think about food. Although my part of the business keeps me up here most of the time, I like to get down on the floor every once in a while just to get the blood running faster and remind myself what this crazy business is all about."

He gave an inappropriate little heh-heh-heh like that was a joke and reached for the pack of cigarettes on his desk. He offered me one and lit up. Nervous? Well, his hand wasn't shaking, but he did seem to need that cigarette.

"And that's where you were when you heard?" I prompted.

"Yes, I came out, and they told me. Of course it was a shock, a deep blow. My first question to them was 'Have you got any idea who did it?' Then I heard they'd found a wallet with a driver's license belonging to this man, Alviero. I said, 'Why, I know him! He's been living as a guest at my father-in-law's home.' So they picked him up. They arrested him when he had the nerve to return to the house." He paused then and looked at me rather sharply. "You knew him, too, didn't you? He was traveling with Ben that day you spent with him."

"Yeah," I said, wrinkling my nose, "kind of an unsavory character."

"And dangerous, too, as it turned out. Well, that was the thing about Ben. He was always too trusting."

"But a good old guy," I put in.

"Yes, wasn't he? I owe a lot to him."

It hung right there for a moment. I believe I was supposed to take that as my cue to leave, but I hung on, smiling sympathetically.

"What brings you to Chicago, Mr. Cervantes?" he asked at last. "Another case?"

"No, I guess you could say I came on an impulse. Like I said, this is the first client I've ever lost. I just wanted to make damned sure they got the one who did it. Then I heard they'd made an arrest, that guy Alviero, so I've just been nosing around a little, checking a few things, seeing the city."

"Well, it certainly looks like they've got the right man!"

"It sure seems that way, doesn't it?" I agreed.

With that, I jumped up out of the chair, but instead of saying my good-bye, I veered off and headed for the windows and the corner view of the Loop they offered.

"I hope you don't mind," I said from over there. "I just had to take a look. Quite a sight."

"Yes, it is," he said. I could tell he wanted to get rid of me.

"I'll bet it's even better without all those clouds." Actually, they were so thick that all but the immediate surroundings were obscured. Even here on the eighteenth floor the height and size of the buildings close by made me feel slightly claustrophobic.

I turned and found Edwards up on his feet. Obviously my time was up. I strode over to him with my hand extended. I pumped his vigorously and thanked him.

"Really good of you to let me stop by like this," I said. "It's really been . . ."

My eye had strayed over to the pictures on his desk. They were just the ordinary family kind, except for one, a big, dramatic black-and-white of Clarissa Edwards in tennis dress, head back, racket poised, ready to smash one over the net. She looked terrific. It could've been Billie Jean King in that picture.

"Say," I exclaimed, "is that Mrs. Edwards? I heard from Ben she played tennis. But that's real pro form there. She must be good."

"She was a top-rated amateur for years and could certainly have gone pro," he said. There was some pride in his voice. "But of course"—he shrugged—"that wouldn't have been suitable."

A neat way of putting it, I thought. Too much money to play for money. Oh, he probably meant in other ways, too. But that was what came to mind.

"Well, tell her hello for me. She's quite a lady. I'm sure she's taking this pretty hard."

"Yes, of course," he said. He bowed his head, looked almost pious for a moment. "Her own flesh and blood."

"Give her my sympathy." I started for the door and called out, "Thanks again." Then I stopped at the door like I'd just remembered something. "By the way," I said, "have you heard from Lieutenant Shinahara of the Santa Monica Police?"

That jolted him just a little. "What? Why . . . why no, I haven't."

"You probably will." Very casually.

I left Roger Edwards's office with a smile on my face. I'd given him something to stew about.

Starting back down the hall, I hadn't gone far when I heard my name called. No, not called, whispered.

"Mr. Cervantes. Mr. Cervantes. Over here."

It was the older woman I'd figured to be Sterling's secretary. I went over to her and nodded a greeting. She held out an envelope to me.

"This would've gone out in the mail," she said. "You may as well take it with you."

I glanced across the aisle and saw that Edwards's secretary was away from her desk. I wondered why this woman was whispering. Anyway, I kept my voice down, too, as I said, "Well . . . thanks," and took the envelope.

"It's your payment," she said, "actually two checks. Mr. Sterling signed the first one before he, well . . . And I signed your expense check. I had power of attorney for this sort of thing."

"Well, really, thank you. I can sure use it, Mrs.—"

"Zelnick, Ina Zelnick. I was his secretary for years—nearly thirty. They're letting me go now; *he* is." A nod toward Edwards's office. "I knew about the little problem with that reward money on the expenses, but I thought rather than hold up the check and make you deal with the people you'd have to deal with, I'd just put it through. It's all there. I know he'd want me to do it this way."

"I think so. I sure hope so. It's very thoughtful of you, Mrs. Zelnick."

"My pleasure, Mr. Cervantes." Then she gave me a little nod and sent me on my way. Halfway down the aisle I turned to give her a wave. But she was back at her computer by then.

I tucked the envelope away and forgot about it.

I took the elevator down to the first-floor lobby of this grand building, and, because I wanted to have a look, I found somebody in a uniform I took to be official and asked where the trading floor was. I felt like I had to see it.

"Fourth floor, sir, but it's been closed for a couple of hours."

"Oh? When does it shut down?"

"Early afternoon; one-fifteen, sir."

"Thanks," I said, "I'll come by tomorrow morning and have a look."

"You do that, sir."

I took a step away and pulled a cigarette from my weekly pack. I put it between my lips and started to light up.

"I'm sorry, sir." It was the man in the blue uniform, suddenly there at my elbow. "I'll have to ask you to enjoy that outside. This is a no-smoking building."

"Really? The whole building? Well, all right. Sorry." And so I went outside and lit up. But I'd noticed that Roger Edwards certainly hadn't hesitated to smoke in his office. I wondered how long he could go on that trading floor, where your blood ran faster (according to him), without sneaking off for a cigarette. I wondered how much of what he'd recited to me—certainly more than I'd asked for—had really been the truth.

It had all but stopped raining. So, taking a fix on the nearby parking lot where I'd left my rented Taurus, I set off for a walk around the Loop area. I started down La Salle Street, which begins—or maybe ends—right there at the Board of Trade Building. Banks, insurance companies, the financial district.

Katy McGucken was as good as her word. On the way back to Twenty-sixth and California she had taken the scenic route, hugging the shore of Lake Michigan along a sort of parkway that took us past block after block of classy old apartment buildings, huge, the kind I thought they had only in New York. Then we drew away from that regal row and swung through an expanse of meadows and trees, bright Irish green in the rain. And from there, not so far ahead, you could see the towers of the Chicago skyline. Coming in on the Hollywood freeway or the 10, downtown L.A. can look pretty impressive, especially at dusk when the lights have just gone on, but it was nothing like this. Even with the rainclouds swirling around the tops of some of the buildings, hiding them, it was really quite a sight. And it remained quite a sight until we were down in among them. Then, except for one shorter open stretch of stores, office buildings, and hotels, with the skyline buildings behind them—"the Loop," said Ms. McGucken—there wasn't much to see except Soldier Field, where the Bears play ball, until we headed west on a freeway and got off near the felony courts and the county jail.

And now here I was, walking through it all, looking up and feeling the light rain about as often as I looked right or left, taking it all in just like a tourist. I had no map. I had no destination. I just wandered.

Where was it? Under the el tracks, along a street of stores, next to a big bookshop, as I remember. I'd been panhandled along the way by a few hard cases and a couple who seemed new at the job. But the guy who was waiting for me there had pulled back in an entryway where the pavement was dry; he was different in a couple of ways. First of all, he was on crutches, leaning up against a wall, just watching the crowd flow by. He was clean, neatly dressed in shabby clothes. I wouldn't have known he was panhandling at all, except when we made eye contact, he nodded, or rather brought his head down like he was pointing, and there at his feet was an upturned hat. He was Latino.

I dropped a dollar into his hat. *"¿Qué tal?"* I greeted him. *"¿Cómo le va?"*

"Está bien," he said. "I could do without the rain."

"It's about over."

"Yeah, but it's still wet. I usually sit down. Been on these crutches all day, seem like."

"How'd you get hurt?"

"Oh . . . industrial accident." He didn't volunteer any details. "I got covered for surgery and the hospital for it. But it's taking a long time to get back to what I was. They say I will. I was on a walker for a while before this, so I'm makin' progress."

"That's good, man."

"Yeah, well, *poco a poco,* you know?"

"You got a place to stay?"

He nodded. "I'm lucky. I share a place. My girlfriend's been carryin' me. I like to contribute something, though. That's why I'm out here." He looked around and shook his head unhappily. "Never been in a situation like this before, man. Main thing is I need a job. Been outta work since I left the hospital. Here . . ."

He dug into his jacket pocket, pulled out a folded sheet of paper, and handed it over to me. It was an employment résumé, intelligently organized and neatly typed; a good photocopy job, too. His name, David Delgado, was up top with a phone number and an address. I tried to get him to take it back.

"Look," I said, "I'm from out of town. You'd do better to give it to somebody else. I'll be leaving here in a few days, maybe, a week at the most."

"No, man, keep it," he insisted. "Maybe you'll meet somebody knows about a job. I just want to get a lot of those in circulation. I got hundreds more."

"Well . . ." I shrugged. "Okay."

"I could do desk work right now. Factory work, well, I gotta wait a while for that, you know? It's hard to be on my feet all day. Like today."

I gave him a serious nod. "I'll see what I can do." Then I dug a little deeper into my pocket and dropped a five in his hat. *"Ay te juacho,"* I said to him, Calo for "I'll be seeing you."

He laughed at that, gave me a thumbs up. "You know that crazy talk, bro? Where you from?"

"California," I said. "L.A."

"I'm from Texas. All us brownfaces are from Texas or California."

"Keep the faith."

"Hasta la fucking *vista."*

I left him, laughing.

That night, in the motel room, I went through all the stuff that Katy McGucken had given me. Although the envelope was fairly thick, there weren't really many documents inside. The coroner's report, lengthy in itself, took up most of the space. There were also the police report, Julio's statement, and the papers pertaining to booking and arraignment. Not all that much to work with.

Finally, after all the detail work, what the coroner's report said was that Benjamin Sterling's death had been caused by repeated blows to the back of the head by a blunt object. The immediate cause of death had come from repeated stress to the medulla oblongata, the brainstem—that part of the brain that automatically controls the routine functions of the body—breathing, heartbeat, and so on. In other words, I guess, the main power switch had been shut off. For my purposes, the real value of the coroner's report was that it fixed the time of death a little more precisely than before: it was now set between noon and 2 P.M.

As for the Julio Alviero file, it consisted of his account of the interrogation, which lasted from approximately 7:30 P.M. to 10:30 P.M.—poor Julio telling the same weak story over and over again for three hours, and his weak alibi. There was a list of the physical evidence, a list consisting of one item, that damned wallet again. Ah, but here was something: the car that Julio had driven that day, a 1990 Thunderbird, had been immediately impounded by the Chicago police. I wondered if they still had it. I bet they'd found it clean.

Julio's statement was just about what he had given me. There were a few more holes in it. He hadn't then been able to remember the name of that first place he'd been in, not even "Tito's something," not even the big Tecate beer sign that he'd told me about. That must have come after hours and hours of thinking and visualizing there in his cell. But there were, of course, great holes in it. Thank God there were. Thank God he'd stuck with it, weak as it was. It was now up to me to see what I could find to fill in the holes.

The booking and arraignment documents? Well, they didn't mean much to me. I'm no lawyer. Maybe I could get Katy McGucken to explain them to me. One thing that jumped out at me from his arraignment, though. Julio Alviero was charged with murder in the first degree. It hadn't happened for a while in the State of Illinois, but murder one was punishable by death by lethal injection or electrocution. The condemned man had his choice.

So, fighting my way through this material, going through parts of it twice and bits of it three times, I was only a little further ahead than I had been before I started. Still, I had an idea what I'd do the next day, and Katy McGucken had left a message at the motel switchboard to the effect that I could pick up "that picture I wanted" tomorrow from ten o'clock on. I'd be there, all right, and the time was right, too. It gave me the chance to do what I had in mind the next morning.

I looked at my watch. It was almost twelve, and that would make it almost ten back in Los Angeles. Which was about the time I'd planned to call Elaine. I wanted to give her more of an explanation than I'd managed with my hurried call from the airport. Thank God I'd remembered to make it. I don't remember exactly what I blurted into the receiver. I wasn't talking to her, anyway, but to her answering machine. I know I said (1) that I was really, really sorry but I couldn't make it that night for our date at Butterfield's; because (2) I was going to Chicago on very urgent business, and as a matter of fact I was at the airport right then; but (3) I'd call when I was settled in Chicago to let her know where I was staying and give her some idea of how long I'd be; and, finally (4) that I really, really wanted to see her just as soon as I got back.

But that's pretty exact, isn't it? Yeah, that's what I told her. Now I was hoping for something better, a conversation, a little back-and-forth maybe, something to warm me up a little and make this job for Julio seem a little less difficult than I knew it would be. I didn't get that. Instead I got her recorded voice. So just like she was my attorney Bernie, I dealt directly with her answering machine.

"Hi," I said, "this is Chico. I'm at the Ohio Inn in Chicago. Missing you. Hoped to talk. Maybe later." I hung up.

That was all I could come up with. I don't know why, probably disappointment at not finding her at home. She was probably over at Barney's talking to some other guy. Or maybe Florence Nightingale was out on another house call.

(Hey, watch it, Chico. Remember what you told yourself when Alicia walked? *Nobody owns anybody.* Cold comfort but true.)

Thinking about it, though, I had to laugh. The male ego was a wonderful thing to behold, wasn't it? Just day before yesterday I was thinking vile thoughts about her, angry at her for trying to psych me out. Now look at me. I was jealously guarding my rights to her. Some switch.

Partly to escape from all this, and partly, too, because the little book fascinated me, I reached over and picked up that copy of the *Tao Te Ching* I'd bought after my encounter with the ghost of Christmas past right there on Sunset. I found myself trying to remember who'd recommended it so strongly, and then it suddenly hit me—it was Elaine, months ago, during one of our first talks at Barney's. That put an interesting spin on it. Maybe she was trying to hand me some advice, indirectly, way back then.

Strange advice. Strange book. I'd always thought it must be one of those spooky Eastern religious texts, thought of Taoism as a religion. Neither idea was quite right. The *Tao Te Ching* seemed to be more a book of conduct, a book of, well, advice. And though it had the ring of authority, the advice it offered was the kind it was just about impossible for me, a guy in my line of work, to follow. I mean, you take this bit; I've just grabbed it out at random:

> True mastery can be gained
> By letting things go their own way.

It's just filled with little gems like that. You know what they used to say back in the sixties—"Go with the flow." I'd be a really great detective if I just let things happen, wouldn't I? No, a detective had to *make* things happen, go out, ask questions, get people to react, stir up some dust. Wasn't that what I was trying to do here?

17

Maybe the trading floor was on the fourth floor, but you couldn't get in unless you were accompanied by a member of the Board of Trade. Visitors like me were advised to go up to the fifth floor, where observation windows looked down on the action, and tours, explaining it all, left at regular intervals throughout the market's short day.

I didn't take the tour. I didn't need to. I got all I needed just by watching. Look, I'll admit I've never gazed upon the floor of the New York Stock Exchange, but what goes on there couldn't be as crazy, or as hectic, as what I witnessed down on the floor below.

Picture a big room, not quite the size of a high school gymnasium. In the middle of it all is a kind of control area a little like the control board in a TV studio, only larger. But the men and women who seem to be overseeing the show are behind computers, and behind them are display monitors like you see in airports, with names and numbers instead of flights and destinations scrolling through them. Up on the walls were other postings or maybe the same ones, I don't know, but the names and numbers were in green and red, bigger, and changing just as fast.

The real madness was there among the traders. There must have been over five hundred of them, all dressed in brightly colored, crazily patterned pull-on jackets, most of them young, some hardly more than kids. They were in huge groups clustered around men who were acting like auctioneers. Some of the traders were waving their arms frantically, giving hand signals, and yelling at the same time; you could hear the din of voices even through the thick glass of the observation windows. The rest of them were talking among themselves, turning to look at the numbers on the big board; then they, in turn, would raise their arms and start yelling. Even with sound diminished, even at some distance, the tension, the level of energy, was so high that you could sense it rising in waves from the trading circles. I guess your blood *would* run faster down there. It was kind of amazing that the buying and selling of commodities, as they called them, would be done in such a wild, haphazard way.

And this one below me, I found out, was just one of three trading floors operated by the Board of Trade. Here it was bonds, precious metals, and currency. I walked down through a series of corridors, past a tour group, and found myself up above the grain floor, where agricultural commodities were traded. It was a larger room set up about the same. There may have been as many traders here, maybe not, yet they were circulating, doing more talking back and forth, and the level of activity in the trading pits wasn't nearly as frantic as at the last stop. Maybe I'd hit on an off day, or maybe trading corn just wasn't as exciting as trading gold.

Asking at the information desk, I found out that the third trading floor, stock options, was actually located in another building. It could be reached ever so conveniently by a walkway over the street, five stories below. Well worth a visit, I was assured. But I figured, what the hell, I'd seen enough. I know nothing about the business of "puts" and "calls" and cared even less. So I took the escalator down, intending to pick up my car and head over to the Felony Courts Building. But when I hit the fourth floor and saw all those guys in their bright jackets moving in and out, I detoured and took a look.

There were turnstiles leading into and out of the restricted area that gave traders access to the three trading floors. Those were activated with plastic cards that those entering and leaving zipped through a groove up at the top. There was a guard sitting, bored, by the turnstiles, watching the ingoing and outcoming traffic with glazed eyes, just making sure, I guess, that nobody jumped the barrier; somehow I was sure that nobody ever had.

I went up to him and said, "I've got a question for you."

"What?" I'd roused him from who knows what daydream. "Oh, yeah, sure. I'll help you if I can."

"The cards those guys use to get in," I said, "are they individually marked?"

"Whatta ya mean?"

"Okay, that guy going through now." He was older and a little softer than the lean and hungry ones I'd seen yelling in the pits. "Now, did his card just let him through the turnstile, or was it coded to identify him personally?"

"You mean, like, it records that trader Joe Smith entered the restricted area at ten forty-eight and ten seconds. Like that?"

"Yeah, that's exactly what I mean."

"Nah." He shook his head emphatically. "I mean, there's a counter in the turnstile that keeps track of the volume, the basic number of people going in and out. But that's all it does. No individual ID."

"Oh, well . . . okay."

"They're working on it, though. I heard them talking about it just the other day. That's a long way off, I'll bet."

"Thanks." I started away, thought of something else, and came back. "One other thing. I was upstairs watching them waving their arms and shouting, and it looked to me like you could only take that so long without feeling some stress. Some of these guys have to be smokers, and this is a no-smoking building. If they want to grab a smoke and cool down, do they really go downstairs and stand in front for that?"

"Some do," he said. Then he gave me a wink. "But, you know, there's places they go, out-of-the-way corners and that. You go into the stairwell between the fourth and fifth floor, and sometimes there's so much cigarette smoke you can hardly find your way. They set off the smoke detectors there a couple of times."

"Well, again, thanks a lot."

"Any time, sir."

So I hopped back on the escalator and continued on down to the building lobby. It seemed to me then that Roger Edwards had an interesting sort of alibi that covered most of the time-of-death period given in the coroner's report. I'm sure he *had* been on the trading floor—maybe all three of them, would have been seen, wandered around, would have talked to people, may even have done a little arm waving himself. But in the constant tumult he could have been gone for a crucial hour and never have been missed—if he'd just gone back to the trading floor and been seen again later. The sleepy-eyed guard certainly couldn't say that Edwards had left for an hour and returned. It was an interesting alibi. It couldn't be proven absolutely, but neither could it be disproven.

Where was the murder weapon? What was the murder weapon?

Great old building. What was it? Art deco, I guess. The lobby fairly gleamed. I crossed the shining marble floor and was just about at the front entrance leading out to La Salle Street when I noticed a woman with a cardboard box in her arms struggling to get out through the door. I ran up and pulled it open for her.

"Thank you," she said, "Oh, Mr. Cervantes. Thank you very much."

It was the lady from upstairs, Sterling's secretary. "My pleasure, Mrs. . . ."

"Zelnick. Ina Zelnick. And it's Ms."

"Of course. I'm sorry." By now we were standing out in front of the building, she with her arms encircling the box, which was about two feet square. "Look," I said, "can I help you with that? Where are you headed?"

"Just off to the parking lot, right down Jackson a block. It'd be awfully nice if you would. It's not heavy, just awkward."

She handed it over to me and we started off together. She was right. It wasn't heavy. But my longer arms managed it much better. The box seemed to rattle lightly with each step I took.

"What's in here?" I asked, not really curious, just filling the space between us.

"A lifetime," she said. Then, correcting herself, "Oh, not really, just thirty years. Ha! Listen to me, *just* thirty years. Not my lifetime, but almost half of it. No gold watch, nothing. Just the odds and ends in that box."

"This is your last day then."

"No doubt about it. Oh, Mr. Edwards made that *perfectly* clear. Honestly, Mr. Cervantes, I can't imagine what I'll do tomorrow morning. I haven't set my alarm clock for years. I just automatically wake up at six and come down here. What am I going to do with the rest of my life?"

"Get another job, maybe?"

"You're joking. At my age?"

"Well . . . how're you fixed? Is money going to be a problem? Excuse me for asking."

"No, I won't be out on the street like the rest of those poor people. I'd say I'm very nicely taken care of, thanks to Mr. Sterling's profit sharing. He really was a good man. It's all so . . . shabby. The way he died, and now this."

We walked on. I glanced over at her. I had the feeling there was something she wanted to say.

Finally, "Mr. Cervantes, I expected you to call last night."

That confused me. "Really? You did?"

"Yes, I put a note in with your checks asking you to call. I was just sure you'd open up the envelope to check the amounts, and you'd see the note."

I laughed at that. "Well, all I can say, Ms. Zelnick, is that you inspire confidence. The envelope's right here in my pocket, unopened. What was it you wanted to tell me?"

"Well, what I wanted to say was this." She stopped suddenly right there on the sidewalk. She wanted to make sure that I gave her my full attention. I stepped over to one side to let a couple pass by. "You know, my desk is quite close to Mr. Edwards's office, and the door was open all that time you were in there. I won't say I was eavesdropping, but I heard it all. I got the sense that you were playing the fool with him." She was sharp. "But Mr. Cervantes, I want you to know he lied to you."

"How, specifically, did he lie, Ms. Zelnick?"

"When he told you he was on the trading floor all day—the trading day, I mean. I won't say he wasn't down there part of the time. I remember him telling Barbara—you remember her, his secretary—that if anything important came up she was to send a runner down. How *she* would know what was important, I can't guess. But then he came back just before noon. Mr. Sterling left around eleven-thirty. The two of them were hardly speaking after that big row they had."

"What big row?"

"Oh, *well,* right after Mr. Sterling came back from California the two of them really got into it. Mr. Sterling's door was closed, but you could hear him all around the office. But I couldn't figure out what it was all about. He was shouting about the Japanese, and gangsters, the war, and there was some Japanese word he said a number of times."

"Would the word be *Yakuza?*"

"That's it! Or that sounds like it, anyway."

"Okay," I said, "I'm sorry I interrupted. Go on, please."

"Oh, well, all right, of course. Where was I? Oh yes, Mr. Edwards came back just before noon—oh, to make some phone calls, I suppose, because he was on the phone quite a bit, but he was smoking, too. He does that all the time, you know. It's against the law to smoke in the building, did you know that?"

"Yes. I'd heard."

"He doesn't care. He just goes right ahead and does it anyway."

My arms were getting tired—not from the weight of the box, just sort of cramped from holding it. I edged us forward a little. "Could we . . . ?"

"Oh, sure." We started walking again. She came very close as we moved along and practically whispered the rest of it. "Anyway, he was there in his office when he got a call from his wife—you know, Mr. Sterling's daughter, Clarissa."

"How did you know it was her?"

"Oh, that Barbara, she practically bellowed it out, the way she does everything. 'Mrs. Edwards on line one'—you know, so the whole office can hear. Well, he couldn't have talked to her for more than a minute, when the next thing I knew he was out of the office like a shot, heading down the hall. And that was the last I saw of him for over an hour."

"When would you say this was? Right around noon? Just a little after?"

She thought about it. "No," she said, "it was later than that—about a quarter after twelve, maybe twenty after, something like that. But when he came back, I can guarantee you he hadn't been down on the trading floor."

"How can you be so sure, Ms. Zelnick?"

"Why, because he'd left without a raincoat or an umbrella or anything. You knew it rained the day all that happened, don't you?"

I nodded.

"Well, Mr. Edwards was absolutely soaked."

"Would you be willing to make a statement about this, Ms. Zelnick? Just what you've told me."

"Oh, I certainly would, Mr. Cervantes." A smile spread over her face. "With *pleasure.*"

I could tell she meant that.

The picture of Julio I had tucked away in my pocket may not have looked much like him, but under the circumstances, it was the best I could do. I'd never seen him look as sad, as defeated, as he did in that photograph, which had been taken when he was booked for the murder of Benjamin Sterling. The lines around his eyes and mouth, the slump in his cheeks made him look twenty years older. Would he even be recognized when I showed the picture around the barrio? Well, it was a chance we had to take.

Who was this "we"? Just Julio and me, I guess. Katy McGucken might be cheering me on from the sidelines, but she was still a spectator, not a player. She'd attached a note to the photo left at the felony courts reception desk, asking me to meet her at Gene's, a bar on California, at six o'clock. She wanted to discuss "the Japanese connection." I was wishing then I hadn't brought it up. But having brought it up, I now had to throw cold water on it.

A check of the phone book had told me that the only Tito's in the 312 area code was Tito's Hacienda at Eighteenth and Blue Island Avenue. That had to be the place that Julio had started on his little binge. That was where I was headed. The neighborhood turned out to be just about as he had described it—a barrio. Nothing like Whittier Boulevard or even lower Sunset, but there were the usual *grocerías, droguerías,* and *carnecerías,* and there, too, was an unlit neon sign proclaiming Tito's Hacienda up high and in the window, Cerveza Tecate.

I parked the car, fed the meter, and went inside. Tito's was more than a bar. It was a nightclub, open in the daytime to pull in business from the neighborhood. It was pretty well filled, considering it was just a little before noon. They start early in Chicago.

Settling down on a barstool, I ordered a Dos Equis, and as I waited for the bartender to come back with it, I prepared my pitch, thinking it through, setting my limits.

He came back. I paid for the beer. No keep-the-change twenty-dollar tip this time. I wasn't buying information. I was establishing an alibi.

I pulled the picture out and put it on the bar in front of him.

"Have you seen this guy?"

"Here, you mean?" The bartender looked at me almost suspiciously.

"Yeah," I said, "here. In the last few days."

"You a cop? Let's see your badge."

"I'm not a cop. I'm a friend of his." That was stretching it a little.

Reluctantly, he bent over the bar and studied the picture. I had attracted a little unwanted attention on either side. The *viejo* on my left and the lush on my right swiveled in my direction and stared.

"Take a good look," I said to the bartender. "It's not a good picture."

Finally the bartender finished studying the photo and said, "If you're such a good friend of his, why don' you know where he is? Why're you lookin' for him? What's this all about?"

"I know where he is," I said. "He's in Cook County Jail. You look at that picture, you know it, too."

He shrugged, gave me a crooked smile and said, "So?"

"So," I said, "I'm looking for a specific day and time of day."

It finally dawned on him. "Oh, you makin' an alibi for him, huh? Okay." He looked back down at the picture. "He was in here."

"Yeah, but when?"

He put a hand to his head and closed his eyes in concentration. "It ain' easy," he said, his eyes still shut. "So many peoples come in here." Maybe he was fishing for a payoff. But no: "Let me take the picture, okay? I show Rosa, the waitress. He was givin' her a hard time. She should remember."

I nodded, and he picked up the photo from the bar.

"Cook County Jail," said the *viejo* next to me, *"estaba allí—dos veces."* He held up two fingers.

"¿A dentro?"

He laughed, an old man's mean cackle. *"Sí, a dentro. Es solamente así que se conece."*

"¿Es malo, no?"

"Todos carceles son malos. Esto es lo peor."

I looked beyond him to the end of the bar and saw the bartender talking to the waitress, pointing at me. She looked up from the picture, which she now held in her hand. There was brief eye contact between us. Then she turned back to the bartender, nodded, and started down the bar toward me.

The old man greeted her. "Hi, Rosa, you beautiful, like always."

She gave him a pat on the shoulder and planted herself between him and me. She thrust out a hip and rested a hand on it. It looked like this was going to be a confrontation.

"So," she said, "you're a friend of his?"

"More or less."

"You from L.A., too?"

"That's right."

"You gonna make me a movie star then, too? You guys from L.A., you all hand out the same shit. What's worse, you think we gonna fall for it!"

Behind her the *viejo* let out with his cackle again. Oh, he was enjoying this.

"I guess Julio didn't make such a good impression on you."

"Oh, he made an impression, all right. He was a first-class pain in the ass. I mean that literally, believe me. He pinched and patted my ass so much he musta thought it belonged to him." She stopped suddenly, like there was a lot more she could say but wanted to get this over with. "What's he up for? Why does he need an alibi?"

"Murder," I said. "Murder One."

At that, she laughed. *"Him?* You're makin' a joke, right?"

"No, he's at Twenty-sixth and California even as we speak, and that's the charge."

"Listen, mister, we get some heavy dudes in here—quiet, dignified, real macho, you know? They could do the big one. In high school, I knew gang guys could do it—one for sure did it, I practically saw it myself. But this guy . . . what's his name?"

"Julio," I said, "Julio Alviero."

"That's right, now I remember, Julio." She handed the picture back to me. "Not him, no way could he have done it—how?"

"He's supposed to have beaten a guy to death."

"Well, I won't even laugh at that. It's ridiculous." Then she looked me straight in the eye and said, "He was here on Monday. He came in about noon, and he staggered out of here a little after one—one-fifteen at the latest."

"You *sure* about his time of departure?"

"Yeah, because I made José cut him off. Isn't that right, José?"

The bartender was suddenly right there with us. "Tha's right, Rosa. I remember now. You said, 'Don't serve him. He's gettin' to be a pain in the ass.' "

She smiled at me. "My words exactly. He'd also had six straight double shots of Cuervo Gold in about an hour. No, Mr. L.A., the best I can do for you is noon to one-fifteen at the outside."

"I'll settle for that," I said. "You be willing to tell that to the cops?"

"Any time. The name is Rosa Quiñones. I work the day shift here every day but Sunday. Get me any time then."

With that, she spun on one stiletto heel and, with her tray tucked under her arm, went off to check on her three tables. I wrote her name down in my little notebook.

"That Rosa," said the bartender, "she's somethin', ain' she?"

"*¡Qué maravilla!*" said the *viejo*.

This time I had to wait for Julio. It had taken a phone call from Katy McGucken, but eventually he was delivered up from the depths of Cook County Jail, blinking, looking curiously right and left. Finally, he focused on me and headed over.

He settled in the chair opposite me. The glass was all that separated us.

"How you doin', homeboy? With the . . . investigation, I mean. You makin' any progress?"

"Some," I said. "I've got you at Tito's Hacienda from noon to one-fifteen—that's all. Not two hours, like you thought."

"Well, I was feelin' no pain. I coulda been wrong about how long I was there."

"Let's agree you were wrong about that. Okay, I've also got you at the coffeeshop—Café Ole, it's called, down at the end of the block from Tito's. The manager said you came in about four o'clock and just drank coffee for about an hour. He remembers you pretty well because they had to clean up the men's room after you threw up in there. He says you left a little after five, only minutes maybe."

"Sounds right."

"*Sounds right?*" I exploded. "Well, where were you between one-fifteen and four o'clock? I was all around that block showing your picture and I couldn't get a response out of anybody. Where *were* you?"

He hung his head. For a moment I thought he was going to

beat his chest and give me a mea culpa. But no: "I think I was in the car," he said.

"In the *car?*"

"Yeah, I think I went in there to take a little nap."

"But you don't remember? You're not sure?"

"No, man, I tol' you, I really woke up in that coffeeshop." He shook his head, remembering. "I really felt *terrible.*"

"Then what makes you think you were in the car all that time?"

"Well, I got this picture in my mind, I couldn't get the car door open. And then . . . yeah, there was something else."

"What was the something else?"

"Fockin' parking ticket. I guess I was at a meter or something."

"You mean there was a parking ticket on the windshield of that car of Sterling's you drove down there?"

"Musta been. When I came out of it there in the coffeeshop I had one in my hand. I don' think I pulled it off anybody else's windshield."

My mind was racing. This looked like the break we needed. "Think now, Julio, what did you do with the ticket?"

"What did I do with it? I threw the fockin' thing away." He thought a moment. "Yeah, I wadded it up and threw it down on the floor. I figured, let Sterling take care of it, something like that. My head wasn't too clear right then, let me tell you."

"And it went out with the trash."

"Yeah, I guess so. Why?"

I felt like the window of opportunity had just slammed right down on my fingers. But wait a minute. When you write a ticket, you also write out a stub, or you keep a copy, however they do it here in Chicago. But somebody, somewhere in the city bureaucracy had a piece of paper with all the information that was on that ticket. Or maybe it was on the computer by now. Whatever. It might be hard to get at, but the information *was* available.

"Why didn't you tell me about this before, Julio?"

He looked at me like I was nuts. "What's the matter with you, homeboy? I'm lookin' at murder one, and I'm supposed to worry about a parking ticket?"

"Listen to me, if the time the ticket was issued is right, then you're covered for Sterling's time of death. You've got an alibi. Not airtight, maybe, but solid. We look at the city's copy of the ticket, we don't need what you threw away. Maybe it'll work out." Then I added, to reassure him, "Probably."

Julio sat, looking at me, gradually deflating. At last, he said, "Oh."

We sat a moment, regarding each other through the wire.

"That wasn't what I came to see you about, though," I said.

"Okay. What?"

"You mentioned a woman from El Salvador." I paged back through the notebook I'd been keeping. "Josefina. You said she might know something about your driver's license, how it got into that wallet."

"Tha's right."

"What's her last name?"

"I was afraid you ask me that. Let's see, let's see." He lowered his head into his hands as he thought. "It was one of those names, it means something in Spanish, you know?" But then he raised his head and looked at me oddly. "Why don' you just call up the house and ask for Josefina?"

"No, I don't think that's such a good idea. If she does know as much as you think she does, then they'll keep her under wraps, at least for a while. I'm going to have to come on with a scam, and for a scam to work I've got to have her last name."

"Molinero," said Julio.

"What?"

"Molinero," he repeated, "that's her name. I just thought of it while you were talkin'."

"Okay," I said, "that works. Molino—windmill, Molinero—miller. Josephine Miller." I wrote it down in the notebook.

Julio gave me a curious smile. "You gotta translate into Ingles to make it real? You somethin' else, you know that, homeboy?"

He had me there, and he knew it. I wasn't going to argue with him. Instead, "What's the best way to get through to her, assuming she won't answer the phone."

"She won't," said Julio. "That's Mrs. Tiller's job. She runs the house."

"What should I say?"

"Let's see, let's see. She's always waitin' to hear from her family—down there, you know? So maybe you could say you're, like, a *primo,* a cousin, you know?"

"Might work."

Then, thinking about it a bit more, he frowned. "I don't know, though. Maybe something else is better."

"Why? What do you mean? What's the matter?"

"Can you do an accent?"

"You mean a Salvadoran accent?"

"Salvadorean. Mex'can, anything. You can speak Spanish to Josefina. It's better that way. But you gotta come up with some kinda accent to fool Mrs. Tiller. An' you speak English more like an Anglo than any homeboy I ever knew."

Gene's was a big, noisy bar just down from the courthouse. Great location. Lawyers love to drink. There must have been forty or fifty of them scattered in the booths and at the tables and the bar. And they were still coming in as I arrived.

I spotted Katy McGucken at the bar with an older man. He looked big, massive, even folded up as he was on the barstool. Maybe he was her boss; maybe they were talking business. I hesitated, not quite sure whether I should interrupt them or not. Then she saw me and waved me over.

"Hi, Chico," she said brightly. "You get what you wanted from Mr. Alviero?"

"More than I expected," I said.

"I'd like you to meet my father."

His feet were on the floor the moment he straightened his legs. He *was* big—about six feet four or five, and anywhere from two hundred fifty to three hundred pounds. Up close, he didn't look much like a lawyer—rougher somehow and tougher. He was well-dressed. The lightweight worsted he wore must have been hand tailored. It draped over his considerable bulk as he stood and made it seem less than it was.

"Very pleased to meet you, sir."

"Likewise."

The hand that wrapped around mine as we shook was just as big as I expected, but softer, and the pressure it offered was just a gentle squeeze.

"Well, Mr. Cervantes, I've heard a lot about you from Katy here." His voice was gruff, but there was a look of amusement in his blue eyes. "And I must say she has great professional respect for you." He reached over and gave her shoulder a playful squeeze.

"Come on, Daddy."

"But still, being her father, and naturally taking an interest in her career, I made inquiries in Los Angeles. And I'm pleased to tell you that you came through with flying colors, so to speak." Maybe he *was* a lawyer. He talked like one.

"Nothing bad," he continued. "And that man in Santa Monica you referred Katy to, Shina . . ."

"Shinahara," I put in.

"That's right, Lieutenant Shinahara. He had some very good things to say about you." He hesitated, then added with a smile, "That's unusual. I suppose I don't have to tell you that yours is not a profession greatly respected in most police departments."

"I guess you could say that, yes."

"So," he said with a little sigh. "I'm here to more or less read you your rights. Simply put, as a private investigator licensed in the State of California, you have none in Illinois. You are here as any private citizen might be, an interested party, a friend of the accused. I hope you understand that."

I nodded. "That's how I've been operating so far."

"Good, and now that you've been informed, that's how you'll continue to operate. Am I correct?"

"You're correct."

"Now, I don't suppose you would have done anything so foolish as to bring a firearm with you into the city of Chicago?"

"Oh, no, I . . ."

It took about two seconds for his big hands to slide down the trunk of my body, along my legs to my ankles. He ended up giving me a pat on the back, the small of my back. I'd never been frisked so quickly, so thoroughly, so inconspicuously in my life. I looked around. He hadn't attracted any attention at all. He'd made it look like he was just bending down to pick up something from the floor. I was impressed.

"Just checking," he said with a wink.

"I understand," I said. Glancing at his daughter, I saw her staring off in another direction, her face a high color, nearly as red as her hair.

"Now, I'm confident you'll stay in bounds, Mr. Cervantes, but even so, it's possible you'll run into difficulty. What you're up to could prove embarrassing to the lads out in Ravenswood Precinct. That, for reasons we don't have to go into here, would suit me fine. But here . . ." He reached into the chest pocket of his suit jacket, pulled out a business card, and handed it over. "Should anything come up, feel free to call me. I'm sure I'll be able to straighten things out."

"Uh . . . thank you . . . very much . . . sir."

"Don't mention it." He pumped my hand again. "A pleasure to meet you, sir. Katy, don't forget to call your mother about Sunday."

"I will, Daddy." Almost inaudible.

"Good-bye, then." He moved with surprising swiftness through the bar crowd to the door. I climbed up on the barstool he'd left vacant and held the card up to read it. CAPTAIN JOHN MCGUCKEN, CHIEF OF DETECTIVES, CHICAGO POLICE DEPARTMENT. All at once I understood a lot better just how Chicago works. I tucked the card away into my wallet.

"I'm *really* sorry about that." She was still red faced.

"Don't be. I thought he was terrific."

"He *is* terrific. And he really is trying to help me. But my God, he didn't have to *frisk* you."

"Best I've ever seen it done."

"Well, he's had a lot of practice. Look, let me buy you a drink, okay?"

"I thought the Public Defender's Office didn't have a place in its budget for private detectives."

"It doesn't. This is personal humiliation I'm working off. It's got nothing to do with business."

So I had the drink. After all the running around I'd done that day, that Cuervo Gold on the rocks tasted pretty good. As I sipped away, I told Katy McGucken all about Tito's Hacienda and Rosa Quinones's offer to swear to Julio's presence there from noon to 1:15.

"Is she on the level?" Katy asked. "Is she a good witness?"

"Absolutely. No bullshit to her at all."

"Okay. That leaves us with forty-five minutes to fill. Theoretically, he could get from Eighteenth and Blue Island to Wilson and Broadway and still do the deed."

"Right. I had no luck anyplace, except the coffeeshop at the end of the block. The manager clocks him in there about four o'clock, which is just about what Julio told me."

"Big gap."

"Right. *But,* when I talked to Julio about this just now, he tells me he thinks he passed out in the car."

"Oh, great."

"No, wait. He got a parking ticket. He threw it away, but it's gotta be on some computer someplace. Depending on when it was issued, it might just fill up the missing forty-five minutes. Is there any way you could check on that?"

She thought a moment. "Sure," she said. "The PD's office has a couple of 'investigators'—retired cops is what they are. They're not much good for anything, but they're perfect for this. I'll get one of them on it tomorrow."

"Good," I said, "there's no way a 'private citizen' could dig into that source. But now you tell me, what did you get from your talk with Lieutenant Shinahara?"

"Well . . . it was interesting."

"I'll bet it was."

"And, like you said, sexy. I mean, the Yakuza, wow!"

"But?"

"But it doesn't really seem to pertain here, does it?"

Hallelujah! I wasn't going to have to talk her out of it after all, it seemed.

"No, it doesn't," I said. "Look, I took it seriously. As a matter of fact, in the only phone conversation I had with Benjamin Sterling before he died—and it turned out to be only an hour or two before he died—I told him to get a bodyguard, hire a local guy, because I thought he was in danger. And I thought he was in danger from the Yakuza. But then, when I heard *how* he died, it didn't tally. They—I mean, the Yakuza—they don't work like that. If he'd died by poisoned dart—that I would've believed. Death by ceremonial sword, you bet! Even a nine-millimeter to the back of the head, I would have figured it was silenced—okay, I could believe that, too. Those guys deal in stealth. Beaten to death? Never, not those guys. No way."

"That's funny," said Katy. "That was exactly Lieutenant Shinahara's reaction. When I described the cause of death, he started to fade. I mean, in the beginning, when I told him Sterling was dead, he tried not to show it, but I could tell he was excited. What he told me immediately was that Sterling had 'greatly insulted' a kind of capo in the organization. But then I told him *how*, and he kind of lost interest. What he said, finally, was that even though you'd promised not to talk about any of this, you were right to tell me what you did, because it was obviously pertinent to our investigation. But that you were especially right in letting him tell it because there was a lot more involved in the case. He couldn't talk about it, he said, because it was going federal."

"Did he say anything about the two attempts on Sterling in Santa Monica?"

"No. I should've asked him about that, too, right?" Katy looked crestfallen, like she'd let me down or something.

"Not necessarily. I don't know how Shinahara feels about them, but I was thinking it over on the plane out here, and I don't even buy them as Yakuza contracts."

"Why not?"

"Because the subcontractor was black, and the Yakuza is not an equal opportunity employer."

"Like the Mafia, huh?"

"Whatever. Look, I don't know how to put this in a nice way, but the Japanese don't think much of black people—American black people, in particular."

"Oh, come on, Chico. I read in the papers about those huge crowds they draw in Japan—I mean, the singers like Whitney Houston and Natalie Cole, and all the jazz people. Buddy Guy even does tours in Japan, and he's just local here in Chicago."

"Yeah, but that's Japanese kids—under thirty, anyway, what they used to call the youth culture. You also read in the paper how some big shot in the government is making off-the-cuff remarks blaming the economic decline—*our* economic decline— on our black population. You know—drugs, welfare, the whole bit."

"Isn't that just one guy? Some conservative?"

"More than one. The Japanese are basically very conservative people. The Yakuza is a very conservative organization. Look, I admit I'm doing a lot of theorizing here, and theories are mostly bullshit. All I can say is that it just doesn't feel right to me. Just say I've got my doubts."

"So, as far as you're concerned, what happened here is tied to what happened in L.A.?"

"Yes, but not with the Yakuza."

A couple of minutes before, she had signaled for another round. The drinks came just then. Katy waited until the bartender had gone, then leaned close.

"Okay," she said, almost in a whisper, "what's your theory of the crime? Who do you like for the perp?"

"Don't do that," I said.

"Don't do what?"

"Don't whisper. You'll have everybody listening in."

They were two deep at the bar now. There was a lot of talk, but it was all at an ordinary conversational level. She looked around, took it all in, and nodded.

"Okay," she said in a normal tone of voice. "According to you, who's the perpetrator?"

"Roger Edwards."

She thought a moment. "I guess you'll have to remind me who he is."

"That's just it," I said. He's Sterling's son-in-law. The cops didn't even take a formal statement from him. He told them who Julio Alviero was, and they went off to pick him up. I went in and saw Edwards, and he gave me some kind of bullshit alibi, like he was trying it out on me, in case the police should ever get around to questioning him." Then I added, "He was also the only one I'm sure knew where we were staying that last night in Santa Monica when the guy delivered the bomb."

"How do you know the alibi was bullshit?"

That was when I told her about my conversation with Ina Zelnick.

Katy was impressed—but reasonable. "You're sure he hasn't given that alibi of his to the police?"

"Pretty sure. Could you check on it?"

"In the discovery process, maybe. But presumably the investigation has continued since then."

"Ha!"

"I know what you mean. Once the cops get their hands on physical evidence like that driver's license . . . But what about motive?"

"Ms. Zelnick said that Edwards and Sterling had a big row in the office a couple of days before Sterling was killed. It was probably about the Yakuza deal. Roger Edwards brought that to him."

"So we're back to the Yakuza again."

She'd spotted a weak point. "Yeah, more or less," I said. "But the two of them never got along. I got that straight from Sterling back in California. I've got the feeling, though, it was also tied up to this factory deal of Sterling's that Julio was involved in. There's also the cui bono factor. Edwards only stood to gain by Sterling's death."

"So the trick is to get Edwards to give his alibi to the cops so this woman, Mrs. . . ."

"Zelnick."

"So Mrs. Zelnick can shoot holes in it."

"Yeah, I guess so. I'm going after some more stuff tomorrow. How much do we have to get to spring Julio?"

"You mean charges dropped?"

"Well . . . yeah."

"A lot more than this, I'm afraid. Even if his alibi checks out, we'd need something to impugn the physical evidence. We'd have to hand the prosecutor a new suspect."

"That's what I'm going after."

"But with the kind of stuff I'm getting from you, listen, I can make a great trial out of this one. I'll go for a jury. Might even get him off."

My problem was, I wanted to be two places at once. It was about eight o'clock, and there I was on my bed in the motel room, postponing dinner until I'd thought my way out of the dilemma.

I'd made up my mind that no matter what, I was going to get to Josefina Molinero and talk to her alone. What I would say, what kind of pressure I could put on her, I wasn't sure. But I knew that talking to her about Julio's driver's license was the logical next step, and I meant to take it.

But I also knew I wanted that skid row hotel on Wilson Avenue canvassed. It wasn't the kind of job I looked forward to. It would probably take all day to do the job right, and maybe longer. I hadn't been aware when I came here that I was on limited time, but evidently I was. Even though I knew I could hold out here quite a while on credit cards, and in a pinch I might even be able to cash one of the Sterling checks at the Chicago bank where it had been issued, it wasn't money, or the lack of it, that was pulling me back to L.A. I didn't know what it was.

Curious about that, I dialed my own number and did the little secret code number that plays back the messages on my machine. Not much at first—a surveillance from a divorce lawyer I probably wouldn't have taken anyway, and a guy who wanted to sell me homeowner's insurance. Then, loud and clear, into my ear, came the voice of Elaine Norgaard.

"Hi, Chico, it's me, Elaine. I don't know about you, man. Here today, off to Chicago tomorrow, what's a girl supposed to think? But yeah, sure, I got your message from the airport, and naturally I was disappointed but naturally I'll survive. I know it must have been important, or you wouldn't have left town the way you did. My instincts tell me you're a pretty dependable guy. Anyway, I called your machine to let you know that I'll be out of town a few days myself. I took some time off at the Shop—long overdue—and I'm heading down to Rosarita Beach. Ever been there? Nice place to go and flake out, especially in the middle of the week when it's empty. I'm going down there to think you over. If that sounds like a threat, it's not. I'm taking William Butler Yeats with me for company—don't worry, I'll take good care of him—so my thoughts will probably all be good. I guess I'm using up a lot of tape, so I'd better wind this up. I'll be back Sunday, and I hope to hear from you then—either from Chicago or, better yet, from down the block. Guess that's all. 'Bye."

If I could have replayed it, I would have—probably half a dozen times. Talk about a letter from home! The sound of her voice, what she had to say—they were all I needed to pull me back home, weren't they?

Maybe not *all* I needed, no. Because the rest of the tape was filled with requests, then increasingly frantic pleas from Casimir that I call him, either at the studio or at home. He helpfully supplied both numbers. I looked at my watch. A little after eight here meant it was a little after six there. I picked up the phone from the nightstand and dialed him at the studio.

No secretary. He was alone. "Hello." Gruffly. "Urbanski."

"Hi, Casimir. It's Chico."

"*Chico!* Where you been? I called and called."

"It's not where I've been. It's where I am. I'm in Chicago. Just got your messages on my machine."

"Jeez, Chicago! Whatta ya doin' there?"

"Some work. It took me out of town the day after I saw you."

"I knew it wasn't like you to leave me hanging. Something big, I swear, or I wouldn't bother you."

"I figured. Go ahead. Tell me about it."

"Oh, jeez, well, look, that certain guy who's been causing us a lotta grief? He, like, wants to make a deal, says it's in our interest, all that shit. He won't say what it is, but he wants to have a meeting on it on Saturday. Only he says if you and Alicia ain't there, then the meeting's off, the deal's off, and he's going right to the gossip sheets with what he's got." He hesitated, then added, "I think he means it."

"What does he want me for? Maybe he wants me to give him a hand."

There was silence at the other end, then, "That ain't funny, Chico."

"No, I guess it wasn't." I thought a moment. "Look, what if I'm stuck here? I don't know if I'll be done by then."

"The old man says he'll make it worth your while."

"Old man Toller? He's back? Who told him?"

"I did."

"Good for you. He's the only one of that bunch with any sense. He wants me there?"

"Yeah, real bad. He asks me two, three times a day if I heard from you yet."

I sighed. "Okay, what time's the meeting called for?"

"Late. Six o'clock in the evening. I don't know what he's got up his mind."

"Look, Casimir, no promises, but I'll try to be there."

"Thanks, Chico. You say so, I know you'll try."

I gave him my phone number at the motel and said good-bye. Then I sat there thinking for about a minute. What should have occurred to me before finally hit me. I went over to the chair where I'd draped my jacket and dug out the papers from the inside left pocket that I'd accumulated in the last couple of days. Among them I found what I was looking for—the neatly typed, well-organized résumé of David Delgado.

I went back to the phone then and punched out the number displayed at the top of the sheet.

18

He was waiting for me, dressed for the occasion in tie and jacket, standing just outside the apartment building when I pulled up. David Delgado moved pretty well on his crutches. He seemed to use them more for assistance than support as he traveled along the cement walkway to the street. Balancing beside the car, he gathered the crutches together, pulled the door open wide, and dropped lightly into the seat beside me. He reached across with his hand and shook mine.

"Glad to see you, man," he said. "Thanks again for remembering me."

He pulled the crutches in beside him.

"Don't mention it," I said. "You can put those in the back, if you want to."

Leaning far over to the outside, he grabbed the handle of the door and pulled it shut.

"No," he said, "I'd rather keep them right here beside me. That way it's easier when I get out."

"Got you." I slipped the Taurus into drive and pulled away.

His address was close to Wilson Avenue, but it was west of where the crummy section began. Maybe Delgado wasn't homeless—and thanks to his girlfriend for that—but he was jobless. I'd looked at his résumé a little more carefully after I talked to him on the phone, and it had given me an interesting picture of him. He'd gone through junior college down in Texas, gotten a certificate for teaching English as a foreign language along the way, worked his way up from a loading dock to a desk job in personnel farther north in St. Louis, and then on to Chicago, where he'd been employed at a number of places, one to three years at a time—inside work, outside work—ending finally last fall at a transformer factory where he listed his job title as shift foreman. The résumé described a steady rise to a toehold in the middle class. The American Dream. But now he'd lost his grip and had tumbled back down. How far down? Only time and luck would tell.

"I never did anything like this before," he said to me as we approached our destination. "You understand that, I hope."

I shrugged. "It's not so hard. You worked in personnel before, didn't you? I saw it on your résumé."

"That's right. Sure."

"Interviewing people?"

"That's right, mostly Spanish-speaking, though."

"Same principles, probably. You try to establish a connection, put them at ease. There are certain things you want to find out, certain questions you want answered, but you don't hit them over the head with them right away. On the other hand, you don't spend an hour talking to each one you interview. Be friendly, be polite, get your questions in, get out."

"You make it sound pretty easy."

"I wouldn't've asked you to try it if I didn't think you could handle it."

I halted the car with my left turn signal on at the narrow street Katy McGucken had taken me down a couple of days before—Clifton, the sign said. A little after nine on a weekday morning, traffic across Broadway should have been pretty light. But still they came. I pointed through the windshield at the building with its crumbling, unscrubbed exterior.

"That's the place," I said. "I want to take you around the back, though."

The break in traffic came. I took the left, made an immediate right down the alley, and saw, as I'd expected, that the yellow bans were down and the cop was gone. I drove to the end of the alley and turned left into the truck yard behind the factory building. Then I turned the car around and switched off the motor. I dug into my pocket and pulled out my pack of dried-out cigarettes. I offered one to Delgado.

He shook his head. "I gave it up. Too expensive."

I lit one, took a puff, then pointed with it to the rear of the old factory building.

"Now, over there, on your side, up on that truck dock—that's where the murder took place. Man about seventy years old hit repeatedly from behind with a heavy metal object. Fell flat, right in front of those double doors. Any questions so far?"

"Yeah, when did this happen?"

"That's important. You've got your eye on the ball. It happened Monday, last Monday, between twelve and a little before two. That's when the coroner's report places the time of death. A couple of guys from the street found the body about two o'clock when they came behind here. And this is important, too; they came back here to get out of the rain. I understand it was raining hard that day."

"Monday?" he said. "You bet it was."

"Okay." I pointed at the rear of the hotel. "You take a look there, and you'll see that most of those back windows have a view down here on the yard. What we're interested in are the people who live in the back. You don't have to go to every room in the hotel. Just the ones in back will be fine. Ask them if they saw anything, anything at all, back here between twelve and two. It wasn't so long ago they wouldn't remember. If they saw a car, try to get the make and color. If they saw two cars, make and color. If they saw more than that, then what exactly did they see? Any questions now?"

He thought a moment. "No, that about covers it, doesn't it?"

I started the car again, drove out of the truck yard, turned down the alley and onto Clifton. I found a place to park not too far from the hotel.

"I'm going in with you to win the hearts and minds," I said.

We got out of the car and set off together. I didn't have to slow down for him at all. He kept right up.

"You brought that notebook along, like I asked?"

"Right in my pocket," he said.

"Take notes, and take names, even if they're Joe Does; names and room numbers."

"Got it."

We turned the corner onto Wilson. I noticed, not for the first time, that there was a bar, an old-fashioned gin mill, right on the ground floor of the hotel, next to the entrance. A couple of hard cases came out of the hotel. We stepped back to let them pass, and we watched them disappear into the bar. I held Delgado back, fished a twenty out of my pocket, and handed it over to him.

"Consider this an advance against expenses," I said. "If all else fails, go into the bar and ask questions. It's okay to buy drinks, but don't give *any* money to potential witnesses, right?"

"Right."

I led the way into the hotel. Delgado followed close behind. At the end of a long corridor, behind a wire cage, was the desk clerk, a man in his fifties—thin, balding, his face creased with lines.

"How do you do, sir?" I said in my most confident manner. "My name is Anthony Cervantes, and this is my associate, David Delgado."

He looked back and forth between the two of us in a puzzled way and nodded.

"With your permission, Mr. Delgado would like to question some of your guests regarding that unfortunate incident of last Monday."

His face remained blank for a moment. Finally: "Oh, you mean the *murder!*"

"Exactly."

"You cops?"

"No, we are not."

"Reporters?"

226

"No, we are simply citizens interested in seeing justice done. Now, I realize this may cause you some inconvenience. Perhaps this would ease that somewhat."

I pushed a fifty-dollar bill halfway through the gap in the wire.

He grabbed at it and grinned cooperatively. "Oh, sure, sure. You can talk to anybody you want to up there. Any of them give you a hard time, just tell them to take it up with Chester at the desk. That's me. Yessir, you just go right ahead. But no rough stuff, right?"

"Absolutely not. Oh, just one more thing. If it's necessary, we'd like to have the chance to use the phone—your phone."

"Sure, sure, no problem."

I took the number and walked Delgado to the elevator. "Just been fixed," Chester called after us.

"Okay," I said, "go get 'em, David. I'll check in with you either by phone or just come by and get you. I don't know how long I'll be. The only way you can get a message to me would be by leaving word at my motel. You've got that number. I'll call in there at least once. Anything else?"

He shook his head.

"You're on your own." I turned away to go.

"Hey," said Delgado, "just one thing."

He was about to get into the elevator. He held the door wedged open with a crutch.

"What's that?"

"You said not to pay anybody, just buy drinks. But you slipped that guy fifty. How come?"

"I said, don't pay any *potential witnesses*. Chester never leaves his cage. He couldn't have seen a thing."

Delgado considered it for a moment. "I see what you mean."

He stepped inside and pulled the crutch in after him. The doors slammed shut. He was on his way.

I've never been to New England, but I've seen pictures. Lake Wood, Illinois, was my idea of what a New England town might look like. Oh, I know those houses out in the East are a lot older, but you take a guy from California like me, and everything built before 1920 looks old to him.

Driving in from the west down what the map told me was Deercross Road, I passed the Public Safety Building—fire station and cop house, all in one flat-roofed building—and the local high school, then found my way into the center of town. It was laid out along railroad tracks, which ran north to south. That surprised me a little until I found out, waiting around town, that it was an Amtrak commuter line that ran direct into the Loop. No slow freights through Lake Wood.

Across from the railroad station was a little artsy-craftsy shopping area, with a discreet sign announcing it as The Olde Market Place. I turned in there and found a parking place along the horseshoe drive that led in and out of the development. Judging from the new condition of the uniform brick construction and the style of the oh-so-tasteful mother-and-child fountain in the middle of it all, olde, in the case of Market Place, seemed to mean no more than ten or twenty years olde. But if not weathered and worn, it *looked* old in the New England style, a little piece of Connecticut right here on the shore of Lake Michigan.

I got out of the car and wandered around the boutiques, looking for a public phone. It wasn't until I got into a sort of side annex, Market Place Court, that I spotted one in front of a restaurant, where inside they seemed to be preparing lackadaisically for the lunch trade. I searched out change, deposited it, and took a deep breath. Since I'd spent long minutes on the drive out here rehearsing what I would say and how I would say it, I felt fairly confident, about as confident as an actor with opening-night jitters.

I listened to the phone ring at the other end of the line. Then somebody picked up.

"Yes? Hello? Edwards residence."

Edwards? Had I copied out the wrong number from my case report?

I must have hesitated a little too long, for the woman spoke up again impatiently: "Who's there, please?"

I went into my act: *"Sí, sí,* yes. Escuse me, please. Ees there

228

now a Señorita Josefina Molinero?" I figured that was about as thick as I could lay it on and still be understood.

"Yes, yes, she's around here somewhere. Who's this?"

"I . . . I yam 'er *primo*, uh, *cómo se dice,* 'er cohsin."

"From her country, are you?" She seemed to have softened a little. "Well, she's always anxious to get news from home. I'll see if I can't find her. You just hold on now."

"Okay. T'ank you."

If Julio was there I would've given him the finger. Did he think I couldn't fool some housekeeper? I was, among my many other talents, an actor—an untapped reservoir there.

But that "Edwards residence" thing worried me. What was that all about?

I waited—more than a minute, less than five, just holding on. Then at last I heard a thud and rattle at the other end that said someone was picking up the phone.

"¿Hallo, sí? ¿Quién es?" It was a sweet voice, but sad and a little distrustful, too—the voice of a victim.

All of a sudden I wasn't sure quite how I ought to approach her. I'd halfway planned to come on strong, kind of confront her on the phone. But at just that moment she sounded like she'd been confronted so often, pushed around, abused, that I thought maybe a more novel approach might be better. Why not try . . . sincerity?

"Señorita Molinero," I began in Spanish, "I am not your cousin. I am not related to you. My name is Antonio Cervantes. But I am a friend of someone who thinks of you as a friend. His name is Julio Alviero."

I heard a sharp intake of breath at the other end. But I kept right on talking.

"At this moment he sits in jail. This is no joking matter. For him, it is a matter of life or death. Julio is almost without hope. *Almost.* He said to me, 'Antonio, you must talk to Josefina Molinero. She may know something that can save me. Josefina is my only hope.' Señorita, do you hear me? Are you listening?"

For a long moment, there was nothing, just the sound of her breathing. Then came a husky, muffled *"Sí."*

And so I pressed on. "Josefina is my only hope. He said that to me. Now, you and I both know him—I have known him since school in Los Angeles. We know that he has his faults, but we know also that he could not do this thing he is accused of. You agree?"

"Yes," she said. "I mean, no, he is not able. It is not in his nature."

"Julio has told me about you. He told me that you are from El Salvador. Have you lost members of your family in the war, the *terrorismo?*"

"Yes, my brother. They took him away in the night."

"You would have saved him if you could?"

"Of course!"

"But that wasn't possible. Now, however, you have the opportunity to save Julio. He believes that only you can do that. I ask only that you meet with me and talk."

Silence, then, "They will not permit me. The señora keeps me like a prisoner here."

"The señora? Which señora is that?"

"The daughter. I think I should not say her name. Someone may hear. She is the one who . . ." Josefina broke off. I was afraid I might lose her. But no. "There is just one possibility. I do the shopping. They drive me to the market. They pick me up. Maybe you could meet me at the Jewel Store."

"Certainly! When?"

"I can't say exactly. It's up to them. Not until after lunch, though. If you could wait there . . ."

"I'll wait. Until I see you, Señorita."

"Until I see you."

When at last I hung up, I felt breathless, spent emotionally. Even though what I said to her was not wholly truthful, it was sincere. I'd spoken with such intensity, and in those few minutes achieved such intimacy with her, that it was almost as if I'd been making love on the telephone. I was sweating. That didn't surprise me. There were tears in my eyes. That surprised me.

I went back to the car, got inside, and lit up another cigarette. It was my second of the day and the last in the pack, so dry that it flared when I put the match to it. It tasted bad, but that didn't matter. What *was* important was that I have something to do, something to occupy me, as I got hold of myself again. I remember distinctly that sitting there in the car I thought for the first time, really, that this thing might break open today, after all.

But I had people to meet, promises to keep, and hours to go before I'd sleep. I jabbed out the cigarette in the ashtray, started the car, and completed the circuit on that horseshoe drive. I turned north on Northern Avenue, drove a couple of blocks, and located the Jewel Store. There was a nice, big parking lot in front of it. I could wait in there when the time came. I looked at my watch. It was only a little after eleven. According to what Josefina Molinero had told me, I had some time to kill, so I decided to check out that address on Sherman Road that was by now well fixed in my mind.

Lake Wood continued to look a lot like my picture of New England as I drove along Sheridan Road, looking for the house. No, it really seemed even more like it than before—the curving road, the college, the dense woods half hiding the houses. For a guy like me, Mexican-American, from California, it was like touring another country. It all felt so foreign to me. I could have been in France or Germany for any sense of belonging I felt.

Along the way, addresses were anywhere from difficult to impossible to read. But somehow I knew I was getting closer to my destination. Somehow, too, I knew when I'd arrived.

The house was up on a rise above the road. I know I've seen bigger places—the Toller mansion off Benedict Canyon would probably exceed this one in floor space—but I'd never seen one as grand. The architect who had designed it, whoever he might have been, had mixed styles shamelessly, maybe at the insistence of the founding father who had built it sometime back around the turn of the century. There were big silolike turrets on either side but also columns supporting a long roof overhanging the entrance. The surprising thing was that it all somehow seemed to work. It was solid, sort of like a castle, but graceful, too. Until last Monday it had belonged to Benjamin Sterling.

I had pulled over to the side of the road for a longer look.

There was a circular drive that led up to the colonnaded entrance from an open gate and low stone walls at road level. In front of the house a white Mercedes sedan was parked, but there was no one to be seen. That suited me just fine. I didn't want to be noticed.

But too late. I had been noticed, all right. I didn't see the police car until just moments before it pulled up behind me. The dome-lights weren't flashing, but I knew this was no time to throw my car into drive and simply take off. That would certainly be considered suspicious. And so, with one eye on the rearview mirror, watching the cop climb out of his car, I grabbed the map off the seat beside me and hastily spread it open between my lap and the steering wheel.

Staring down at the map, turning it this way and that, I managed to look surprised when the expected knock came on the window next to me. I rolled it down.

"You gave me quite a start, officer."

"Your driver's license please, sir." He'd probably practiced that great stone face of his in front of a mirror.

Carefully, so as not to give him any sudden worry, I reached into the inside pocket of my jacket and pulled out my wallet with two fingers.

"Anything wrong?" I asked.

"Remove the driver's license from your wallet."

I had every intention of doing that anyway. I didn't want him to see my p.i. license. It came out easily. He took it from me and studied it, frowning his disapproval.

"California, huh?" He held onto the license. "I noticed the Hertz sticker on the bumper. This is a rented car?"

This guy was bucking for detective.

"Well, yes," I said, "that's right."

"May I see the rental papers, please?"

Again, slowly enough to satisfy him, I reached into the other side of my jacket and pulled out the Hertz papers.

"Remove them from the jacket, please."

Only then would he accept them. He held up the license and

compared the information on the two. Then, with a stern nod, he handed them back.

"What was your reason for stopping here, sir?"

"To look at the map," I said. "I seem to have gotten lost—or at least turned around."

He looked down at it, unfolded before me. "Well, you won't find anything on that side. You're looking at the map of Chicago there."

"That explains my problem then." I said it like I meant it and began the awkward work of turning over the open map. But then I stopped. "Maybe you can help me, officer. How do I get onto Deercross Road?"

Almost reluctantly, he provided directions that I really didn't need. But I thanked him anyway, reassembled rental papers and wallet, and tucked them away. In the side mirror, I watched him trudge back to his patrol car. Then I slipped the Taurus into drive and pulled away at a modest speed.

For a while I thought he was going to stay on my tail all the way out of town. But no, after the first two turns, he left me on my own. Even so, I continued on toward Deercross, keeping a close watch in the rearview. Finally, assured I had been left alone, I made my way back to Northern Avenue and the parking lot of the Jewel Store.

Burying the car deep in the middle of it, I climbed out and began looking for a public phone. There was one just about where you might expect, right next to the entrance. It was then not quite noon. I dug out Katy McGucken's card and punched out her phone number. It turned out to be a long-distance call—not surprising; I was miles out of the city—so I put it on my charge card and waited.

"Ah, Chico," she said at the sound of my voice, "I've got good news for you."

"That's what I want to hear."

"I asked Mr. Ryan to handle this. He's the best we've got around here. Anyway, he really came through. He got the number of the Sterling car off the impound sheet—you know, when the forensic guys went over it for blood and didn't find any. So with that, he went right into the computer bank and pulled the ticket out. Chico, it was issued at one forty-two that day— physically impossible, under the best traffic conditions, to have made a round-trip to Wilson Avenue and back to Eighteenth."

"Great!"

"Not only that, but Mr. Ryan went out looking for the parking violations officer who issued the ticket. He found her, and she told him she remembered writing one there on Blue Island about that time because there was a guy stretched out on the front seat. She'd heard once about a ticket being issued with a dead man at the wheel—"

"Yeah, that happened in L.A."

"Anyway, she wanted to make sure this guy wasn't dead. So she opened up the car door and gave him a shake. He stirred. She smelled the booze. So she locked the door and shut it."

Of course—Julio's drunken impression that he'd had trouble getting the door open. It was locked. That's why.

"That's it, Chico! His alibi checks out to the last detail. I'd like to see any prosecutor try to put a hole in it." Katy sounded excited, like she was on the chase or something. "But what about you? Where are you? What're you up to?"

"Well," I said, "I've got somebody checking out that hotel on Wilson. You remember? The one that had a back view to the loading dock?"

"I remember."

"And right now I'm out in Lake Wood."

"Lake Wood?"

Briefly, I told her about Josefina Molinero, that she had something to say, and that I was going to meet her here at this supermarket, of all places.

"You want me to come out there?"

"No, I'm going to bring her to you, if I can talk her into it."

"Good luck," Katy said. "I won't budge from here until I see you, or at least hear from you."

We left it at that.

I thought a moment, then dialed my motel and asked the desk man if I had any messages.

"Uh, well, yes sir, you do," he said. "I took it myself about eleven-thirty. It's pretty strange, though."

"What is it? Who's it from?"

"It's from David, that's how he gave his name. And it's just one word—'Bingo.' You understand that? He left a number, though. You want it?"

It was the number of the hotel on Wilson. I called it and got Chester. Announcing myself as Mr. Cervantes, I asked if my associate, Mr. Delgado, was available.

"Oh, sure thing. He's right here."

There was a brief wrangle between them as Delgado demanded privacy. Most of what was said came in loud and clear through the receiver. Finally, Delgado said, "Here, Chester, add this to your collection and take a walk."

There was silence for a moment, then, "It's David, Chico. Okay to talk now."

"What did you do? Give him the twenty just to get rid of him?"

"Nah, he isn't worth it. I gave him ten of my own. *Maricón*. Anyway, I got somebody for you. Good witness, old guy, has to stay in a wheelchair, so he spends most of the time right there in the room. I hit it off with him right away because of the crutches. Says he saw it all, even though he didn't see it real clear because of the rain and the distance, and the fact he didn't know what he was watching until after it happened."

"All right, what was it he saw?"

"Part of it you're not going to believe."

"Try me."

"Well, right around noon, this car shows up—white, foreign job, he's not sure of the make, but big. It parks up close to the loading dock and nobody gets out for a while. It's raining hard, see. Then two people get out and run up on the loading dock. They talk for a while there out of the rain. Then one of them runs back to the car and opens up the trunk, grabs out an umbrella but doesn't open it up, just runs back up to the loading dock with it still wrapped up. It turns out there's some kind of metal bar inside it—sounded like it'd be a tire iron or a lug wrench. Anyway, when the one guy has his back turned, out it comes, and he gets it over the back of the head—*bam!* He goes down, but he gets it about five or six more times. Now, this is the part you're not going to believe."

"Go ahead."

"The one who did it, who knocked the guy over the head—it was a *woman!* It had to be a woman or a guy in drag—you know, skirt, long hair, wearing heels, and shorter than the man, too. The old guy's sure it was a woman. Can you believe it?"

I felt disorganized. "I have to," I said at last. My mind was racing. Why had I resisted the idea so? Why had I decided to ignore facts, clues?

"Chico, you still there?"

"Yeah," I said, "I'm still here. Listen, how come the old guy didn't come forward with this? What's his excuse?"

"All I can say is, he's a *very* old guy, well up in his eighties, crippled, lives on a disability pension, and I think he was just afraid to deal with the system."

"Well, stay with him. Keep him company. It may be hours before I get there. Don't let him change his mind."

"Right. His name is Frank Avery, and he's in room twenty-seven." As I was writing it down, Delgado said, "Jesus, Chico . . ."

"What is it?"

"I hope I never get like that—old, alone, in a tiny little room. Afraid."

"We all hope that, David. We all hope that."

I had been sitting in the rental car for about an hour right there in the middle of the parking lot. It was a good location in a couple of ways. First of all, it gave me a good view of the entrance to the supermarket. True enough, I hadn't seen a picture of Josefina, hadn't even gotten a proper description of her from Julio, but I had a good idea how she would look. In my mind's eye I pictured her as young, in her twenties, but maybe a little older; she'd have that Central American look—short, high-waisted, round-faced, looking more Indian than Spanish. Since I hadn't seen anyone, male or female, who seemed even mildly Latino since I drove into town, it seemed to me she wouldn't be very hard to spot.

Not only did I have a clear sight line to the entrance, I was also pretty well hidden. The cars around me came and went. But when they came, they tucked in close to mine, and when they went, it was never very long until another came. So I sat and watched and waited.

As I did, I kept asking myself why I had ignored Clarissa Edwards for so long, really looked the other way until I couldn't do that any longer. David Delgado and the old man—what was his name?—Frank Avery forced me to look at her and at my own stubborn stupidity.

Maybe it was part of the old macho thing again. Maybe it all tracked back to that. Men want to believe in women. We tell ourselves that even if they're not all saints, at least they're not capable of the kind of violence we deal in all the time—gang stuff, wars, the kind of casual nastiness that's referred to as domestic violence, the aggressiveness we bring into dealing with other men. Yet occasionally, not often, we see it explode in women, and when we do, we're always surprised, just as I was surprised by what Delgado had reported.

And, well, I was sort of disappointed, too. Because, after all, I'd been with her those two days as we searched for her father. Looking back, knowing what I did now, I'd have to say that her attitude at various times was sort of inappropriate. She was friendly, almost chipper, when she came to L.A. to make that trip out to the county morgue to identify the body she'd been told was her father's. As she stayed on to look for him with me, she seemed to get sullen. Her reaction to the story of Ben Sterling at Tarawa was just plain wrong. She only brightened when he turned up again—so they could have another go at him, I guess. But still, I rode with her, I talked with her, and she seemed to me then to be honestly concerned for him. How wrong I was; *dishonestly* concerned was more like it.

What drove me nuts as I thought back about it all was that that rookie detective, that Neanderthal Lorenzen had read it almost right in the beginning. The only thing he got wrong was me as the hit man. She'd hired me as the finger man: my job was to find Benjamin Sterling, get him into plain sight, and make a good target of him.

Sterling himself had said that she had the killer instinct that her husband lacked. She was an athlete and obviously had the strength to beat a man to death. And the cui bono factor pointed to her just as directly as it did to Roger. Her father could have dissipated millions of the family fortune in the manufacture of fishing reels.

So there I was, sitting behind the wheel of the car, staring out the windshield, asking myself pretty basic questions about my ability to see what now seemed pretty obvious, reflecting upon my shortcomings in the line of work I'd chosen too long ago to quit.

Then, surprising me a little, a white Mercedes four-door sedan appeared in front of the entrance to the store. Somehow, I hadn't expected *that* car. It stopped, stayed only long enough to let off a passenger, a woman. She turned and watched the car pull away, giving me a clear look at her. Although she was a good twenty-five or thirty yards away and not quite the woman I had pictured, everything I saw told me she must be Josefina—and besides, she'd arrived in a white Mercedes just like the one I'd seen parked in front of the Sterling mansion. Where was it? I turned, stretched, and managed to catch a glimpse of it exiting the parking lot, turning right, and disappearing down Northern Avenue. Reassured, I jumped out of the car, looked for Josefina again, and found her gone. I had taken my eyes off her for only seconds. She had to be inside the store, but just to make certain, I made a careful sweep of the lot, looking for her and keeping my eye open for a white Mercedes that might have U-turned back into view. Satisfied, I shut the door of the Taurus and set out with an energetic stride for the entrance of the Jewel Store.

By the time I made it inside, I was pumped, ready, the adrenaline pulsing into my system like fuel into a supercharged engine.

I didn't bother with a shopping cart. I didn't even reach over to grab a basket as I hurried past a pile of them. No need to pose as a shopper. I was there to find Josefina Molinero and get her out of there just as quickly as I could.

238
—

Up one aisle and down another. Maybe I should have really searched the lot. Maybe she had ducked around the corner just to get out of sight.

But no, she was over there in the produce section, picking over heads of lettuce. Calmly? No, she was flashing looks left and right. Her shopping cart was empty. Josefina was taller than I'd expected and looked more Spanish than Indian. Was it her? Yes. She looked scared.

When she saw me, her eyes widened. She stood there, a floppy head of butter lettuce the size of a softball in her hand, and then she nodded. I walked over to her.

"Señorita Molinero?"

"Sí."

"Antonio Cervantes. *Su servidor.*" Keep it proper.

Automatically, she put her hand forward and shook mine, an odd gesture under the circumstances but no more so than my greeting. "*Mucho gusto,*" she said, completing the formalities. Thinking about this later, I decided that we weren't just showing that we were of good family and knew how to conduct ourselves, we were trying to inspire, and demonstrating, a degree of trust.

I continued in Spanish: "We must leave this place."

"*Tengo miedo,*" she said. I am afraid.

"You have reason to be," I said. "I have just heard—"

"I think she knows—Señora Edwards. She drove me here. That is not the usual thing. She repeated the threat."

"What is the threat? Tell me."

"She says, if I tell that I took Julio's driver's license and gave it to her, she will have me sent back to El Salvador."

"You did take it then?"

"Yes, of course. Again the threat. If I do not get the driver's license or something with his name and picture, she would denounce me to the Migra. I have no green card, no documents. I am very illegal. I did not know how she would use it. *Dios mio,* her own father!"

Through all this, she had held that head of lettuce out between us, gesturing with it. By now it was squeezed down to baseball size. I took it from her and put it back on the pile.

"If you go back in that house, no matter what you do, she will probably kill you," I said.

"I know. She is moving in—she and her husband. She says the house is hers now. I am afraid to be alone with her. I am afraid to eat, for poison. I am afraid." She was quietly flustered, near tears.

"Bueno, vamonós."

I took her by the elbow, meeting no resistance, and led her out of the produce section and to the front of the store. Then, holding tight to her hand, I moved us through the shortest checkout line, begging pardon as I went, calling to the checker that an emergency had come up. In another moment we were outside, moving at a fast trot for the Taurus.

"Where are we going?" she panted beside me.

"To Chicago, to the police, to Julio's lawyer." I hadn't quite decided yet.

But she accepted it and got in the car. I shut the door after her and was moving around to the driver's side. Then, just about in front of the car, I noticed a couple about 10 yards away going toward the store. They were noticing me. Suddenly the woman pointed in my direction and screamed. The man started toward me. Puzzled, trying to figure this out, I turned around.

And there was Clare Edwards poised to deliver a forehand smash to my head.

I leaped back. Whatever she had in her right hand—black, metal—whizzed down past my head.

But I lost my balance. I found myself on my back on the blacktop, looking up at her as she stumbled slightly, then bent to deliver another blow. As it came down—there was a clang on the pavement—I rolled twice to my right and scrambled to my feet.

She came at me, feet wide apart, holding the tire iron with a two-handed grip. She swung a long, looping one at my middle. I might have dodged it completely, but when I fell back I came up against the fender of the car next to mine, so that it just grazed my jacket and shirt.

But now she moved in, sure that she had me pinned down against the fender of that car. I caught my first glimpse of her face.

Where I expected to see anger, rage, what I saw instead was nothing. The expression she wore was no expression at all, cold and impersonal, a competitor's face.

Then here it came, another forehand smash, except that as her arm moved forward, a hand grasped her wrist at the top of the arc, and though that didn't stop the downward sweep completely, it slowed her, shortened the swing, brought it under control. I was able to dance away from the car.

The hand belonged to the man who had moved to help me when the woman with him screamed. They struggled, the two of them, Clare holding her own for the first moment or two by the strength of—what? her conviction, I guess. But he was taller, stronger, and had leverage on her, and he was forcing her down.

But suddenly she broke away and delivered him a sharp thwack on the left arm between the shoulder and the elbow. That's when I grabbed her from behind and circled my hands under her upraised arms and clasped my fingers together behind her neck. I forced her head down and down in a full nelson as she flailed wildly with the tire iron. I had her just about bent double when my rescuer stepped forward and wrenched the weapon from her hand and stepped back with it.

"Are you all right?" I called to him. "That was quite a knock she gave you on the arm."

"I'm not sure," he said. "It's numb. I can move it pretty well, though, so I guess it's not broken."

She was mumbling something from down below. I couldn't understand her.

"Mister, I don't know how to thank you."

"She would've killed you," he said. There was something close to awe in his voice. "I had to do something."

She was twisting beneath me. "You think I should let her go?"

He studied her for a moment, considering the question. "No," he said, "not until the cops come. My wife called in a nine-one-one."

We had gathered quite a crowd around us. Most simply gawked. One or two brave souls stepped forward, bent down, and attempted to identify the woman I held in such an awkward posture in front of me. They were friendly, for the most part. If the latecomers objected to what they saw, they soon had the situation explained to them by those who had witnessed the action. My rescuer's wife had rejoined him. As they talked together, he rubbed his arm carefully, probably trying to get some feeling back into it. I spotted Josefina back a bit from the edge of the crowd. She smiled at me. I winked at her.

Then a siren came close and closer. It shut off as the police car turned into the Jewel parking lot. The crowd parted, and the cruiser rolled to a stop just about two car lengths away. I released Clare Edwards, and she crumpled to the pavement. I stepped back from her.

The cop who jumped out of the car was the same one who had given me a rousting outside Sterling's place. He drew his gun, a great big Colt Python .357, and pointed it straight at me, two-handed.

"Don't you move, mister," he snarled at me.

"Hey, wait a minute," said my rescuer, waving the tire iron at the cop. "You better listen to what happened."

"Shut up, you. I'll take care of this."

"Listen . . ."

The cop threw him a fierce look. Clare Edwards was just then struggling to her feet.

"You all right, Mrs. Edwards? This is the guy, the same guy I called you about who was hanging around out in front of your father's house. You know him?"

"Uh . . . yes, yes. He's . . . a . . . hit man from Los Angeles. He tried to murder my father out there. He tried to murder me just now."

"This is *ridiculous!*" screamed my friend.

There were cries of "No! No!" from the crowd and a couple of boos. She looked around angrily, but the noise continued.

"You hear that?" Waving the tire iron again. "She hit me with this thing. There are lots of witnesses to what happened. Aren't you going to take names at least?"

"Why don't you just go home, mister? All the rest of you people, get out of here. The fun's over." He waved his .357

around a bit carelessly. There were more boos from the crowd. "Mrs. Edwards, I'm afraid I'm going to have to ask you to come to the station so we can get this guy booked and in a holding cell."

"Certainly, officer." She strode off, chin up, toward that white Mercedes, wherever it was. The cop turned and watched her go.

Up to that time, of course, I'd had nothing to say. But I beckoned to Josefina, who now looked a bit fearful. Before the cop could stop me, I had my wallet out and out of it took Katy McGucken's card. I gave the card and the car keys to her.

"Can you drive?" I asked in Spanish.

She nodded.

"Take the car. Go to this lawyer in Chicago. Tell her what you told me. That man"—pointing to my good samaritan—"will tell you how to get there." I hoped he knew the way.

The cop pushed her away roughly. "What'd you give her?"

"My car keys. I told her to drive it to the station. You're impounding it, aren't you?"

That seemed to confuse him. "Uh . . . yeah. Probably."

"Well, she's saving you some trouble."

"I . . . *guess* that's all right. You seem to know a lot about this, buddy. How come?"

"I put in ten years on the LAPD."

"A rogue cop, huh? Well, how about that."

The crowd was beginning to disperse. Cars pulled away. The cop didn't seem to notice that one of them was the Taurus and Josefina was at the wheel. He jammed the gun in my back—not smart, even with the safety on—and pushed me toward the patrol car.

As he threw the rear door open, I turned to him and said, "What's the matter? No cuffs? You haven't read me my rights. You haven't arrested me yet. What's the charge?"

"Get in."

"You're just taking me in for questioning. Isn't that right?"

"Get in."

I got in.

All the way to the Public Safety Building I had to listen to him tell me through the wire mesh separating front seat from back just what terrific people the Edwardses were—"leading citizens" he called them—and how it wasn't smart to mess with them. But I could tell that he was beginning to worry about his performance back at the parking lot, and worry even more about the mess that awaited him at the station.

"Ever been sued for false arrest?" I asked him.

"Just shut up, will you?"

"But what do I know? I'm just an ex-cop who hasn't been arrested yet. Right?"

"Shut up."

As soon as we stepped into the station, going in from the rear through the motor pool, I turned to him and asked, politely, "May I use the telephone?"

"What a minute. I'll have to ask."

He left me with nobody particularly in charge. A dispatcher looked at me questioningly, and all I could do was shrug. He shrugged back.

The cop who'd brought me in returned and took me forward into a large room with a number of desks, all but a couple of them empty.

"You can use any of the phones here," he said. "Just don't take too long. I or one of the detectives will be questioning you pretty soon. If you're calling a lawyer, better get him out here."

I didn't call a lawyer. I called John McGucken.

First I told him what David Delgado got from Frank Avery in that hotel on Wilson Avenue. Did I know the address? The room the witness was in? I gave him the information I had written down.

Then I told him about Josefina Molinero and her part in it all—the threat to denounce her to Immigration, our meeting in the supermarket, and the attack in the parking lot.

"Wait a minute," said McGucken. "This woman, Sterling's daughter, she went after you with a tire iron in broad daylight with people around?"

"That's just what she did."

"Well, what happened?"

I gave him, well, not exactly a play-by-play account but a brief, colorful narrative that handed full credit to my rescuer. Then I told him that I had sent Josefina off in the rental car to Twenty-sixth and California to give a statement on what she knew.

"Good," he said. "But how come you didn't go with her? Where are you now?"

"I'm at the Lake Wood police station."

"How come? To swear out a complaint against Sterling's daughter?"

"No, she's supposed to swear out a complaint against me. It's sort of complicated," I said. "But I'd hate to see her just walk out of here at this point—a witness that places her at the scene, Josefina's story. This is the time to bag her. If she walks, I'm not sure what she'd do."

"What do you mean?"

"I think she's unstable."

"Unstable? You mean nuts?"

"She's acting like it, isn't she? I mean, the way she went after me in front of all those people." I hesitated. "So look, if you could get somebody out here to put the squeeze on her, it'd really be helpful."

"I'll see what I can do about that. Stall them." With that, McGucken said an abrupt good-bye and hung up.

I had been on the telephone so long that I wondered why nobody at the station had pulled me off. But then, when I got up front where all the talk was coming from, I understood. Clare Edwards was there, holding forth, and the cop from the parking lot was sitting there at a computer, hanging on her every word, taking it all down. She was really in her element, recovered completely from her little setback. What she had to say was pure fiction, of course—ah, but the *way* she said it! Her delivery was commanding, her voice confident. You could tell just listening that she was one of Lake Wood's leading citizens, and the cop at the computer was clearly one of the citizens she led.

Unfortunately, like most in his profession, the officer's skill at the keyboard was strictly of the two-finger variety. And so it was necessary, from time to time, for him to interrupt her performance and ask her to repeat things, or give him just a moment to get it down just the way she said it.

I took advantage of one of these brief silences. "Great story, Mrs. Edwards," I said. "You got any witnesses to back it up?"

The cop glared at me. "You keep quiet! You'll have your chance to make a statement."

"Well, I *hope* you won't believe anything *he* has to say." She threw me the kind of look she might have given a nasty piece of garbage on the sidewalk. "He's one of that Mexican gang who . . ." She trailed off in confusion. "Wait a minute. Where is she?"

"Where is who, Mrs. Edwards?" The cop seemed puzzled.

"The girl, what's-her-name, Josefina. Didn't you arrest her, too?"

"Well, no. She was supposed to drive this guy's car over from the Jewel Store." He turned to me. "Why isn't she here yet?"

"I don't know," I replied, all innocence. "Maybe she lost her way."

"But you've *got* to get her!" She was suddenly screaming at the cop. "She's one of them. And I'll tell you something else. She's an *illegal immigrant!* You should arrest her for that. Get her out of the country *fast*. They're pouring in on us. You've got to do something about it."

"Uh, Mrs. Edwards, that's a federal matter. Maybe we should just stick to what happened in the parking lot."

"I've got something to say about that."

It was the guy who had wrestled the tire iron away from Clare Edwards. And he was still carrying it with him. He had just come through the door with his wife in time to hear that last bit.

"Oh, it's you again," said the cop.

"You're damned right it's me again. I would have been here sooner," he said, turning to me, "but we stopped off at the doctor's so he could have a look at this arm of mine."

"There are broken capillaries," said his wife, "and some nerve damage."

"Which means," he said, "that I'm going to have a hell of a

bruise, and I won't really feel anything in that arm for a while. Not broken, though."

"Well, you'll have to wait your turn," the cop said.

"Gladly."

The two of them moved over closer to me. "Didn't exactly get your name in all the commotion," he whispered and offered his hand.

"Antonio Cervantes," I said, "from Los Angeles. Words cannot express, et cetera, et cetera."

As we shook hands, he said, "Bob Epstein, and this is my wife, Leah. We just moved here from Evanston."

"We *thought* it'd be a nice, quiet place to live." She rolled her eyes expressively.

The three of us listened as Clare Edwards continued with her recitation. No, now it was more on the order of a paranoiac tirade. She began on the Mexican conspiracy, the brown menace from the South, and somehow she managed to include the Jews in it, too. On and on the woman went.

Even the cop looked uncomfortable. "Uh, Mrs. Edwards, if you could just get on to what happened when this guy attacked you in the parking lot."

"I'm coming to that."

Epstein leaned close and whispered, "Is she sane?"

"Well, it's sort of open to doubt. She used that tire iron you've got in your hand to murder her father."

"She *what?*" The tire iron jumped in his hand. He almost dropped it. Bob and Leah Epstein exchanged looks.

"Mister," said the cop, "if you're not quiet, I'm going to have to ask you and your wife to step outside." Then he went back to his two-fingered tapping on the computer keyboard.

He whispered in my ear again: "I noticed hair and dried gunk on it. I thought maybe she'd connected with you." He held it up for my inspection. It was just as he said. She hadn't even bothered to wash it off.

"Don't let her have it, whatever you do," I whispered back to him. "If we can just stall her here long enough, some cops may be coming out from Chicago to take her in for questioning."

"What's that?" Epstein asked with a sly smile. "You're asking a lawyer to stall? Just watch this."

He handed the tire iron to his wife, who took it only reluctantly. Then he stepped forward, and in a deeper tone than I'd heard from him before then, he said, "There's something I'd like to interject at this point."

"Isn't he wonderful?" whispered Leah Epstein.

In a way, that's just what he was. There wasn't much to what he said in the way of content—there didn't need to be—but his style was really terrific. Essentially, it was a courtroom performance. There he was, about thirty-five, tall and lean, dressed for a day off in jeans and checked shirt, and he began trying the case right there in front of the cop—no, *pitching* it to him, electing him judge. The cop was annoyed at first, then gradually seemed flattered by the attention. Epstein didn't just butt in and try to tell what really happened there in front of the Jewel store. Sure, he interrupted, and frequently, but it was with questions: What time was it that she first drove up to the entrance and let Ms. Molinero off to do the shopping? Could Mrs. Edwards perhaps be more exact than that? Did Ms. Molinero have a shopping list?

At about this time, I remember the cop made an effort to shut him up. "Look, these are just details. Can't we get on with this?"

"Oh, I know, officer. But details like this often prove very important later on, should a complaint come to trial. Preliminary reports are *very* important."

"Well . . . that's true, Mr. . . . Mr. . . ."

"Epstein."

"Epstein!" echoed Clare Edwards. "That's all we need—a Jew lawyer!"

"Oh, I'm sure you don't want that remark on the record," he said sympathetically. "Do you, Mrs. Edwards?"

In this way Epstein managed to stretch what might have taken her five minutes to fifteen or twenty. Who knows how long it could have gone on? But something happened at that point that ended the game. Something that quieted even Clare Edwards.

It was a noise, a faint and familiar wuk-wuk-wuk off in the distance, the sound of a helicopter. But it grew closer and closer and louder and louder, until it was a roar that overwhelmed us all. The cop rose from his seat at the computer. Clare Edwards looked around the room a bit wild-eyed, as if she was searching for someplace to hide. Just then she did look a bit crazy.

And then, when the decibels had peaked, another sound came, maybe felt rather than heard. There was a grinding and settling directly above us. The helicopter had landed on the roof.

But the roar continued for almost a minute more. Just about the moment it shut off, the large figure of a man appeared at the back of the room. He strode forward and paused about 10 feet away. He looked deeply serious as he hitched up his pants, passed a look around at the group of us, and then addressed the cop.

"My name is John McGucken," he said. "I'm chief of detectives for the Chicago Police Department. I would like to see your chief of police. And if a Mrs. Clarissa Edwards is here, I would take it as a favor if you detained her so that I might question her in the matter of Benjamin Sterling."

19

I was ticketed on American Airlines flight 83 from Chicago to Los Angeles. Calling in late the night before from the motel, I found out there was space available and made my reservation. It meant a long wait in the ticket line there at O'Hare, but I was prepared for that. I got there early, having deposited the Taurus with Hertz, kicked my carry-on bag along as I moved slowly forward to a ticket agent, and was at last able to exchange my open return for a boarding pass on flight 83.

I don't know about you, but to me all airports seem alike. No, it's more than that. Once you step inside those magically opening automatic doors, no matter whether they're in Los Angeles or San Francisco or Chicago, it's like you're entering another world, another place, or maybe a nonplace—it's Airportland.

In Airportland people don't talk much. Even couples and families don't have much to say among themselves. What they do is wait. They sit, staring off at distant points, avoiding eye contact with others. Or they wander like ghosts through those Airportland shops, which are all the same from one city to the next, thumbing magazines, handling souvenirs, killing time.

I'd found a bookshop (in just about every particular, except the book titles displayed, like another I'd once visited at La Guardia). There I was browsing diligently, determined to find some relief from the passive fatalism of Lao-tzu. I'd been through his little book a dozen times by then, impressed and attracted in spite of myself, and resisting it for all I was worth. I needed something else.

By the time I'd worked my way through paperback fiction and into biography, I realized that I was being paged. I heard my name repeated a couple of times, then listened as I was asked to return to the American Airlines ticketing desk. I went. Had I been bumped? Were they really awfully sorry to inform me that their computer had misinformed them?

So, expecting the worst, I got a lift when I rounded the corner and spotted Katy McGucken's unmistakable mop of red curls bright as a beacon in the middle of that crowd at the desk. She was looking around for me.

"Chico!" she called when she spotted me. "I came to see you off."

"You do this for all your visitors?"

"No," she said, grabbing my arm at the elbow and giving it a hug, "you're special." Then, as we set off together, more or less in step, she expanded on that: "You really are, you know that? I mean, how many guys would come here all the way from Los Angeles and do the leg work the cops should have done—and do it to help out somebody they don't even like much?"

"Oh, Julio's okay, I guess. Like most of us—imperfect. In a way, he was right, though. I probably *was* the only one who could help him."

"No," said Katy, "what he said was, you were the only one who could *save* him."

"St. Jude himself!"

"Julio's out now," she said. "Everything finished up so late last night that I had to wait till this morning to get somebody from the prosecutor's office to sign off on it before I put it in front of a judge."

"Charges dropped?"

"Charges dropped. I wasn't there to welcome him out, but I understand that Josefina was."

"Interesting. What's he going to do for money? Back out on the street?"

She laughed one of those Irish laughs, worldly-wise beyond her years. "No," she said, "I don't think so." Then she looked around and lowered her voice. "Strictly off the record, it seems there's a sort of emergency fund to discourage victims of false arrest from bringing suit. He was also met by somebody with a nice fat envelope, a little something to help him toward reestablishing himself in the community. You think he'll go back to Los Angeles?"

"No," I said, "definitely not."

"You think he'll stay out of trouble?"

"Your guess is as good as mine."

We'd reached the electronic inspection point. I tossed my carry-on bag onto the conveyor for an X ray, and she dropped her purse on behind it. She walked right through the metal detector—women always do—but I had to empty my pockets of keys, Swiss Army Knife, and change before I managed to pass on my second try.

Then we were off again, heading for the departure gate.

"My father told me to tell you that anytime you want a job on the force, you've got it. I think he really means it, too."

"I'm flattered," I said—and I certainly was. "I've never seen anybody take a situation in hand the way he did. That entrance in the helicopter, just for starters."

"It was the fastest way to get there."

"Yeah, but it was impressive. And his attitude was just right, too. He was very diplomatic with those Lake Wood cops. He got the chief's permission to interrogate her right there at the station, then asked him to sit in on it."

"And that way he got better cooperation from Mrs. Edwards."

"At least the first time through her story. Then he called you and made sure that Josefina told you what she'd told me, and talked to the cops he'd sent to see old Mr. Avery. Then he goes back into the room with Mrs. Edwards and chops her story up into little tiny pieces. It was really just a case of the irresistible force and the immovable object. Eventually she gave."

"But he told me last night," said Katy, "that she was tough to break, unreasonably tough. She seemed to think that if she just kept insisting, then she could have it her way. He said that he really does think she's jumped the track—the way she went after you in daylight in front of witnesses, all that. A good lawyer can probably get her off on an insanity plea. Maybe she'll hire that fellow who saved your neck in the parking lot. He's good, all right."

"Epstein? Who knows?" I said. "There was definitely premeditation on her part—getting Julio's driver's license and so on." I thought a moment. "What about her husband?"

"They've got him in for questioning right now."

"He's in on it, I'm pretty sure. My bet is that he lined up those two attempted hits in Santa Monica. It'd be interesting to know who his contact was. . . . Hey, wait a minute."

"What's the matter?"

I pulled out my ticket and looked at the boarding pass. "I thought maybe we'd passed my departure gate. But it's the next one down. You really didn't have to come all the way out here to O'Hare, you know."

"I know, but I felt like I owed you something—even if you did take away my first real shot at a trial I could win."

"Sorry about that."

"Don't be."

They were calling the early boarders onto the flight. Katy looked around and noted the general movement toward the boarding gate.

"Well, I guess I'll leave you here," she said. "No sense hanging around until they call your seat number."

"Thank your father for me. Thank him a lot for that helicopter ride back into town. That was quite a view of Chicago I got."

"You may be seeing more of it."

"Why? What do you mean?"

"You'll make a terrific witness for the prosecution, Chico."
With that, she gave me a kiss on the cheek and started back down

the corridor. About halfway to the next gate, she turned, gave me a big Irish grin, and waved good-bye.

So it was back to the *Tao Te Ching*. I had thumbed through the copy of *Esquire* that the stewardess gave me, spent about half an hour with it or a little more, without finding much to hold me. I had a drink before lunch and picked at my food. Then, once the tray had been hauled away, I pulled the little book out of the bag I had stored under the seat just in front of me. That must have been someplace over Arkansas or eastern Colorado. I opened it up and began to read.

I don't know why, but this time the little poems, thoughts, sermons, whatever they are, seemed to make more sense to me. All that meant, of course, was that I was in a more receptive mood. With the weight of Julio off my shoulders, the experience of Chicago behind me, I was willing to settle back and let this strangely attractive view of life pull me in. It began to seem that what old Lao-tzu was presenting was not so much a passive approach as a sense of being above it all. You took the cards you were dealt, played them as sensibly as you knew how, didn't crow if you won, and didn't complain if you lost. There were better ways to read it, I'm sure, but right then and now, this one satisfied me. It sort of went along with what I'd learned growing up in Boyle Heights—learned from my father's example, too.

Then, not quite halfway into the book, I came across one that I'd read probably a dozen times before without really responding to. The part that got to me was in the middle.

> Thus the Master is available to all people
> and doesn't reject anyone.
> He is ready to use all situations
> and doesn't waste anything.
> This is called embodying the light.
>
> What is a good man but a bad man's teacher?
> What is a bad man but a good man's job?

Well, I certainly wasn't a master, and I didn't know about embodying the light, but the part in between was a good summary of the right sort of MO for a guy in my kind of work. And that last line about a bad man being a good man's job, that fit, too. Julio wasn't really a bad man, neither was I especially a good one, but he'd been my job, all right. He made me an offer I couldn't refuse.

I must have gone on from there, but not very far. My mind kept returning to those lines. I went back once to reread them and thought about them some more. Then, suddenly, I wasn't thinking about anything at all. The drink I'd had before lunch, the closeness of the cabin put me under completely. The book dropped to my lap. I was asleep.

Those last two lines echoed in my dreams. When they came, they were sort of threatening—no, not sort of at all, they really were threatening. It was, I don't know, sort of a montage of Thomas Jarrett, and Saheed was in there, too. I got that view of Saheed that I'd seen through the bookstore window, a smile close to a sneer, and then, as I looked at him, he vanished, which in effect was what had happened when I ran out and looked for him on the street. But this time it happened right before my eyes—he simply, suddenly wasn't there. But Thomas Jarrett was the star of the show. I saw him as I had first seen him at Newport Beach—naked, calling for a towel as he stepped out of the bathtub. Then, suddenly, there he was, grinning at me from that picture in the *Los Angeles Times*. Is a good man a bad man's teacher? He laughed at the idea, turned to me within the picture, and simply laughed. Is a bad man a good man's job? He mouthed the question, then laughed at me. There were other pictures—Jarrett pacing around his living room, negotiating some kind of crazy deal with me that he had no intention of honoring. Alicia was in that picture, too, wide-eyed, frightened, looking from me to him, sure that I was selling her out.

"Hey, hey, buddy, better wake up, huh?"

"No . . . no . . . what?"

It was the guy in the seat next to mine, in his sixties, a bald businessman kind of guy. He was shaking me awake, looking concerned. "You okay?" he asked.

I sat there, blinking. "Yeah," I said. "Yeah, I guess so."

"You must've been having some kind of nightmare. All of a sudden you started thrashing around, saying 'No, no,' and I thought, well, I better wake you up."

I took a deep breath and let it out in a sigh. "Thanks. Yeah, thanks. I'm glad you did."

"We all have them. It's . . . it's the stress."

Still groggy, I was looking around, trying to orient myself, get a grip on reality. Those images of Jarrett were still with me, and that frightened face of Alicia's. "I think I'd better get up and walk around," I said to the businessman beside me. I unbuckled and pushed out of my seat.

"That'd probably do you some good."

I touched him on the shoulder. "Thanks again," I said. Then, moving as firmly as anyone could along the floor of an object moving at 500 miles an hour through the stratosphere, I made my way to the back of the plane. I found one of the toilets open, went in, and ran water in the basin. It was sort of lukewarm. That was all right. I splashed it over my face, gently rubbed it around my eyes. That felt good. I toweled off then and stood for a moment, looking at myself in the mirror.

Same old face, the one I'd shaved this morning at the motel back in Chicago. I tried to smile at it, but I couldn't. That dream I'd had stopped me from smiling. It told me that something bad lay ahead, an ordeal, and that I'd be lucky to get through it in one piece. I remembered those severed hands and my lame joke to Casimir. It was something I could have said only at a distance of 2,500 miles—a safe distance. Well, in another hour or so, I'd be in the middle of it again, with no jokes, no distance, nothing at all to insulate me from Thomas Jarrett. But what could he do to me, to Alicia, to any of us right there at the studio? Well, I'd find out soon enough.

Casimir Urbanski was waiting right there at the gate. As I came down the jetway, I saw him, taller than I'd realized—a full head above the crowd around him. He stepped forward, gave me a slap on my shoulder, and made a grab at my bag. I let him take it. In his big hand, it seemed to shrink to the size of a purse.

We'd walked some distance when he turned to me and said, "You have a good flight?" Casimir never was good at small talk. Or maybe he just wasn't in the mood right then.

"So-so."

He shrugged and nodded, more or less in a single large gesture. Then he said nothing more until we got outside at ground level. A Mercedes limousine was waiting there. I was surprised when he guided me over to it. I hadn't quite expected anything that grand.

"It's the studio's," he said. I didn't for a moment think it was his.

The chauffeur jumped out to open the door. Casimir waved him away and threw it open himself.

"We got a stop to make on the way," he said. "Plenty of time, though."

I settled in at the far end of the wide seat. Casimir slid in beside me. He grabbed my arm and gave it a squeeze but said nothing. The limo pulled away silently, and in another moment we entered the flow of traffic and headed toward Century Boulevard and the 405. Traffic was light. It was Saturday, after all.

Out there on the freeway I turned to him and asked, "You know anything more about this?"

He held up a finger, signaling me to wait, then pushed a button that raised a pane of glass to a nice tight fit between the driver and us. "Just he said he's got a deal to offer us is all."

"I think you said that much on the telephone."

"Well, that's all then."

"What's old man Toller say about this?"

"He says, listen to Jarrett, then decide, because maybe we got more bargaining room than we think. He's gonna be at the meeting."

"That's good." I held back a moment and then asked the obvious question. "Any idea why I have to be there?"

"No. Just, like I told you, you're not there, the meeting's off."

That didn't help much. I knew that Uschi and Hans-Dieter

would gladly hand me over to Jarrett as host...
cooked up. I could count on Casimir, but I c...
hundred percent sure of old Heinrich Toller, ...
nominally the boss of the studio. More like an a...
lately.

We rode along in silence for a few more miles ...
just ahead. That was when Casimir, looking straigh...
'I really don't like this, Chief. I got a bad feeling ...
"That makes two of us."
"You want to jump off anywhere along here, Sa...
Boulevard, or Wilshire, I'll tell them you weren't on th...
I thought about that.
"No," I said at last, "I've come this far. Might as well ...
way."
The driver turned off at Sunset, headed west and into ...
wood. After a couple more turns south and west the driver p...
up in front of a big new apartment building, not quite luxury ...
definitely upscale.
I turned to Casimir, eyebrows upraised, inquiring.
"Alicia wants to see you," he said. "She's coming along, too,
so don't take too long." He looked at his watch. "About five
minutes, okay? She should be ready to go."
"You're not coming up?"
"No, you go alone. That's how she wanted it."
And so I got out of the car and headed up three steps to the
entrance. The name on the bell was here, Ramirez; I don't know
what else I expected. I rang it, and only seconds later I was buzzed
through the security door. She must have been waiting for me.

But it wasn't Alicia who opened the door to her apartment. It
was an older woman. She was tall, a bit heavyset, but attractive in
the stern, dignified way of some Mexican women. She wore a
simple black dress that fell well beneath her knees and no jewelry.
I remember wondering at first sight if she was in mourning.

She gave me a solemn smile. "You are Señor Cervantes, of
course," she said in Spanish.

I said I was.

"Please come in. I will make sure Alicia knows you have

arrived." She closed the door and disappeared down a hallway. I knew that woman's face but couldn't place it. Who was she? It seemed to me I'd talked with her, had dealings with her, sometime in the not-too-distant past.

She had left me in a sort of vestibule that opened onto the living room. I leaned in and looked. It was beige-carpeted and furnished with indistinctly modern pieces. There were no pictures on the walls. The place, neat as a pin, had even less personality than a Holiday Inn room. It was hard to believe anyone lived here, much less Miss Chaos herself.

I heard a door open, the sound of a baby making noises in imitation of talk, and then the click of heels on tile. I looked. It was Alicia, all right.

"*Hola, Chico.*" She kissed me timidly on the cheek.

"Hello, Alicia."

"*Por favor, en español. La alemana comprende ingles. Ella no comprende español.*"

"Okay," I said, and then continuing in Spanish: "So, the big meeting tonight. You know anything about it?"

"Nothing."

"And I no more than you."

I took a step back and looked her over. She was dressed for business in a dark suit and under it a no-nonsense white blouse. This was an entirely new version of Alicia. I'd never seen it before.

"You like what you see?"

"You've lost weight."

"For the camera. It makes you look fatter."

"You look great."

"Oh, Chico," touching me on the arm, "you *always* think I look great, even when I was nine months big with Marilyn." She laughed. Then, suddenly serious. "Would you like to see her?"

"I would like to see her. Yes."

She beckoned me to follow. "This way," she said and then led me down the hall to the kitchen.

A big, dark-haired, dark-eyed baby nearly a year old sat strapped in a high chair, being fed by a big, blond-haired, blue-

259

eyed young woman in her twenties. The woman jumped to her feet and stood stiffly, almost at attention.

"I would like to present Fraülein Erika Holzer," said Alicia in English, and to Fraülein Holzer: "Antonio Cervantes."

The woman reached forward and pumped my hand. I'd forgotten how hot the Germans were on shaking hands.

"Fery pleassed to meet you," she said.

"And I you," I said, trying to match her politeness for politeness. "A beautiful baby. She looks very healthy."

"Oh, fery, fery healthy."

I bent down to Marilyn. Our eyes met. She reached out to me. I let her grab a finger.

"She remembers you," said Alicia in Spanish.

"You think so?"

"*Claro.*" She stepped over and grabbed a paper towel off the roll nearby, separated Marilyn's hand from my finger, and gave my finger a wipe. "Babies are always so messy," she said, holding onto my hand a little longer than was absolutely necessary. "Come, let's go into the living room."

At the door I turned back to the German girl. "I can tell you're doing a wonderful job," I said to her.

"Oh, dank you, dank you." She seemed really happy at my polite praise, smiling and nodding eagerly.

"Good-bye, then."

She nodded one great final nod and sent me on my way.

I followed Alicia down the hallway to the living room. She sat down on the massive sofa. I took a chair opposite her.

"I saw your show," I said.

She brightened. "You like it?"

"It's as everyone says, you're marvelous in it."

"Ah, thank you, Chico. I know you would not say that if it wasn't from the heart."

True enough. I didn't tell her what I thought of the show, though. But hey, I'd probably lie about that if she wanted me to.

"Well," I said, "you're a success, a great success. You got what you wanted. I congratulate you. Sincerely."

She stared at me for a long moment and said at last, "No, not everything I wanted. I miss you, Chico. You saw—Marilyn misses you, too. I was bad, I was wrong, the way I left you. I know that now, and I knew it then. But Chico, I want this thing so *bad*. You can never understand how bad I wanted it."

"Yeah, well, maybe I understand." My throat was beginning to tighten up. "It's okay, really."

"No, Chico, it's not okay." She stared down at her hands. "I ask you to forgive me."

"I . . . I forgive you."

Then, looking me straight in the eyes. Oh, Jesus, those eyes of hers! "You think, after this business tonight, we could try again?"

This was it, wasn't it? What I'd hoped for and what I'd feared. I had to give some answer, and it took all I had to give the one I meant. I cleared my throat a couple of times and at last managed to say, "I'm not sure that will be possible."

"All right, maybe you have someone new now. I don't know. But you think about it, please."

I was saved from answering that by the doorbell. Three loud, long rings. I stood up. "That would be Casimir," I said. "It's time to go."

She rose, gave a tug to her suit jacket, and smoothed her skirt. "Think about what I say."

And at that moment the older woman appeared and handed Alicia a small, dark purse that seemed to match her suit. Then the woman moved to the door. I noticed she had a purse slung over her shoulder.

"Chico, you remember my friend Concepción? You met her in Culiacán."

"Of course. I thought she looked familiar." I nodded. "Señora."

"She's coming with us."

Concepción gave me that same solemn smile I'd seen earlier, then she threw open the door.

Alicia called out a good-bye to Fraülein Holzer, and we filed out into the hall. It wasn't until we were halfway down the stairs that I remembered that Concepción was the madam of the Gallo Inmortal, the house in Culiacán where I had first met Alicia.

20

By the time we were all gathered in Ursula Toller's office, there was quite a crowd—Ursula, of course, and old man Toller, Hans-Dieter, Casimir, Alicia, Concepción, and me. Extra chairs had been brought into the big office. There was no telling how many Jarrett might bring with him.

The big question mark for me was Concepción. Why was she here? Had she become a permanent member of Alicia's household? What need did she fill? I would have expected Alicia to cut ties completely with her former life. Maybe she had made it easy for Jarrett to dig up dirt on her.

There was no general discussion, no speculation on what might be expected, no tactics planned for negotiation, because the truth was, nobody knew what to expect, and Jarrett had made it clear that he had no intention of negotiating. Uschi and Hans-Dieter were deep in a whispered conversation. Casimir stood close to them, listening, saying nothing. Alicia and Concepción sat together and said very little; I got the idea they'd talked it all over before.

What was I doing? Making myself as inconspicuous as possible, standing by a window, looking down across the empty studio, wondering how long this would take, wishing it was over.

I was surprised by a touch on my shoulder. I turned and found Heinrich Toller there, his hand out to me.

"So, DeQuincey." That was his nickname for me, origin too complicated to explain.

"Glad to see you again," I said. We shook hands. "It's been a while."

"Yes. Too long." He held onto my hand, clapped his left over it. "You know," he said, "all these people who work for me, I can't count on them. But you, I can always count on. You always deliver—sometimes a little more than we want, but you deliver. How much is this going to cost me?"

"I have no idea. Maybe nothing, maybe a lot."

"Fair enough. We work it out, *ja?*" He stood with me, looking out the window at the darkness moving in over the Majestic lot. "He chose his time right, this man Jarrett. There is only one film shooting here, and they wrapped for the day an hour ago. Administrative people gone for the day, a few people in production offices. The place is as empty as it will ever be."

"Which gives him the advantage?"

"Not necessarily."

The phone rang. Ursula Toller leaped to it.

"Yes," she said, "yes? Hello?" A pause, then, "All right, direct him to the administration building and up to my office. Oh, and . . . what kind of car is he driving?" A brief pause. "Thank you."

She hung up and looked around at the rest of us. "That was the gate," she announced. "There are two of them. They're in a Jaguar."

Why should it matter what kind of car they're in? What was she up to?

She began shouting out orders. "Father, you come back here and sit behind the desk with me. Cervantes, get out in the hall. Show them you are here and make them feel welcome. Alicia, come up and sit by the desk, next to this man Jarrett. Casimir, where are you going?"

"Out in the hall with Chico."

He took me only as far as the outer office and there pulled me over to the secretary's desk. From under his jacket he pulled a nickel-plated .357 magnum, his old service revolver, and found an open drawer. He put it inside.

"Now, look," he said, "this is going to be in here, like. Safety's off. Round under the hammer. I got the feeling they'll frisk us over, you know? No *way* they're gonna take you outta here. You know where this is, you get at it if you got, like, a chance. You don't, I get it and I go after you. You're covered, you know?"

I nodded. "I'm covered. Thanks, Casimir."

"We'll handle it, Chico." He clapped me on the shoulder and went back into Uschi's office.

Out in the hall, I had just enough time for a few ironic reflections on Uschi's command, "make them feel welcome." What did she have in mind? A ceremonial bow? A salaam? Did she think that the manners she had been taught at that Swiss finishing school would make an impression on a gangster like Thomas Jarrett? Then I thought about it some more and decided that maybe the two of them, Jarrett and Uschi, had a lot in common.

There were footsteps on the stairs. And then there they were—Saheed first, holding an Uzi that he must have brought in under the raincoat he wore. He pointed it at me. I put my hands up, palms out, to show they were empty. He nodded, and Jarrett appeared, carrying a briefcase, grinning reflexively at me. You couldn't really call it a smile.

"Well, Cervantes," he said as they approached, "you made it. I was afraid we might have to abort this little meeting, which of course I would have done if you hadn't been present." He was speaking in that phony-affable way of his, still wearing the grin.

Saheed patted me down awkwardly, one-handed, the Uzi cocked up and away from me. I wondered if he'd ever fired that thing.

Through all this Jarrett kept talking. "You know, Cervantes, we had our eyes on you—Saheed made sure you knew that—but you disappeared on us. We thought perhaps we'd given you too big a scare. You might never come back. So we're especially glad to see you could make it this evening."

Finished, Saheed gave another nod to Jarrett to indicate I was clean. Then he took a step back.

"Well," Jarret said to me, "haven't you got anything to say for yourself?"

"Sure. Come on in."

I waved them forward and led the way into the inner office. As I passed the secretary's desk, I gave one of those sweeping, swift, oh-so-casual glances at the drawer where Casimir had stuck his .357. It was easy to spot, still slightly open.

Everybody was standing when we entered the room. Uschi circled her desk and stepped forward, offering her hand to Jarrett. Maybe this was more than just the old German handshake routine. Maybe she recognized in him a spiritual brother. I'm not sure what they said to each other; they were a little too far away, their voices too low for me to tell. But she was, if not smiling, then speaking with animation that had nothing to do with anger.

Casimir's hunch was right. Saheed frisked all the men just as he had me—awkwardly—then went through the purses of the women present. Satisfied, he called over to Jarrett, "Nothing here. You go ahead now."

"Fine, Saheed. Will you all please take the seats that Miss Toller has provided?" Jesus, I thought, he's going to make a presentation!

There was a bit of milling around then—there were, after all, nine of us there—but soon we settled in places around the desk, facing the Tollers and Jarrett.

"Where do you want me, Meester Jarrett?" Saheed asked.

"In the back, I think. You can keep an eye on everyone there."

"Sure t'ing. Nothing happens I don't see."

Saheed settled in behind me and a little to the left. I watched him sink down into one of the more comfortable chairs back near the door and lay the Uzi carefully over his knees. Then I saw that Concepción was watching him, too. She even managed a smile at him—not the grave one she'd shown me earlier, but something a little more professionally flirtatious. He smiled back.

My eyes roamed over the group. The only contact I made was with Casimir, and that only briefly. His eyes flickered sharply at me, then continued their intense concentration on Jarrett—hatred, pure Polish hatred.

Jarrett put his briefcase up on the desk, unbuttoned his suit jacket, adjusted his tie, and began roaming around the room.

"Now, most of you don't know me," he began. "But I've had an interesting life—two separate careers. I've been both a businessman—in oil, when there was still money to be made in it outside the Middle East—and a gangster. Oh yes, I won't mince words, that's what I was for a few years, a supplier of substances for which there is a great demand in this country. I know there are some who might say that these two careers were really one and the same, that a businessman, particularly in a rough-and-tumble business like oil, really is a sort of gangster. And it's true, there are similarities. For instance, I brought to my second career a certain skill in organization, a passion for strict accounting, and a willingness to negotiate that had made me successful in business. They made me successful once again.

"Ah, but there are differences, too. Don't let anyone tell you there aren't. I found that the second career awakened my baser instincts. But that wasn't all. I also found that to enjoy any degree of success in it, I had to act upon those instincts—give them free rein, play the monster, eliminate the competition . . . completely. What was expected of me I soon found I enjoyed. I don't mind telling you that it's great for the ego, gives you a powerful sense of, well, *freedom* to have the power of life and death over a person—well, many persons.

"So for years I prospered in my second career. I had an organization in Mexico, enjoyed a firm working relationship with people in Colombia, things went well."

Then he paused at last in what had been a flowing, uninterrupted monologue. Had he rehearsed this? But even this temporary halt, it turned out, was for effect.

"Until *that man*"—pointing at me from across the room; I was sitting apart from the rest of them, so there was no doubt who he meant—"ruined it all, all that I'd worked for, all that I'd achieved. And he was aided by *this woman.*" He pointed down now at Alicia; he was quite close to her, practically standing over her. He stood looking from me to her and back again, glowering like a judge about ready to pass the death sentence.

But then he resumed his tour of the room, becoming reasonable again, almost playful.

"Now, among those baser instincts, in some ways the most important of them all for anyone engaging in criminal pursuits is the desire for revenge. It must be fed. It's the other's fear of revenge that keeps you a player in that game. So, I admit it, I was planning my revenge on these two. Killing wouldn't do—too easy. Why not wait until they had something they wanted, then take it away from them? The baby? Well, that was a possibility, but finally you people provided the answer with this show of yours—*Lupe*, of course. I gathered my material on your star—it wasn't all that difficult—presented my offer to you: money or publication. As far as I was concerned, it was a win-win situation. I stood to gain either way. I would either make a nice, tidy sum or would have the pleasure of destroying this woman Ramirez completely.

"But you know, I read the newspapers, too. I became aware that this show of hers, *Lupe*, is a big hit. I even watched it myself, and I understood why the public might like something like that. And so I began thinking like a businessman once again—and high time, too."

He was back at the desk now, opening up his briefcase, laying copies of a document across the desk, four copies in all. Then he finished with that and kept right on talking.

"Now, I've been briefed on the television business. I'm fully aware that even when a show is a hit, you don't go into profit until the third season, something like that. Nevertheless, I'm willing to invest in the show. I'll take that chance. What I have to invest, of course, is the information I've gathered on the star, although that, of course, is not how the contract reads. When you agree to the terms and sign the contract, I would be neutralized as a threat. Why should I want to destroy the star of the show when I'm part owner? Go ahead, read the contract. I drew it up myself. I may have graduated in the bottom ten percent of my class, but I did go to Stanford Law."

He stepped back away from the desk then and with a sort of florid gesture presented the contract to them. Ursula Toller and her father each grabbed up a copy. Hans-Dieter jumped up and took one, then began skimming it impatiently.

"Aber mein Gott!" croaked Uschi. "You want twenty-five percent!"

"That's what it says," said Jarrett firmly.

Everybody was up now. Casimir grabbed up the remaining copy from the desk and began studying hard. Concepción walked up to Saheed and began whispering urgently. It looked as if she was negotiating a trip to the ladies' room. He let her go. She stepped around him and out the door.

Alicia came over to me.

"What does this mean, Chico, this thing in the contracts?"

"It means you'll be working for him—for Jarrett."

"You mean this? Is it true?"

"Well," I said, "just listen to them."

They—the German contingent, anyway—were all talking at once, shouting at each other *auf deutsch,* shouting at Jarrett in English. And Jarrett, for his part, had blown his cool; he was shouting back at them. Casimir stepped back from the rest, saw me standing with Alicia, and offered us the copy of the contract he'd been looking at. I shook my head, no. I wanted no part of this.

"Didn't I say the terms of the contract were not negotiable?" Jarrett demanded.

"No, you *didn't!"* cried Hans-Dieter petulantly.

"Yes I did!" insisted Jarrett.

They went back and forth like that for a while. Ursula Toller added her wail to the confusion of voices: "But twenty-five percent is *criminal.* It cuts out any chance we have to make a profit. Perhaps ten percent, but—"

"I never heard of such a thing," shouted her father. "A *non-*negotiable contract. From Hitler maybe, but . . . *Unerhört! Einfach unerhört!"*

But Jarrett outshouted them all: "I said *on the telephone* that my terms would have to be accepted. Doesn't that mean nonnegotiable?" He had lost control, and he knew it.

But old man Toller, standing at the desk now, looking much

taller than his five feet, five inches, answered that: "But that was surely a negotiating ploy. In any deal, there is room for negotiation. That is the essence of business!"

Jarrett became silent for a long moment. It gave me time to look around and notice that Concepción had come back. She moved up toward the front of the room.

At last he said, "Negotiation *is* the essence of business," echoing Toller. "I've said as much myself many times." Then abruptly he began his pacing again, stopped, whirled around, and said, "All right, what do you suggest?"

The yelling began again, but Jarrett refused to listen to anyone but Heinrich Toller. The two began shouting demands, offers, and counteroffers at each other, and only minutes later they had rewritten the contract. Jarrett settled for eighteen percent, but in addition would be given office space and staff on the Majestic lot for his production company, and a budget of $250,000 per year for the development of motion picture and television projects. Suddenly Jarrett was a player. He seemed delighted.

They worked hastily on the four copies, changing numbers, adding clauses, initialing—and, finally, signing.

"I'm also demanding droit du seigneur with regard to our star," Jarrett joked, nodding at Alicia, "but I don't see how that could actually be written in."

Hans-Dieter had a good, hearty laugh at that. "Very good! Droit du seigneur—no, it wouldn't stand up in court." Great guffaws.

Then they shook hands. The three of them actually shook hands with that creep. Casimir and I looked at each other, shook our heads, and turned away, embarassed—even if *they* weren't.

Then Jarrett stood off to one side and waited for silence.

"Just one more matter unattended to, if you don't mind. Please?" They all turned toward him. "Thank you. And you may have guessed that my unfinished business has to do with Mr. Cervantes right over there." He pointed at me. "Now, I asked—well, actually, insisted—that he be here tonight for a very specific reason. For just as I put aside my desire for revenge with regard to Ms. Ramirez, I've decided to do that now also in Cervantes's case."

He paused, almost as though he was expecting a round of applause for that. If he was, he didn't get it, so he pressed on. "For a long time after the ruination he brought upon me, I brooded on it and gave him credit only for dumb luck in what he'd done—just blundered through, I told myself. But if I'm thinking more like a businessman in recognizing the opportunity offered in this deal we've just concluded, I think I've also become more objective about Mr. Cervantes. I'm willing to admit that although he *was* lucky, he also showed considerable resourcefulness and tenacity, and this is just the sort of man I want on *my* team. So . . ." He paused, again for effect. "Antonio Cervantes is working for me now. He'll be well paid by you"—turning to the Tollers—"since he'll be on my personal staff. And he'll no longer have to grub away at that dirty little business he's in, peeking in keyholes and so on." He beamed a winner's smile at me from across the room.

Others had sat down. I was still on my feet. I started toward him but got control of myself and stopped after a step or two. Not completely under control, though, because when I started to speak to him I found myself shouting. "I don't want your job, Jarrett. I wouldn't work for you if I had to."

"But that's just it. You do have to. No option. You've been drafted, so to speak." He looked around. "Isn't that so, Saheed?" He frowned. "Saheed?"

I turned and looked. Saheed was still sitting in that chair by the door, the Uzi there in his lap, his hands cupped over it. But his head was down like he was deep in thought or something.

Jarrett approached him briskly. "Have you gone to sleep, or what?" There was something between surprise and annoyance in his tone.

The others got up and followed him, out of curiosity, I supposed. I stood where I was.

Jarrett gave him a shake.

Saheed's head almost fell off.

Or that's how it seemed when his head flopped back with a jerk and exposed a grinning, deep gash across his throat. The Uzi clattered to the floor.

Jarrett looked around, wild-eyed. But before he could move, something strange happened. Concepción stepped forward and threw her left arm around his neck. It was an embrace. I thought for an instant she was going to kiss him. But then she pulled away, and I saw the knife in her hand and the spreading red spot in the middle of his white shirt.

His eyes went dull. He staggered and fell. Concepción dropped to her knees, pulled back Jarrett's chin, and brought the blade swiftly across his throat.

"Lift him up!" screamed Ursula Toller. "Don't let him bleed on the carpet."

Casimir and I buried the two of them in a single grave up in the mountains. It was hard work. The hole had to be deep. Coyotes would dig up anything they scented in a shallow grave.

Casimir proved those muscles of his weren't just for show. He dug away in a robotlike rhythm, not too fast and not too slow, a real peasant's pace. I kept up with him for about half the job, but when it came time for one of us to jump down in the hole and dig deeper, he did it without a word. I hauled the bodies out of the van and got them ready for burial. That meant I unrolled them from the canvas we had them wrapped in when we carried them out of Uschi's office; I stripped them and scraped the skin off the pads of their fingers with my Swiss Army knife. By the time I finished all that, Casimir had pulled himself out of the pit. He gave me a questioning look, and I nodded. We grabbed hands and feet and tossed in first one and then the other. I don't even remember who went on top of who.

After we filled up the hole we took a few minutes to replace the brush and weeds, and by the time we finished, it looked about the way it had before we started digging. Then we gathered up the tools and tossed them into the van, along with the canvas and the clothes. We looked around the area carefully to make sure we were leaving nothing behind.

Satisfied, I nodded and said, "Follow me."

271

I drove the Jaguar; Casimir drove the van. I led the way to a chop shop I knew about in the Valley. It was a good forty-five-minute haul from the remote spot in the mountains, but Casimir stayed behind me all the way. When we got to our destination it was about 1:30 in the morning. The yard dogs behind the chain-link fence made a lot of noise as we worked, but there was nobody around to ask us why we were taking the license plates off the car, or emptying the glove compartment. I pulled the car key off Jarrett's key ring and left it in the ignition. Since I'd worn the gloves that Hans-Dieter supplied through all this, I didn't bother to do a wipe on the inside of the car. They'd find it in the morning, a gift. I thought they'd have the good sense to cut it up for parts.

I climbed into the van beside Casimir, and he got us out of there. The barking of the dogs was still sounding in our ears as he turned on to the main road.

We had a long drive ahead of us. We talked.

"You know anything about this beforehand?" I asked Casimir.

"Not a thing," he said.

I believed him. He wouldn't have gone through that business of planting his service revolver in the outer office if he had known what was planned.

"I had a bad feeling about it going in, though," he said. "Remember? I even said so in the limo when I picked you up at the airport."

"I remember." I said nothing more for a block or two. But then, "I guess we were the only ones out of the loop."

"You think even the old man?"

"Yeah, even him."

"And Alicia?"

"Oh, definitely Alicia. It must have been her idea to bring Concepción up from Mexico. I think Ursula dreamed up the way to handle the situation, and Alicia gave her the means."

"You think that's how it was? Hans-Dieter and the old man just going along with it?"

"Yeah," I said. "Yeah, I do."

He thought about that a moment, then nodded and said, "Yeah, me too." He glanced over at me. "Jesus, huh?"

"So that whole business about negotiating the contract, that was just I guess what you'd call a diversion. To stall Jarrett and keep him occupied while Concepción did her number on Saheed."

"She sure worked quiet."

"She sure did."

Another block-long pause. "And we're the cleanup crew," said Casimir. "They sure took off in a lotta different directions."

"Suits me," I said: "I never want to see any of them again."

"Not even Alicia?"

"Not even her. Maybe especially not her."

"I gotta work with them, though."

"Well, believe me, buddy, even if your movie flops, which I hope it doesn't, you'll keep right on producing as long as the Tollers are there at Majestic. You know where the bodies are buried."

"But they got something on me, too. Accessory onto the fact."

"On me, too. Everybody's got something on everybody."

"Messy. Too many people involved. You think it's gonna work?"

I gave that some thought. Finally, I said, "Yeah, I do. Number one, Jarrett worked alone. Saheed was the only one he trusted. There may have been a couple of *pistoleros* back at that ranch of his. There probably were. But when they see the boss isn't coming back, they'll just disappear—south, probably. If they knew about the blackmail scam, they won't push it. They probably didn't, though. It's a question of how well Jarrett hid the stuff he had on Alicia, whether it comes to light, and, for that matter, if it ever really existed. He never showed copies of what he had, did he?"

"No, and Alicia says there wasn't any pictures. Pictures was impossible."

I felt especially relieved at that. I don't know why. "Number two," I said, "we buried them pretty deep up there where it's pretty lonely. Could you find that place again?"

"No, not me."

"I'm not sure I could either. Not the exact spot. The way I see it, we'll just have to wait it out. Jarrett's disappearance is going to cause a stir. Old Southern California family and all that shit. But the feds and the cops know he was dirty. They'll probably figure it was drug stuff and let it die."

Then there was a long stretch when we said nothing at all. We swung onto the freeway. Miles went by. But I could tell Casimir was building up to something. Finally, he came out with it.

"But Chico," he said, "I gotta sleep with her."

"Your problem, Casimir—and hers. But look at it this way. I don't like to admit it exactly, but Ursula did me a favor. She saved Alicia and that show of hers. Jarrett deserved to die, if anybody did. It was probably the best way to handle it."

21

The thing about Butterfield's is, you'd never guess it was there.
It's a big restaurant with a Sunset Boulevard address, right below
La Cienega. But nobody ever comes in that way. You enter from
the back, through the parking lot just off Olive. When you climb
up the stairs from there to the restaurant proper, you find yourself
in a big garden with candlelit tables all around, people sitting there
about as relaxed as they ever get in Los Angeles, and waiters and
waitresses passing among them, dispensing wine, food, and good
cheer, while up above, though the traffic rumbles on Sunset, all
you hear around you there in the garden is the murmur of
conversation and the tinkle of wineglasses, knives, and forks.

Elaine and I had been there well over an hour, and our conversation was still murmuring right along. She wanted to hear all
about Chicago, Julio, Clare Edwards, Katy McGucken, all of it.
I mean, she *really* wanted to hear about it. She kept asking me
questions. When dinner was set before us, and I tried to change
the subject and ask her about Rosarita Beach, she wouldn't let
me. She wanted all the details on Chicago.

Well, it beat talking about what Casimir and I had been up to
the night before. She wasn't going to hear about that from me.

But I really didn't have much more to tell—a little, maybe, but not much.

The waitress came around, poured the rest of the wine out in our glasses, and dumped the bottle down neck first in the ice bucket. Coffee? No, Elaine said she had a nice glow on and wanted to keep that. An after-dinner drink? Elaine declined, said she had Courvoisier and lots of bottles of sticky sweet stuff at her place. So I asked for the check.

"Julio called me up today," I told her.

"*Really?* What did he say? He was pretty grateful, right?"

"Elaine, Julio doesn't think in those terms exactly. But yeah, considering it was Julio, considering the situation, I guess you could say he was pretty grateful. But he called me up to tell me they couldn't ship Josefina back to El Salvador."

"Great! How come?"

"Because they were going to get married. Going down to City Hall to take out the marriage license, all that stuff. I said, 'Julio, is this the real thing, or are you just getting married to keep her here in the country?' And he said, 'Homeboy, you met her, right? She's pretty nice? She looks good? And she went to bat for me, right? Well, I found out all I need to know about being alone down there in Santa Monica. I'll make her a good husband.' "

"Oh, that's nice, that's really nice."

"So then I called David Delgado to tell him the check was in the mail, and he was getting a bonus. And he says, 'Oh yeah, the old check-is-in-the-mail scam. I've heard that one before.' Just bullshitting around, you know. And we talked awhile. He really sounded pretty good. Once he gets off those crutches, he'll be okay. I'm sure he will."

"Face it, Chico. You're a hero." She was teasing me.

"Yeah, I was a hero on another job not so long ago. I didn't make much on that one, either."

"Okay, listen," she said, "when I said you were a hero I was doing what they call back home 'kidding on the square.' You know, kidding but meaning it, too. Because yeah, I think you are a hero to those two guys. It's okay if I think you're a hero, too, isn't it?"

I didn't say anything to that. I didn't know what to say. Hero? I wanted to be a superhero for her. Jesus, I wanted to be Superman for Elaine Norgaard.

"I haven't had any heroes for a long time," she said. "I need one pretty bad."

I reached across the table and took her hand. A couple of minutes later we were on our way to her place.